BATTLETECH:
A QUESTION OF SURVIVAL

BY BRYAN YOUNG

BATTLETECH: A QUESTION OF SURVIVAL
By Bryan Young
Cover art by Eldon Cowgur
Interior art by Alan Blackwell, Doug Chaffee, Brent Evans, Harri Kallio, Chris Lewis,
    Duane Loose, Chris Lowrey, Justin Nelson, Matt Plog, David White
Cover design by David Kerber

Printed in USA.

Published by Catalyst Game Labs,
an imprint of InMediaRes Productions, LLC
5003 Main St. #110 • Tacoma, WA 98407

*This is for those who carry on, for the activists
and radicals who, despite the odds,
do the work of making the world a better place.*

THE INNER SPHERE: 3151

It's been more than a thousand years since humankind took flight from Terra and traversed the stars. On their sojourn, they colonized thousands of planets across a region of space known as the Inner Sphere. As with any expansion of territory, war and strife followed. Various factions consolidated into interstellar empires known as Great Houses. They vied for overall control, going to war with each other, fighting off and on for centuries. The chief weapon of these wars were BattleMechs, giant walking tanks with more firepower than a small army.

The Dark Age—brought on in 3132 by the collapse of the hyperpulse generator network, a system that allowed quick communication across occupied space—saw open conflicts erupt across the Inner Sphere. Terra and its surrounding systems had been governed by the Republic of the Sphere; a beleaguered nation founded by the charismatic Devlin Stone. The armies of the Great Houses, free-fighting mercenaries, and warmongering Clans all sought to seize control of Terra.

The Clans are descendants of the Star League Defense Force, the largest military force in human history, which left the Inner Sphere under the leadership of SLDF Commanding General Aleksandr Kerensky in 2784. After a fierce civil war broke out, far from the Inner Sphere, Kerensky's son Nicholas formed his loyalists into the twenty Clans, creating the brutal caste system and warrior mentality that they're now so well known for. In the year 3049, the Clans returned to the Inner Sphere with superior firepower and technology, ready to liberate Terra and serve as the defenders of humanity once more.

But thanks to the machinations of ComStar and the valiant forces of the Inner Sphere, the Clan invasion was halted before reaching Terra.

The Clans remained in the Inner Sphere for the next century, squabbling among each other until they could make a play for Terra. The prevailing Clan would become the ilClan, taking charge of all the Clans. The forces of the Inner Sphere didn't rest during this time; the Republic sealed off Terra and several neighboring systems behind the "Fortress Wall," impenetrable to hyperspace travel.

Clan Ghost Bear spent this time integrating into the Free Rasalhague Republic, blending the way of the Clans with the way of the Inner Sphere and eventually forming the Rasalhague Dominion, where the Clan and native-born Rasalhagians live together, largely in harmony and equal status.

Clan Wolf, on the other hand, built up forces and pressed into the Inner Sphere, bent on capturing Terra. Clan Jade Falcon did much the same, but with a much more destructive bloodlust.

In 3151, Khan Alaric Ward of Clan Wolf discovered a way through the Fortress Wall and raced to Terra, with Khan Malvina Hazen of Clan Jade Falcon close behind. Both Clans emptied the worlds of their Inner Sphere Occupation Zones, leaving only token garrison forces, solahma *troops past their prime, and* sibkos *full of children in training.*

On Terra, the historic rivalry between the Wolves and the Jade Falcons played out as they decimated the forces of the Republic of the Sphere, claiming Terra for the Clans. The two Clans then fought a Trial of Possession for the right to proclaim themselves the ilClan. Clan Wolf won, practically destroying the Jade Falcons. Malvina Hazen was killed, and Alaric Ward declared himself both the ilKhan and the First Lord of a reborn Star League.

The remaining Clans must decide how they will react. Will they bend the knee to the new ilClan? Or will they resist? The few Jade Falcons remaining in the Occupation Zone have received no word of the fate of their leaders from Terra, and scrabble to keep their dominions together.

For Clan Ghost Bear, the decision is much more difficult, as they're entrenched in the civilian system of government and can't simply decide to follow—or ignore—the new First Lord. Before the Clans can decide, they must pay their respects to the ilKhan of the ilClan, Alaric Ward of Clan Wolf...

"When there is no enemy within, the enemies outside cannot hurt you."

—OLD TERRAN PROVERB

PROLOGUE

KERENSKY SPACEPORT
UNITY CITY, PUGET SOUND
NORTH AMERICA
TERRA
23 MAY 3151

Dalia Bekker had seen a lot in her twenty-five years as the Khan of Clan Ghost Bear. She'd seen a lot more in her seventy years of life, but none of it had prepared her for the feeling of setting foot on Terra for the first time. Those first steps brought a feeling of exhilaration and a dizziness, too. As though the history of the place and the importance of her walking on the planet could crush her with its gravitas.

The spring air was crisp, and the coast brought with it the smell of the sea and the pine scent of the Pacific Northwest. During her descent, she'd surveyed the damage done to the planet during the Battle of Terra over the previous five months and wished her visit was happening under better circumstances. Still, she had to hand it to Clan Wolf: they'd done it, even if she would have preferred to leave Terra as it was, and see all the Clans integrate into their areas as effectively as Clan Ghost Bear had.

She walked along the landing platform toward the spaceport proper, her saKhan Roy Jorgensson in tow.

It was time they paid their respects.

Before they left for Terra, Bekker had informed Prince Miraborg of the situation and the need for them to go. Being a Ghost Bear as well as the fourth elected Prince in charge of the Rasalhague Dominion, he understood what was at stake and why Bekker and Jorgensson had to do this.

Duty.

And it was duty that sent them walking out to greet Alaric Ward, Khan of Clan Wolf, newly ascended ilKhan of the Clans, and soon to be self-appointed First Lord of the Star League reborn.

Alaric Ward looked every bit of his forty years, practically a child in Bekker's eyes, but a warrior nonetheless. And one with the grit and skill to accomplish what she never thought would be possible while the Fortress Wall stood. The sun made a shadow of the crescent scar on Ward's left eye, giving him a menacing look that belied the smile he greeted them with. His long blond hair had been pulled back into a neat ponytail, and he wore a new uniform that told her he'd chosen it to both reflect the Star League uniforms of old, but with a blend of Wolfish sensibility. Olive green fabric spread across his well-muscled torso, edged with black trim that reached high up onto his neck from his shoulders. Ward bore the symbol of the Star League rather than that of Clan Wolf, leaving that designation to the pins on his collar. To Bekker, this felt like a preview of his intentions.

Bekker did not return his smile.

"Khan Dalia Bekker and saKhan Roy Jorgensson of Clan Ghost Bear," Ward said, stretching his arms wide. "It is my pleasure to welcome you to Terra."

"Congratulations," Bekker said, nodding her head curtly.

"Congratulations, indeed," Jorgensson said behind her.

For both of them, this was a matter of honor, not necessarily one of joy.

"How are things in the Ghost Bear Dominion?" Alaric asked, clearly knowing full well what he was asking.

"Rasalhague is well, ilKhan Ward."

"Splendid," he said, smiling wide. "This victory was one you shared—your Clan's blood fought and died valiantly on Terra as part of Clan Wolf. Indeed, we would not be standing here if your Bloodnamed brother Ramiel Bekker had not been part of the offensive."

At the mention of Ramiel Bekker, Ward grew somber, stiffening like a board, but Khan Bekker couldn't tell if the emotion was genuine or an act. Everything about Ward felt phony to her.

"Is he here?" Jorgensson asked. "I would like to pay my respects."

"Alas, the WarBear died like a true warrior this past March." Ward's voice cracked as he spoke. More affectation? Or genuine loss? She couldn't say. "It feels like a lifetime ago. We've accomplished so much since then, and have so much more to do."

"No doubt," Khan Bekker said, remembering the younger Bekker fondly from their few interactions. *If only the Ghost Bears had been able to keep him...* "I am saddened to hear of the loss of the great WarBear. Whether bearing the mark of Bear or Wolf, he was Ghost Bear family and a true Clan Warrior, the like of which the Inner Sphere had never known."

"*Seyla*," the ilKhan said softly, a sliver of sincerity shining through the clouds of his affectations.

They stood there in the somber moment for what felt like an eternity.

Regardless of the folly of destruction and political machinations that had driven the Clans to Terra and cost Ramiel Bekker his life, they were here now, and all would do their duty.

The Ghost Bear Khan took in a deep breath and broke the silence with polite reservation. "You likely have much to do. We do not wish to keep you."

"Indeed, there are many arrangements to be made, and I am glad you will be here for the ceremony. Afterward, we will talk and make plans."

"As you please, ilKhan, we would not miss the opportunity."

"My thanks." The ilKhan gripped Bekker on the shoulder and nodded warmly to her, then he was gone, off to greet another Khan or sanction more political machinations. Whatever it was, Bekker wasn't sure she trusted him, all things being equal and him being a Wolf, after all. Ghost Bears were slow to change— and even slower to let go of ancient, not-named grudges.

As soon as the ilKhan was out of earshot and they were on their way to their appointed quarters, Jorgensson spoke. "He is not at all like I imagined him."

"And how did you imagine him?"

"A difficult question."

"I refuse to bear a saKhan who is afraid of difficult questions."

"I imagined him bigger somehow. Larger than life. And smarter, perhaps?"

Khan Bekker allowed herself a slight smile. "Kerensky help us all if he was."

"And how do you think he will react to our predicament?"

"I doubt he will be pleased, but who knows with a man as driven as Alaric Ward. We have our own oaths to keep, however, and only time will tell."

THE CITADEL
UNITY CITY, PUGET SOUND
NORTH AMERICA
TERRA
25 MAY 3151

The hospitality of Clan Wolf had not lacked whatsoever. Khan Dalia Bekker and saKhan Roy Jorgensson had luxurious accommodations built originally for tourists that were almost embarrassing for Clan warriors, and they wanted for nothing. Food came regularly, every meal a feast. All they had to sit through was the ceremony that made Alaric Ward the First Lord of the Star League.

The ceremony itself was full of pomp and circumstance, and designed to let all of the attending Clan Khans know how important Ward felt his position was. To Dalia Bekker's eyes, he looked somehow hurt during the ceremony. Like the weight of a thousand worlds bore down on his shoulders, and he'd thought himself Atlas, but found he'd been Sisyphus all along. His face stayed grim through the entire ritual, as though he could power his way into the gravitas he felt it required.

She had to admit, the Court of the Star League on Terra—an ornate complex that was part sprawling revivalist government facility and part museum of Star League history—was enough to feel impressive on its own, and his pageant was designed to add to its stone carved solemnity.

But it was all just a show.

Why else wait to meet with the Khans until they'd witnessed his ascent?

"We have been summoned," her saKhan told her afterward.

"Of course we have. He plays politics with a flair for the dramatic, but never forget it is just politics."

"That certainly appears to be the case."

And with that, they left.

The meeting room was furnished as decadently as the rooms the ilKhan had assigned the Ghost Bear Khans. A wide table of polished cherry wood sat in the center. High-backed chairs surrounded it. Waiting for the ilKhan, Bekker found time to stand at the wall, staring at the tapestry work. The scene was familiar to Bekker, and a chill ran across her back.

"What is it?" Jorgensson asked.

Bekker waved a hand at the tapestry her saKhan had not paid a bit of attention to. "This is a rendering of the Annihilation of the Not-Named Clan."

Jorgensson's brow furrowed. "We do not even speak their names. Why would there be a tapestry of it here?"

"Made special. For our benefit." Bekker ran her fingers along the artistic draping and found it smooth, feeling new. It depicted a *Timber Wolf* destroying a *Conjurer* with ruby-colored lasers on a blackened landscape with the first blue rays of dawn behind them. It didn't matter how anachronistic it was; the coloring on the *Conjurer* was unmistakable. Knowing the walls had ears, she did not say to her saKhan that it was meant to throw them off balance and remind them of their place. Ideally, he had come to the same conclusion already.

Hundreds of years prior, the Ghost Bears had sought the honor of destroying the Not-Named Clan and participated in that Trial of Annihilation with the other Clans. When a Ghost Bear Star Captain had spotted a *sibko* of Not-Named children evading the Wolves, the Bear acted out of pity and let them escape. This shame had been passed down for centuries.

The tapestry was a reminder of their rivalry. Of their position. Bekker smiled again. It fazed her not a bit. "No deed be left undone, they shall not escape the Bear again," she said quietly, quoting the Oath of Acceptance.

The tapestry did not matter. If Alaric Ward wanted to broach the taboo and have his fun, he was ilKhan now and had won Terra, what was it to her? She had a duty to the Rasalhague Dominion and an oath to the Ghost Bears to uphold.

"Khan Bekker, saKhan Jorgensson," came a voice at the door. The ilKhan, Alaric Ward, was dressed in his new uniform of the First Lord, though with an added floor-length cape, black and flowing. "I am so glad to see you both."

Bekker turned from the tapestry, hands folded neatly behind her back. She bowed politely. "IlKhan."

Jorgensson did likewise until the ilKhan bid them to sit.

"I am sure you have many things to tend to in the Dominion, and I do not wish to keep you long."

"Of course, my ilKhan," Bekker said.

"Then you feel no need to dispute my position?" Alaric said.

Bekker cocked her head slightly. "We sit on Terra, which you conquered. Does that not make you ilKhan?"

"I am glad we speak the same language. I will want a complete accounting of the holdings of the Ghost Bears so that we might add the might of the Dominion to the new Star League."

Now Bekker clasped her hands in front of her on the shining table, doing her best to hide her exasperation. *He must know less about the Ghost Bears than I thought.* Where to begin, she was not entirely sure.

She cleared her throat. "As you are no doubt aware, ilKhan, the Ghost Bears have become integrated into the Rasalhague Dominion. The two are one, natives of the Dominion and Clan alike. Were it up to me alone to move Bears from our Den into the new Star League, we would do so without hesitation. But I cannot make decisions for Bears or Rasalhague by fiat. I must consult with Prince Miraborg, and we must let the population have a say in the decision."

Alaric Ward's face looked chiseled from stone. Silence permeated the room, as if the ilKhan were waiting for her to change her answer before he would even deign to respond. "We support you, absolutely," she added. "If you require the Ghost Bears in an emergency, I have been authorized to pledge our support, but joining the Star League requires a vote."

"Are you not Khan of the Ghost Bears?"

"Indeed I am."

Alaric brow took on the faintest of furrows. "And the Ghost Bears have ceded their power to...what? A prince?"

"Prince Miraborg *is* a Ghost Bear, but sits as the ruler of the civilian population. The Ghost Bears are integrated into the military, and I am the leader of the military. I report to the Prince and he acts as a commander in chief, but in internal Clan matters, the word of the Ghost Bear Khan is law. In external civilian matters and politics, or matters that effect the entire Dominion, we get a vote, but do not get involved. Though we might not see eye to eye on this, this is how we envisioned the Clans to work under the teachings of Kerensky. Our role as the Clans was never to subjugate the worlds of the Inner Sphere, but integrate into them and protect them. Though there are enemies at our borders, the Rasalhague Dominion is free of threats, and the people enjoy that freedom. The Draconis Combine at our border knows what folly it is to cross us, and the rest of the old Houses know as well. We have fulfilled the mandate of the Clans in the Inner Sphere."

Ward crooked a finger to his lips, thinking. Then, after a deep breath, his eyes locked with Bekker's. "And yet you ignored Terra, the cradle of humanity."

Personally, Bekker felt the power came from the people of the Inner Sphere, rather than any specific geographic quirk of Terra, but admitted its importance to the parts of their culture they still shared. And the tapestry served as a good reminder of the balancing act she performed. "We are here when called," she said.

Seeming to come to a conclusion, Alaric leaned forward. "Take your vote, then. Perhaps there is some wisdom in the way of the Ghost Bears and the Dominion. And any Clan that could produce a man as gifted as the WarBear deserves at least some benefit of the doubt. But I warn you not to delay. The Inner Sphere is full of strife we will have to quell as the new Star League expands."

"*Aff*, it is a Republic you have, ilKhan, if it can be kept. We will take our leave and organize a vote. I will bring the results to you personally."

"See to it that you do, Khan Dalia Bekker," Ward replied. "The very future of the Ghost Bears depends on it."

And perhaps he is right, she thought as she and SaKhan Jorgensson rose to leave.

CHAPTER 1

As far as he knew, Jiyi Chistu was the last Bloodnamed Jade Falcon Warrior left.

Word from Terra had been sparse, but the interrogations of the self-styled former Governor—Scientist General Axle—proved all their dreams of taking Terra had become a nightmare. The Wolves were victorious, and there had been no direct word from the Jade Falcons, if any even survived.

That they'd been so thoroughly devastated saddened Jiyi, but he had almost expected such a result from the self-styled Chingis Khan Malvina Hazen. There was a reason he'd spent so many years quietly subverting her, and her imbalance as a leader was near the top of the list. The very top of the list was the Mongol Doctrine, her propensity to destroy everything in her path and scorch her allies as well as her enemies if the whim took her. It was no way to lead.

For years, Jiyi assumed it would lead to the extinction of Clan Jade Falcon. He wished he had not been so right.

From the balcony atop the governor's mansion, he looked out over Sudeten's capital, Hammarr, and found the city a fitting metaphor.

It had been destroyed twenty-five years earlier, burned to the ground, with nearly every inhabitant killed. Leveled by Khan Malvina Hazen after her reckless war against Khan Jana Pryde. A warning to those that supported the ex-Khan. She had used the WarShip *Emerald Talon* as her missile to level the city, and she had not missed. Thankfully, humans are sturdier and more stubborn than that. It had taken decades, but the people of Sudeten had rebuilt it, despite Hazen's cruelty. And just like the city, it was as good a place as any for Jiyi to rebuild Clan Jade Falcon from the ground up.

During the reconstruction efforts, pieces of the *Emerald Talon* had been unearthed and salvaged or incorporated into building designs. It gave the city a mix of old and new as they recreated it to the best of their ability. And after twenty-five years, it was safe to say Hammarr had bounced back.

And, like their capitol, so would the Jade Falcons.

"Khan Chistu?" a voice asked.

Jiyi was miles away, still thinking about a thousand things: his recent ascent to Khan, the state he'd found Sudeten in, the crushing news that the Jade Falcons had been defeated. He hadn't realized how demanding it was to be Khan until he found the position thrust upon him.

"Yes, Star Captain Quinn." Jiyi turned to regard her. "Where were we?"

"The personnel issue." Star Captain Quinn stood at the sliding glass doorway at the balcony's entrance, one foot in the office and another on the deck. Dressed in the olive-green uniform of the Jade Falcons with the khaki tie and emerald trim, she looked the part of an officer, but still looked a little uncomfortable with her new post. She had been a mere MechWarrior in Chistu's Trinary for only a few weeks before the call to Terra came; having been transferred to his unit for actions that had made her appear *dezgra*. Jiyi hardly found a refusal to kill civilians in pursuit of the Mongol Doctrine *dezgra*, but he was grateful for the new blood. Her promotion came as a surprise to her, but he had always believed in getting the best person for the job, whether that be *solahma*, purported *dezgra*, or even a civilian.

"Right, the personnel issue," Jiyi said as they walked into the office together. "How could I forget?"

"We are the Jade Falcons now, and we are but a Trinary at this moment, with twice that many 'Mechs, though no one to pilot them. There are Warriors we found garrisoned here..."

Jiyi sighed. "All *solahma* infantry."

"*Aff.* There are a few who might be able to pilot a 'Mech, but I would not wager my life on more than that." Quinn stood at the receiving end of the Khan's desk as she continued reporting, waiting for a signal to sit or remain standing. "The factories of Sudeten will be able to produce many BattleMechs, more than we can currently use. But some good news comes from the academies. The *sibko* training facilities here have Jade Falcon fledglings, though they are not as close to graduation as we would hope."

Jiyi eased into his chair behind the desk and bade his subordinate to sit as well. Both leather chairs were old, reclaimed from the wreckage of Hammarr. "How far along?"

"The oldest are fourteen. They near graduation, but it will be a few years yet before they are Warriors."

He smiled broadly. "Then let us be sure that there is a Clan waiting for them when they reach their trials."

"*Aff*, my Khan." Star Captain Quinn had the severe look of a Jade Falcon from the Hazen bloodline, like a much younger version of Malvina but without the scar, and her hair had remained a dark blonde, showing no signs of graying white. Instead of being ready to pounce viciously at the slightest displeasure, Quinn appeared eager to help, with a suggestion almost always on her lips, only held back by the trauma of bad leadership in her past.

"Speak your mind, Star Commander," Jiyi said. "We need every good idea we can get."

"We have more infantry than MechWarriors."

"*Aff.* That sounds more like a comment than a suggestion."

"How many could be trained to pilot a 'Mech? We will face challenges sooner than later. On every edge of our border—and even from within—our enemies look at the holdings of Jade Falcon as easy pickings. We are nestled in the capital and have 'Mechs to hold off attacks for now. But it is only a matter of time before they come here unless we do something. In an invasion, a Jade Falcon in a 'Mech is worth a hundred Falcon infantry. Why not bring some of them up?"

"I imagine there are some who only barely failed their trials?"

"*Aff.* I have taken the liberty to assemble a list of candidates from the infantry for us to promote and make MechWarriors." Star Captain Quinn placed a noteputer on the desk and slid it across to the Khan.

"Hmm..." Jiyi stroked his chin, not accepting the tablet, but not ignoring it either.

"I do not believe we have any other choice, my Khan."

"It is not that I do not agree with you. I do, but I wonder if that will take more time than we have. And resources. Who will train them?"

"I can. I will fight alongside them. But I do not think we can afford *not* to."

He thought long and hard about that, easing backward in the chair and running his fingers through his mop of curly brown hair, trying to tame its chaos. "How many?"

"I have identified ten candidates. Not many in the grand scheme for infantry, but enough to field two Stars of 'Mechs."

"We will be lucky to get one Star out of it. You say they all have failed in becoming MechWarriors. Who is to say they will not fail again?"

"Fair point."

"So let us assume we get one Star out of it. That is a good start, but nowhere near enough. And how many of the infantry are nearing their prime or past?"

"You have proved effective at whipping *dezgra* and *solahma* warriors into shape, why not again?"

Jiyi sighed. "You said yourself, what choice do we have?"

"I have your permission, then?"

"The order is given. As long as they pass a Trial of Position, they can have a BattleMech. But we cannot put all of our hopes into a Star of infantry playing MechWarriors. We need more options."

"*Aff.*"

"We have VaultShip *Gamma*, which means we have resources to trade. It is something worth defending, and Sudeten has all the 'Mech factories we could want, with defensible positions as long as our opponents have no more gall than my predecessor. But we must extend our talons further."

"Aff." Star Captain Quinn never quite settled into her seat, but remained at a sort of attention as she watched him think. He knew people liked to do that, hoping to divine his thought process, to gain an advantage. He liked to think of himself as impenetrable, if only because he paused to think. He had known far too many Warriors or would-be Warriors who had fallen to his intellect merely because they reacted with instinct rather than forethought.

Though there was nothing wrong with instinct at times.

That was what the Falconers in their *créche* had tried to instill in them: the instincts of a Warrior. But Jiyi had been only one of three in his *sibko* to survive to a Trial of Position, let alone earn a Bloodname. And in both cases, Jiyi made it through not because of instincts, but because he had stopped to think. To outwit.

It had served him well in the past.

And it would serve him well now as he set out to rebuild Clan Jade Falcon from the ashes left by Malvina Hazen.

Quinn, his second in command and one of the few fighting-age Trueborns in his cadre, was much more at home with troops than in an office, and he needed to give her a task that would focus her strengths.

"Make it so," he said. "Oversee their Trial and train those who pass. I will make preparations to defend Sudeten in the meantime, and then I will have a voyage to make."

"Oh?"

He had a list of planets from the Occupation Zone close enough to be brought into the fold. More importantly, many of them were garrisoned, and he would be able to add those warriors to his *touman.* Though he went through the calculus in his head, all he said to Star Captain Quinn was, *"Aff.* And when I go, I plan to leave Merchant Jodine in charge of Sudeten."

Quinn blinked.

He knew what she would be thinking and smiled warmly, speaking so she had no need to conjure a response. "I assure you, it is not a reflection on your duty or ability. First, you will be occupied seeing to the defense of the planet. Second, will you not be training a new group of MechWarriors? You will have your hands quite full, if I am not mistaken."

"*Aff*," she said through gritted teeth.

"I know you distrust the merchant caste, or feel them beneath you..." he let that sentence trail off like a question, and left it for her to answer.

She nodded. "*Aff.* I am a Warrior."

"So are they, in their way." Jiyi smiled when he noticed her face sour. "And I know what you are thinking. That I have spent too much time among the merchants instead of with Warriors. And there is some truth in that thinking, but it does not offer the whole picture. Tell me, what is your opinion of Merchant Jodine?"

"I believe she would run screaming from a battlefield."

"But their battlefield is merely different than ours. She would run screaming from our battlefield in a 'Mech much the same you and I might if we had to keep a budget and barter for goods across the Rasalhague Dominion, as she has done. Make no mistake: they are Jade Falcon, through and through. Where our weapons are BattleMechs and the ways of war, theirs are the laws of supply and demand and economics. These weapons are just as potent. You can kill a world or a people by starving it of goods as easily as under the heel of a Cluster of 'Mechs."

Quinn remained silent, obviously thinking about his answer. Perhaps she was not convinced, but Jiyi felt confident in his rightness. It had taken him quite a while to come to that understanding, but that came from age, maturity, and experience. Quinn was younger than him by almost two decades, and had barely served as a fledged Falcon for a couple of years. She had not seen enough or done enough to know better.

She was the most promising Trueborn left in the Jade Falcons that did not bear the name Jiyi Chistu. She had been his de facto saKhan since his recent rise to Khan, and perhaps she would truly earn that position one day, but right now she was still as green as a spring meadow.

Merchant Jodine was much more his match, but as a merchant, she could not take the mantle of saKhan, so he had a vital member of a lower caste as his left hand and an adolescent Falcon as his right.

Ideal?

No.

But he could think his way out of any challenge. He would have to.

"Now go, Star Captain Quinn. Make the reborn Jade Falcons proud, and perhaps we will live to fight another day."

"*Aff,* my Khan."

CHAPTER 2

CITY HALL
ANTIMONY
QUARELL
RASALHAGUE DOMINION
07 JULY 3151

Vote Day was a solemn occasion, and for Star Colonel Emilio Hall, the decision was an easy one. The Ghost Bears had integrated into the Rasalhague Dominion, and had no need to integrate into the ilClan and the new Star League Defense Force. It would throw everything they had fought for and won into question. Besides, how long would the SLDF even exist in its current form?

But he knew many Ghost Bears and citizens of the Dominion felt joining was imperative. For a lot of Ghost Bears, it was a sense of wanting to fulfill some old-fashioned sense of destiny. For the common folk of the Dominion, it came from a desire to be a part of something bigger.

Emilio Hall did not begrudge anyone those reasons, but he had found the Ghost Bears had evolved beyond the need for the rigid structures of the Clans and their misguided ideals about destiny and conquering. The Ghost Bears protected the planets they had found themselves ingrained with, and there were more than enough Clans to go around the Inner Sphere. To his mind, they were fulfilling the same purpose, but with more nobility and democracy.

It was while studying the works of a long-dead Terran philosopher and statesperson that Hall discovered the core of his own philosophy regarding this vote. "Laws and institutions must go hand in hand with the progress of the human mind. As that becomes more developed, more enlightened, as new discoveries are made, new truths discovered and manners and opinions change, with the change of circumstances, institutions must advance also to keep pace with the times. We might as well require a man to wear still the coat which fitted him when a boy as civilized society to remain ever under the regimen of their barbarous ancestors."

Thomas Jefferson was a barbarous ancestor the same as Nicholas Kerensky, and just because they had met the challenges of their own time and place, there was no need to lionize them for their devotion to the structures of their day. They worked well enough for some in their time and place, but their time and place were long gone, and there were better examples to lead.

The Ghost Bears had found a new tailored coat for a more advanced and civilized society.

And that was how Emilio had chosen to vote.

He stood in line on the steps of Antimony's City Hall, the morning sun shining bright across the steps of the old granite building, waiting to cast his ballot alongside others, the line spilling out across the ferrocrete plaza, with a fountain centered in the middle. Emilio wore his finest dress uniform for such an occasion, a well-fitted coat of sky blue with navy blue trim covering a navy shirt and black necktie. He had dark curly hair, and his brown face had been clean shaven for the occasion. There were other Ghost Bears in line to vote as well, but the vast majority were non-Clan.

He could not tell if he was grateful the media was absent or not. On one hand, there was no good in making a circus of the vote. On the other hand, the top-ranking member of the military on Quarell casting his vote in an orderly fashion with no strife or argument occurring could be a powerful example for the folks of the planet. Emilio had worn his uniform to set an example of a Ghost Bear, and thought being an ambassador to civilians of the Rasalhague Dominion was always a correct choice. It helped bolster their position in the Dominion and let everyone know they'd made the right choice to join together the way they had.

"It's a lot of uncertainty, isn't it?" said a woman in line behind him.

Emilio turned to look, wondering if it was him she was speaking to, but she seemed to be speaking to no one in particular. Perhaps it was merely an invitation to talk. She looked as though she'd seen many long years in the Dominion.

He nodded to her. "*Aff*," he said. "But that is life in the Inner Sphere, is it not? One uncertainty after another."

"You can say that again—" She eyed the epaulets and stripes that proclaimed his rank. "—Star Colonel."

The conversation withered. Small talk was never a strength of Emilio's, nor was it a strength of any Clan member, even assimilated as a Ghost Bear could be. But the woman started again. "It's not often you see someone ranked as high as you in line with the rest of us."

"Our votes all count the same."

"That's what they say. Or that *is* what they say, rather. Sorry for the contractions."

"Think nothing of it. Though it is respectful in our culture to speak formally without contractions, there is no edict that places that responsibility on you."

"Aye, aye, but it's—it *is*—still a matter of respect though, isn't...is it not?"

The Star Colonel smiled. "Fair enough, though I confess I take no offense."

"That is good to know." The woman's eyes narrowed. "Which way are you voting? To join or refuse?"

Emilio shrugged his broad shoulders, not wanting to sway any opinions. That was not his place. "Perhaps I am still deciding."

"We're coming up fast, you better decide soon." She laughed, pointing to the entrance of the ornate building. Carved into the building's stone columns, quarried from the local antimony mines, were figures representing the old 'Mechs of the Star League Defense Force that had been garrisoned on Quarell in the last years of their existence, long before Kerensky had left and formed the clans.

Indeed, there were only a few people ahead of them before they reached the inside and the sign-in table, and then would be given access to the voting booth proper.

"I hope we join," the woman said. "I think unification is the best way to keep us out of wars. If we're all the same folks with the same government and the same protectors, we're likely to stay out of wars if there's no one to war with."

"I understand. I have only been assigned here a few years. When was the last time Quarell was at war?"

"Oh, long before my time. We've traded hands now and again, but there hasn't been much fighting. Not here. Here it's all politics."

"There is truth in that." Hall turned back toward the front of the line, waiting his turn.

The woman would not leave well enough alone now. "I tell you, though, my sister is a refuser, and we have just about stopped talking about it. I can't even believe someone could be selfish enough to think we should just stay here, isolated, and risk losing everything we have, our very way of life."

"Is that how you see it?" Emilio asked, turning back to her.

The woman nodded. "I mean, the worst part is that she's just so obnoxious about it. And she's the sort that no matter how many different ways you explain it to her, she never understands. It just boils my blood that she would be so foolish. I mean, we grew up together. I thought I knew her better than that, but I guess I didn't."

"The beliefs of people are not merely shaped by their upbringing," Hall said.

A man further in line behind the woman spoke up, inserting himself into the conversation. "Really?" he said to her. "You'd join the Wolves on Terra, and you think *she's* the foolish one? Clan Wolf was in charge here for a while and broke everything. It didn't work. It wasn't until we joined the Rasalhague Dominion that we got a fair shake and a say. And she wants to just give that up to hand it back to the Wolves? It doesn't make any sense."

Emilio turned back toward the door, wanting to extricate himself from the argument. The two kept at it bitterly. His thoughts turned to how the argument would play out within the ranks of the Warriors in Clan Ghost Bear, and he dreaded to think of the violence that could result.

Surely, there was no love for Clan Wolf amongst the Ghost Bears, their rivalry legendary for centuries, but the Bears of the Dominion would simply have to come to peace with whatever decision was made. It would be easy enough for Emilio; he would abide by whatever decision was handed down by the vote. But for Warriors, peace was not often a word in their vocabulary.

Emilio believed in democracy, and he did not think either choice would be to the detriment of the Ghost Bears. If they joined with Clan Wolf and the Star League, they would fashion a new coat and find a way to make that new system better. If they refused, and stayed the Rasalhague Dominion and kept to their borders, the people in their charge would remain safe, and the Ghost Bears would continue to fulfill their purpose.

It was Emilio's turn to check in to vote. He took his dress hat off and tucked it underneath his left arm as he entered the building.

"Name, please?" the person on the other side of the table asked, more concerned with the data on their noteputer than the person standing before them.

"Star Colonel Emilio Hall." Emilio's posture straightened as he spoke.

The poll worker tapped a few keys on their screen and then looked up to the Star Colonel. "You are verified, Star Colonel Emilio Hall. Your voting booth is right that way."

"My thanks," the Star Colonel said, heading in to perform the duty sacred to anyone who held the power of the vote important.

CHAPTER 3

COPPERTON
QUARELL
RASALHAGUE DOMINION
07 JULY 3151

Alexis angled her *Bear Cub* through the trees, hoping they would obscure her from the enemy long enough to spring the trap.

"Thomasin, Sophie, I'm in position in the trees," Alexis said over the radio.

"Copy that," Thomasin replied, his voice confident and sure. Alexis would even go so far as to say arrogant. But that was what many Trueborns tended to be like, even if they did not mean it.

"As you suggested, I will lure them in your direction," Sophie said.

All three of them piloted *Bear Cub*s. At 25 tons, the light 'Mechs were no match for the single 100-ton *Kodiak* they faced—but that was the challenge. They had already lost two 'Mechs from their Star, which, on paper, made it a fair fight in terms of total weight on either side, but the *Kodiak* had obliterated them right at the beginning of the battle, before they could be useful. It was down to the three of them—or Alexis—to find a way to victory.

With Lewis and Anna out of commission, that left Alexis, Thomasin, and Sophie in charge of winning this simulated 'Mech version of a Clawing ritual. That *Kodiak* wasn't going to go easy on them any more than a ghost bear on Strana Mechty. Alexis knew it really came down to her. Thomasin and Sophie were Trueborns, and both had a pretty rigid way of thinking. As a freeborn, Alexis was a little more flexible.

"Sophie, be sure to keep juking. You don't want to be an easy target for him," she said.

"Understood."

"Thomasin, get into the copse of trees across from me and wait. Once we are in position, Sophie will lead the *Kodiak* through the cleared swamp. Its heavier chassis will weigh it down in the water. We are lighter and faster and will be able to outmaneuver it."

"This feels *dezgra*," Thomasin said.

"There is no dishonor in winning at any cost."

Begrudgingly, Thomasin agreed. *"Aff."*

"As soon as the *Kodiak* has its back turned, we'll strafe it from behind and then fade back into the trees. It is the only way we can deal enough damage to win here."

"Aff," Thomasin again said reluctantly.

She knew he didn't like the plan, but he wouldn't have agreed to it unless he had a better one. And with their three *Bear Cub*s so far outclassed, there really wasn't any other option if they wanted to win. Sure, they could lose with their "honor" intact—whatever that meant—or they could stick together, work together, and win.

"Thomasin, you in position?" Sophie asked. The sound of a weapon impact came through her radio along with her voice. The *Kodiak* had hit her. Alexis glanced down at her readouts and found Sophie's *Bear Cub* flashing yellow across the torso.

"Aff," he said again.

Looking out through the trees, across the swamp land between them, and into the trees Thomasin hid in, Alexis couldn't make out any sign of his 'Mech, which is exactly what she wanted.

"Do it, Sophie!"

Without a word, Sophie launched the plan into action. Alexis watched her Starmate's *Bear Cub* race through the swamp, deftly maneuvering through the quagmire.

The lumbering *Kodiak* arrived shortly thereafter, slowed significantly in the wetlands. It had a harder time pulling its massive legs up to take each ponderous step forward.

"Now?" Thomasin asked. He probably didn't even realize he had essentially acquiesced command to Alexis. But the plan was hers, so it made sense that he would just stick with her being in charge. And if anything went wrong, she was sure he would pass the blame on to her.

"No," Alexis said. "Wait until its back is turned. Then we hit it from behind, one at a time. Then get to the trees on the other side. Then we'll do it again. And we'll keep doing it until we can take it down."

"*Aff.* Now?"

"*Neg.*"

The *Kodiak* lumbered forward, crossing Alexis' viewscreen.

"Now?" Thomasin asked, his patience wearing thin.

"*Neg.*"

The *Kodiak* moved ahead even further. It would have trouble turning to fire upon them if they were quick.

Alexis gave the order: "Now!"

She shoved her *Bear Cub* forward and burst through the cover of the trees. Twisting her torso a full 30° to keep her legs aimed at the tree cover and her weapons aimed at the *Kodiak's* rear flank, Alexis let loose. Smoke filled her view as her short-range missiles spiraled forth, crashing into the *Kodiak's* backside in a cacophony of explosions. Then she opened fire with her medium lasers, the golden flashes of light boiling metal off her enemy's armor.

Thomasin turned and did likewise with his missiles and lasers. His missiles impacted against the back of the *Kodiak's* arms, but his lasers scorched the middle of the *Kodiak's* back.

And then they were on the move again.

Thomasin's *Bear Cub* crossed Alexis and before the *Kodiak* could effectively turn around to attack them, they both faded back into the jungle.

"Sophie, as soon as it turns around to deal with us, hit it again."

"*Aff.*"

As the *Kodiak* made its slow turn, working to locate Thomasin and Alexis, Sophie made her run. Another salvo of missiles crackled across the *Kodiak's* back, followed by the golden flash of her medium lasers.

"Be sure to watch your heat using your lasers," Sophie called out. "I am coming up on tolerances now."

The *Kodiak* had no idea which way to turn or pick a target, while Alexis did the math of its position and hers.

"Alexis, it is still coming for us," Thomasin said.

"I can see that. Sophie, hit it again."

"Aff."

Calculating the odds, Alexis wondered how much damage it could take before they disabled it. As Sophie's second salvo ripped into its back, the pilot had to be at least feeling it. Where Alexis' team lacked an advantage in weight and armor, they made up for it in numbers. They had the *Kodiak* pinned in a kill box and surrounded.

Alexis grinned.

They had the bastard right where she wanted him.

"Okay, listen up." She couldn't contain the glee in her voice. "I am going to come out and draw its fire. Thomasin, move south and get behind it again. You two hit it with everything you have from behind, and that armor will crack open like an egg."

The *Kodiak* extended its claws out and fired into the woods in Thomasin's direction with all eight of its medium lasers. The dense, wet wood refused to go up in flames, but the pilot certainly removed quite a bit of Thomasin's cover.

Thomasin objected to the plan. "That *Kodiak* will tear you apart. That Ultra-class autocannon will destroy you in one shot, just as it did Lewis and Anna."

"Maybe. But I will play the odds. We just need to win. If I go down, you two can still take him and that is what matters. If you do your jobs right, we have a chance to disable it before it gets even one more shot off at me. He already seems distracted enough by you, Thomasin."

"Aff," he said.

"Sophie?"

"Let us end this," Sophie said.

"On my mark," Alexis said through a smile. She loved nothing more than the exhilaration of a plan coming together and the feeling of pulling one over on someone.

"Mark!" Alexis charged forward through the trees. As soon as she reached the edge of the clearing, she opened fire with her SRMs and the lasers. She hit the huge assault 'Mech—at this range, it was almost impossible to miss—but the armor on the *Kodiak*'s arm and torso didn't even look scratched.

The *Kodiak* pivoted to engage her on its other side, still trudging through the deep bog water.

Thomasin's *Bear Cub* burst out from the trees directly behind the *Kodiak*, and the first salvo of Sophie's renewed attack rippled explosions across its back.

Alexis planted her *Bear Cub*'s feet into the ground and fired again. The best thing to do was to give the *Kodiak* a target it couldn't ignore. It would fire until it destroyed her, sure as anything.

But that meant leaving its back exposed long enough for Sophie and Thomasin to finish the job.

Like a monster, the *Kodiak* reached its clawed hands toward Alexis and opened fire with its medium lasers. When the lasers fired, Alexis blinked. The *Kodiak* had missed with all of them!

Thomasin and Sophie had hit it again from behind.

"I think we got its gyro—it's having a hard time moving," Thomasin said, which explained the *Kodiak*'s completely wasted shot.

"I have one more hit before my *Bear Cub* overheats," Sophie said.

"Stick to missiles and plant your feet in the water. It will help," Alexis called to her, hitting her firing stud again now that she had been given one more chance to distract her enemy.

Her lasers cut into the armor of the *Kodiak*'s left hand, dripping molten steel into the puddles of swamp below it, boiling the water on contact, steam rising into the air. Alexis hoped the damage had disrupted its lasers. Anything she could do to disable any of its weapons would give her, Thomasin, and Sophie a better chance of coming out on top of this engagement.

Her heart skipped when the *Kodiak* trained its Ultra autocannon on her.

"Thomasin, Sophie, you have this. Hit it *now!*"

Alexis sidestepped, hoping to dodge, but the *Kodiak* tracked her movement to the side.

It fired right at her.

Direct hit.

Her screen went black, and she slumped forward. Had she made a mistake? Or did she do the right thing?

The lights in her simulator pod came back on, and the door opened beside her.

Waiting on the other side was her *Ursari*—her simulator trainer—Star Commander Diego. He was an imposing Ghost Bear Warrior who wore concern for those in his charge as readily as his bushy mustache. "That was a very risky maneuver, cub."

"*Aff,* but it paid off...right?"

"You fight like a pickpocket, that much is clear. We will see if your gambit was successful." The Star Captain pointed to the monitors in the simulator hall. The rest of the cadets from the trial who had already been eliminated from the simulation, Lewis and Anna among them, stood around watching the rest of the battle play out on the vidscreens.

Smarting from the assessment of her combat style, Alexis crawled out of the training pod and looked up to the view of the battle for herself.

Thomasin and Sophie were doing their best. After the *Kodiak* had taken out Alexis, it had turned to target Thomasin. Sophie kept her distance, and kept firing missiles at her enemy until she ran out of ammunition.

By the time the *Kodiak* lined up a shot against Thomasin's *Bear Cub,* Thomasin had finished the work on its left arm, severing it from the assault 'Mech. Sophie's heat must have fallen enough, because she let loose with her lasers again.

"Come on, Sophie," Alexis said to herself.

The *Kodiak* aimed its Ultra autocannon at Thomasin, and Alexis felt the breath go out of the room. A pin drop would have been audible, no question.

A golden flash consumed the screen—

—and the *Kodiak* slumped over, its back melting into slag.

The room erupted in cheers and applause, and Alexis could finally take a breath as a smile spread across her face.

They did it.

Thomasin and Sophie's pods opened, and they emerged to hurrahs and glory befitting them. Alexis leaped forward to congratulate them with a broad smile. "I am so glad you got him!"

"It was all you," Thomasin told her, and she shrugged. "It was nothing."

"It was all me, actually," Sophie chided as Alexis pulled her into a hug. "And that's fine, Daniel is going to be really peeved."

Before Alexis could agree, Star Commander Diego shushed them all. Then, he looked down at his noteputer and tapped a few buttons before looking up at the cadets of the *sibko*. "The Bear Claw Star was successful in eliminating Cub Daniel in the *Kodiak*, well done. However, they lost three of their number. Cubs Lewis, Anna, and Alexis, what have you to say for yourselves?"

Lewis and Anna had nothing to say, and so they didn't. But one of them had to say something, though, so Alexis took a step forward. "I distracted the *Kodiak* long enough to allow Cubs Thomasin and Sophie to take it down. It was my plan that worked, and we won the day."

"But at the cost of yourself and your *Bear Cub*."

"*Aff*. Sometimes a sacrifice is necessary for a victory." Speaking so matter-of-factly made Alexis feel a bit flushed with defiance, wondering how much of her freebirth was showing in her attitude.

The *Ursari* shifted his attention to Sophie. "Cub Sophie, you overheated at the end, wasting your last shot on the *Kodiak*."

"*Aff*," Sophie said, matching the defiance Alexis offered. "Cub Thomasin would have perished had I not."

"Do not allow your 'Mechs to overheat if you can help it. *Aff*, in this simulation there was but one enemy 'Mech, but in reality, there could always be others, and you do not want to be caught unawares."

"*Aff, Ursari*."

"And you, Cub Thomasin." The Star Captain turned to the last survivor of Alexis' Star. "Well done."

Alexis smiled, proud of Thomasin.

But then the Star Captain turned his attention to Daniel who was indeed angry. "Cub Daniel, you had the advantage in weight and weapons. Why did you let them neutralize those advantages?"

Alex's eyes narrowed, annoyed. Daniel was obnoxious, but she got the distinct impression the *Ursari* was purposely trying to make him their enemy.

Daniel, standing straight and arrogant, didn't need help being their enemy. He was among the oldest of the Bearclaws, a favorite among the *Ursari,* and he hated freeborn Ghost Bears like Alexis with every cell in his body. His angular jaw, ice blue eyes, and brown hair made the very model of the Bourjon blood line. "They were applying *dezgra* tactics."

"A reason," Star Captain Diego said. "Not an excuse."

Alexis caught Daniel side-eyeing her, angry. He took a breath, ready to protest further, but was interrupted by the simulator hall doors opening wide.

Star Captain Sasha Ivankova stepped inside. "Cadets," she said in a booming voice. "I have watched your progress, and you have done well. Instead of hand-to-hand training today, we will be making a special trip."

Alexis almost expected a murmur from the rest of the *sibko*—she'd been with them long enough to know they often had a hard time keeping quiet—but the severity of their Den Mother kept them silent. They all straightened nervously at the sight of Star Captain Ivankova.

"We will be heading to the civilian government center," she continued. "Where you will all be given a chance to cast a ballot for Vote Day. Since you are all of voting age and everyone of voting age, Clan and non-Clan, alike is allowed a vote in the Dominion, you will fulfill this duty. It is up to all of us whether or not we join the ilClan or refuse, and remain part of the Rasalhague Dominion instead."

The whole idea of the vote made Alexis nervous. It had already caused arguments that veered close to fistfights in the *sibko* barracks. All of Alexis' *sibmates* were excited to vote, one way or the other, and to be honest, Alexis was glad she even got a vote. After the life she'd led before joining with the *sibko,* she couldn't believe she could do anything respectable like that at all. But at the same time, she wished they had no call to vote on something so contentious. Everyone thought they were right, no matter how much they disagreed, and it made everyone want to take a swing at each other.

She'd finally found her family, and she didn't want to see anything as ridiculous as Inner Sphere politics tear it apart.

"Now," the Den Mother said, "change out of your training gear and put on something presentable. We need to be an example of the Ghost Bear *sibko* program. We will meet at the transports at 1400 hours. Is that understood?"

"Aff, *Star Captain!*" came a rousing chorus of adolescent voices.

But Alexis' response was half-hearted.

CHAPTER 4

FALCON'S RUN TRAINING FACILITY
OUTSKIRTS OF HAMMARR
SUDETEN
JADE FALCON OCCUPATION ZONE
09 AUGUST 3151

Dawn stood at attention, in a line with the other nine candidates she had served with in the Jade Falcon infantry and Elementals. Some were past their prime, *solahma* Warriors eager for one last chance to prove themselves. Others were younger, like Dawn, but had simply missed their Trials by a hair's breadth, and ended up in the paramilitary police instead of in the cockpit of a 'Mech.

Dawn did not wonder why she was there. She knew why.

Clan Jade Falcon was on the brink of extinction.

That was the only reason such a motley crew would be granted the chance to become MechWarriors once again.

She had no intention of blowing it.

Not this time.

Star Captain Quinn stood at the end of the line, waiting for their new Khan's approval of her work. The Khan, minted just weeks prior in the wake of the chaos from the disastrous march to Terra, walked up and down the line inspecting them. Dawn felt a pang of regret that the Jade Falcons had not won the ilClanship, but if she could do her part with the new Khan, she would be able to help bring the Jade Falcons back to a position of power with a leader they could believe in.

Khan Jiyi Chistu came to Dawn and looked her up and down. His eyes looked right through her, and she could practically see the gears turning in his head. He was handsome enough, if not a little bland to look at. Dark curly hair, scruff on his cheeks, classic scar across his eye. Those scars seemed standard issue for Jade Falcons. Dawn did her best not to stare, though.

Finally, he broke the silence. "How long have you been in the paramilitary police?"

"Three years, my Khan."

"Young, then. What kept you from becoming a MechWarrior?"

"The first opponent in my Trial of Position forced a free-for-all. I argued that it was dishonorable, but was overruled." There was no sense in explaining to him why those above her hated her and singled her out and forced her into the paramilitary police, even though she had been born and bred to be a MechWarrior. It would only sound like an excuse. They had conspired against her to prevent her from becoming one. But she had the last laugh. They were all presumably dead on Terra, and here she was, standing before her Khan.

"But you made no kill? Else you would not be here, *quiaff*?"

"That was how the official record was written, my Khan, but as I said, I protested, and my Trial of Grievance was refused."

"And the one who forced the free-for-all?"

Dawn's voice chilled. "Dead."

"And how do you like the paramilitary police?"

"I prefer a 'Mech."

"We all do. It is what makes us Jade Falcons." The Khan furrowed his brow, then scratched the stubble under his chin. "And you are willing to participate in another Trial of Position for a chance to get back into a 'Mech and serve your Clan?"

"*Aff*," Dawn said. The word itself felt inadequate to the task. Too small. Dawn had no desire to put on a paramilitary police uniform ever again. She had not been bred for that task whatsoever, she did not like it. There was nothing like sitting in the command couch of a 'Mech and bringing dozens of tons of technology to a fight.

Exhilarating was the only word she could think to use. And that's how she felt, thinking about the chance to do it again. She hated that the opportunity arose from the near extinction of her Clan, but she was a Jade Falcon, and would fight to the death in any situation and make the most of it.

"Splendid," the Khan said, then moved on to the next soldier.

Once the troops were inspected sufficiently, the Khan had a few words with the Star Captain Dawn could not hear.

The Khan's quiet reserve did nothing to help her guess whether he was pleased or not. His countenance gave nothing away, which she supposed was a good quality to have in the Khan leading the shattered remnants of the Clan into battle and renewal.

He and the Star Captain wrapped up their conversation or debate or whatever it was, neither of them betraying anything. Then the Khan stood before the assembled Warriors, folding his hands behind his back and looking at each one of them in turn.

"Jade Falcons assembled before me," he said, his voice booming, "today, things are different. They are different for our Clan, and they are different for us individually. You know this. You all know the precarious situation we are in. There are Wolves at our gate. Enemies all around us. And we must fight for our very existence. Things that have served us well over the years now work to our disadvantage.

"I will not dissemble. None of you are my first choice to pilot a BattleMech..."

He paused after he said that to stare right into Dawn with his storm-blue eyes. His choice of words was meant to elicit a reaction, and she had tried to keep as perfectly still, as she had during her inspection. She wanted to prove she had the sangfroid to become a MechWarrior with her second chance. But her fears betrayed her under his withering gaze and cutting remark. A shiver raced up her spine.

He broke his gaze and shifted his piercing stare to someone else. "As Khan, it is on me to look at the resources we have and the resources we need to best serve and defend the Clan. You are what I have. MechWarriors are what I need."

The Khan executed a perfect about-face and paced in front of the assembled line, keeping his hands at ease behind his back. "This is unorthodox, what we are going to do. But, as they say, desperate times call for desperate measures. I wanted to come out and see you because I want you to know that you have the support of your Khan. Being promoted to MechWarrior is not something that will be taken from you as soon as our *sibko*s begin graduating and taking their own Trials of Position. I came out here to personally assure you that if you survive these Trials to the satisfaction of Star Captain Quinn, then you will have earned the right to stand alongside the legends of the Jade Falcons for your deeds from that moment forward."

His stare lasered into Dawn once more as he said this, inspiring a sense of duty and honor she had not felt since getting downgraded from a 'Mech to a mere badge. "You will do everything in your power to become a MechWarrior worthy of the 'Mechs we will assign you. You will survive. And you will fight. The situation is dire. We are all that is left of Clan Jade Falcon, and we are rebuilding. We are in the best possible position to do so with the hand we have been dealt, but it will not be easy. Nothing you do will be easy. Do not expect it to be. The path we all have ahead of us will be difficult. But if you do this, you will bring glory to us all, *quiaff*?"

"AFF!" the recruits all responded, vigorously, Dawn included. She was part of something again.

"*Quiaff?*" the Khan said again, louder this time.

"*AFF!*" they all barked again, louder as well.

Electricity sparked through Dawn's soul, roused by the feeling of togetherness she thought she had lost. She would be a MechWarrior. She would make her Khan proud. There was no other way forward for her. Dawn would succeed or die trying.

"Good." Khan Jiyi Chistu stopped in front of them, then extended a hand toward Star Captain Quinn. "I leave you in the capable hands of Star Captain Quinn. She will oversee your Trials and ensure that only the best of you will become MechWarriors in the new Jade Falcons. I would offer you all luck, but you are Jade Falcons, and have no use for something as fickle as luck."

The Khan left them there, still standing at attention. That's when Star Captain Quinn stepped in front of them all, replacing the Khan as the focus of their attention. She took a moment looking them over. More theater to stress them out or test their patience.

Finally, she spoke, "The Khan believes in all of you. I do not. Not yet. You will have to earn that. But for now, we will see what you know about piloting a BattleMech."

Dawn suppressed a grin.

This was going to be *fun.*

The simulator couch reeked of old sweat and past failure, and Dawn could not be more dismayed with her situation. She had assumed her days in a simulator were over when she had completed her *sibko* training.

She wanted to feel a real 'Mech under her control.

But if the simulator got her to that point, she would have to go through any simulation they required of her and do it with aplomb.

"Recruits," Star Captain Quinn's voice came through over the comm, "let us see what you are made of. Activate your simulated 'Mechs and show us what you can do."

The ignition sequence for the simulator was not that different from the 'Mech she'd trained in, an aging *Gyrfalcon* like the Khan preferred to pilot. She had no problem starting her virtual 'Mech right away and pushed it into the field where the other 'Mechs were lined up. She looked around on her HUD, hoping to see the other BattleMechs roar to life, but none did.

Soon enough, one of her fellows came online. And then another. But after five minutes, only three of them had been able to get the 'Mechs going, and only Dawn had been able to do it so quickly.

With derision dripping from her voice, Star Captain Quinn got back on the radio. "Those of you who have been able to activate your 'Mechs, weapons ready. For those of you who have been unable to do so, you have exactly one minute before your 'Mechs are fired upon. MechWarrior Dawn, the first to engage their 'Mech, will lead the attack. Do I make myself understood?"

"Aff!" came the chorus of would be MechWarriors.

"Then let the countdown begin."

Dawn gripped the control stick and thumbed the firing stud, thinking this simulated exercise would not be so bad after all.

CHAPTER 5

KODIAK POINT
GHOST BEAR HEADQUARTERS
ANTIMONY
QUARELL
10 JULY 3151

Star Colonel Emilio Hall needed to focus and blow off steam, so the martial arts studio at Kodiak Point was the right place for him to go. He began by meditating, and then went through drills of movement. Slow, deliberate, and Aikido-like, but he did not practice Aikido.

He was much more an adherent of Jeet Kune Do. The philosophy of it appealed to him. It drew on everything from martial arts and boxing to fencing and tree chopping. The core philosophy was to intercept your opponent by discovering their intent, in thought or deed. Determine where they would strike, and be there first.

It centered him and allowed him to focus on his problems while utilizing something that would help keep him combat-ready. It did not matter how high in the ranks he climbed; as a Clan Warrior and a Ghost Bear, he had to be ready for anything, in a 'Mech or otherwise.

The tension and frustration of the Vote and the changing nature of the Inner Sphere worried him. No matter how the Vote turned out, life for the Ghost Bears and the Rasalhague Dominion would be irrevocably altered by the actions of Clan Wolf. Whether they stayed or went, nothing would be the same. If they went, they would be stuck under the whims of the Wolf ilClan. If they stayed, at some point they would have a new enemy and a new front of battle. Alaric Ward, the new ilKhan, had upset the balance of everything they had fought for under the guise of an ancient tenet of the Clans that would no longer serve them. Damage was already done.

Though he closed his eyes to focus, he sensed a significant change in the room.

A presence.

An intrusion.

The emptiness was infinite when he practiced. The introduction of a second presence felt as obvious as a gunshot piercing it. The intensity of her presence told him exactly who it was before she broke the silence with her voice. "Star Colonel," she said from the door at the edge of the dojo.

Star Captain Allison Rand. She served as Emilio's second-in-command.

"Yes, Star Captain?" he said without opening his eyes.

"The votes of Quarell have been certified after the final recount."

"And?"

"The Dominion is on the road to joining the Star League. We have won on Quarell."

He kept his posture, refusing to deflate with her words. Emilio was careful not to reveal his opinion about the vote. The last thing he wanted to do was get in a protracted debate with his second-in-command. He had nothing to prove, and she was prone to such theatrics.

"Joining won on this planet, at least. There are many worlds in Rasalhague, and not all think alike. We will see how the vote turns out across the Dominion. We are but one Bear in the den."

"I cannot help but notice," the Star Captain said, the curiosity in her voice like a question from a precocious child, "how you hedge every time I claim our victory."

"Victory means different things to different people, Star Captain." Finishing the flourish of his arms and fists in front of him, he pulled them back close to his body and straightened his posture from the fighting stance. "We all view it differently."

"I see," she said.

He turned to regard her. Her brow was furrowed, the information collating in her mind. Her uniform was neat, crisp at each crease. The only crooked lines about her were the jagged lines of the ponytail of blond hair that rested on her shoulder in an orderly mess. One of her brown eyebrows raised up as she made the connections. She knew where he stood now, wanting to refuse the call and make sure the Dominion remained safe and whole. He supposed that would be his cross to bear.

"You have won," he said, "and that is all that matters. I look forward to joining the Star League if that is the ultimate decision of the Dominion. That I got a vote and a say, the same as anyone else, is a testament to the superiority of our system. But I would be lying if I said I did not have my reservations."

Star Captain Rand held her tongue. She had that much respect for him, at least.

"How is the populace handling it?" he asked.

"There are protests here and there, but at this point, by and large, the refusers are accepting the vote."

"I would expect nothing less. That is what votes are for. They have had their voice heard and will submit to the judgement of the greater populace. How close was it?"

"We—" She stopped and corrected herself. "The measure passed by less than a thousand votes."

"In the region?"

"Planetwide."

"Oh," was all Emilio could say. It was close. Razor-thin. But the fact that the protests were not more widespread was positive. "That is not what you came here to tell me though, *quiaff*?"

"*Aff.*"

"What is it, then?" Emilio pulled the dangling black ribbon of his blue gi's belt and tightened it.

"We have been selected to host a cross-training exercise on Quarell."

"Sounds like fun."

"Indeed. It is spread across *sibko*s, both here and from other worlds. Come October, we will host as many as four additional *sibko*s of cubs on Quarell. They have sent a list of preparations we must make."

Emilio smoothed the close scruff of a beard on his chin. "War games, then?"

"*Aff.* Among other tests. We have been told to coordinate with the local government to empty a city for live-fire exercises."

"They will love that."

"*Aff.* I expect we will eventually decide on a place that will be suitable. But time is short." The Star Captain looked at the noteputer she had brought with her. "I have a list of suitable options available for you."

"Splendid. But not much time to pull it off? Not ideal, but we will manage. When do the other *sibko*s begin arriving?"

"September."

"Wonderful. This comes from the Den Mothers? Or the Khans?"

"Both."

"I would have thought they had more important things to worry about. This happens occasionally, though. Every three to six years or so. Perhaps they felt the time was right, given the situation."

"There is nothing more important than the next generation of Ghost Bears, is there?"

But Emilio did not answer. He merely resumed his defensive stance.

"Do you wish to spar, Star Colonel?" There was a knife's edge in her voice he had heard so often. Did she want to prove her point in a sparring match rather than a Circle of Equals?

The stakes were definitely lower this way.

"*Aff.*" A difference of political opinion was not worth a Circle of Equals. Not this one, anyway. And besides, if anyone should have been interested in such a Circle, it should have been him. His side had lost the vote on Quarell. There was still a chance the rest of the Dominion would see the reason he did. It would be close, though.

Sense lost by less than a thousand votes on Quarell, but it could win by a thousand more elsewhere.

As Star Captain Rand got into her own gi for the sparring match, Emilio tried to cast aside the disappointment of the vote and focus on the task ahead with the *sibkos*. They would play host to hundreds of young Cubs. And if there was one thing he knew about young Cubs, it was they could be a handful at that age. They would all be seventeen or eighteen, ready to burst with energy. They all had something to prove, Trueborn and freeborn alike.

He remembered what it was like to have something to prove so earnestly matched with the dread of not being able to make it. As a Cub, Emilio was convinced he would die before he took his Trial of Position. And when the date of his Trial had come, he became convinced he would die during the Trial. When he survived, he assumed he would die in battle before he got a Bloodname.

None of it was true. It was simply one of the tricks the adolescent Warrior mind played on itself.

He no longer thought he would die before the next benchmark in his life.

But he had reached the rank of Star Colonel, and did not know how many more benchmarks he would meet. Some part of him hoped he *did* die before he fell into retirement. Perhaps he could travel the stars and make his great work the greater glory of the Ghost Bears, spreading democratic ideals the way merchants spread resources in their VaultShips.

The Star Colonel turned back to Rand, who had changed quickly into the gi.

She faced off against him with a deep forward stance. "Are you ready, Star Colonel?"

"Aff." Star Colonel Emilio Hall could read every move she could possibly make from that stance and distance, and he smiled.

In all their interactions, he found her style easy to read. Like a book. She chose the most aggressive moves she could, wasted a lot of effort making attacks bigger than she needed to. She was also quick to anger and got erratic when enraged. Patience and calm would win out over her every time.

"Are you ready?" he asked.

She nodded.

Then, with a knowing grin, he said, "Very well then. Let the fight begin."

CHAPTER 6

HAMMARR SPACEPORT LANDING PAD
HAMMARR
SUDETEN
02 SEPTEMBER 3151

Khan Jiyi Chistu smiled broadly as Jodine, the Jade Falcon Merchant Factor in charge of the entire Merchant caste, walked toward him on the landing platform. The ship behind her was small, an in-atmosphere vessel that brought her from another hemisphere. She had been shoring up contracts on the Jarho Islands.

Jodine's cape swept to one side, and the shape of her tight-curled locks of ebony hair followed with it. Her dark face, much darker than Jiyi's, appeared in grim silhouette at a distance, and he knew she had equally grim tidings they had to discuss.

The wind on the platform blew at Jiyi's curls and pressed his uniform tighter to his body. "Merchant Jodine," he said, spreading his arms to her, almost as though he were going to hug her.

"My Khan," she offered back respectfully, ignoring his gesture.

"What news have you brought me? You would not have traveled all this way if you had nothing to report."

"*Aff.* My merchants have heard rumblings about the recall order we received, requesting we move to Alyina before we decided to head here instead."

He nodded. "This order and its provenance have weighed heavy on my mind."

"Mine also. There is other news as well."

"Walk with me." The Khan directed her toward the spaceport complex, and they walked together, talking over the gusts of wind. "Tell me what you have learned."

As she changed direction, Jodine brushed away the wisps of hair that had flown into her face. "The recall order was a play for power, as we suspected, but not from our enemies as we guessed. The Jade Falcon Merchant Factor Marena has given herself the title Syndic. She has not publicly denounced the Jade Falcons yet, but she has declared herself the Merchant Queen of Alyina, and formed what she is calling the Alyina Merchant League."

"She is Trueborn, is she not?"

"*Aff.* And she was the source of the recall order. It appears as though she has decided to take the rest of the VaultShips and consolidate control of the Jade Falcon income generation."

Jiyi's stomach twisted. Without Marena, it would be almost impossible to finance the reconstruction of the Jade Falcons. "It is good that we still have you, and that you still control VaultShip *Gamma*."

"*Aff.*"

"And surely, you have no intention of joining with Marena?"

"*Neg.*"

Jiyi smiled. "But you considered it?"

Jodine cocked her head as she regarded him. "I wondered what glory it could bring me or the Jade Falcons, but I realized having influence with the Khan of my Clan would be more beneficial."

"My ear is always yours, Jodine."

"And that is why I am here instead of fleeing to Alyina. But they are making their play, since what you have is all that is left of the Clan. If she knows how things are here on Sudeten, she will count on you not surviving."

"She is wrong."

"I believe that, too. What will you do about her?"

Jiyi stepped up to the doors of the spaceport complex and they slid open. He smiled and changed the subject, leading them to the escalator inside. "What other news did you bring me?"

"Vedet Brewer has resurfaced."

"The former Archon of the Lyran Commonwealth? Who lost that title without managing to die in the process?"

"*Aff.*"

"A vulture, picking at the bones of the wounded Jade Falcon."

"*Aff.* He has taken one of our worlds in the Occupation Zone and declared himself Duke of the Vesper Marches. He is inviting disaffected Lyrans to join and live under his protection in these marches. A new alliance."

"Lovely." Jiyi sighed. Every loss meant more work and a more difficult job of rebuilding. "Where is his new capital?"

"Melissia."

"Of course."

The Lyran Commonwealth had held Melissia until a decade ago, when the Jade Falcons had taken control of it. The Fifth Talons were stationed there, but they were subject to the invasion order. They had emptied the planet, leaving it defenseless, and headed to Terra to their doom.

At the top of the long escalator, Jiyi led Jodine through a long passageway that opened onto a bar and near-empty balcony that overlooked the landing pads. He paused to speak with the bartender. With a nod from the Khan, the bartender knew exactly what to do and went about preparing drinks.

"That is not all," Jodine said as they settled at a table on the balcony. The wind had subsided some, but enough remained to flutter their hair in the gentle breeze. "Arcturus has also fallen."

"With the Falcons weak, it is not unexpected." Jiyi felt even more attacked by this news. Arcturus had also been a holding of the Lyrans once, though they had lost it to Clan Wolf more than half a century prior. The Falcons had taken it from the Wolves just a few years ago. If memory served him, the Thirteenth Falcon Dragoons had been assigned to protect the planet before being recalled to Terra, where they must have met their doom alongside the rest of the Jade Falcon *touman. Such a waste.* "What else do you know of this loss?"

"A number of Arcturan Guards have gone rogue and have taken a number of planets from the Occupation Zone, using Arcturus as their base of operations."

"Naturally."

The bartender arrived with a noteputer and a pair of drinks. Four pungent shots of mezcal, two each for the Khan and the Merchant Factor.

Jiyi raised the shot in front of him in a salute, and Jodine did likewise. They downed the golden liquid together.

"Excellent," Jodine said, savoring the shot. "But not as good as what we have on VaultShip *Gamma*."

"I have never had better than that, but trust me, I look."

Logging into his own noteputer, Jiyi and pulled up a map of the Jade Falcon Occupation zone. With the new information, he made alterations, showing each erosion in his Clan's territory as he spoke. "So, Alyina is gone, left to the devices of our former Merchant Factor."

"Aff."

"And we have lost Arcturus to renegades, and Melissia has fallen to a vulture."

"That is the long and the short of it."

Jiyi studied the map for a long while. The less he spoke, the less he had to worry about anyone divining his true intentions, though that never stopped them from asking. Jodine was more restrained than most, but eventually she succumbed as well.

"What is the plan, my Khan?"

"I must go."

"My Khan?"

"I knew we would be under attack," Jiyi said. "With the Jade Falcons' fall at Terra, it is natural—even understandable—that we would suffer losses. They look at our carcass like scavengers, not realizing we are still alive while they pick our bones. They will discover fight in us, though we may need to retract our borders for the time being." He zoomed out the map even further.

"Will you strike at the so-called Merchant Queen then, bring her back into the fold?" Jodine asked.

"Neg."

"*Neg?*" Jodine blinked, confused.

"We need allies. I will send her an invitation to discuss the future of the Clan. It is no wonder she made the play she did if she thought the Jade Falcons were no more. Indeed, it is more than likely that you or I would have done the same in her place. No, we make peace with her and utilize her resources. We will not lose Alyina and the rest of the VaultShips; they will once again be part of the Jade Falcon holdings."

"They are merchants, though. I am afraid they will not have the Warriors you need. Nor the information to both fend off the other threats and keep the Jade Falcon Occupation Zone whole."

"You are correct. Which is why you will remain here on Sudeten, in charge. Keep VaultShip *Gamma* close, as we cannot afford to lose it. I must leave immediately."

"Where will you go?"

Jiyi raised his second shot of mezcal. "To sound the Jade Falcon's call."

CHAPTER 7

BEARCLAW SIBKO TRAINING FACILITY
COPPERTON
QUARELL
RASALHAGUE DOMINION
03 SEPTEMBER 3151

Downtime in a Ghost Bear *sibko* was rare, but when Alexis did get it, she relished it. It was something she never had before getting thrown into the Ghost Bear way of life. She couldn't afford downtime back then.

Doing nothing made her feel warm and fuzzy. Especially when she nestled into a bunk between Thomasin or Sophie. It was best when it was the both of them. During this particular downtime, Thomasin sat at the edge of the bunk while Alexis nestled into Sophie's arms, wishing they had time to "couple," as the Clans called it.

Coupling hadn't necessarily been encouraged or discouraged. The Den Mother and the other *Ursari* treated it as sort of a given. They were all given medication to prevent reproduction just in case their particular pairings made that a possibility, which wasn't always the case. No matter how much Sophie and Alexis coupled, there was no chance of reproducing. And no matter how many times Thomasin had spent coupling with any of their male *sibmates*, they weren't going to reproduce, either. The *Ursari* didn't care who the *sibkin* made their connections with, because that togetherness made them all feel safe and taken care of as they found some comfort in each other's arms.

"Thomasin," Sophie said, "why are you not lying with us?"

Thomasin, his back to Alexis and Sophie, just shrugged.

"Are you okay?" Alexis said.

"Things are fine."

"Then, again I ask, why are you not lying with us? We only have ten minutes until our next drill."

Thomasin turned and faced them, crossing his legs on the bed. "We have this cross-training, and then we will have our Trials. I have a hard time reconciling it."

"Which part?" Sophie asked.

But Alexis knew. She had the same reservations.

"The Den Mother focuses on the aspect of our shared bonds so much. We are a family. How can we fight them in our Blooding? Yes, we must prove ourselves superior to become Warriors, but I do not want to kill any of our *sibkin*."

"I have similar anxieties," said Alexis. "How can we remain together, but have to fight each other so viciously?"

"It is the way of the Clans," Sophie said.

Alexis nestled deeper into the crook of Sophie's arms. "There has to be a better way."

Thomasin smoothed the patch of gray-blue blanket in front of him. "Maybe there is a better way, or maybe this is the best it can get. How far away from the teachings of Kerensky can we stray and still remain a Clan?"

Alexis dreaded when the conversations took these turns. Inevitably, they would always come to the vote. Thomasin had been a very vocal joiner, and had a deep, specific disdain for anyone he learned had voted to refuse.

"I have no idea why anyone would want to move further and further away from what it means to be a Clan," he said, "but they manage to find ways to come closer and closer to that."

Sophie rolled her eyes. "Focus on the *sibko* training, Thomasin. There is nothing left to worry about. The vote is over, at least on Quarell, and we won. The refusers will have to live with their betrayal."

Sophie groaned in annoyance when the bell for the next drill rang out through the halls, but Alexis sighed in relief. She had successfully dodged the conversation since Vote Day and just smiled and nodded with Thomasin. She had finally found a home with the Ghost Bears, one she never had before, and didn't want to risk it for anything.

Her frustration mounted, though. She'd been promised to find belonging, and she had, but she didn't want things to change. Alexis had read about the prognostications about the ilClan and the Inner Sphere and Terra, and about Clan Wolf as well. Nothing about the situation made her feel like things would become better and more caring if they had to join the Star League.

So she had voted to refuse.

But that ability to vote made her feel special in her place and position within the Ghost Bears, which she hadn't expected.

As long as Thomasin didn't lead a mob against all the refusers he found, she could keep her little family.

The drill alarm continued, and Sophie dragged herself up from the bed, tearing herself from Alexis' arms. "Let's go."

But Alexis didn't want Sophie to go any more than she wanted to go to the drill.

Now that she'd found downtime, she never wanted to give it up.

When Thomasin stood next, Alexis knew she would have to get up, too.

The bell continued its incessant drone. It wouldn't stop until they were all in the field, ready to fight.

**BEARCLAW TRAINING FIELD
COPPERTON
QUARELL
RASALHAGUE DOMINION**

Standing at attention in the rain wasn't Alexis' idea of worthwhile training, and she far preferred the predictable to the unexpected, but she supposed they had to learn to fight in all climates and weather conditions. This particular training field was broad and flat, covered in dirt that quickly became mud.

To her credit, Den Mother Sasha Ivankova stood in the rain with them, barking orders at them. "Which *sibko* is going to win the cross-training exercises?"

"*The Bearclaws!*" they all shouted.

"And why are you going to win?"

"*We are the best!*"

"The correct answer."

The Den Mother didn't even seem to notice the elements. The rain came down at a slant through the wind, and she walked as though she were sauntering alone in a forest on a clear day. She set quite an example. Alexis hoped to please her with her own stoicism in adversity.

The rain flew from the Den Mother's face when she snapped her gaze to the other direction, looking at one of Alexis' *sibkin* further down the line. Daniel. "Who among you wants to earn five extra points for this exercise? And the glory that goes with it?"

Alexis would be damned if it was Daniel.

If she had a problem, he usually caused it. He hated her, as he hated all the freeborns in the *crèche*. He shared no sense of family with those who had found other ways into the Bearclaws, and constantly tried to stop their progress. He also used every opportunity, ranging from subtle to overt, to make life more difficult for the freeborns, Alexis especially. Sometimes it would be as simple as tripping her on the way to the mess. Other times it would be angling to make her look bad in exercises, going out of his way to get her eliminated first. It infuriated him that Alexis still performed as well as she had, though, and she took great pleasure in that.

The Den Mother clearly favored him, which is why he never got in trouble. And maybe she thought this exercise would be well suited for him to gain points.

He wouldn't get any if Alexis had anything to say about it.

The Den Mother continued, gesturing up to the rigging in the distance. "At the top of that structure is a flag. The first one who brings it to me will be awarded the five points and no more drilling for the day."

Alexis resisted the urge to wipe the rain from her eyes, and squinted to get a better look. It was a simple outline of a structure. Two wooden beams ten meters high and about three meters apart were set into the ground. They were connected by a third beam at the top, giving the structure the look of some solidity. Three ropes dangled down from the top and the flag whipped in the wind atop a slim pole at the apex of the high beam.

"Am I understood?"

"AFF!" the entire *sibko* shouted.

"Then begin. May the best Bear win."

The Star Captain stepped aside and let chaos ensue.

The field was already well-worn dirt from their exercises, and with the rain it had all turned to mud. As soon as she set the cubs at their goal, it became a mad scramble through the mud, slipping and sliding, and tearing into each other, each of them jockeying for some advantage.

All except for Alexis.

She remained at attention, not moving a millimeter.

She merely watched the bedlam. Elbows were thrown. Her *sibkin* growled and snarled at one another like animals. They all wanted those five points.

But Alexis watched for her opening.

"Are you seeking rest or glory?" Star Captain Ivankova asked Alexis with a sneer in her voice.

"Glory, of course. I am just waiting for the right time to strike. Slow and steady wins the race."

The Den Mother huffed. "Just like a thief."

Alexis ignored the slight and watched.

With her *sibko* in front of her, huddled into a disorderly scrum and practically killing each other to get to the ropes first, she sought an opening to make her move. By the time the first of her *sibkin* made it to the ropes, they had already been pulled down by the mob. A new cub made it to the rope with regularity, reaching up, trying to get enough of a grip to pull themselves out of the mess, but each time, they were yanked down and shoved back into the cold mud.

Alexis took a deep breath and began her march.

She didn't run, and was careful not to slip in the mud. By the time she could see her kin more clearly through the rain, they were all covered in mud, head to toe. She couldn't tell Thomasin and Sophie from any of the rest, but she had made up her mind about how to proceed.

As she got closer, Alexis sped up into a jog, still careful to keep her footing. By the time she reached the edges of the *sibko*, she was practically sprinting.

Planting a foot on the back of a fellow cub, she launched forward and stepped on another of her *sibkin*, this one even closer. Then, she leaped for the rope, a full 2 meters off the ground, higher than anyone else had made it. She grabbed on and didn't wait to quit swinging before working to shimmy up the rope.

A roar from below sounded an awful lot like Daniel. "How *dare* you!"

It might have been a mistake to glance back down as she climbed, but Alexis got the distinct impression it was his back she had leaped up from. He wiped the mud from his eyes and pointed up at Alexis as she ascended.

"Pull her down!"

But every time someone grabbed one of the ropes below Alexis, they were immediately pulled back down. When it was Daniel's turn, Alexis assumed Thomasin and Sophie wrenched him back down to the ground. Though they were both Trueborn, they did not share Daniel's bigotry and reviled his arrogance, so they relished his defeats as much as Alexis did.

The wind and rain whipped at Alexis' face, and she wiped cold drops from her eyes with her sleeve while still reaching up the rope. The thick jute felt harsh against her hands, it had swelled in the rain to where she heard the twist of it squeak with pressure. Reaching higher, she pulled herself up further.

Just one more meter...

The rope below her swung harshly, almost pulling her out of balance.

Glancing down, Alexis saw cub climbing up beneath her, but someone yanked them backward. They hadn't let the rope go.

Alexis paused for a moment, waiting for some of the movement to subside, but the fight below her was so pitched now she didn't think she would get that chance. The only thing to do was press forward. At least if she failed now, the crowd would break her fall and she would have made it further than anyone else.

Clawing her way up, Alexis gripped the top beam and flung her legs across. The beam was 30 centimeters wide, just narrow enough to make losing her balance and breaking her neck in the fall a possibility. Alexis figured that was half the point. Only one of their *sibko* had died in the training so far, but she had heard stories of other Clans where surviving your *sibko* training was remarkable.

Using the flagpole—which she found to be sturdy, cold— Alexis pulled herself to a standing position on the high beam. There was no other way for her to reach the flag otherwise. Climbing up the rope, the structure felt sturdy enough because she expected to be swinging, but in the rain and with the rumble going on beneath her feet, Alexis had not felt anything more treacherous.

Alexis smiled as she grabbed the small plastic flag clipped to the top. She raised it over her head in victory, letting it flap in the wind for a moment before stuffing it into her pocket.

Turning around and looking down at the mess beneath her and the field of mud beyond leading to the Den Mother, Alexis felt a stone drop in her stomach.

She got the flag, sure, but that was only half the task. She still had to get it back to the Star Captain. And not a single person below, fighting for the flag in the first place, was going to make that easy on her.

Doing rough calculations in her head, Alexis formed a plan and sure as hell hoped it would work.

The three ropes leading up to the top were now dangling free. Kneeling down and keeping a hand on the flagpole, Alexis reached out and gripped the center rope beneath her. It remained taut as the melee continued beneath her and the rest of the cubs did their best to keep the rope gripped in their hands, but she pulled on it as hard as she could.

As soon as the rope had enough slack to yank, she jerked up hard.

Someone down there must have realized what she was doing, because the shouting got more intense and another cub clambered halfway up the rope to her right, and no one seemed to be stopping them.

Letting go of the flagpole, Alexis pulled the rest of the rope up as quickly as she could with both hands. Other cubs jumped to reach it as it flew upward, but they couldn't catch it fast enough.

Alexis turned her back to the Den Mother and arranged the rope so she could make a jump for it, eying the cub coming up the other line fast.

"Now or never," she told herself.

She found the spot of rope at about the right length, gripped tight, looping the rough cord around her hands, and leaping into space. Pushing off the structure, Alexis aimed for as wide an arc as she could before the force of gravity brought her swinging back toward the shouting *sibko*. They prepared to intercept her, muddied arms raised, but her feet were above the level of their heads as she flew by. Their heads whipped back to see her let go of the rope at the apex of her swing.

Alexis' arms pinwheeled as she struggled to right herself in mid-air and her legs started pumping, trying to absorb the momentum of her leap. Her feet slid forward and her heart jumped. If they caught her, they would tear her apart, and she would lose the flag, the points, the glory, and the right to gloat over the Trueborns.

Righting herself, even on the slippery ground, Alexis ignored the calls to violence behind her and launched into as much of a sprint as she could, given the sticky nature of the field of mud.

It was too late for the rest.

Alexis neared the Den Mother and reached into her pocket for the flag—but she couldn't feel it.

Panic hit her and she dug deeper into her pocket. She realized it was probably still there, she just couldn't feel her fingers in the frigid rain.

She would need to find it if she wanted to win. The mob of the rest of the *sibko* barreled toward her like an assault 'Mech on a mission of destruction.

The Den Mother had reproach writ large on her face, standing there in the rain, waiting for Alexis to produce *something*.

"It is here!" Alexis said, careful to enunciate each word. Contracting words with her *sibkin* felt acceptable, but she'd never dream of doing it in front of the Star Captain. That would be a supreme sign of disrespect and Alexis couldn't afford to lose the points, even though she was about to gain five more. "I promise."

"One would think you would be better at picking your own pocket," the Den Mother said.

Alexis suppressed a growl and finally found the flag, whipped it from her pocket, and presented it to the Den Mother.

"Here you are, Star Captain," she said, smiling wide. "As requested."

"Very well." Star Captain Ivankova snatched the flag from Alexis' hands, regarded it as though it were a piece of contraband, and raised a hand to the oncoming freight train of *sibkin*.

"It is finished! To attention!" she shouted, stopping their forward momentum. They pulled themselves apart and fell in.

Alexis looked the least muddied of the assembly and she worked hard to keep her irrepressible grin from showing, lest she get into trouble.

"Like a thief, Alexis has won the challenge, the points, and the glory, but victory is victory. She will clean up and report to her bunk. The rest of you, report to the gymnasium for laps. Now."

There were groans, but Alexis couldn't help but feel pleased with herself as the others passed her by, heading to the gym.

It wasn't until a brutish, muddy hand shoved Alexis from behind that the smile left her face. She was too busy falling face-first into the mud.

The arrogant laugh emanating from behind her could only belong to one person.

Daniel.

Like the Ghost Bear she hoped to be, Alexis roared and picked herself back up, ready to destroy him.

"Alexis," the Den Mother bellowed. "Before me, now."

"*Aff*," she said begrudgingly, turning her back on Daniel and heading over to the Star Captain.

"Daniel," the Den Mother said, "to the gymnasium."

"*Aff*," he said, and left the Den Mother and cub to stand there in the rain.

"Alexis, you did well. You earned your five points."

"That is all?" Alexis seethed. She could have called for a Circle of Equals, but she had a sneaking suspicion Star Captain Ivankova would have put a stop to that anyway. For a woman who preached so much about family and the ideals of the Ghost Bears and the Dominion, she made her disdain for Alexis well-known.

"That is all," the Den Mother sneered. "Now go."

"Aff."

And Alexis went.

CHAPTER 8

FELDSPAR
QUARELL
RASALHAGUE DOMINION
08 SEPTEMBER 3151

Feldspar was as out of the way as a city on Quarell could be. Nestled in a low valley and surrounded by hills, a road led out of it in each direction. The tiny airport could not accommodate space vehicles or DropShips. The feldspar mines in the surrounding hills had dried up ages ago, and the only people who remained did so out of habit.

It made sense to Star Colonel Emilio Hall why Feldspar had been voted to become the site of the war games, but logic would not make much difference to those living there. The land had been bought up by the government all around the town, and the neighboring towns as well. They'd all been evacuated over the last few years for some industrial initiative that had been voted on and accepted, but Feldspar had been the lone holdout. They didn't want to leave their home. Why would they want to be evacuated and displaced?

The mayor had been pleading his case for the last half-decade, and was committed to slowing the process, but the war games had accelerated the timetable.

It would show the locals the proper respect to discuss things with them in advance and let them know the Dominion military was there to help them evacuate the area.

The hover car bearing Emilio pulled up in front of the house of the mayor, the largest residence in the town. At one point, Feldspar had been home to as many as twenty thousand people, mostly miners, and the mayor's mansion had been built by one of the original founders of the town. It was streamlined series of modern boxes and lots of windows. For a town that mined rocks, that much glass certainly made a statement.

"Here we are, Star Colonel," the driver said through the intercom between the cab and the passenger compartment.

"Splendid." Emilio got out of the hover car and found no one outside to greet him. Another statement, this one intentional.

He decided he wouldn't simply stand there and wait for a greeting. The walk was longer than it looked, as it was on a slight incline, and led to a set of five stairs that came to the box of a first level.

Looking through the glass of the front window, Emilio saw the mayor sitting in a high-backed chair in the front room, facing away from the front door and keeping his view fixed out the window. He must have been eighty years old if he was a day, with a shock of tight white curls that contrasted brightly with his dark skin. Through the door, Emilio heard a chime announcing his arrival.

"Come in," the man said loud enough for Emilio to hear through the glass.

Emilio opened the hulking wooden door and stepped across the threshold, taking off his cap as he did so. The front room was decorated for official receptions. The mayor had created a welcoming atmosphere, with warm colors and lush, velvet drapes. The old wood floor looked well-loved and recently polished.

"Star Colonel, please forgive me for not standing," the mayor said, making no effort to turn around and regard Emilio. Then, he gestured to the matching high-backed chair across the low table from him. A vase atop it sprouted fresh cut flowers that added a pleasant scent to the room. "Please, feel free to sit."

"Of course." Emilio took the graciously offered seat in the plush chair. He was not accustomed to the comfort, and wondered if this was how every far-flung city on Quarell lived.

Before Emilio could start, the mayor raised a hand. "Would you like anything to drink? Coffee? Tea, perhaps?"

"Coffee would be fine."

The mayor tapped a few buttons on the arm of his chair before folding his hands in front of him. They were bony and frail, but as he clasped them, Emilio saw strength in them, too.

"Mayor Stelfreeze, I understand you wished to see me about the evacuation."

"*Aff.* That is what you say, yes?"

"*Aff.* Indeed."

"Good. Because I would like to be respectful in my request." The mayor's eyes, milky with age, had a ferocity to them Hall could respect as well. "I respect the Dominion. I respect the Ghost Bears. And I respect what they do for us."

"I am sure you do. But I also ask, respectfully, that you no longer hold up the evacuation."

At that, the mayor leaned forward. "I do not respect the vote to hold your war games here. Nor did I respect the vote to displace us in the first place, some five years ago."

The Star Colonel took in a breath, ready to respond, but an aide arrived with a tray of steaming coffee, delivering a mug to the Star Colonel and the mayor both.

The cup felt warm in Emilio's hands as he sipped, finding the coffee to be quite good. A surprise, to be sure.

"We grow it here," said the mayor. "In the hills. After the mines dried up, coffee became our trade."

"It is very good."

"I am glad that you enjoy it. There may not be much of it left."

"Mayor Stelfreeze, I would like to assure you that the Dominion has already committed to relocating your people to New Feldspar. It is more than half-built, and nearly ready for you. It is just not safe for you all to stay here while we have the cross-training exercises scheduled."

"I am sure you will all do your best and the cross-training will be a success, and the next generation of Ghost Bears will defend the Dominion as true Warriors."

"*Aff.*"

"Then I would like to call for a Trial of Refusal."

The words hung in the air between them and Emilio deflated, wishing things had not come to this. But this was about their very way of life and their homes. If he had learned anything about civilians, it was that they did not like being displaced.

"That is your right," he said finally. This was part of the integration of the Ghost Bears and the Rasalhague Dominion: civilians could call for Trials of Refusal against political decisions they disagreed with. It happened so rarely, though, that Emilio had not thought it would happen here.

But that spark of life in the old man's eyes should have prepared him for it. "The vote was split eighty-twenty," Stelfreeze said, "so I propose the Dominion forces field four 'Mechs to our one. And the field of battle would be Lime Kiln Gulch, beyond the foothills of our abandoned mines."

"And you have a champion in mind?"

"*Aff,*" the old man said as though he had been a Clanner all his life. "I propose that you be our champion."

Emilio's eyes widened at the suggestion. He smoothed the beard around the corners of his mouth. "This would definitely put me in a difficult spot, you understand."

"More difficult than losing your home? Packing up your entire life and leaving so you can watch a pack of cubs blow your ancestral homes to smithereens? More difficult than that?"

Some part deep inside Emilio burned to take on the challenge, to prove himself and to prove a point. Sometimes the victors of a vote *did* make a terrible decision, and they should be called to account. And maybe he wanted to prove to those beneath him that he had the tactical acumen and 'Mech piloting skills to take down four 'Mechs on his own. But the odds were not in his favor. The Dominion would choose the sharpest, most talented MechWarriors on Quarell to face the challenge, and Emilio would be humiliated. There was no upside to agreeing to the Trial—only honor dictated that he did.

"I believe you have the honor to fight to win for us, even if you do not believe in our cause," said the mayor. "I would fight myself, but I haven't been behind the controls of a 'Mech in forty years. And even then, it was an AgroMech. And a MiningMech before that."

Emilio sipped his coffee. "I appreciate your zeal and spirit. It does you credit and great honor, but the vote is cast, and you know that I—or any champion—would have very little chance of winning with those odds."

"But we would send a message that we went down with a fight."

The Star Colonel could not argue with that logic. And if there were no more questions of their obstinance, then the evacuation that had already been held up for years would go along smoothly once and for all.

Emilio snapped his fingers. "Very well, you can have your Trial. And I will be your champion. I will do everything in my power to win, but were I to lose, you will pack up and leave?"

"With no further objection."

Emilio took a last sip of coffee and placed the mug down on the table between them. "I will make the preparations. Time is of the essence. We will hold the Trial tomorrow."

"I look forward to it," Stelfreeze said. "You are a man of great honor."

Emilio stood and left, exchanging final pleasantries with the mayor and wondering just how in the world he would break this news to those under his command.

LIME KILN GULCH
QUARELL
RASALHAGUE DOMINION
09 SEPTEMBER 3151

Positioned at the south end of the gulch with a wall to his back, Star Colonel Emilio Hall settled into his command couch, waiting for the formal Trial to begin.

He would start at one end of the gulch and the rest would start at the other side. He racked his brain, hoping to find some advantage, some quirk of the landscape he could use to even the odds. He would fight against Star Captain Allison Rand and three others, handpicked by the civilian council: MechWarriors Justin, Reinhart, and Gurdel.

Instead of his usual *Ursus II*, he had opted to field a *Kodiak* in this Trial. Having an assault 'Mech would sand some of the rough edge from the long odds and put him on slightly better footing. At least it would look like a valiant fight.

Star Captain Rand preferred to pilot a 60-ton *Kuma* that had a more consistent range of fire than the *Ursus II*s that Justin and Reinhart would be fielding. The *Ursus II*s were 50 tons and boasted jump jets. They were well rounded 'Mechs that offered a lot of options at any range, but it did not help when they wanted to stick with a distant range and pour the heat onto a single target. They had to keep moving and get in close over time for maximum effectiveness.

The easiest of the targets would be the *Ursus II*s. The problem would be MechWarrior Gurdel's 95-ton *Executioner*. The *Executioner*'s Gauss rifle rounds alone could travel most of the distance of the Gulch, so Hall would need to be careful. His honor demanded that he do his best to win, and getting taken out at long range by the *Executioner* before he had defeated even a single 'Mech was not an option.

He would need to find somewhere to keep under cover and strike, a den to conceal himself in until the right time came. Separating his enemies somehow would be key. Finding a way to get them alone, one on one, would be his best chance. Otherwise, he had lost already.

"I still cannot believe we are being forced to do this, Star Colonel," Star Captain Rand said over the radio. "The losers had their chance to vote, and it was not even close. This is a mockery of a Trial. What would they have us do if you somehow manage to win? Just find another town somewhere else? It makes no sense."

"That was what we agreed upon, however unlikely or unwieldy that result would be. They deserve the honor of having their voice heard and to use every tool at their disposal to redress their grievances. This is part of our *rede*, which we have extended to these civilians. Would you break that?"

She did not respond for so long he wondered if the line had been broken, but then her voice came back with a tinge of annoyance. *"Neg."*

"Do not expect me to go easy either," he said. "Honor demands this be a legitimate Trial, one-sided as though it might be."

"Though I find this a waste of our time, I would never expect you to go easy."

"Good." He could not tell if there was sarcasm in her voice or not.

A voice cut in over the both of them. It belonged to Erika Gulbrand, the Prime Minister of Quarell. "The Trial is set to begin. Does either party have any last words beforehand?"

"*Neg*." Star Captain Rand said.

The Star Colonel bristled a bit. Normally he would be the one overseeing such a Trial, but having been dragged into it, the right fell to the civilian authority on the planet to act as an impartial third party. Ultimately, though, it was all for show, and he did not care. "I hope those who feel wronged are made whole by what happens here today."

"Well said, Star Colonel," the Prime Minister said. "I hope all involved find that solace as well. Now, on my mark, we will begin."

Emilio took in a deep, meditative breath and imagined how Allison Rand would command the battle. She would keep the *Executioner* back. Her *Kuma* would keep a middling position, and she would send Justin and Reinhart in advance to close in. If they could draw him out, then he would be fodder for the *Executioner* and the *Kuma*'s better maneuverability.

So that was what he would try to disrupt. Just like in his martial arts training, he would attack the point where they were coming at him, and divine their intent to use against them.

"The Trial begins," the Prime Minister said.

And then the radio squelched off.

Being alone without allies meant he had no one to talk to and no one to listen to. And the Star Captain would not be so foolish as to broadcast her plans on an open signal.

Scanning the surrounding rocks and craggy areas on his HUD, the Star Colonel spotted an old mine off to his right side and pushed his gigantic *Kodiak* in that direction. If he could get into the cave long enough to flank one of the *Ursus II*s, it would give him enough time to chip away at the force arrayed against him.

It was easier for Emilio to push through the black and gray-leaved trees than it was to angle around them, but he did when he could so as not to leave so obvious a trail. The rocks of the cliff were chalky white and the layers that had been stripped revealed rust-red rock beneath. In the middle of the sheer face stood the mouth of a cave, the perfect den for Emilio's trap. It looked big enough for him to walk into without having to cut away the rock with his lasers. He did not want to fire anything if he did not have to, for fear of giving away his position.

Some part deep inside of Emilio hated everything about the stratagem he had chosen. The Clan way was to stand and fight upright, to the death if necessary, and the Ghost Bears respected this credo as much, if not more, than any other Clan. But he was not just fighting for himself. He fought for a cause, his *rede,* and so much more. He *had* to do his best and he *had* to put in a performance so strong that no one would doubt he had tried his hardest.

Walking his massive *Kodiak* backward into the cave, all he had to do was power down and wait for the enemy to pass by. The gulch could not be more than 50 meters wide, and the cave itself was at least 200 meters from his starting point. The top speed of the *Ursus II* was about 65 kilometers per hour, and if they were moving at top speed from their starting point, it would not be long before they reached the end of the gulch. It would take a little longer than that to navigate the trees if they got into the bush, but it was likely they would stick to the dry creek bed in the center. Naturally, that was where they would want to keep Emilio because it could mean a straight shot from a Gauss rifle.

"Come on, Rand," he said. "Let us see what you are planning."

After a few moments, Emilio wondered if he had missed something. *Where are they?* The gulch was not that wide; he should have been able to see anything as soon as it came by.

He clung to the shadows, hoping he would not be found out before he was able to spring his trap. With the fusion reactor off, the cooling vest actually felt cold against his skin. Shivering,

Emilio tightened his hands around the control sticks and steeled himself against the wait.

He closed his eyes and took in a deep breath, clearing his head, imagining that his body was going through the moves and forms of his martial arts training. It centered him and put him in the warrior's mindset. Time sped and slowed at the same time, vanishing in either direction. And when Emilio finally opened his eyes, there was a target before him.

Reinhart's *Ursus II* stood in the monochromatic trees at a far enough distance that Emilio would need to strike fast if he were to get him. But he did not want a single target. If he was going to strike fast and hard, he wanted his element of surprise to work for at least two 'Mechs.

Patience.

Restraining himself, Emilio waited. He looked over the *Ursus II* and it felt a bit like an out-of-body experience. That was the sort of 'Mech he preferred to fight in. Seeing it from the outside was like the vertigo of seeing that back of your head in a live security camera. It never looked right. The blue and gray paint of the Beta Galaxy's standard arctic camouflage shone bright in the coal-colored foliage. He could make out the unit insignia of the Fourteenth Battle Cluster on the shoulder pauldrons of the *Ursus II:* a black bear, claws bloodied, roaring over a blue star.

It was never Emilio's hope to attack one of his own, but a Trial was a Trial, and he had to fulfill his oath.

He pinpointed everywhere he could aim his lasers to disable the *Ursus II* without needlessly killing Reinhart. The Trial had not demanded that anyone die, so Emilio would aim to keep everyone—himself especially—alive to fight another day.

His attention darted up to movement beyond Reinhart. And there it was: Justin's *Ursus II.* Exactly as he'd predicted. Justin was on the other side of the riverbed, hoping to catch Emilio in it and herd him toward the center.

Had it really not crossed their minds that he would not play by their rules?

The *Kodiak* roared on and life returned to the limbs and joints of Emilio's 'Mech. Before Reinhart had a chance to turn at the surprising blip on their screen, Emilio raised the arms of his *Kodiak* and stepped forward. With all eight of his medium lasers, he lashed out at Reinhart's side, boiling chunks of armor from the *Ursus II*'s left arm and leg and spilling molten metal across the foliage, burning up trees, shrubs, and grass. Then, pulling the trigger on the control stick, Emilio fired the Ultra autocannon, scoring another direct hit in the *Ursus II*'s left arm, blowing it into useless pieces and wobbling the whole 'Mech, ready to tip.

Feeling the heat build up, Emilio charged to cover the distance between himself and the *Ursus II* before it could get its bearings. With a forceful shove on his way by, he threw Reinhart's *Ursus II* further off balance until it crashed into the dry riverbed on its one good arm.

One down. At least for now.

Emilio could always go back and finish Reinhart's 'Mech off, but there was still Justin to deal with, not to mention Gurdel and Star Captain Rand.

They must have been in radio communication, obviously, because Justin spun to their left and put Emilio into their field of fire.

Ordinarily, Emilio would have come to a halt to take a shot at his opponent, but the riverbed was exactly where they wanted him, so that would be the place he would not go. Instead, he kept moving, across the deadly riparian area.

The *Ursus II* fired a volley of missiles, spiraling in smoke behind Emilio, missing completely, and exploding into the trees and rock beyond. They fired their medium lasers as well, golden flashes of light that missed their mark entirely.

Emilio half-hoped that Justin 's missed shots would inadvertently hit Reinhart, but they were Ghost Bears. He would have no such luck.

Once he felt secure enough in the dense foliage across the way, Emilio wheeled the *Kodiak* around in a large pivot, forcing Justin to do the same before either of them could take a shot.

With Justin and Reinhart in obvious radio communication with Gurdel and Rand, it was only a matter of time before the latter two would arrive to pin him into a corner. But he would have the advantage once more if he could simply deal with the second *Ursus II*.

Justin got the first shot off, lining it up faster than Emilio could. It made sense; Justin was already mid-turn and Emilio's *Kodiak* had to shake off its momentum and completely change direction. They fired another spate of missiles, choking the field between them with smoke. They peppered against the *Kodiak*'s torso, doing damage, but not enough for Emilio to worry yet. He could take many hits before falling.

Not that he wanted to take *any*, but he was under no illusions about how this would all end.

Justin's lasers fired next, turning bits of the *Kodiak*'s torso armor into slag, dripping down the ground in hot splashes.

Lining up his own shot, Emilio fired his Ultra autocannon and medium lasers. The report from the autocannon boomed loud and the shot crashed right into the torso of the *Ursus II*, just below the cockpit. Emilio would have aimed higher if he were not fighting a fellow Ghost Bear.

The lasers incinerated swaths of armor across Justin's torso and right arm. The 100-ton *Kodiak* in a one-on-one fight against the *Ursus II* was going to tear it apart sooner than later, and it was to Justin's credit that they stood their ground and fired again, taking only the time to widen the stance of their legs, trying to prevent the same fate as Reinhart. For his part, Reinhart flailed in the riverbed, doing his best to get back to his feet, but with an arm missing, it was not going to happen quickly.

Lasers from the *Ursus II* cooked the *Kodiak*'s torso, and the heat soared even higher in Emilio's cockpit. For a split second, he wondered if overheating was actually going to be a concern during the Trial. It might if he lasted long enough.

He fired once more at the *Ursus II*, unloading everything he had for that particular range and putting his heat sensors deep into the red. The Ultra autocannon round snapped through the armor of Justin's right arm and penetrated into the internal structure. If Emilio was lucky, it would take at least some of their weapons offline and give him a fighting chance, even if he came close to cooking alive. The eight medium lasers from his clawed hands let loose a ferocious assault, boiling off the rest of the armor from the *Ursus II*'s torso, also revealing the 'Mech's innards.

That's when the *Kodiak* lurched forward involuntarily. Emilio had been hit. Hard.

Likely the *Executioner*'s Gauss rifle.

Metal crunched loud around him, and Emilio practically felt it on his own body. The blinking yellow damage readouts on his HUD confirmed the story. The Gauss rifle was the only weapon on the field that could do that much damage to his rear quarter. He had thought he would have more time before they caught up. They were not playing it safe; Star Captain Rand was trying to end things quickly. Of course she was. She had no desire to be there, any more than Emilio did.

The turquoise flash of a large laser brightened Emilio's viewscreen. That was Rand herself in the fray. They must have not waited that long to discern Emilio's position and strategy.

The damage indicators on the *Kodiak*'s rear quarter flashed from yellow to orange after the damage from the laser. Emilio scanned the topographical map for blips that would give him an indication of what direction they were attacking from. It told him they were in the trees against the rocks behind him. Despite the cover, they were still deadly accurate. He would be proud if his life was not in danger.

Since they could do more damage to him than the *Ursus II*, he turned to meet them, exposing his back to the damaged 'Mech.

They were only blips on his heads-up display rather than actual foes. He had no visual lock on them whatsoever.

A Gauss rifle round cracked the front of the *Kodiak*'s torso. Had it been a blow on his own fleshy body, it would have definitely penetrated straight through him. Fortunately, the front armor on the 'Mech was made of much sterner stuff than even a Gauss rifle could tear asunder in a single shot.

The brilliant green flash of the *Kuma*'s lasers was a larger problem. According to the display schematic, Emilio's center mass had taken another sizable hit. The armor was being flensed from the *Kodiak*'s chest, one hit at a time.

But still, he could not quite see them.

When an explosion rocked the back of his *Kodiak*, he knew he needed to press forward, no longer leaving his back exposed to the hurting *Ursus II*. It had not moved, leaving him to wonder if it could move at all anymore.

Emilio willed the 'Mech forward, using his lasers to cut through the trees, hoping he could cause some incidental damage on the way to his targets. If he was lucky, perhaps he could start a conflagration. He hoped the heatsinks in the *Kodiak* were good enough that he would not overheat by being a little extravagant in his use of the lasers, but it was a risk he had to take.

The distance to the radar blips decreased as he got closer to the *Kuma* and the *Executioner*—and they got closer to him. They must have realized he was not going to leave himself open in the riverbed, and were charging through the trees at him.

He felt another faint explosion at his back and watched a volley of missiles fly by his cockpit from behind. The *Ursus II* was definitely not getting any closer, and his back would be safe for the time being.

Emilio's viewscreen tinted blue-green again with the blast of the *Kuma*'s large laser, and the front torso display on his HUD flashed from green to yellow. Between the Gauss rifle and that damn laser, he was not going to last long.

Another shot came at him, and he still could not see its origin.

Then, on the periphery of his vision, he caught a glance of the one of his targets. The *Kuma,* a bulky, humanoid-style 'Mech with a bucket head, was ahead and off to his right.

Rand.

Changing direction, Emilio went right for her, stopping long enough to open fire with everything he had. First his Ultra autocannon—a miss. Then the eight medium lasers, with mixed results. Certainly not enough to deal a killing blow.

A great *crack* of the Gauss rifle from his left side gave him a good idea of the *Executioner*'s position. But he had to pick a target. The *Kuma* was the unlucky one right now.

Outclassed by 50 tons, and trading fire back and forth across two arcs, the end came quickly. The *Executioner*'s Gauss rifle battered Emilio's left arm until he could not raise it to aim his lasers anymore. Then, the *Kuma* cracked open his front torso and the heat became unbearable.

By the time it was over, he'd blasted off one of the *Kuma*'s arms, but not enough to stop it. Disappointment blossomed in Emilio's chest, but that was overcome with gratitude that the Trial was finished. He should have been able to find a way to take them.

Thankfully, they had disabled the *Kodiak* rather than destroy it with him inside. He had fought as hard as he could, but the odds were too great.

When they finally pried him out of the 'Mech, the Prime Minister was there to shake his hand and thank him.

"I hope Mayor Stelfreeze is satisfied," Emilio said.

"He is disappointed, but appreciates your effort," the Prime Minister said. "It took great honor to fight as hard as you did. But it was a lost cause. They all knew it. They simply wanted their voices heard."

The Star Colonel wiped the sweat from his brow. "Then, with their voices heard, I hope it brings them some peace."

"It will. I am sure of it." The Prime Minister looked over their shoulder and Emilio turned to see what she saw. Star Captain Rand approached, dressed in her MechWarrior garb, carrying her neurohelmet, and dripping sweat from every pore.

"I will leave you to it, Star Colonel," the Prime Minister said. "Your transport awaits."

Emilio nodded respectfully to the Prime Minister, and then turned his attention to his second.

"You fought well, Star Colonel," she said.

"As did you."

"I thought I was a goner. And those *Ursus II*'s will likely need to be scrapped. There will be no dishonor in your loss here. Fighting and doing your best was honor enough for the position these civilians put you in."

"I appreciate that. But now that it is done, I would like you to oversee the evacuation personally."

"*Me?*" She seemed genuinely surprised. Or perhaps she simply thought the job was beneath her.

"*Aff.* It will carry great meaning if you, who won the Trial, oversee the results of it. They will feel respected, even in the loss. We can afford no more ill will. We need to show the *sibko*s that are coming here to prove themselves how real Ghost Bears comport themselves with honor."

"Of course, Star Colonel." She couldn't hide the snarl on her lip.

"Then go to. I will see you back at Kodiak Point."

"*Aff*, Star Colonel."

Emilio let out a breath and headed back to the transport, wondering what else could go wrong on Quarell.

CHAPTER 9

FALCON'S RUN TRAINING FACILITY
OUTSKIRTS OF HAMMARR
SUDETEN
JADE FALCON OCCUPATION ZONE
10 SEPTEMBER 3151

Holding the medallion strung around her neck tightly with one hand and toying with the 'Mech controls with the other, Dawn sat eagerly in the command couch of the *Locust IIC 4*, waiting for her Trial of Position to begin. It was not often that a Jade Falcon got a second chance at becoming a MechWarrior, and Dawn was not going to fail. Even in such a ridiculous 'Mech.

*Locust IIC 4*s were light 'Mechs, weighing 25 tons. There were seven 'Mechs in the field, per the tradition of a Trial of Position. All were *Locust IIC 4*s. Clans abhorred waste and, according to Star Captain Quinn, these were not going to be fielded in battle any time soon. They were in various states of disrepair, some were missing some of their armor, others missing weapons here or there. Dawn figured they would have been nothing more than spare parts, but instead they would be used in the Trial.

Dawn and her fellow Fledgling, an older Warrior named Hosteen, began the Trial on one end of the field. Spaced evenly before them across the rolling hills of the training field, just out of range, were the six other *Locust IIC 4*s, each one piloted by a fledged Jade Falcon MechWarrior. Those in the field would remain completely still until engaged. As was the tradition of

Clan Trials of Position, each would-be MechWarrior would face off against one foe at a time. After defeating one, she would have to move on to the next, defeating up to three of them. But if any of the static combatants in reserve were attacked or hit by fire, a free-for-all would ensue.

All Dawn had to do was make a single kill to become a MechWarrior. She did not have to *actually* kill the opposing MechWarrior, though that did sometimes happen in the Trials, but she had to disable their 'Mech enough for it to be counted as a kill.

With the dire straits Jade Falcon found itself in, she was surprised the Trial of Position was not being held in a simulator, but then, she also had not known of the stockpile of *Locust IIC 4*s Star Captain Quinn was sitting on.

Though they were more heavily armored than a standard Inner Sphere *Locust, Locust IIC 4*s were light on armor by Clan standards, and only boasted an extended-range medium laser atop its head and a battery of small, short-range lasers on each shoulder. They were essentially armed cockpits on mechanized raptor legs.

They were fast and maneuverable, topping out at over 120 kilometers per hour. Dawn would need to be fast on her feet and deadly accurate in her aim. The wrong hit at the wrong angle would crush her dreams of being a MechWarrior forever, but a well-placed shot would cement them into reality. Added to that, she had to be careful not to hit one of the dormant 'Mechs. That was how she had lost the first time, and she would not let that mistake happen again. She wasn't the one who had engaged the free-for-all the last time, and she'd be damn sure she wouldn't this time.

"Dawn and Hosteen," boomed Star Captain Quinn's voice over the comm, "you have trained and drilled your whole lives for this moment, doubly so in these last weeks. This is when we see if you become true Jade Falcon MechWarriors. There are six MechWarriors before you, three each, waiting to prevent you from fulfilling your destiny. Will you let them? You have but to score one kill to become a MechWarrior. But Khan Jiyi Chistu says that, given our *rede* and history, if you kill two, you *will* be given the rank of Star Commander. Three, and you'll be a Star

Captain, equaling me in rank, regardless of everything that has come before. *Quiaff*?"

"*Aff!*" Dawn barked. Excitement filled her. She knew she needed to get at least one kill, but the possibility of higher rank and the honor that accompanied it ran a thrill of what could be right up her spine.

Hosteen's response came just a moment later, filled with a hunger equal to hers.

"Then let the Trial begin."

Dawn's *Locust IIC 4* roared to life, rumbling her in the seat. The engine was so large, everything felt as though it vibrated down to her teeth.

The first order of business was to get moving. She and Hosteen were just out of range of each other. Instead of heading straight for the first 'Mech in the Trial, she cut across the hilly field toward Hosteen's area before double-backing and heading toward the opposing *Locust IIC 4.* She did not want to risk a stray hit activating any other 'Mechs and the new approach angle made it all but certain neither she nor her opponent would risk a stray shot into the other half of the Trial.

Taking in a deep, calming breath, Dawn felt it there in her heart, right where her righteous fury resided: she was meant to be a MechWarrior, and that meant things would be okay. She was going to win.

She felt it with every molecule of her will.

Gripping the control stick and racing her *Locust IIC 4* in the direction of its target, she felt that determined fury in every step.

The opposing *Locust IIC 4* lined up with Dawn on a collision course. She juked to the left and fired her lasers, flashing yellow-gold, but they missed.

Her opponent returned fire, but they were firing at where Dawn *had been,* not where she was now. She kept one eye on the *Locust IIC 4* in front of her on her viewscreen and another eye on the radar readout, offering blips of distance and position for the other 'Mechs on the field. She closed in on her enemy *fast.*

Behind her, Hosteen and his opponent raced in circles. His strategy seemed to be to stay out of range and move in only when he had a clear shot.

Dawn could not worry about that, though. She only kept tabs on them to ensure she was not going to get shot in the back or that he was going to cause a free-for-all.

She pulled the trigger once more. The lasers lanced out toward the opposing 'Mech. One missed, but the other tagged one of the fast-moving legs.

"Damn it," Dawn said. She hoped she would have taken this 'Mech out by now.

It was the only thing that stood in the way of her dreams. She did not even need to take down the others. This was harder than she had thought it would be, and she did not have any time to waste. She did not need a rank or position, she just needed to stay in the cockpit of a 'Mech.

Her field of view scorched with the brightness of a laser hit. The cockpit cooked and her damage readouts for the center mass of her 'Mech blinked from green to yellow.

No way she could take another hit like that. Two at the most, and she would be out.

"You will *not* take this away from me," she snarled, hoping to channel that indignation into ability.

Dawn's opponent changed directions, trying to come at her from a different vector, forcing her to pick a firing solution that would provoke the 'Mechs behind them.

"No, you are not doing that." Dawn kept moving forward beyond her speedy enemy and made a U-turn to come right at the *Locust IIC 4*. "Get back here."

Lining up her arms with the targeting reticule, Dawn let loose, firing both of her lasers.

The golden glow of laser heat cooked off chunks of the opposing *Locust IIC 4*'s cockpit, but they returned fire that was just as vicious and accurate. Standing fast, it did not matter to Dawn that the heat in her 'Mech rose or that the damage indicator screamed. She had not initiated a free-for-all and doubted she could take many more hits; the only thing that mattered was taking down her opponent and becoming a MechWarrior.

I am right to want this, she told herself. *This is where I am meant to be.*

Dawn fired again, strafing to the left as she tried to keep out of the heat death of laser fire. The lasers hit again, turning the rest of the cockpit and the actuator on her *Locust IIC 4*'s left leg into molten slag.

Looking down at her HUD and damage indicators, they screamed that she could not take much more damage. Flashing red lights appeared all over the 'Mech's schematic, showing her that death was close, maybe even from the next shot...

But the next shot from the 'Mech across the field did not come.

Narrowing her eyes and taking a closer, magnified look at the *Locust IIC 4* on her viewscreen, it was apparent the enemy had come to a halt. Looking down at the map on the HUD, the 'Mech's heat indicator on the directional radar winked out.

She had done it!

The number of kills tallied on her display clicked up to one, making it official.

Elation overtook Dawn. She could not repress her smile—until dread took over once more.

She would have to face off against more foes, and with no armor and a 'Mech already close to overheating.

But Dawn was a MechWarrior now, and she would not die so soon after her new career had begun.

Her next opponent activated their 'Mech and descended from the crest of the hill. Dawn needed to remain mobile. Despite the blaring heat warnings, she pushed her *Locust IIC 4* straight toward her first kill. If she could use it as cover between herself and her next opponent, they would not be able take potshots at her. That would at least buy her time to reduce the heat in her 'Mech and give her a chance to fight back.

The MechWarrior swooped down the hill like a hawk after its prey, but must have realized what she was doing. Instead of continuing to rush forward, both 'Mechs circled and sidestepped, with Dawn trying to stay hidden in cover while the enemy's 'Mech feinted and juked back and forth on its way, hoping to grab some advantage. It was already on high ground and had suffered no damage, so it had every advantage.

Glancing down, Dawn saw the blips representing her and her opponent circling her kill, but then saw the other two 'Mechs in the exercise heading her way. They were not supposed to interfere with each other's Trials unless it turned into a free-for-all, which was something Dawn was still hoping very much to avoid.

Ignore them, she told herself. *Focus on your target.*

Running out of space between herself and her cover, Dawn sprinted past the motionless *Locust IIC 4* and lined up a shot.

She fired every laser she had, heat be damned. If she could make this one shot, she'd get a rank and that would make all the difference in her life. Another golden flash lit up her viewscreen, and then she lost power. Her HUD dimmed, and her *Locust IIC 4* tripped on its own momentum, crashing forward into the ground.

Flipping switches and turning dials, she did everything she could to get her 'Mech back into service and get the power back, but there was nothing. Something had been severed or melted.

She didn't know if she had made the kill or not.

Touching another button, she managed to get her radio to sizzle back to life. "—Dawn, do you copy?" The voice belonged to Star Captain Quinn.

"This is Dawn," she replied.

"You made it, then."

"*Aff.*"

"Then congratulations. You made two kills, and have been promoted to the rank of Star Commander."

A swell of emotion overtook her to the point where she couldn't quite believe the words she was hearing. "Star Commander?"

"*Aff.* Now let us get you out of your 'Mech."

It didn't matter how much the straps of her couch cut into her. It didn't matter that sweat poured from her brow and soaked through the scant clothes she wore. It didn't matter that Dawn thought she might have a concussion. She smiled, gratefully rubbing her medallion between her thumb and forefinger. None of it mattered, because she was a MechWarrior now.

CHAPTER 10

BEARCLAW SIBKO TRAINING FACILITY
COPPERTON
QUARELL
RASALHAGUE DOMINION
12 SEPTEMBER 3151

The entire Bearclaw *sibko* stood at attention in their barracks, each cub waiting in front of their bunk and footlocker. Alexis kept her eyes straight ahead and did her best to keep from getting distracted by any of her fellow *sibkin* and their cold gazes.

Life on the street had given her an uncanny ability to maintain a singular focus, but it also made her nervous when she could not check behind her back. It did not matter that she was reasonably safe in the place where she slept, surrounded by people who, in theory, would never betray her. But she still had that nagging feeling of something left unseen or undone behind her.

It was an instinct that had kept her alive; she did not know how to shake it. So, at attention she stood, hoping the inspection would be over before the flesh on her back crawled right off her body.

"Bearclaws," called their Den Mother, Star Captain Sasha Ivankova, from the front of the room. "Today, we will be receiving the first of the other *sibkos* that will be challenging you in our exercises. The Mektid Bear *sibko* arrived on Quarell yesterday and will be bunked here. Over the coming weeks, we will be joined by many other *sibkos*. The Porbjorns, our fellow

Quarellian *sibko*, will play host to the Dragonbears. The others, the Bjornsons, Berserkers, and Werebears, will be housed in Antimony, with the Ghost Bear leadership on Quarell in the capital. It is a great honor to be participating in such an exercise, and I am sure you will do nothing that will bring dishonor to the Bearclaws, *quiaff*?"

"AFF!" they all replied.

"Now, *Ursari*," the Den Mother called out to the other instructors ringed around the room, "it is time for our regular inspection. Nothing here will bring us shame or dishonor; we will find no contraband and nothing that is forbidden, *quiaff*?"

"AFF!" the *Ursari* shouted from around the bunkhouse. Their voices were deeper, with a more defined growl.

Alexis kept her eyes forward and tried to ignore the creeping fear at her back. She had nothing to be frightened of. There was no contraband in her footlocker; her bedding was crisp and straight, and her uniform was perfect. Thomasin and Sophie, likewise, would not have a problem either. The three of them were fastidious, though Thomasin was the least so.

She liked patterns and the unsurprising, because she could always see the pattern and bend it to her whim. She hated that there were so many unknowns around her beyond that.

More than anything, she wished the entire enterprise was over so she could spend some of her downtime with her two friends. It felt like it had been weeks since they had been able to relax. They had polished *everything* in the complex twice. Alexis could not figure out why they were so adamant about cleanliness with another *sibko* arriving. Combat readiness seemed far more important. Wouldn't drilling and more teaching do more good than polishing the toilets in the head to a glimmer?

"Bear Cub Alexis," the Star Captain said. "I presume we will find everything in order in your footlocker?"

"*Aff*, Star Captain!" Alexis responded coolly.

She had nothing to fear.

But that didn't stop her from feeling vulnerable as the Den Mother stepped behind her and flung open her footlocker. Alexis heard Ivankova riffle through the neatly packed belongings, not that there was that much. As cadets, they were not allowed many possessions. Merely a few changes of clothes, a noteputer for doing homework, personal toiletries, and little else.

Alexis kept her breathing steady and her demeanor cool. She wouldn't risk upsetting the Den Mother with an outburst or a hair on her head out of place. Ivankova disliked her enough as it was. Of course, a "random" inspection would give her a reason to fling Alexis' stuff everywhere.

Alexis never understood what it was that Ivankova did not like about her. Freeborns were afforded much more freedom, latitude, and acceptance amongst the vast majority of Ghost Bears and subjects of the Rasalhague Dominion. Alexis always just assumed the Star Captain had another reason for despising her, but she could never figure out what.

Unless it was the fact that she excelled and showed up the Trueborns as often as she could.

It was a point of pride for Alexis that she was in the top five of her class, but that also made her a target.

"Alexis," Ivankova's intoned gravely behind her.

"Yes, Star Captain," Alexis said firmly. What she would be reprimanded for this time?

"What is this?"

Alexis' brow furrowed. *What is what?*

Confused, she said nothing.

Ivankova stepped around to the front of Alexis, so they could all lay eyes on the *what* in question: a codex bracelet. Each Clan member wore a bracelet that identified their battle history and accomplishments. Trueborn warriors had their genetic code embedded in theirs as well, to record their deeds for future generations and as proof to compete for their Bloodnames.

Alexis shifted her left wrist slightly, checking to make sure her codex was still there under her uniform. She wore it everywhere and had practically forgotten it. Failing to wear it would have definitely caused a problem with the Den Mother. Having it stuffed in her footlocker doubly so.

But her own codex was locked tight around her wrist, exactly where it was supposed to be.

With no more information than the Den Mother had, it seemed like a good plan for Alexis to stick to the truth and straight forward answers. "It appears to be a codex, Star Captain Ivankova!"

"I can see that, cadet. Do not patronize me. Whose codex is it?"

Dread licked at Alexis' heart like flames. "I...I don't know, Star Captain."

The flames in Alexis' heart reflected back at her in the eyes of Den Mother Ivankova. "Excuse me, cadet?"

"I mean, I *do not* know, Star Captain!" Alexis said, correcting herself. She was so damned confused. Why would anyone's codex be in her footlocker?

"Then why was it in your footlocker?"

"Again, I do not know, Star Captain!"

The Star Captain raised the codex up over her head and spun around, looking at all of the assembled cadets. "Who is missing their codex?"

One by one, each of Alexis' *sibkin* checked their wrists, pulling their sleeves up to see. Even Thomasin and Sophie did so, looking as confused about it as Alexis was.

"I am," said a voice from five bunks over.

Daniel.

Of course.

"Bear Cub Daniel, to me."

"*Aff!*" he said, toddling over to her with innocent eyes and feigned confusion, an obedient little teacher's pet.

The whole display made Alexis sick as she began putting together what was going on. He had planted it in her footlocker. There could be no other explanation. Alexis saw right through his feigned surprise, and she could only hope their Den Mother could as well.

Examining the bracelet more closely, the Star Captain confirmed that the codex was, indeed, Daniel's. "It was careless of you to let this go missing."

"*Aff,*" he said, trying his hardest to remain at attention and seem innocent.

Surat *bastard*, Alexis thought, trying to keep herself from saying anything that would worsen the trouble she was already in.

"You will need to be more careful, Daniel." The Star Captain side-eyed Alexis hard. "Especially with a sneak-thief in your midst."

The flames in Alexis' heart turned from dread to anger, boiling her blood like magma, ready to erupt like a volcano. She bit at the end of her tongue, holding herself back from falling into the trap that had been so carefully—or clumsily—set for her.

Ivankova turned to Alexis, the burning in her eyes telling Alexis everything she needed to know about what the Den Mother thought had really happened. Alexis' presumed guilt was writ on her *Ursari*'s face as immutably as a stone carving. "What do you have to say for yourself, cadet?"

"I have no idea how it ended up in my footlocker, Star Captain Ivankova."

"A likely story. At the very least, you admit to not being in control of your own gear?"

Alexis did not say anything to that. Anything she did would only be used against her further. With the Star Captain turned to Alexis, Daniel stood beyond her, shaking his head, a smug grin on his face.

Alexis took in a deep breath and blinked, trying to keep from murdering him. She did not have to say anything, though.

The Star Captain turned to Daniel, whose smile vanished. "Cadet Daniel, you really lost control of your codex? This record is your life, and you would so casually misplace it?"

"Neg," Daniel said. "It was Alexis, she—"

"—how long has it been missing, cadet?"

He was about to answer, but caught himself. "I...I do not know."

"Could it have been missing for an hour?"

He shrugged. *"Aff?"*

"Could it have been missing for a week?"

"I do not think so..."

But he did not sound so sure. How could he? The entire thing was his idea and his will. He knew *exactly* when the codex left his wrist. He couldn't exactly confess to trying to frame her and get her in trouble, though.

And it seemed very apparent to Alexis that the Den Mother knew it.

"I will not judge which of you is more at fault for this outrage," the Star Captain said, "but you both will pay for it, I assure you. With me, both of you."

"Aff!" Alexis said, simultaneously with Daniel.

They both fell in behind the Den Mother as she marched them out of the barracks.

The fire in Alexis' heart doubled in size, enough for her rage at Daniel and the injustice being done to her, and enough for the dread of whatever the Den Mother had planned for them.

Alexis stood at attention in front of the Den Mother's desk, right beside Daniel. She braced for the fury of the woman in charge of her training, and did her best to allow the smoldering anger inside her to subside so that she did not get into any more trouble than she already was.

Daniel's own anger was palpable.

Alexis could only imagine how furious he must have been, being the Den Mother's favorite cub, yet getting swept up in punishment from his own plan to get Alexis in trouble.

He should have chosen someone else's codex instead of his own.

A ridiculous mistake. If you were going to frame someone for something and didn't want it traced back to you, you never got personally involved with the evidence. That was an easy edict of the street, but maybe the Trueborns had a lot to learn about street smarts.

"I expect better of both of you," Star Captain Sasha Ivankova said. "You are both at the very top of the class, competing back and forth for the top spot, and should know better than to engage in such chicanery. And you, Daniel, how could you allow your codex to be lost? That is unthinkable. Completely. Alexis deserves some understanding, given how she came to us, but you? You are a Trueborn, and should not lower yourself to such ridiculous behavior."

Alexis wanted so badly to scream that she had nothing to do with it, that it had been planted on her, that she was framed, but something about the look on the Den Mother's face told her any pleas or protests would go ignored.

And perhaps the Den Mother was right. Alexis should have known better and kept better control of her gear. But something about the entire exchange bothered her as well. She had wanted a family when she joined the Ghost Bears. She would not have been so eager if she had not been promised such when Star Captain Aoi Bekker had brought her into the Bearclaws all those years ago. "Family is what an enterprising young person such as yourself needs," she had told her.

But her idea of family hadn't included backstabbers like Daniel. And bitter Den Mothers like Star Captain Ivankova.

"Star Captain Ivankova," Daniel said. "I do not think I should be held to account because this thief stole my codex."

"You do not seem to grasp the gravity of what you have lost, Cadet Daniel. And for that, you and the thief will share the same punishment. Allowing your codex to be lost in the first place is every bit as grave an offense as stealing one."

Daniel winced, shutting his mouth. Clearly, he hadn't thought his little scheme through. Alexis was glad that at least he would get some comeuppance for trying to frame her.

"First, I will be taking ten points from both of you. And you will both lose all of your free time today. You will make up the barracks for the Mektid Bear *sibko* in the gymnasium. This was to be the afternoon activity for the entire crèche, but you two will do it on your own. You will make every bed. You will scrub every head. You will make sure *nothing* is out of place for them when they arrive. And if it is not done to my satisfaction, you will lose more points and have more duties to carry out."

There was a catch of breath at the end of the Den Mother's statement that made Alexis certain there was more.

But Ivankova kept them both in suspense a moment longer. Finally, her lip curled up deviously. "And the two of you must not speak to each other while you do it. For every word you speak to each other, you will lose another point. I will station an *Ursari* there to ensure my will is obeyed. *Quiaff?*"

"*Aff!*" they both said.

Alexis seethed, but at least she wouldn't have to talk to him.

COPPERTON
QUARELL
RASALHAGUE DOMINION
13 SEPTEMBER 3151

"What a dishonorable swine," Thomasin said to Alexis between sips of his mocha. "I cannot believe he would even try such a thing."

The three of them—Alexis, Thomasin, and Sophie—sat at an outdoor cafe in downtown Copperton, enjoying the first free bit of leisure time they had been given in what seemed like ages. They were supposed to be mingling with the Mektid Bears and showing them around, but everyone pretty much went about their day as though they'd received day passes to the small mining town in the mountains.

"He isn't worth worrying about," Alexis said.

"He really did not say a word the entire time you two prepared the room?" Sophie blew on her steaming mocha and looked out across the main street. The quaint shops and wooden boardwalk felt like they had come out of a completely different time, a stark contrast to the life they led at the school. Everything there was gleaming metal and hard lines. Here, it all felt natural and lived in. It felt more like home to Alexis. It was on streets like these where she had survived until she'd been tossed into the Bearclaws in the first place.

"He started to once," said Alexis, "but when the *Ursari* docked him a point, he kept his mouth shut."

"And you did not say anything?" Thomasin asked.

Alexis wrapped her hands around her mug of steaming coffee and chocolate. "Nope."

"I do not think I could have done it." Thomasin leaned back on the hind legs of his chair. "I would have screamed at him at the very least. More likely I would have knocked his block off. You really cannot let him get away with that kind of stuff any longer."

"I do not plan to," Alexis grumbled. Though she had nothing specific planned, she allowed Thomasin and Sophie to think she did. And if anyone else were listening, they would know Daniel could look forward to some other sort of comeuppance.

"I think he is jealous that I do better than him, even though I am freeborn."

"That sort of thinking feels ancient," Thomasin said. "Freeborn warriors play such a vital part of the Unity Council and help mediate between the Trueborns and the civilians. Not to mention Prince Miraborg himself is a freeborn. Freeborns have a sacred duty in the Dominion to break those deadlocks."

"Speaking of deadlocks..." Sophie gulped down her mocha and swept her shimmering brown hair out of her face. "Did you hear about the vote?"

"No," Alexis said. She had been busy making up bunks for the Mektid Bears.

"Seems like we are officially joining the Star League Defense Force." Sophie offered no joy or sadness at delivering the news. It simply was. She eyed her empty cup with the same intensity as her discussion of the vote.

For Alexis, all she could feel was relief. At least it was over, and it hadn't driven them all apart in the way she feared it would.

"It was a close vote, though," Thomasin said, dashing her hopes. "I have a hard time believing it, but it is what it is. I am glad. We will have a fine time navigating those waters."

"What do you mean? The vote is over, and we will all move on from here." Alexis still didn't have the best grasp of Ghost Bear politics inside the Rasalhague Dominion. When she fended for herself, before she joined the *sibko*, politics seemed as far away as the sun and as relevant as a class on ballroom dancing.

Sophie leaned in closer to the table and hushed her voice. "The Mektid Bear who told us about the vote was a refuser, and they happened to break it to a group of joiners in the Bearclaws. Apparently, they started a bit of a tussle."

"Are they suddenly not Ghost Bears all of a sudden? What happened to us being family?"

Thomasin crashed forward, bringing all four chair legs back down to the ground. "I mean, families have disagreements. And some of these refusers are just really pissed they lost, especially since it was so close."

"It's definitely not the joiners being sore winners?" Alexis asked. "Because when the joiners won here on Quarell, it seemed like there was a lot of gloating against the protestors and the folks who lost."

"*Aff*," Sophie said, wrapping an arm around Alexis as though sensing her discomfort and knowing she needed an extra bit of soothing. "It is both."

"I do not like it," Alexis said, grateful for Sophie's touch. "I think both sides have valid points, and even if we disagree, we are all Ghost Bears."

Thomasin leaned in, too, lowering his voice as though he were a spy. "I would not say that so loud. Some of these people are ready to fight."

Alexis wondered why anyone would get mad to the point of violence over a vote—any vote. "Over a simple vote?"

"Some believe politics is an act of violence every bit as devastating as an attack in one of our 'Mechs," Thomasin said. "And they believe exerting the will of the majority on the minority is nothing short of tyranny."

"But that's the whole nature of our system," Alexis said, wondering if ignoring all of it and going back to living on the street would be less of a headache. "Isn't majority consensus and a careful evaluation of both sides the entire point?"

"In many ways, yes." Sophie nuzzled against Alexis, head on her shoulder, but her voice had an edge to it. "It is easy to throw your hands up and say *both sides*, but sometimes, one side is advocating something so horrible or violent or to the detriment of everyone else that they are not really equal. They're oppressors. And staying neutral is actually supporting the oppressor."

Alexis deflated beneath Sophie's nuzzles and sipped the rest of her drink. The kick of cinnamon and cardamom at the end complimented the deep chocolate and coffee taste. She would not drink anything else if she could. "They must have taught these classes before I joined."

Thomasin and Sophie both laughed.

"What is so funny over there?" came a voice from the sidewalk.

Alexis groaned.

Daniel.

He stood there on the sidewalk with two other *sibkin* from the Bearclaws and a pair of Mektid Bears in their own uniforms, tinted more gray than the blue of the Bearclaws.

"Oh, nothing you would get," Sophie said to him with an arrogant grin.

Daniel's eyes narrowed. "Say that again to my face."

"I did," Sophie said sharply.

But before that could process in Daniel's tiny mind, Thomasin stood. "Hey *stravag, w*hat she meant to say was we better not catch you framing Alexis again for something you did. Ever."

"Hey," Alexis said, raising a hand between the two of them. "I can fight my own battles."

"*Aff,*" Thomasin said to Alexis, walking toward Daniel on the sidewalk. "But we do not stay neutral, and we do not let bullies get away with bullying, *quiaff*?"

"*Aff,*" Alexis said. "But—"

—before Alexis could say anything else, Thomasin punched Daniel right in the face, knocking him to the ground. Daniel's friends in the Bearclaws and the Mektid Bears all stood there motionless, mouths agape.

"Try nonsense like that again, and you'll meet me in a Circle of Equals," Thomasin said.

It was doubtful Daniel heard him, though.

He'd been knocked out cold.

CHAPTER 11

GOVERNOR'S MANSION
HAMMARR
SUDETEN
JADE FALCON OCCUPATION ZONE
05 OCTOBER 3151

Through his travels, Khan Jiyi Chistu had started to think of the de facto Jade Falcons headquarters in the ornate governor's mansion as home. It felt good to walk through the halls. More than anything, it felt good to no longer be trapped in a DropShip. Perhaps he had grown too accustomed to the relative luxury of his post on VaultShip *Gamma*, but being on-planet and in a place of comfort was nice. Especially in a palatial estate like the one they'd rebuilt for the planetary governor that his Falcons now occupied.

He turned through the corridor, his booted steps heavy on the aged wooden floor, recounting his travels in his head. He would need to give a clear report to those in his command he had left in charge. As soon as he got within communications range, he had appointed a time and place to brief them and was anxious to deliver that briefing. He had gone and solved some of their problems, but the more he learned about their problems and the Inner Sphere in general, the larger their problems became.

He pushed open the door to the conference room—a wide room with an oaken, oval table surrounded by modern chairs and a view of the city beyond—and strode inside. Merchant

Factor Jodine sat on one side of the table, and Star Captain Quinn on the other. Under better circumstances, every seat would be filled with advisors and other high-level Jade Falcon Warriors, but such was the sorry state his predecessor had left the Clan in. They had next to nothing, which made the situation seem all the more desperate.

Both Quinn and Jodine rose to greet him as he entered, showing their new Khan the proper respect.

"Please, sit. We have much to discuss," he said, taking his own seat at the head of the table. "But first, I wish to know how things have been on Sudeten in my absence."

He turned to Star Captain Quinn first. She cleared her throat and looked up from the noteputer sitting in front of her. "The first batch of new MechWarriors have passed their Trials of Position. You were correct, we ended up with a single Star, but at this point an extra Star of Warriors is better than nothing. There are a couple among them that are competent, and will actually make fine MechWarriors with more training. There is a more detailed report in your files, should you wish to review it."

"Excellent. That is exactly what I want to hear. In a time with little good news, this pleases me. And you, Merchant Factor Jodine?"

Merchant Factor Jodine moved a wisp of curly hair from her forehead and pinned it behind her ear. "The factories are operating at capacity, and we will have a new batch of BattleMechs off the assembly line every month if we can keep the factories supplied. However, the mines are producing below capacity; we need more workers. So much of the generational knowledge is lost. There were other losses in the mines on some parts of the planet. But we are doing what we can. Our techs are training new workers, and new facilities are brought back online every day. But we need supplies and raw materials in addition to the workers and techs to deal with them."

"I have some news that might help with that," said Jiyi. "In my travels, I visited Dompaire. They will be increasing their shipments of supplies and raw materials to us forthwith. There were also two Stars worth of Warriors I was able to bring. The *solahma* Star Captain in charge of Dompaire was not thrilled about losing so many to me, but he acquiesced in the end. The rebirth and reconstruction of the Jade Falcons is worth more than his ego. There was also a Star's worth of Warriors who passed simulated Trials of Position on Graus. So we have almost an entire Trinary to outfit with new 'Mechs from Sudeten."

"I will be sure to add these Warriors to our *touman* and get them into our training rotation," Star Captain Quinn said, taking note. "They are *solahma* as well?"

"*Aff,*" Jiyi said. "Most, anyway. A few are freeborn who have never fought in a 'Mech before. But they will fight and they will die for the Jade Falcons, such is their *rede*. Such is ours."

"*Aff,* my Khan," the Star Captain said.

"I am also expecting infantry reinforcements from Graus. The population there is greater than here. They were my first stop in surveying the wreckage of the Occupation Zone. Star Captain Cosmo is there, left in charge of recruiting and rebuilding the infantry. He knows we are owed two Clusters of infantry, trained and equipped, by the end of the year."

"Very good, my Khan," Quinn said, taking notes on everything they discussed.

"We are still in a tenuous position. And we need to focus on creating new *sibkos* here on Sudeten. That should be our top priority. While I respect freeborns and *solahma*, our leadership core needs to be Trueborn and of a proper Warrior's age, lest we fade into obscurity or become annihilated and stricken from the histories of the Clans."

Merchant Factor Jodine tilted her head. "What would it take to kickstart the Iron Wombs here on Sudeten to start new *sibko*s?"

"We would have to find them first. Many were lost in Malvina Hazen's attack, as Hammarr was home to most of the facilities that bred Trueborns. Perhaps we can fabricate new facilities. The Scientist caste here will help. Perhaps we can trade for some, Merchant Factor."

"Perhaps."

"Has there been any word from elsewhere? Have we seen anyone else joining or leaving the fold?"

Quinn and Jodine exchanged a knowing look that told Jiyi *something* had come in. But which of them would speak up first?

Star Captain Quinn finally did. "We did receive a message, my Khan. A holorecording."

Merchant Factor Jodine held disappointment on her face and hunched in her shoulders. "It is from Alyina and Syndic Marena."

"Ah, Marena has finally responded to my request to join forces?"

"Not exactly," Star Captain Quinn replied, cueing up the recording. "You will want to see for yourself."

The lights in the room dimmed at Quinn's command and the holoprojector at the center of the table whirred to life. There, a meter-tall version of the self-styled Merchant Queen of Alyina, Marena, appeared. She wore a uniform Jiyi did not recognize. More like a civilian than a Clan merchant, but it was fashionable enough for a culture he knew nothing about. Even through the blue glow of the projection, he could tell her hair was whitening at the roots.

Her already ice-blue eyes pierced through him even more brilliantly in the projected image. She held herself with confidence, paused there in the moment, waiting for Star Captain Quinn to play the message.

"Go ahead, Star Captain."

"*Aff*, my Khan." Quinn pressed *play*.

The Merchant Queen came to life, warmth written on her face and posture. She gestured with her hands as she spoke, creating a welcoming atmosphere in her immediate vicinity. She spoke with a voice that made Jiyi want to like her, despite the message she might be delivering.

"*Jiyi Chistu,*" she began. "*I appreciate your offer to join Clan Jade Falcon and come back into the fold. I have spent many weeks considering your offer, but I regret to inform you that the holdings of the Alyina Mercantile League are leaving the hierarchy and dominion of the Clans entirely. Alyina is severing all ties and claims to Clan Jade Falcon, and the Mercantile League renounces it completely.*"

Jiyi took in a sharp breath and held it, trying to stem the tide of the loss he felt with this news.

The Merchant Queen's message continued.

"We never wish to be dominated by the Warrior caste again, especially one as inept and needlessly wasteful as Clan Jade Falcon has become under Malvina Hazen's rule."

He could not argue with her reasoning or assessment of Malvina Hazen. He had come to believe very much the same thing about her. What he could not agree with was what Marena said next.

"But Malvina Hazen is dead, and with her die the Jade Falcons. I would refer to you as a Khan of a dead Clan as soon as I would refer to Nicholas Kerensky as a great man. Neither will happen any time soon. In fact, you cannot even be Khan, because as you know, your rede insists that a Khan be elected by the Clan Council, and not a ragtag group of left-behind Warriors, solahma, and freeborns.

"This is not a slight against you. I find it admirable that you are doing what you can with what you have. Truly, you have the spirit of a Warrior. But I do not believe Warriors should be at the top of the decision-making process for so many people. A Warrior sees only war as a solution to everything, and when you pilot a BattleMech, every problem is one you think you can defeat by shooting at it. The Inner Sphere and the people that Kerensky swore to eventually defend by creating the Clans need something better to defend them.

"So, here is my offer, since I do respect you and what you are doing: join me. I know that will be difficult for you to stomach. Do not make a decision right now, but consider it. If you were to join me, I would make you the commander of the Alyina Merchant League's combined military. Sudeten, Graus, Dompaire, and the other worlds in your grasp are only tenuously so. Soon you will face larger, more powerful foes, picking meat from the Falcon carcass. I know how dangerous things are for you now and how precarious your position is. You have more 'Mechs than Warriors, and Warriors are not simply grown and trained overnight. You are in a perfect position to join the AML and we can help sell that excess for the security you fight for.

"I expect a response before the year comes to a close. If you agree to join me, no blood need be spilled. If the

new year arrives and I receive no response from you, I will assume you have rejected my offer, and we will meet in conflict sooner or later, though that is decidedly not my desire. I wish you the best of luck, Jiyi Chistu, whichever choice you make."

The image of Marena bowed slightly, then winked off. Then, the lights returned to full power in the room.

Jiyi Chistu could not quite believe what he had just heard.

Star Captain Quinn and Merchant Factor Jodine remained silent, letting Jiyi catch his breath after that body blow of a message knocked the proverbial wind from him.

"Well," he said after a moment, trying to smile, "at least we know where she stands."

Merchant Factor Jodine stifled a chuckle. The Star Captain either did not find the remark funny, or was better at hiding it than her merchant-caste counterpart.

"When did this message arrive?"

"Just this week, via JumpShip," Star Captain Quinn said.

"So, she took time to consider the offer?"

"It would seem so, my Khan." Star Captain Quinn looked right into him, and he knew without having to ask that she was worried he would accept her offer. The strain in her eyes and across her face said it all.

"This definitely exacerbates our problems. I am wondering what the two of you would counsel?" Jiyi asked, opening the floor.

"We reject her offer," Star Captain Quinn said, "and when we are at the full strength, we show her what happens when people turn their back on the Clans."

Jiyi nodded curtly. It was very much the response of a warrior. "Merchant Factor?"

"I doubt she would have sent such a message from a place of weakness. She must believe she has a force equal to the Jade Falcons' current *touman*. Enough to defend herself, but not enough to attack with any certainty of winning..."

"...else she would not have sent a message; she would have simply invaded," Jiyi said, finishing Jodine's theory.

"Therefore, it is likely she has had some Falcons defect already, or has decided to hire mercenaries," Star Captain

Quinn added. "If she is rejecting the rest of the Clan teachings, it would come as no surprise. Or she has assembled a military that combines the best of both. In any case, she has just made it that much more difficult for Clan Jade Falcon to survive."

"If I submit, the Falcons simply cease to be," Jiyi said. The mere thought nearly panicked him. "If I reject her, I open a war on yet another front. We are currently in a position to fight a war on zero fronts, and yet she would force us to choose from these options."

"Then what will you do, my Khan?"

Jiyi wondered how long they could hold out at their current strength. What he needed was a miracle and it seemed as though the Merchant Queen had just accelerated his timeline for a plan he needed yesterday. "We will answer her by the end of the year. In the meantime, we must solve the problem of our Warrior and *sibko* shortage. That is what we will focus on. No solution is too extreme if it yields results."

"*Aff,* my Khan."

Khan Jiyi rose from the conference table. "Thank you both."

And he left, wondering where in the Inner Sphere he could get his hands on an entire *sibko's* worth of trained Warriors, fast. The very fate of Clan Jade Falcon depended on it.

CHAPTER 12

KODIAK POINT
GHOST BEAR HEADQUARTERS
ANTIMONY
QUARELL
06 OCTOBER 3151

"Welcome to Quarell, Star Commander Kaede Sullivan. I am Star Colonel Emilio Hall, the ranking Ghost Bear Warrior on the planet. It is my pleasure to welcome you and the Dragonbear *sibko* for these exercises."

The breeze tugged at Star Colonel Hall's cape. The wind in front of Kodiak Point was always a little rough, coming in off the lake and funneling through the mountains.

Star Commander Sullivan met Emilio's smile with her own brilliant one as she stepped off the hover transport. "I am sure the pleasure will be all ours, Star Colonel."

"Please, let us get your cubs quartered and I will give you the tour."

The hover transport unloaded a dozen Dragonbears in sharp uniforms, all kids—too young to look like real Warriors, eager to see a new world. Emilio wondered if that awe ever wore off. He'd been to a dozen different planets in his life, and he saw the astonishment of it reflected in their faces.

"How are things on Thun?" he asked Sullivan.

"Thun is well, Star Colonel," she said, her strides elegant as they walked. "The protests from the planet-wide vote seem to be subsiding."

"The vote?"

"*Aff.* There has not been protests like this since the merger of the Clan into the Dominion. But it is more manageable this time, I think. We left just as word came from the Dominion-wide vote, and I hope the protests did not reignite."

"Which way did Thun vote?"

"To refuse, but only narrowly. The feeling of having the vote overturned by the rest of the Dominion weighed heavily in the minds of the protesters. The first spate of protests were from the joiners, angry they lost. This new wave may well be the refusers, angry to feel as though the rest of the Dominion is overturning their vote."

"It is all very polarizing."

"*Aff,*" Sullivan said. "Quite. Were there protests here?"

"A few. Some refusers."

"Quarell voted to join?" Sullivan asked.

"*Aff.*"

"Strange times."

Emilio watched the last of the cadets troop off the hover truck and head toward the main entrance of Kodiak Point, guarded by a granite statue of a Ghost Bear from Strana Mechty. "Strange times indeed."

The first place Emilio brought the cadets was the barracks they had fashioned from the mess. It was an easy conversion to make. The Dragonbears, being the first to arrive, would bunk there, giving them the first crack at food every morning. After the cadets had settled and dropped their duffle bags off at their bunks, Emilio led them all to the main 'Mech bay at Kodiak Point.

Easily the largest on Quarell, Kodiak Point housed almost half of the Fourteenth Battle Cluster, consisting of thirty 'Mechs of Trinary Command and the Ninety-Sixth Battle Trinary, as well as the Tango Fighter Star. The rest were housed strategically across the planet, within easy reach of their own DropShips in the event of a mass mobilization. Being on the border of Jade Falcon space—*former* Jade Falcon space, Emilio reminded himself—meant they had to be prepared for anything. The Falcons had not been above encroaching on the Dominion. They had not taken the merger between the Free Rasalhague

Republic and the Ghost Bears very well. The animosity grew worse with hardliners like Malvina Hazen in charge.

If there was one thing Emilio was grateful for, it was that at least the Jade Falcons had not taken Terra. If the Ghost Bears were going to join the ilClan, letting Malvina decide how every other Clan would be treated would have been nothing short of disaster. He had long dreamed of dealing a significant blow to the Jade Falcons, and though he was grateful they had been all but wiped out, he was disappointed he could not take something from them and use it to bring glory to the Ghost Bears. Perhaps the Dominion could eventually expand its reach into the former Occupation Zone, but that would likely be long after Emilio had retired.

"Star Colonel?" a voice asked. Sullivan again.

"Oh, my apologies." Emilio realized he had been miles away, thinking about politics. He cursed himself inwardly and looked back to the cubs walking behind him, looking out on the finest force of 'Mechs they had likely ever seen. "Welcome to the pride of Kodiak Point," he told the Dragonbears.

The huge bay reeked of oil and machine parts. There was a low, sustained rumble from all the techs wandering around. It took a lot of maintenance to keep 'Mechs as fine as the Fourteenth's in tip-top order.

All of the BattleMechs were divided into their Stars and arranged in order. They looked out on the center of the bay, and the doors beyond would let them step out into the fine Quarellian air. In the center of the bay was the *Kodiak* Emilio had piloted in the Trial of Refusal. Still battered and missing huge chunks of its armor, it was nearer to fighting shape than it had been at the end of battle he had fought.

The sight was met with muted *oohs* and *ahhs*.

No matter how many 'Mech bays Emilio visited, he had never seen one more impressive than this. Although it had been built more than three decades ago, it gleamed as if it was brand new. The only sign that it had aged were the stains of oil, greases, coolants, and lubricants in some of the maintenance bays.

"This is the *Kodiak* you used in that Trial of Refusal?" Sullivan asked in front of the cubs.

"You heard about that?" Emilio's eyes narrowed. He figured that would not warrant mentioning to anyone save the folks of Feldspar. They were the only ones affected by his actions, and he still wished he could have pulled out a victory for them, despite the headaches it would have caused him.

"*Aff.* When coming in from orbit, we heard some of the latest news and Star Captain Allison Rand included it in her report."

"I bet she did."

"She was very complimentary of your skills. You faced four MechWarriors by yourself. It was an honorable thing."

One of the cubs stepped toward them. A young woman of about seventeen, as most of the cubs traveling to participate in the exercises would be. The patch on her coverall gave her name as *Valkyrie*. She had that hesitating look that said she wanted to ask a question.

When she raised her hand, Sullivan turned and nodded at her. "Yes, Cadet Valkyrie?"

"I had a question for you, Star Colonel." She straightened her posture, as if at attention.

It was as likely as anything she had never spoken to anyone as highly ranked as a Star Colonel before.

"Go ahead," he said.

"What do you like about piloting the *Kodiak*?"

Emilio grinned. There was always an opportunity for a teaching moment when dealing with *sibko* cadets. "I will be honest and say it is not my preferred choice of 'Mech. It is a little heavy for my tastes, but I chose it for the Trial because of the situation. As with anything, you need to survey the battle ahead of you and choose the right tool, the right strike, the right response to the challenge. Know the intent of your enemy and you will know the best way to strike back. I knew I would be facing four 'Mechs. I would be outclassed and outweighed no matter what I did. But the *Kodiak* had enough armor and firepower to take several hits, even from most of them at once."

"So you were intent on winning," Sullivan asked, letting her curiosity lead, "despite the overwhelming odds and curious nature of the Trial?"

"I believe in Trials, even if I do not believe in the particular cause this one was fought for. And, as the Star Captain must have put in their report, I was chosen as champion of the people of Feldspar and agreed. It would have been a dishonor on myself, on the Ghost Bears, and the Dominion itself if I did not fight to win."

"*Aff*," Sullivan said.

Valkyrie raised her hand again. "What 'Mech *do* you prefer to pilot, Star Colonel?"

"Come," he said. "I will show you."

Emilio marched Sullivan, Valkyrie, and any of the others who wanted to follow to the first bay of the Command Trinary, where his 'Mech was housed.

It was quite a distance, the 'Mechs needing as much space as they did, but they finally arrived. A bulky *Ursus II*, glimmering in the Arctic camouflage of Beta Galaxy. Its name was *Callisto*, and he loved it as much as any MechWarrior could.

He loved taking it up in its jump jets, feeling that moment of weightlessness, and then descending back down to the ground. He loved firing its missiles and lasers at any range; he loved how maneuverable it was.

In his mind, *Callisto* was a work of art.

But clearly, it was not as impressive to the assembled cadets of the Dragonbears, especially since the first 'Mech they had seen was the *Kodiak*, which was twice the size of his *Callisto*. The *Ursus II* lacked the menacing claws, too. Cubs and cadets were always drawn to the *Kodiak* and the claws. It looked fierce, but they were too young to realize that ferocity did not always come in the packages they expected.

"You prefer...this to the *Kodiak*, Star Colonel?" Valkyrie asked. "An *Ursus II*, *quiaff*?"

"*Aff*."

"But it has half the firepower and armor of the *Kodiak*—"

"The Clans are taught to abhor waste," he said. "And in my studies, I have learned that economy of attack is often a matter of simplicity. 'Simplicity is the shortest distance between two points.' It means choosing the right tool for the right task, never one larger and more wasteful than is needed. In most cases, *Callisto* is more than enough of a 'Mech for the situations I am in. When I have need of a larger 'Mech, I choose one."

"But what if the situation changes on the field, and you do not have time to change 'Mechs?" Valkyrie blurted.

Sullivan's face reddened at the impertinence of the cub in her command. "Cadet Valkyrie, you forget yourself."

"No," Emilio said, raising a hand and interceding on her behalf. "It is a fair question. And these cubs are here to learn and be the best, *quiaff*?"

"*Aff*, Star Colonel, but—"

"She seeks to learn. And that is to be encouraged, regardless of what rank her teacher holds. For we are all teachers." Emilio turned to Valkyrie and tried to radiate warmth to counteract the reproach of her *Ursari*. "First off, Cadet Valkyrie, you have to remember that as a Star Colonel in command of other 'Mechs, the right 'Mech for the job does not always have to be mine. That is ego, and something many Clan Warriors struggle with: understanding that you cannot do everything on your own. I have my subordinates—my Ghost Bear family—to call upon if I am the wrong instrument for a job. And no matter the size of the 'Mech, I will defend the Ghost Bears and the Rasalhague Dominion with my life. I will attack those who oppose us just as viciously. But this is the 'Mech I feel most comfortable and lethal in. It is in this *Ursus II* that I will face off against any foe." He looked up at *Callisto* with a loving twinkle in his eye. "And it is a great monster to be reckoned with. I fear for those who would accept my *batchall* while I am inside it."

"That makes sense. Thank you, Star Colonel."

"It is my pleasure, Cadet Valkyrie. Be free with your questions. Especially about 'Mechs and combat. I much prefer that to other topics of conversation." Emilio gave Sullivan a sideways glance and half a knowing grin.

"Who would you guess would be the next enemy to fall before you then, Star Colonel?" Valkyrie asked.

"Well, the Rasalhague Dominion has enemies at every border. And with us joining the Star League Defense Force, the enemies of the Inner Sphere become our enemies. They can lurk anywhere." Emilio winked slyly. "But *Callisto* and I, we will be ready for them."

CHAPTER 13

THE FALCON'S NEST BATTLEMECH FACILITY
HAMMARR
SUDETEN
JADE FALCON OCCUPATION ZONE
07 OCTOBER 3151

"If only we could solve all of our problems on our own, eh?" Jiyi Chistu, Khan of the Jade Falcons, stood before *Emerald*, his 55-ton *Gyrfalcon,* admiring it, wishing he had a reason to be piloting it. He felt more at home on the command couch of his 'Mech than he did at the desk of a Khan, handling all of the political machinations that position implied. He came down here to think, and he always did his best thinking with his 'Mech. It brought him a measure of solace to be with it.

Running his hands along *Emerald's* metal talons, he felt his strength return, as though the physical connection to the 'Mech reminded him of where he was happiest. It had been a long season, and the coming winter would likely be longer still, thanks to Sudeten's standard weather patterns.

Looking up, he admired the sharp beak on the head and the tips of the wings. *Emerald* was a handsome 'Mech. But he could not clear his mind of the problems before him. The Merchants of Jade Falcon had abandoned the Clan, declaring themselves independent. At best, they cost him the resources they held, and their cooperation. At worst, they risked starting a war if they could hire enough mercenary companies.

Worse still, the borders of the Jade Falcon Occupation Zone had been further chipped away, and there were enemies lurking on every planet and behind every jump path.

Terra had fallen, and the Jade Falcons had lost. No help would come from the Wolves and their so-called ilClan.

Jiyi Chistu had no friends and allies save for those around him, and even then, their ranks were few. Malvina had been so sure of her claim to Terra she had left nothing behind. Nothing but Jiyi and a token resistance. When they wrote the history books about the Jade Falcons, there would be entire chapters devoted to how they were destroyed by Malvina Hazen's hubris.

Jiyi could only hope they would also include chapters about how he had saved them, pulled them back from the brink and kept them alive. And he could only hope he actually *would* be able to save them. That precipice they stood on was so vast, and the deep beyond it contained nothing but failure. How could he keep them upright—and not just upright now, but upright for generations?

The Jade Falcons themselves hung in the balance. If he could not rebuild them in time to fend off their gathering enemies, they would be remembered like the Smoke Jaguars: a cautionary tale told to children about what happens to Clans that delve too greedily into the Inner Sphere.

He looked his 'Mech up and down and swore he would use it to rebuild the Jade Falcons, 'Mech by 'Mech, brick by brick if he had to. Failure was simply not an option.

"My Khan," said Star Captain Quinn. "There is news for you."

Jiyi glanced over at the Star Captain. She waited at attention, straight-backed and ready to deal with anything that came her way. He wished she was not so green behind the ears. But soon, she would have all the experience she could handle, and more. He just hoped she was up to the task.

"Tell me you have solved all of our *touman* problems."

"*Neg.* But there is an agent of the Watch here to report to you."

"The Watch? They're here?"

"*Aff.* They bring news from the Rasalhague Dominion and Terra."

"Let us not keep them waiting, then."

"*Aff,* my Khan."

Star Captain Quinn had a car waiting at the 'Mech facility, waiting to take them to the governor's mansion.

"I worry for the future of the Jade Falcons," she said after a long bout of silence in the car.

"As should we all," Jiyi said.

"I feel like we are on borrowed time. Like we were not supposed to survive, and we are doing so despite the circumstances arrayed against us."

"That may all be true."

"I want you to know I appreciate what you are doing for the Jade Falcons. You are the right person to meet this moment."

Jiyi smiled. "I want you to know that *I* appreciate what *you* are doing. You are training our MechWarriors and helping rebuild the next generation. We will survive. Not just because of me or my decisions, but because of your work, too. No one will forget that."

Quinn had no response to that other than an embarrassed look. She was hard on herself, and did not like praise. Jiyi truly believed she represented the best of what he had.

"Your belief in me means everything, my Khan," she finally told him as they pulled up the long drive to the mansion.

"You have no reason to doubt it." Jiyi chuckled softly. "Just do not make me regret it either."

"I would never dream of it, my Khan."

Star Captain Quinn led him to the study of the governor's mansion, full of books and noteputers full of aged information. Jiyi wondered where all the books had come from, since the city had been destroyed, but he assumed it was an expensive fancy of one of the interim mayors between the destruction of Hammarr and its current occupant.

Seated at the fireplace was a hooded figure who rose at the sound of the door opening.

"Khan Jiyi Chistu," Star Captain Quinn announced, "this is Watch Agent Colmari. Watch Agent Colmari, this is your Khan, Jiyi Chistu, savior of the Jade Falcons."

Colmari pulled the hood off, revealing a woman beneath. She looked quite unassuming and ordinary; Jiyi felt she had a face perfect for spy work. "It is an honor, my Khan. After reports from Terra, I feared there would be no Falcons left to report to, but when I heard you had ascended to the Khanship, I knew I had to finish collecting my information and bring it to you."

"Indeed, the reports of the demise of the Jade Falcons have been greatly exaggerated."

"I am glad to hear it, my Khan."

Jiyi sat down in the high-backed chair opposite Colmari's. "Please, sit and report."

Colmari nodded and eased back into her chair. "I serve in the Rasalhague Dominion."

Jiyi nodded. "What you report will benefit us greatly if it is of value."

"I believe it is." She produced a noteputer from the folds of her robe and tapped on it. "After my report, I will turn over this noteputer with a copy of all of my files. You will be able to go through them more in depth than any conversation can get into, but there is trouble brewing in the Dominion."

"Trouble brews everywhere in the Inner Sphere, but I wonder if we can turn it to our advantage."

"The chief event playing out now are protests and strife across all of the Dominion worlds. As you are aware, they do not act like other Clans. They integrated fully into the Rasalhague Dominion. They are not vassals of the civilian government; they still uphold many Clan traditions, but they answer to the civilian government."

"I have spent much time in the Dominion stationed aboard VaultShip *Gamma*."

"So you know civilians get a say in Clan affairs?"

"To a point. But what is yours?"

"When the ilKhan demanded the Ghost Bears join the new Star League Defense Force, the Bear Khans explained they would like to, but they had to put it to a vote first. Not just among Trueborn Clan Warriors, but the entire populace. They were given the choice to join or refuse."

Jiyi knew how difficult it was to run a Clan in the first place, but he could not imagine having to do so with so much bureaucracy that any decision would need to be put to a vote of all the castes, let alone the Warriors. "I presume they voted to join?"

"Only just. The vote was evenly divided across worlds, and it has caused a great amount of consternation. There were planets where the refusers won and protested because the Dominion-wide vote went against them. There were planets where joiners protested because the refusers won, and then it stopped when all the votes were tallied. But as far as our network of information states, there was no world in the Dominion where the vote was not close. On the planets of Rasalhague and Alshain, both with populations of billions and where the civilian and Clan governments are housed, the votes dividing the two sides numbered in the hundreds. There have been accusations of vote tampering and illegalities. They are in disarray, even if things seemed to have calmed down recently."

"So, the Ghost Bears, and the Dominion itself, are joining the Star League. Fascinating." Jiyi was not quite sure if that helped his cause or hurt it. If the Ghost Bears remained outside of the Star League, they might set their eyes on their common borders and see an easy way to expand, especially given their border with the Draconis Combine. But since they joined, would Alaric Ward order them to finish off the Jade Falcons and the job he had started on Terra? Anything was possible.

The gears turned in Jiyi's head. First the Vesper Marches and the Tamar Pact—as the rogue Arcturans were calling themselves—the breaking off of Syndic Marena and her Alyina Merchant League, then this. With the Ghost Bears likely to come after him, it was more than he could defend against if any two of them decided he was a problem worth dealing with. Or even one, if it were simply the Ghost Bears. Their Clan had not gone to Terra and lost everything. Their Clan had not participated in the various wars and battles that had taken so much strength and energy from the other Clans battling for the promised land. They had simply built up into an invincible juggernaut in Rasalhague. And Jiyi was in the unenviable position of being exactly where they would want him if the ilKhan wished to destroy the remnants of the Jade Falcons reborn. And the ilClan would do it, too, given what had happened the last time the Ghost Bears dishonored themselves in the final hunt against the Not-Named Clan.

"And no word of the Jade Falcons who left for Terra?"

"*Neg.* Reports from Terra read more like fairy tales written by Wolves. No actionable intelligence. The only common thread is that the Jade Falcons were obliterated."

"It is as we feared." Jiyi frowned, crooking a finger over his lips, desperately seeking some silver lining in the clouds of disaster gathering above him.

"I am afraid so," Watch Agent Colmari said. "And there was something else. It felt urgent to tell you when we had less information, but it turned out to be nothing."

"Let me be the judge of that," Jiyi said. Nothing was inconsequential, and if she thought it was important enough at the start, perhaps her dismissal of it could have been a feint of the Ghost Bears.

"We believed we had been tracking an attack heading for the Jade Falcon Occupation Zone. DropShips from across the Dominion began moving toward the border and seemed to be rallying on Quarell, where the Ghost Bears have their Fourteenth Battle Cluster headquartered."

Jiyi thought hard about the map of the worlds surrounding them. Quarell was just a few jumps away, and definitely on the border between the Falcons and the Bears.

"We assumed this was an attack force," said Colmari.

"But you decided otherwise?"

"*Aff.* It turns out that they are holding a cross-training on Quarell. The DropShips were full of Ghost Bear cubs. A *sibko* cross-training event. They are all competing on the planet. The movement was merely groups of children from strategic worlds, gathering on the border for war games. Nothing to worry about. There will be no attack. At least not imminently, and not from Quarell."

Jiyi blinked. Watch Agent Colmari clearly had no idea the value of the information she just delivered.

"How many?" he asked, wondering if this could be the solution to his Warrior deficit.

"Sir?"

"How many cadets? How many are on Quarell? And when do the exercises end?"

"Oh, there are a hundred there at least, from at least a half-dozen different *sibkos*. It seems as though this is their last big training before their Trials of Position. And the games are scheduled to take place through November and into December."

Jiyi's mind spun with the possibilities. This was exactly what he needed, but he would need to mobilize forces quickly to take them. First, however, he had to deal with the Watch Agent. "Excellent. You have done well with your report, Watch Agent Colmari."

Jiyi glanced at Star Captain Quinn, whose wide eyes told him she must have understood the importance of this information as well. She stepped in and reached for the Watch Agent's noteputer. "We will have the rest of the data analyzed," Quinn said, taking the tablet. "You have our thanks."

Jiyi stood from his chair and looked expectantly at the Watch Agent until she got the hint to reciprocate and stood as well. Ordinarily, one of these debriefings would last much longer, but with the information he had just received, there was no time.

Confusion was clear on her face. She seemed to get the idea that she had offered him something of value, but she could not determine what. It did not matter if she understood, though. Probably better if she did not at all. That way, she could not give anything away.

"The Jade Falcons owe you a debt, Watch Agent Colmari."

"We are all Jade Falcons."

"*Seyla,*" he said as she stepped to the other side of the study's door. "Until we see each other again, Watch Agent. Best of luck on your next dispatch."

Jiyi shut the door and spun around, a smile on his face broader than the wingspan of his *Gyrfalcon.* Stepping further into the room, he waited until he heard her footsteps vanish down the hall. Then he said to Star Captain Quinn, "Muster the troops."

"You do not really mean to—"

"We leave tonight. How many do we have ready to fight, right now?"

"There are three Trinaries at the most. And one is made up of new recruits. Those you brought and those we promoted before you left. And we will have more infantry and Elementals that you might want to bring into this battle rather than seasoned 'Mech pilots. We will need to leave at least a Trinary for defense."

"Two Trinaries will have to do."

"How do you expect to drop in on the Ghost Bear Fourteenth Battle Cluster and walk away with *sibkos* full of recruits?"

"A Trial of Possession."

"That is not how those work, my Khan, and you know that. They will never agree."

Jiyi folded his arms, but he felt an excitement inside him. "The future of the Jade Falcons depends on it. Allow me to work out the details. But we will make them an offer they find too good to refuse."

"And if it does not work?"

"Then the Jade Falcons are finished anyway. Now go. Time is short, and the journey is long."

"Yes, my Khan." Star Captain Quinn left double-quick, following the Watch Agent's path out the door.

Khan Jiyi Chistu stared into the crackling fire, surrounded by the books and plunder from the rest of Sudeten. What exactly could he use to entice the Ghost Bears into a Trial? He had to figure it out. Come hell or high water, those *sibkos* were going to be Jade Falcons before the year was over.

CHAPTER 14

FALCON'S RUN TRAINING FACILITY
OUTSKIRTS OF HAMMARR
SUDETEN
JADE FALCON OCCUPATION ZONE
07 OCTOBER 3151

"What the hell?" Star Commander Dawn said as the lights winked out on her simulator session. None of the controls responded to her moves, and the simulated ignition switch would not turn the 'Mech back over.

The door opened, and the bright light of the outer room spilled into the pod, revealing a room full of other newly minted MechWarriors from her Star standing around, wondering why the simulation had ended. Stepping out and looking around, Dawn was just as confused.

"Is this some kind of drill or something?" she asked the MechWarrior next to her, Siamion. A tall mountain of a man who had served in the infantry with her and made the jump to MechWarrior in their Trial of Position.

He just shrugged. "They have told us nothing."

"Here it comes," Dawn said as Star Captain Quinn stepped into the room. The assembled MechWarriors all stood up straight, waiting for an explanation.

"MechWarriors," said Star Captain Quinn. Dawn had great difficulty divining the nature of her countenance, unable to decide if it was grim or excited. "The time has come. We are mobilizing now. You are to report to the DropShip at Hammarr

Spaceport within the hour. This is a confidential mission. You will speak to no one between here and there, and you will say nothing of this mobilization, *quiaff*?"

"AFF!" they all parroted back.

Dawn's brow furrowed. Unless the situation was impossibly desperate, they would not send her ragtag group into a battle so soon. Yes, they had trained, and yes, they had done well in their simulations, but there were other, far more seasoned Stars of MechWarriors on Sudeten. Something must have gone wrong, and that never boded well. Now that she was in charge of a Star, she couldn't imagine sending them into battle so green. They simply weren't ready, which she took as a failure of her own. After all, it was her job to prepare them.

"You will be briefed aboard the DropShip," Star Captain Quinn said. "And you will receive your 'Mech assignments onboard as well. There will be much drilling during the voyage. I expect you to not fail me. Is that understood?"

"AFF, *Star Captain!*" they all said.

OVERLORD-C-CLASS DROPSHIP *FALCON'S SHADOW*
HAMMARR SPACEPORT
JADE FALCON OCCUPATION ZONE
07 OCTOBER 3151

The crew of the DropShip had shown Dawn and the rest of their Star to their billets, where they were given instructions to leave their belongings and report to the briefing room immediately. The only belongings they had been able to take were their uniforms and any nominal personal items.

The only personal effect Dawn had to speak of was a modest necklace she had picked up after flunking her original Trial of Position, and she wore it around her neck. The merchant she purchased it from told her it was the mark of Jude, the patron saint of lost causes.

She had not removed it from her neck since.

Fortunately, Saint Jude, or divine providence, or the cosmic luck of the galaxy had put her back on the path of being a MechWarrior.

Dawn rubbed it between her thumb and forefinger for good luck. Clan Warriors—MechWarriors especially—should be careful of trusting in luck, but after losing her shot, she'd had nothing left to lose but her life. Now that she had what she wanted, she could not deny the effect, placebo or otherwise. And if this St. Jude supported her lost cause, then who was she to argue?

MechWarrior Hosteen, who had won his position alongside Dawn, sidled up to her as they moved through the bunks of their billet and through the corridors to the briefing room. He was a big man, and older than she had imagined he would be when first they had met outside of their 'Mechs. "Do you know what is going on?"

"*Neg*," Dawn said. She thought she was going to be asking that same question a lot. "But it must be important if they're taking us all."

"Or desperate."

"Likely both." Dawn turned the corner and found a jagged line of MechWarriors all heading to the briefing room.

The briefing room itself was organized as a semi-circle of rows of seats facing a podium and a screen, a different kind of theater of war. There were more than enough seats for every MechWarrior an *Overlord-C* could carry, 45 in all, which made Dawn wonder if the DropShip was not carrying its full capacity and complement, or if they were still waiting to take on more MechWarriors. She had seen Elementals boarding, but had not seen any of them in the briefing room. Would they be briefed later in the same room, or separately elsewhere? She had not spent any time in DropShips as a MechWarrior; she was curious to find out.

Hosteen shuffled in through the row of seats and sat down beside her. Siamion sat down right in front of her. It felt good to get to know more folks as they had been training, and it felt good to feel like part of a group again. Once she had left her friends in the paramilitary, they had treated her like she was different. Their shoulders were cold, and they never seemed to have time for her, though she did not have much time to spend with them anyway, mainly because Star Captain Quinn drilled them so often, both before and after the Trials of Position. But here? She was finally part of the group she wanted to be in.

The chatter in the room grew as it filled.

Hosteen leaned in close to her. "This seems like a lot of MechWarriors all in one place."

"Is it the whole *touman*?" Dawn asked.

"I would hope not. The Khan is bold, but not foolish enough to put the whole *touman* in one ship."

Siamion leaned back in their chair to join their conversation. "There are still at least a few MechWarriors planet-side. At least a few Stars' worth. It is likely and sensible that a defense is left on Sudeten."

"We must have, I would think," Hosteen said. "I mean, it would not do well to leave our home base and come back to find we have no home at all."

"*Aff*," Dawn said. "I am positive the Khan is doing what is best. It is just that with the situation we are in, what is best might not always be what is wise." She looked down at her MechWarrior jumpsuit—the standard Falcon uniform in emerald-green, with short sleeves, accentuated by black knee-high boots—and wondered about the wisdom of her own promotion. *Definitely best.* She also hoped it was wise.

Star Captain Quinn entered the briefing room with a noteputer, moved purposefully across the presentation area, and set it on the podium. The Jade Falcon crest, the emerald falcon with a sword in its talons, appeared on the screen behind her as she fiddled with the connection between the noteputer and the presentation monitor.

Star Captain Quinn looked up at those assembled with a face as cold as the Ice Hellion Plateau and the chatter in the room dropped as fast as the temperature in that arctic waste. Dawn got the hint and kept her mouth shut.

When the hush consumed the room entirely, the Star Captain scanned the room, looking deeply into each one of the MechWarriors there. A shiver ran down Dawn's back when Quinn met her eyes.

"Jade Falcons," Star Captain Quinn said finally. "You are here not because you are the best."

Dawn tilted her head and furrowed her brow. That did not sound like the usual sort of pep talk.

"You are here," the Star Captain continued, "because you are the best we *have*. The Jade Falcons have lost everything but us. And so we might not be the best in this moment, but we have to rise to the occasion. And we must do it fast. The survival of Clan Jade Falcon depends on it. Are you ready?"

"AFF!" the room bellowed like thunder.

"You have been selected for an impossible mission deep into territory that harbors no love for Jade Falcons. And we will win!"

"AFF!" they all said again. Dawn felt the word rumble in her chest. The coldness within her was replaced with an unusual warmth. Something she had not felt in a long time. At least not since the Clan had fallen apart.

Star Captain Quinn looked down at the chronometer on her wrist. "This ship leaves at the top of the hour, and we will be ready to meet anything that we find on the other side. Now, I will turn you over to your Khan, Jiyi Chistu."

Dawn looked over to the other side of the screen; she had not even noticed the Khan standing there. His arms were folded, and he had a grim countenance. He slowly walked to the podium.

"Jade Falcons," he said, looking up at all of them. "We have a momentous task in front of us. I would not say it is impossible, though it might seem so to some. Star Captain Quinn has not led you astray in her characterization of the job ahead. You must know that she is my right hand. My left, Merchant Factor Jodine, remains behind on Sudeten to defend our base of operations. Though she bears the rank of Star Captain, Quinn has proved herself time and again. Once we are through this trial, I have no doubt she will earn her Bloodname when we focus again on such things. And though she has not been voted to the rank, at this moment, Star Captain Quinn is the closest thing to a saKhan the Jade Falcons have. I expect you all to treat her accordingly, *quiaff*?"

"AFF!" Dawn shouted with the other thirty or so Mech-Warriors in the room. But she could not have heard him right. Was a Merchant Factor really commanding Clan defenses? The Khan had sandwiched that bit of information in between two other important statements.

Did he hope we would not notice?

Before Dawn could think too much about the unorthodox practice of elevating members of the merchant caste and compare that to her own situation, the Khan continued his rallying speech.

"What have we mustered you for? That must be the question at the top of your minds. The answer is this: we will be partaking in a Trial of Possession for a number of *sibko* cadets. Scores of them. A hundred or more, if we succeed as brilliantly as I assume we will. We will replenish our ranks and make the Jade Falcons strong once more. Over the coming weeks, I will train you to fight like you have never fought before. Our enemy is the Ghost Bears. The Fourteenth Battle Cluster, to be specific. And they will not be easily defeated."

There was a low murmur in the room, and Dawn shared their confused curiosity. Would they still be Jade Falcons if half of them had been raised as Ghost Bears? That could change the face of the Clan forever.

The Khan continued, "We cannot meet them as Jade Falcons have traditionally taken the battlefield. We will do something new and altogether surprising. And, in exchange, we will bring home with us the next generation of Jade Falcons who will help us elevate our Clan back to the prominent position where it belongs. Our journey will take weeks. And, at the end of the journey, you will all become experts in a new kind of combat, one that leaves behind the Mongol Doctrine and the way Jade Falcons have traditionally swooped in and destroyed everything in sight. The Ghost Bears will be expecting that, so we will fight against them in a way they have never faced before, tailored to play into both their biases and instincts."

Taking it all in, Dawn could not quite believe what she heard. By the sound of murmurs around her, it seemed the other MechWarriors shared her incredulity. *Did he just say the entire Ghost Bear Fourteenth Battle Cluster?*

It did not make sense. How would they, a couple of Trinaries at best, take on one of the most elite Clusters of the Ghost Bear *touman*?

"I would not ask you to do this," the Khan continued, "if it were not of the utmost importance and vital to the survival of the Jade Falcons. We have a plan, and it will work, so long as we all work together."

The Khan's eyes softened, even the one damaged by the scar, and the right side of his mouth hooked into a sly grin. "We are Jade Falcons, are we not? In the words of one of our earliest Khans, Patricia Bailey, it is 'our great destiny to see Clan Jade Falcon thrive, to see it live beyond us all, and to do that, sometimes our trajectory bends below us like the path of the Eden Serpents we hunt.' And if that is not a call for us to bend our traditional paths to hunt the prey we seek, I do not know what is. Khan Bailey meant that our traditions and our most closely held beliefs can change, too. For if they do not, there will be no Jade Falcons left to rid the Inner Sphere of the Eden Serpents that look to take everything from us, *quiaff*?"

"AFF!" they all roared. Even Dawn, feeling a thrill of excitement and swell of emotion radiate from the room and the Khan's words.

When the room quieted again, the Khan lowered his tone and leaned in as though he were about to tell them all a great secret. "We will be victorious. And it will be together that we do so. Your strength is my strength. My strength is the strength of the Jade Falcons. But that victory will take much work. Are you willing to do that work?"

They had to survive. If the Jade Falcons did not make it through this Trial, what else did Dawn have left? *"Aff!"* Dawn said again, along with everyone else who wanted to see a future for the Jade Falcons.

This time, she meant it more than she ever had before.

"Then go to, my Falcons. Strap in and stay strong. We leave immediately for the Rasalhague Dominion."

CHAPTER 15

LYKOURGOS ARENA
ANTIMONY
QUARELL
RASALHAGUE DOMINION
10 OCTOBER 3151

Alexis stood on the field of the Lykourgos Arena alongside her *sibkin,* surrounded by other Ghost Bear cadets from Quarell and elsewhere, watching the monitors overhead for a closer look at the proceedings. The cameras were trained on the dais at the end of the arena and the stadium was filled with onlookers, Clan and native alike. Most were from Quarell, but others had traveled with their local *sibko*s to support and cheer on their comrades.

Everyone wanted to watch a good competition and root for their home team.

She tried not to think about how easy it would be to get away with so much sneaky wealth redistribution in a crowd that size and so loud and distracted. Maybe she knew some of the kids in the crowd out there doing just that. But that life was behind her now. She had to look ahead.

Alexis kept still, trying not to look around too much, but the surroundings really were awe-inspiring. The screens hanging above the arena were the biggest she had ever seen. Streamers and bunting hung overhead, all in the standard Ghost Bear colors: primarily blues, blacks, and whites, but with many other accent colors.

Above and behind the dais was the biggest of the banners with the Ghost Bear emblem emblazoned across it: a screaming ghost bear, surrounded in a circle by six swooshes of its clawed arms, all set on a black field with the entire image ringed in a gold. It was supposed to represent their unity, and Alexis wanted so badly for it to mean that for her. It had for a time, but now it all just felt so...superficial.

"Welcome, sibko *cadets, to the Quarell Cross-Training Exercises and War Games of 3151."* Star Colonel Emilio Hall stood at the podium on the dais to make his remarks. Since he was the highest-ranking Ghost Bear on Quarell, the duties must have fallen to him to play host. His dark, curly hair was practically tame, and his brown face looked freshly shaved. Alexis thought of him as some sort of distant grandfather in her growing Ghost Bear family.

"This is the first time they have been held here on Quarell," the Star Colonel continued, *"and the first that have been held in six years. As many of you know, they happen only occasionally. The last combined Ghost Bear* sibko *exercises and games were held in 3145 on Jabuka. We welcome all of you who have traveled from so far away to participate or to watch. For you cadets, cubs ready to become Ghost Bears, this will be one of the final challenges in your training."*

Alexis wondered why they weren't held every year. Or with regularity, like how the Terran Olympics were held every two years, switching seasons of sports each time. It seemed like the sort of thing that every cadet would want to participate in.

She certainly wanted to.

And she was lucky she was able to, after what Thomasin had done to Daniel.

Glancing over the line of other Bearclaws, she saw Daniel at the end, right next to the Den Mother. Even at that distance, Alexis could see his blackened eye had healed completely. She wished it hadn't, though. It didn't matter that Daniel had deserved it; Thomasin should have known better. And of course, Daniel had been dragged straight back to the Den Mother and there was an inquiry. At first, the Den Mother wanted to punish Alexis, but when it was clear she hadn't actually done anything, and Thomasin—a Trueborn—had been the one to throw the punch, suddenly it was easy to brush aside. She told all of them to forget about the infighting and concentrate on the upcoming games.

But Alexis, Thomasin, and Sophie had been forced to earn back their place in the games. They each had to earn ten extra points between then and the opening ceremony. Each. Only then would they be allowed to compete. It was difficult, especially with how much the Den Mother had hated them, but they all worked hard to do it. Had Alexis been the one to throw the punch, she would have been barred from the games completely. Instead, she struggled to earn the points. Extra duties and winning competitions were about the only way she could earn them, since the *Ursari* never seemed to award her points for having the right answer or being exemplary in classes like they did for Daniel. Even Thomasin and Sophie seemed to have an easier time than she did.

Alexis had found a family in Thomasin and Sophie, but her treatment by the Den Mother hadn't made her feel anything like that was the case. Alexis didn't feel as though they treated her much like anything but a black sheep. *And don't bears eat sheep?*

"Our first events will be war games in simulators. Others will include actual 'Mech races and combat, as well as strategic war games designed to test your battlefield tactics on a grand scale. At the end of the month, the two sibkos *with the most points will compete in a live-fire exercise in the remote town of Feldspar and surrounding areas which have been evacuated. The leading* sibko *will lead the attack, the trailing* sibko *will mount the defense. It will be to the credit of your Den Parents and* Ursari *to see one of your* sibkos *become champions."*

Star Colonel Hall waited for the roar of the crowd to die down before beginning the introductions. As the Star Colonel introduced each *sibko*, spotlights lit up the cadets, dimming the rest of the arena. The crowd applauded politely for the visitors, but roared when he announced the hometown *sibko*s. *"From Jabuka, we have the Berserkers* sibko. *From Quarell, the Bearclaws and the Porbjorns* sibkos. *From Carse, the Bjornsons* sibko. *From Thun, we have the Dragonbears* sibko. *Straight from Lothan, we have the Mektid Bears* sibko. *And, finally, from Fort Louden, the Werebears* sibko."*

Alexis hated the feeling of having the bright light shine on her, so much more comfortable in the dark with the light on the others. Maybe it was just her upbringing causing that anxiety. She liked being the best, but she did not necessarily like everyone else knowing it. And the Bearclaw *Ursari* were doing their best to pick on her or praise her to make sure she never forgot how good she was. Her life with her new family felt so much more uncomplicated when no one realized she was the best of the group.

Once the applause for the cadets died down, the Star Colonel continued. "Each of you cubs are on the path to fully entering the Ghost Bear Clan as a warrior in the Rasalhague Military. Trueborn or freeborn, it makes no difference. You are all members of the Dominion, and Ghost Bears at heart. Remember that regardless of these competitions here, you are one of us, and we will defend you no matter what, just as you will defend us, *quiaff*?"

The entire arena shouted back: "AFF!"

"Good luck, cadets. And may the best *sibko* win."

Eventually the applause died down after each *sibko* was led out of the arena one at a time, ending with the Bearclaws. Alexis hated that they had to go last. Between the intervals of games and who got announced when, there didn't seem to be any rhyme or reason to what they did, and Alexis preferred the predictable. It made it easier to get in and out with whatever objective she wanted.

The hover transport for the Bearclaws was waiting to take them immediately to their first event in the games. Once they'd all taken their seats, the *Ursari* at the front of the bus, led by Star Captain Sasha Ivankova, stood to brief them. "We are heading to a simulator room, where you will be assigned into a Trinary. One of you has been selected to act as the commander of the unit from a central control room. We have been paired against the Dragonbears from Thun—the only other *sibko* in the games that can match our sixteen cadets. This exercise will place you in direct opposition to them. It will be a fight down to the last 'Mech. We score points for each 'Mech we destroy and each 'Mech of our own that remains standing at the end. Like any situation, it behooves us to do as much damage as possible and take as little as we can."

From her seat on the transport nestled between Thomasin and Sophie, Alexis imagined herself operating the whole battle from the command station, but something told her that whatever criteria was chosen for that position, she would not meet it.

The *Ursari* behind the Den Mother, Star Commander Diego, stepped forward and carried on the briefing as the city outside the transport's windows gave way to the country. "The 'Mechs in the simulated Stars will be randomly assigned once you get into your simulator, but will be equally matched against the opposing team based on an algorithm that determines combat value and weight. Each Star will consist of an assault 'Mech, a heavy, a medium, and two lights. All will be 'Mechs you are familiar with or trained on, common to Ghost Bears."

Who would be in charge? It almost did not matter who piloted the 'Mechs if the orders and strategies they were given did not make sense.

Star Captain Ivankova stepped forward again and looked right at Alexis. "I know what many of you are thinking, and you are wondering which of you will command. It was a split decision, but the *Ursari* have chosen one amongst you to lead. It was not my first choice, but I am sure they will do an adequate job."

Alexis looked around, wondering which of her *sibkin* would be called for the honor. But she was surprised when Star Commander Diego said, "Cadet Alexis."

Her eyes widened.

"What?" Daniel said loudly from across the transport bus.

His angered incredulity almost made her disbelief and panic at the massive job before her almost worth it.

"You will have your chance, Cadet Daniel," Ivankova assured him.

Of course she'd be right there to soothe his hurt feelings.

"When we reach the central hub for the simulators," *Ursari* Diego continued, ignoring the drama unfolding, "Cadet Alexis will follow me to the command center. The rest of you will follow your Den Mother to the simulation pods and meet your 'Mech assignments."

Thomasin leaned in to whisper, "Congratulations."

"You are going to do great," Sophie added. "There is no way we will lose."

But Alexis knew *something* could go wrong. Especially with Daniel nursing that sort of third-degree burn.

SIMULATOR CENTER
OUTSKIRTS OF ANTIMONY
QUARELL
RASALHAGUE DOMINION

It wasn't long before they arrived at the expansive warehouse on the outskirts of Antimony. As they got off the transport, single file, Star Captain Ivankova pulled Alexis out of line and to the side.

"So, you will be the one representing us in command."

"*Aff*, Star Captain."

"I warn you, cadet, do not be too eager for the rigors of command. You may find it does not suit you the way you think it should."

Alexis wasn't sure if that was a threat, or just the Den Mother trying to give her a pep talk. That was the problem with the Star Captain. *Everything* sounded like a threat.

"I will do my best, Star Captain."

"I am sure you will," Ivankova said. "Let us hope it is good enough. Your *sibkin* will not take kindly to your failure."

"And neither will I," Alexis said.

"Cadet Alexis," Star Commander Diego said at the end of the line, coming up behind her. "Are you ready?"

Alexis did not break eye contact with the Den Mother as she answered, "*Aff*, Star Commander."

The Star Commander put a hand on Alexis' shoulder, and she finally turned toward the building. He walked her toward the door behind the others of the *sibko*, but Alexis couldn't help glancing over her shoulder.

The last thing she saw before entering the building was Star Captain Ivankova, arms crossed in front of her chest and her eyes fixed in an icy glare.

"Do not mind her," *Ursari* Diego said as they entered the simulator complex.

"She voted against me, *quiaff*?"

"*Aff.*"

"For Daniel?"

"*Aff.*"

"I see."

"Do not take it personally," he said, leading her up a back staircase. "The rest of the *Ursari* see you and your worth. As do most of your *sibkin.*"

"Do they hate me because I am freeborn?"

"For a couple, perhaps. But not for everyone. For most, it means very little these days. I have told you before that those attitudes died decades ago. Sometimes, being good at what you do is enough for people to dislike you."

"They seem pretty alive for something that died that long ago."

"Sometimes families are difficult."

Alexis nodded. It was something she was starting to learn.

"When you go in, you will be alone, isolated from your opponents. All you will have access to is the battlefield data sent in by the 'Mechs at your command, and a simulation of satellite data, giving you an overview of the terrain. You will have to trust yourself, Bear Cub."

"*Aff.*" If there was one thing Alexis could do, it was to try to trust herself. But would everyone else trust her?

Alexis and the Star Captain reached a door at the end of a long, dim hallway leading to the control room. In front of the door stood a Ghost Bear Elemental.

"This is it," Star Commander Diego said. "You will do your best, and that will be good enough. The Bearclaws believe in you."

That acceptance and vote of confidence from the Star Commander blossomed in her chest, bolstering her. "Thank you, Star Commander."

Diego turned to the Elemental. "This is Cadet Alexis, representing the Bearclaw *sibko*, reporting for the simulation."

The Elemental, a man who looked like a massive bear regardless of his Clan, nodded and stepped aside, granting them access.

Before Alexis stepped in, she turned to her *Ursari* one last time. "Will everyone be watching?"

"*Aff.* Across Quarell and, eventually, it will spread across the Dominion, but try not to worry about that. Focus on the task. Your family is with you."

That made her feel stronger.

Certainly better than anything the Den Mother said.

Alexis sat down at the console, put on her headset, and found herself still grateful to be part of something bigger than herself, regardless of the setbacks—and the alleged family members who stood in her way.

CHAPTER 16

Star Colonel Emilio Hall sat in a private box at the top of the arena, waiting for the *sibko* games to begin. Below him was a stunning view of the packed arena and the monitors that would display the events. The voices of civilian media personalities who would call the action as it happened boomed through the arena. It was as much a sport as anything; they were broadcasting the games across the planet, and recordings would then travel throughout the Dominion and elsewhere. Not just to the planets fielding *sibkos*, but even into the hands of the Khan and the Prince.

What better way to prove their unity than by competitive sport?

Seated next to Hall was his second, Star Captain Allison Rand. "You should be proud of the games, Star Colonel."

"I am, but the work is not mine. There are hundreds of people who did far more than I did. We merely supervise and advise. You did more, surely. It is you who should be proud."

"I am. There are Watch Agents from around the Sphere here, as sure as anything, and they will report back that the Ghost Bears are strong—and that opposing the Rasalhague Dominion and the new Star League will be futile, now and for years to come."

The Star Colonel nodded. He saw her trying to bait the bear, reminding him of the vote and trying to spark an argument.

It wouldn't work. He merely *harrumphed.*

"I need you to understand," she said, her tone sharp and almost accusing, "that I will do anything to keep the Ghost Bears strong, doubly so that we are joining the Star League. And I will not let anything stand in my way."

"As would any Ghost Bear," he said, trying to divine her meaning and diffuse the activation he sensed in her.

But the start of the games and the announcers saved him from having to elaborate further. The screens flashed to a display of the command centers for the Bearclaws and the Dragonbears. The court of the arena projected a holographic map in 3D that showed the overview of the simulated battle area and the two Trinaries of imaginary Ghost Bear 'Mechs lining up to blast each other into smithereens.

"Commanding the Dragonbears," the announcer's voice echoed through the arena and the box, *"is Cadet Linus. His entire* sibko *hails from the planet Thun, deep in the Rasalhague Dominion."*

The screen showed young Linus sitting at a command console, looking at an overhead view of the map, much the same as the one in the arena below, but centered over the Dragonbear positions. Trees and fog kept the rest of the map obscured from him. The image wiped across to a view of a young woman.

"For the Bearclaws, commanding will be Cadet Alexis, a freeborn hailing from right here on Quarell!"

The crowd cheered at the mention of their own planet.

"In this game, these two commanders will lead a Trinary of 'Mechs into battle. Each team will score a possible 5 points per 'Mech they destroy and a possible 1 point for each 'Mech that remains standing at the end of the exercise. Each cadet has been randomly assigned to their 'Mech, so this should prove to be a very interesting contest."

"It is always fascinating," Rand said, "to see what the next generation does with their battle tactics. Do they adhere to the traditions they have learned? Or do they adopt the unorthodox?"

Like a game of chess, the Dragonbears set out a pair of light 'Mechs to scout. A wise enough move, except the Bearclaws had planned for that, and had long-range 'Mechs in position ready to take them down.

As the fireworks began below, the crowd grew excited, palpably so. Emilio could even feel it way up in the box. "There is always much to learn from the young. Even when they stick to tradition, they find new ways to interpret it."

Rand nodded. "That is how the Ghost Bears have always done it. Stuck to traditions and found new ways. It was what brought us to Rasalhague and what delivers us to our foretold destiny to the Star League."

Emilio had no interest in arguing politics, so he let the announcer's voice fill the space between them.

"The Bearclaws have taken an early ten-point lead, taking down both of the scouts, but that allowed the Dragonbears to identify an entire Bearclaw Star taking cover in a ravine, and are maneuvering the rest of that depleted Star out to meet them. It also seems as though the Dragonbears have inadvertently engaged a free-for-all, leaving both commanders to their own devices in managing the battle without the constraints of honorable combat."

Rand scoffed at that last statement, but Emilio could not understand why. "Who do you like in this fight?" she asked.

"Whoever wins, we all win, *quiaff*? We test the entire next generation. They are all Ghost Bears. The ingenuity of the best of them is our victory as much as the loss of the least of them is our defeat. So, I like them all."

"You are completely neutral on everything."

Emilio laughed nervously, edged in discomfort, reflected laser light from the battle flashing against his face. "I mean, the cadets in these *sibkos* represent a future for all of us. But if I had to pick between the two, I would choose the Bearclaws. They are from Quarell, and it is always good to curry favor with the local sentiment, *quiaff*?"

"*Aff.*"

"And what of you?"

"The Dragonbears. I met with their *Ursari* and watched them train since they arrived. They are fierce, and will not be put down so easily. They will do whatever it takes to win, as any Ghost Bear should."

One of the Bearclaw 'Mechs dropped. It flashed by on the screen so quickly, Emilio couldn't even track what sort of 'Mech it was, but it had been reduced to slag. Emilio pointed to the scoreboard, seeing the scores now matched at fifty. "It looks like they have caught up easily enough. But I imagine the Bearclaws will give them a fight for their lives."

A Dragonbear 'Mech fell under the withering fire of a Bearclaw, then the Bearclaw faded back into the ravine. "I would expect nothing less of any Ghost Bear *sibko.*"

He watched the score increase for the Bearclaws. "It astounds me how quickly a Star of 'Mechs can just evaporate in a battle."

"It is definitely easier when the battle is simulated."

"*Aff.*"

Rand rubbed her hands together. "Care to put a wager on it?"

Emilio glanced at her. She seemed serious enough. "I am not much of a gambler."

"Oh, come now, Star Colonel, I am sure you have put a wager down on a Trial of Possession if you felt the odds were right."

He thought about the list of things he would actually wager on. The lives of people he could protect. To take something away from an opposing force to reduce their ability to make war. But he would have to control the terms of the engagement. "I would, if I thought I had some control of the outcome, and the risk was worth the reward. But on something like this?" He waved his hand dismissively over the arena. "This is enjoyable enough on its own. And anything can happen with cadets like this. May as well flip coins."

He noticed Rand giving him a long side-eye, but he could not discern if she was skeptical of him or somehow disappointed with him. He had noticed that as soon as she had divined his position on the vote, she treated him differently, as though every question she asked from that moment forward was leading in a specific way. But he could not quite determine which way. Was she leading him into some sort of trap to remove him as the head of the Fourteenth Battle Cluster? That sort of ambition was unlike any Ghost Bear, but he could not rule it out completely.

And he would definitely not put it past her. She was intensely patriotic to the point of jingoism, and had risen through the ranks quickly, no doubt buoyed by that devotion.

As he put his mind to the problems Rand could represent, Emilio turned his attention back to the war games. Each side had exchanged the lead several times, back and forth, until there was only a scattered Star left on either side.

"It is getting interesting," Rand said, but he did not know if she meant the growing distance between them, or the game itself. But then she added, "It will definitely be close."

The screen above zoomed in on the two commander cadets—Linus and Alexis. Each showed signs of strain, but both were still determined, calling out orders and doing their best to lead their *sibko* to victory. They seemed evenly matched in ability and, aside from the standard rookie mistakes one would expect to see from Warriors so young, both were admirably competent. He had seen worse moves from more seasoned Ghost Bears, and they had still lived to tell about it. Emilio felt that idea was worth celebrating: the Ghost Bears had produced a fine crop of cadets this year, and they would be joining the Star League with an excellent advantage.

But he worried about how many of them would be sent off to fight wars across the Inner Sphere and the Periphery, all based on the whims of the ilKhan.

He had cast his vote and so had the cadets. They would all meet the obligations of the vote on their own.

Emilio looked over to the Star Captain and furrowed his brow. Her nefarious plan had worked. She had got him thinking about the vote, even though he had been determined not to.

"I cannot believe this!" came the voice of the announcer, echoing across the box from the arena. *"The Dragonbears are charging the ravine where the Bearclaws' last 'Mechs are taking refuge. And do not forget: the tenets of* zellbrigen *are out the window! Anything can happen! Linus seems to be moving in with everything he has in a final gambit..."*

"Still do not care to wager?" Rand asked.

Emilio only laughed.

He was too busy enjoying the match.

SIMULATOR CENTER
OUTSKIRTS OF ANTIMONY
QUARELL
RASALHAGUE DOMINION

Alexis smiled, watching the remaining Dragonbear 'Mechs walk right into her trap. Cautiously approaching the ravine, they were going to edge in and try to root them out. But Alexis was creating a kill box just inside, and all her MechWarriors had to do was be patient.

"Okay, everyone. They're edging closer to you. Just hold fast in your positions and wait for my mark to fire."

"*Aff,*" Thomasin said. Sophie repeated the affirmation. Jezebel and Zoe followed after.

But there was one voice she did not hear.

"Daniel, do you copy that?"

Of course it was Daniel.

But there was nothing on the other end of the comm.

"Daniel, do you read me?"

Still nothing. Looking down to her map, Alexis saw his *Kodiak*, the last assault 'Mech they had, moving forward from his position.

"Daniel, we have one chance to win this, and you cannot win against them on your own. They have already broken the rules of combat, any one of us going out on our own will get destroyed. Get back into position, now."

But the 'Mech on the map was undeterred, the *Kodiak* kept walking to the mouth of the ravine. Alexis watched as the Dragonbear 'Mechs approached the mouth as well. They started firing, and Daniel fired back.

Alexis couldn't comprehend what was happening. She had placed her team in the perfect position; they just needed to be patient, and let their opponents come to them. But Daniel had just walked out there as though he could win the battle single-handedly, as though the Dragonbears did not have their own assault 'Mech, an *Executioner,* just standing there, ready to destroy anything that came out of the ravine. "What are you *doing*?"

"We can win this!" Daniel shouted through the comm.

She could hear the lasers and missiles firing through the radio, along with Daniel's grunts and groans.

"Daniel, you are going to lose this for us."

"I have this, Alexis. You were going to lose it, but I have this."

He did *not* have it.

Alexis watched as all five Dragonbear 'Mechs opened up on Daniel's *Kodiak.* He blasted one of the attacking *Bear Cub*s with his Ultra autocannon and took it down, but his armor was melting down faster than he could take the others.

It was not ideal, but she had to send the others in to help, or it would be a total rout. His was the biggest 'Mech in her arsenal, and they would be hopelessly outmatched if they could not pour on the fire to support him.

"The rest of you, get out there. Support Daniel."

"But they just have to come to us," Thomasin said.

"I know that, but Daniel is not pulling back. If you want to help, you need to get out there and do it *now.*"

"Aff," Thomasin said, but the reluctance came through the radio. The rest of the 'Mechs in her command funneled to the end of the ravine and fanned out from the opening. If Daniel had stopped short thirty meters closer to the end, he would have boxed in any help she could have given, and it would have spelled certain doom for all of them. Alexis was grateful for at least that one small favor in Daniel's stupidity.

They exchanged volleys of fire with the Dragonbears. It was going to be close. They could still pull it off, though.

Daniel shifted the firing arc of his battered, smoking *Kodiak*—now showing much more internal structure than armor plate—to deal with the *Executioner.* She didn't know how his 'Mech could even be standing, let alone putting up a fight. But right there in front of him, with the *Executioner* staring down at the rest of the Bearclaws. At the mouth of the ravine was where their fate and the rest of the battle would be decided.

Fuming was all Alexis could do now.

She had had it.

The victory had been hers outright, but Daniel had snatched it from her and forced her to react to his bullheaded action. It was enough to make her scream. Did Daniel even realize they were on the same team, in the same *sibko*, or even in the same Clan? He sure didn't act like any *sibkin* she ever wanted.

"That *Executioner* is still holding strong. Thomasin, give some fire support."

"I will do my best. I am engaged with the remaining *Bear Cub.*"

"I see, but that *Bear Cub* does not have enough to take you down in the time it takes to concentrate your fire. And Daniel is about to go down."

"*Aff,*" Thomasin said dutifully.

But Daniel cut in, "*Neg,* Thomasin. I have this! The *Executioner* is mine! You cannot take this kill from me."

"Ignore him, Thomasin. *Zellbrigen* does not apply here. Engage."

"*Aff.*"

She watched Thomasin's *Mad Dog Mk III* engage the *Executioner,* just as Daniel's *Kodiak* began blinking red. "Daniel, you are about to lose your 'Mech. If you are going to take the *Executioner,* now is the time."

"I have it, I have it," he snapped.

But the red flashing lights on her command console winked off. And Daniel was out.

Alexis growled. She could have used Daniel's help, but instead he had taken himself off the board. "Everyone, focus all weapons on the *Executioner.* Daniel is out and that is your biggest opponent. The mission is to win, *quiaff?*"

"Aff!" they all said, obeying much better than Daniel had.

The *Executioner* lit up on her display and then winked off. Relief washed over her, but only for a moment. They were still down and behind. Outgunned and outweighed. Glancing over to the scores, they were inching closer and closer. Single points were adding up here and there on both sides as the 'Mechs duked it out and sloughed armor from each other.

At least it was a show for the audiences of Quarell.

"Sophie, watch your right!"

"I am on it," she replied. "I am giving this *stravag* Dragonbear the time of his life!"

But then Sophie's *Rime Otter* flashed red, and then off. She was out. Her voice winked out in mid-sentence, and Alexis had to laugh. Otherwise she would cry, and that did not seem like something befitting a Ghost Bear.

"Thomasin, you have lost Sophie. Jezebel, Zoe, you are going to have to provide support. Thomasin, paint the targets."

"Aff."

The last three members of Alexis' remaining Star went to work.

More shots traded back and forth. Armor boiled and exploded off the simulated 'Mechs, spraying across the faux battlefield.

"I am down, I am down!" Zoe yelled as her dot winked off the battlefield.

But she had taken a Dragonbear with her.

"Zoe is out," Jezebel said. "And there are only two left."

"You want to lure them into a kill box," Alexis said. "Pull back to the mouth of the ravine, you take the north side, Thomasin, take the south. It is the only way we might be able to split their attention."

Dutifully, they followed her orders, and Alexis saw that reflected on her map. *If only Daniel had been so obedient...*

Together, Thomasin and Jezebel were able to whittle down the Dragonbear *Executioner,* but as it fell, so did Jezebel.

"Come on, Thomasin, you can do this." But Alexis saw his dot on her map a furious, flashing red. She knew he didn't have much left at all.

"I think I have them," Thomasin said excitedly, scoring another hit.

But then Alexis couldn't hear his voice at all. "Thomasin? Thomasin!"

Looking down at her panel, she realized what had happened. He'd been tagged out.

The Bearclaws, under Alexis' command, had done well, only losing the game by 6 points. The only surviving Dragonbear 'Mech, a *Mad Dog Mk III,* had so little structural integrity remaining, it could be blown over in the wind. But the Dragonbears had scored a perfect 75 points for the complete annihilation of their foe, and an extra point for their surviving 'Mech. That gave them a solid 76 points.

The Bearclaws had only destroyed fourteen 'Mechs, giving them 70 points. The damage done to the *Mad Dog Mk III* was severe enough to give them 4 more points, leaving Alexis' side with a final score of 74.

It should have been a higher score. *We should have won.*

Alexis should have assumed Daniel would not submit to her orders, and based her strategy around that as an eventuality. She hoped the rest of the *sibko* would not hold the loss against her. She had done all she could, and they should see that.

The console before her shut down, and the lights in the room came up.

Alexis stood up, feeling weary as the adrenaline of the battle subsided, and turned as the door opened.

Standing there, with a disapproving look on her face, was her Den Mother. Star Captain Sasha Ivankova.

"Well, Alexis, it seems as though you are *not* fit for command after all. If only the rest of the *Ursari* had listened, we would have been victorious."

She wanted to tell the Den Mother it didn't matter; that the score was close enough it would not affect them too badly in the final standings. Other *sibkos* would *have* to do worse.

But silence was best with the Den Mother, especially when she was in this kind of mood.

She had a way of turning words around on people.

"Now, to decide your punishment." Star Captain Ivankova grinned wide enough it seemed to Alexis that she was glad the Bearclaws had lost.

Alexis tightened her jaw. There was no use in arguing. "Yes, Star Captain," she said. But what she really meant was, *"Bring it on, Den Mother. I can take whatever you can dish out. Even if I shouldn't have to."*

CHAPTER 17

COMITATUS-CLASS JUMPSHIP *ALIS FALCONIS*
RECHARGE STATION
BLAIR ATHOLL
JADE FALCON OCCUPATION ZONE
12 OCTOBER 3151

"I want you all comfortable in assault 'Mechs," Khan Jiyi Chistu said into the comm to the MechWarriors in the simulator pods aboard the *Alis Falconis.* "Ranged weaponry will be a key to our superiority against the Ghost Bears. I spent much time in the Dominion during my assignment to VaultShip *Gamma*, and the last thing they will expect from Jade Falcons is devastating long-range assaults."

Jiyi sat beside Star Captain Quinn, who pulled the proverbial levers behind the simulation, determining the terrain and weather conditions for the training. She was good at it. She would have made an excellent Falconer in charge of a Jade Falcon *sibko.* Maybe her destiny was not to be his *saKhan*, but instead would see her in charge of the training across the Jade Falcon worlds. It seemed to be her calling.

"For these exercises," Jiyi said, "we will be simulating the most common terrain types and weather patterns you will encounter at our target destination."

Quinn nodded and added more parameters to the simulation.

"We will also be programming targets based on how Ghost Bears behave in situations against common Jade Falcon tactics. They will field 'Mechs that are highly maneuverable and easy to hide under cover, expecting us to swoop in on them. So for this simulation, you will have target practice in a stationary assault 'Mech, picking off the lighter, faster 'Mechs one at a time. Are you ready to begin?"

"*Aff!*" The MechWarriors acknowledged Jiyi's orders and began their fight as soon as Star Captain Quinn started the simulation.

Jiyi leaned back in his chair to monitor the progress.

"You really think this will work, my Khan?" Quinn asked, only briefly taking her eyes from the simulator controls.

"Would I have put everything in motion on this voyage to Quarell if I did not?"

"A fair question. But this gambit implies that you like to gamble."

"*Neg,*" Jiyi said. "I vehemently do not like to gamble. Especially not with the future of the Jade Falcons hanging in the balance."

"You would not call a weeks-long voyage culminating in an incursion inside the Rasalhague Dominion to poke a sleeping bear a gamble?"

"Ghost Bears are still Clanfolk, and they will still respond to a Trial of Possession. If we cannot lure them into playing the game we wish to play, then we simply leave."

"And then, I suppose, all we will have lost is time."

"To a point, but only if you believe the training we are doing is not worthwhile. Bears always take the bait. They will *not* refuse the negotiation. We *will* have our Trial, and we will win our new Warriors, and Jade Falcon will be strong."

"I will lead where you follow, my Khan."

Jiyi folded his hands behind his head, smiling broadly. "I know. And I appreciate it, truly." He sat back up straight and looked back down to the console to see just how his MechWarriors were doing.

Star Commander Dawn tried sidestepping in her *Turkina,* but found the Khan had been true to his word about their being stationary for the exercise. The only way to move her aiming reticule was with the *Turkina*'s torso and arm actuators. Her feet remained stubbornly planted on the ground.

The targets were a steady stream of approaching *Grendel*s, *Rime Otter*s, and *Bear Cub*s. Dawn and the nine other MechWarriors on either side of her stood there, fixed as if their feet were set in hardened ferrocrete.

"Should we call out our targets?" asked another Mech-Warrior.

Dawn recognized the voice of Hosteen. *"Aff,"* she replied.

"Aff," said a cascade of voices from her Star and the other Star they were training with.

"I have the *Bear Cub* marked one," Dawn said, marking it as *"one"* on her HUD, then transmitting that data so it would appear as her target on all of their HUDs.

"I have the *Rime Otter* marked two," Hosteen called.

"Grendel marked three," came another voice, on down the line until they had each picked a target. After all ten Jade Falcons chose their targets, five 'Mechs remained unclaimed. All fifteen spilled out from their spawning point and charged their firing line.

Dawn opened fire on the *Bear Cub*, starting with her extended-range PPCs, blasting from a distance. It moved so fast that she missed with the first azure bolt, but readjusted her aim and led just a little bit further.

Hitting the firing stud, Dawn fired a volley of long-range missiles at the target. They corkscrewed across the battlefield, joining a half-dozen other volleys sent from other Jade Falcon 'Mechs to their own targets. Dawn's missiles peppered the *Bear Cub*'s torso and arms, exploding on contact. Chunks of armor flew from the light 'Mech, but she was going to have to hit it again. Pulling the trigger on her control stick, Dawn fired her particle projector cannons, triangulating her aim where the *Bear Cub* would be in a moment.

Direct hit!

She cut the *Bear Cub*'s armor right off the torso, cracking the inside open.

It tried to keep moving forward, but crashed face-down into the desert grassland.

She chose another target,—a boxy 'Mech with long legs, a triangular torso, and a long cannon for a right arm—and called it out to the rest. "I have the *Grendel* marked eleven!"

As she opened fire on the approaching 'Mech, Dawn glanced around at how the others were faring. She was one of the few who had put down their first target. Behind the first wave, a parade of blue-painted Ghost Bears rushed straight for them. They were still too far out of range with their own weapons to bother firing anything yet, but the Falcons would be besieged with enemy fire any moment now.

The plan to call out individual targets and take one each was only going to work if they actually made good on their promises.

"*Rime Otter* marked seven is down!" another MechWarrior said. "Marking *Bear Cub* as twelve!"

Dawn missed her second shot against the *Grendel*. It had a different speed and gait from the *Bear Cub*, so leading it was more difficult. *No. Not more difficult*, she told herself. *Just different.*

"*Rime Otter* marked two is down," Hosteen called. "I'm tagging the farther *Grendel* as thirteen."

Dawn fired her PPC again and missed her elusive *Grendel*, but the shot sliced into the armor of the *Rime Otter* coming up behind it. "Damn it," she muttered. If this had been an honorable Trial, that would have dropped the strict rules of *zellbrigen*, and they would have been facing a brawling melee.

By that time, the front 'Mechs had gotten into weapon range and opened fire against the line of Jade Falcon 'Mechs, frozen in place by the simulator's parameters.

"I am taking heavy fire!" one of Dawn's compatriots shouted.

Another second, and another half-dozen of them would be in range to fire.

But that was when Dawn noticed as they cut one 'Mech down, another appeared at the starting point and began its charge forward.

This exercise would never end—at least, not until the Jade Falcons were obliterated.

The Ghost Bear 'Mechs concentrated their fire against the lead 'Mech in the Jade Falcon formations. With seven Ghost Bears in range, it took two hits from each of them and the forward most Jade Falcons 'Mech was obliterated before their very eyes. Dawn hoped her group could accomplish whatever it was the Khan wanted them to before she lost everyone.

The *Grendel* she had tagged toppled under the force of her withering fire, the ice-blue blast of the PPC turning its insides to slag, leaving it unable to stand. By the time she called another target, there were only six Jade Falcon 'Mechs left on the line.

"We cannot let them get behind us," Dawn said.

"What do you propose?" asked another Falcon Warrior.

"It is already a free-for-all. We cannot claim targets for ourselves." Dawn spoke as she fired again, letting another battery of long-range missiles fly. "We have to work in teams of two or three and concentrate fire on 'Mechs that get too close. If too many get too close, we will not be able to repel them."

MechWarrior Hosteen agreed. "We have little choice."

"Split off into pairs," Dawn said. "Hosteen and I will be Alpha. Let us hit the closest target. Bravo, you hit the second closest. Charlie, the third, and so on."

"It is not the Clan way," one of the other MechWarriors— Natalya—objected, just as another of their number went offline, destroyed by the simulated Ghost Bears.

But Dawn knew the answer to that. "If we do not survive and win these battles, we will not have a Clan at all, *quiaff*?"

"*Aff,*" Natalya grudgingly replied.

"The Jade Falcons are what we make of them," she said. "The Clan is being born anew and we adhere to our *rede*. We abhor waste, and we do what it takes to win."

"*Seyla,*" Hosteen said.

"*Seyla,*" Natalya and half a dozen others repeated.

Dawn targeted the closest 'Mech and lined up a shot. "So let us try it this way."

"*Aff!*" came the responses.

And so they fought on. They kept the enemy 'Mechs from swarming them until they ran out of missiles and their heat got out of control, and their rate of fire slowed considerably.

But Dawn didn't care if they were all destroyed. She knew how to beat the simulation the next time. The whole group of them how to work together better. And she felt a lot more competent in the cockpit of a *Turkina* now, even if she hadn't been able to move in the damn thing.

But when she could, she would be unstoppable.

Dawn smiled; she actually pitied whatever Ghost Bears would be sent against the Jade Falcons.

Dawn found the gravity ring of the *Alis Falconis* took some work to get used to. It was one thing to be in a simulator pod, moving around like a 'Mech might. The mess hall, on the other hand, was more difficult. She didn't feel quite at home inside her own body, and every step she took felt too light.

Shoveling food into her mouth, she felt as though she had to swallow twice as hard to get it to move down into her gullet.

She sat in the back corner of the room, hoping she could get through the meal unnoticed. Based on Natalya's reaction to her shift in tactics, she couldn't imagine anyone wanting to talk to her.

When Natalya came in to get her meal, Dawn avoided eye contact. She just wanted to eat in peace.

That felt impossible when Natalya took her tray and headed straight in Dawn' direction.

"Natalya," Dawn said curtly, keeping her eyes down. She hoped she would just keep walking by. Since Dawn was in the back corner of the room, though, there was very little chance of that happening.

"Star Commander Dawn," Natalya said.

Dawn saw Hosteen come into the mess and her eyes caught his, hoping he might come over to rescue her from the potentially awkward conversation. He made his way toward them.

Natalya stood there, not saying anything.

She could not tell if Natalya was unable to speak for some reason, or could not choke back the rage enough to speak to her. In either case, Dawn knew that whatever Natalya said, it was going to be bad.

Hosteen, gripping their tray of food in one hand, sauntered over to Dawn's table and sat down on the bench next to her, just as Natalya finally broke her silence. "I just wanted to tell you I am glad you were in command. You were right."

Dawn blinked, convinced she heard Natalya wrong. "What?"

"I was wrong to challenge you," Natalya said. "Would it be all right with you if I joined you?"

"Please," Dawn said, motioning to the seat in front of her, never in a million years thinking that she would be the person people clamored to sit with. But she was a Star Commander now. And it really looked like she knew what she was doing.

Dawn hoped she would never let them down.

CHAPTER 18

BEARCLAW SIBKO TRAINING FACILITY
COPPERTON
QUARELL
RASALHAGUE DOMINION
25 OCTOBER 3151

Lying in the barracks after lights out, Alexis stared at the scoreboard on her noteputer and still could not believe two things: the Bearclaws were in fourth place and Daniel's nose was not broken.

Of the six *sibko*s, they were *fourth.*

It was so close, too. Only four points separated them from the Porbjorns in first place. Second place belonged to the Mektid Bears, and the Bearclaws would have held that spot if Daniel had not pulled that stunt in their first event. And they would have been in first had Lewis and Anna not allowed their 'Mechs to overheat in the relay event across the continent. As it was, they would have to overcome the Porbjorns, the Mektid Bears, *and* the Dragonbears, then hope the Berserkers and Bjornsons did not come up from behind.

There was nothing she could do to change that.

She had been not eligible to participate in the events of the previous two days. Being the largest of the *sibkos* sometimes meant not all of the cadets could compete in some of the events. And the Den Mother had held Alexis personally responsible for their defeat on the first day, and had done everything she could to keep Alexis from finding any more ways to mess things up.

It did not matter how much the other *Ursari* vouched for her or interceded, the Den Mother just kept sidelining Alexis wherever and however she could.

The Den Mother had provoked frustration and fury from the rest of the *sibko* for holding Alexis responsible instead of Daniel. The others had wanted to engage Daniel in a Circle of Equals and knock him senseless—or worse—for not following her orders and costing their *sibko* the first match. Thomasin and Sophie had led the push to beat him senseless for it, but Alexis told them to knock it off. If the Den Mother wasn't punishing Daniel for his insubordination for a reason, the reason was likely a trap Alexis would rather not walk into.

Instead, she tried to quiet her mind and focus on the scores and what the next trial might be. She *wanted* to participate, and she wanted the Bearclaws to win, even if that meant Daniel won, too. They were the best of the *sibkos*, people like Star Captain Ivankova just couldn't seem to see it.

A noise across the barracks startled her into shutting off her noteputer for fear of someone seeing the light from the screen. The last thing she needed to get in trouble for was being awake past curfew.

But what did they expect?

They were all so anxious about the games. Not as anxious as they would be for their own Trials of Position, but anxious nonetheless. None of them had ever had this many eyes on them before.

As the beam from the flashlight passed over her, Alexis shut her eyes and drew in a quick breath, offering her most reasonable facsimile of sleep. She doubted she would get in *that* much trouble for being awake and busy. Unless it was the Den Mother doing the looking, in which case Alexis was done for. If a meteorite crashed through the facility from the sky and landed two bunks over, Alexis was confident she would be the one blamed for the disturbance.

It did not seem like a way to run a *sibko*, let alone a family.

Listening to the night watch shuffle through the barracks, Alexis figured it was time to go to sleep anyway. In case she got picked for the next event, she wanted to be well-rested. And she wanted no trouble to come to her.

But her closed eyes brought her fitful dreams and thoughts. She had agreed all those years ago to join the Ghost Bears because they were a family. There was no other Clan that would offer that to her, but more than ever it felt as though the Ghost Bears were being torn apart.

The vote pushed it to the brink. She could not have imagined how poorly people would react to a simple vote when they didn't get their way. Didn't they believe in the system anymore? Maybe she didn't have all the information about joining the Star League or leaving it, but there was no reason to get into a physical altercation because of it. That was exactly what had happened.

She had never seen protesters before in her life.

What was there even *to* protest?

Even living on the street and picking pockets wasn't worth a protest. The social workers who had replaced much of the police force kept her fed when they could catch her. And they hadn't tried to stuff her into a foster home, though maybe she should have taken them up on their offers.

She had never thought about joining up with a Clan before. She hadn't even realized it was an option. The only thing on her mind the day she had joined was the fat wallet of the Ghost Bear whose pocket she had decided to pick. He was the one who caught her hand mid-pluck, then pulled her around in front of him.

And when he saw her, he laughed.

He offered no anger or reproach. He did not seem to even care that she had gone for his wallet. Maybe there wasn't even any Bear-Krona inside of it. Now that she knew better, she wouldn't even be able to guess what a Star Colonel like that would have been carrying around.

Behind his laughter was a kindly face.

"Hello there," he'd said.

"Hello yourself," Alexis had told him.

But he only laughed harder. "Where did you come from?"

"The street," was all she said. She had no other answer.

"I like your moxie. It amuses me."

She dodged his questions for what felt like an eternity, until he brought her into one of the social worker stations in

Antimony's downtown. He had lured her there with a free meal, more than she'd eaten in a week. She ate so much she almost puked. She remained tight-lipped during the feast, but they had a file on her. He promised no more questions, only food, but the social workers told him who she was before she could protest. He was a Star Colonel; of course they'd listen to him over her.

"They tell me you do not have a family," he said, sitting down across from her as she shoveled food into her face in the brightly lit and overly sterile intake station. It felt like a hospital, and she figured that was why most kids avoided the stations like they were a disease.

"I have some."

"Who?"

"My friends."

"The ones who left you the second I grabbed you?"

That shut her up. Where *had* they gone. They'd all disappeared, and she had been left on her own.

"Would you like to have a family?"

"What's that supposed to mean?"

"It means you could become a Ghost Bear. We are a family. We will take care of you. But in return, you will need to learn to become a MechWarrior and leave your life on the street behind. Is that something that you might be interested in?"

Alexis had no idea what a Ghost Bear family would be like, but she signed up. She was hungry, and they promised to feed her every day. And if she could have a meal every day without having to beg, borrow, or steal for it, it would be worth it. She was only ten. Not going hungry was all that mattered.

She loved being a Ghost Bear. They fed her regularly, the food was good, the clothes were clean. Friends were easy to come by. There was a rocky beginning to all of it, of course. A culture shock, to be sure. It took her a long time to stop looking into every refuse bin for food. Alexis made sure to keep one eye on all of her belongings, for fear they would be stolen, not realizing that was just not how things worked there. For a time, she tried sleeping *under* her cot when things got to be too much.

But as soon as Thomasin and Sophie had clicked with her, it had been smooth sailing for the most part. The Ghost Bear culture only showed occasional signs of cracking. It wasn't until talk of the vote that the inflamed attitudes of everyone started coming out. In her earlier days, she was assured that bigotry against freeborns had been relegated to the past. Suddenly, the vote had brought out the worst in those who had harbored such hateful attitudes and so many bigots suddenly felt like it was okay to wear their prejudice on their sleeve. It was so disheartening to see that their Den Mother was one of them.

Alexis saw red until she saw black, and sleep took her.

She awoke to the pre-recorded sound of a roaring bear through the public address system. *"Attention cadets, the next event will be starting in thirty minutes. Get ready. You will all be participating, Bearclaws and Mektid Bears alike."*

By the time they were on their feet, Sophie put a hand on Alexis' shoulder. "You doing okay?"

Alexis shrugged.

"You look like you have not slept."

"Maybe I haven't. It's way earlier than we normally get up, *quiaff*?"

Sophie shook her head. *"Aff.* I worry about you, Alex. Something is wrong."

"I am fine."

"You do not look fine."

"I have been through much worse than any of this. They can throw anything they want at us and I am sure I will live, *quiaff*?"

"Aff." Sophie smiled and took Alexis' hands into hers, her fingers were soft and sent a thrill up Alexis' back.

She regarded Sophie wryly. "Do I even want to know what event they will have us competing in?"

"Whatever it is," Thomasin said, wrapping his arms around Sophie and Alexis by the neck, "we are going to kick it in the teeth and make it beg for mercy."

PYKON RIVER DELTA
QUARELL
RASALHAGUE DOMINION
26 OCTOBER 3151, 0600 HOURS

"You have *got* to be kidding me."

For Alexis, the rain in the dark might have been the worst part of the exercise. She expected that at the very least she would be in a 'Mech or a simulator room for all of the games. That dismay was followed closely by the fact they all wore what felt like a hundred kilograms of gear on their backs. The third worst part was the native water moccasin snakes that lived in the marshy areas surrounding the Pykon River—the ones that killed a farmer or two every year for as long as there were farmers and fishers in the delta.

The last worst thing was the mission itself. They had to sneak through an enemy perimeter without being spotted. The Porbjorns were in first place, and had the honor of the defensive position in the game. If the Bearclaws could slip more than half of their *sibko* across the to the finish line undetected, they would outscore the Porbjorns *and* move up at least a place or two in the rankings.

It was incumbent on all of them to do their best, but something told Alexis another rift was brewing as they stalked the swamps of the Pykon River Delta.

"How in the world are we going to get past their perimeter?" Zoe asked.

They had only been let loose into the area thirty minutes prior and were struggling to find a path forward.

"We go this way. We cling to the fringes, stay out of sight," Alexis said. To her, it felt obvious, but of course there was someone to argue.

"What makes you think you should be in charge?" Daniel asked loudly, wiping mud from his eyes.

"Nothing makes me think I should be in charge, but how else do you expect to slip through if not by staying hidden? You want to just waltz in there?"

"I studied the maps before we left. We have to go this way, it is the only way through." Daniel pointed straight for the Porbjorn's center line.

"That is suicide, Daniel," Alexis said, "and we will lose this as sure as anything."

"Go whichever way you want," Daniel said. Then, louder to the rest of the *sibko*, he gestured with his arms to follow. "The rest of you, follow me. We will leave the thief to go her own way."

Alexis let out a low, grizzly growl. "Fine, you all go that way. But if I am the sneak-thief, don't you think it would make more sense to follow me on a stealth mission? I have far more experience than Daniel at staying hidden, *quiaff*?"

"Aff," Thomasin agreed. "None of us know how to do that better than you, Alex."

Alexis nodded to him, thanking him for the support.

Daniel sneered. "Fine. If you want to follow this freeborn into defeat, be my guest."

"Do not think we have forgotten who walked us into defeat before, Daniel." Sophie pointed an accusing finger at him. "You cost us the first event, no matter what the Den Mother says. Thomasin and I were there. You felt like you knew better than the rest of us, and we had to try to fight them to a draw."

Lewis nodded. "We would be in first place, defending the line, if you had only listened, Daniel."

"No, that is not how it was," Kaleo said from behind Daniel. "He tried to save us from losing. Alexis would have had us hide in the ravine until the Dragonbears hunted us down one by one and slaughtered us. He is the only reason it was as close as it was."

As soon as he said it, two other *sibkin* joined in arguing about Daniel's superiority over Alexis. Their words cut Alexis. Every time one of them spoke up to side with her or Daniel, all she felt was shame. *She* was the one splitting up her family. Kaleo was her *sibkin* just as much as Thomasin and Sophie. Why was he turning against her? Why were *any* of them arguing at all?

Alexis roared when she could take no more. "Why are we arguing? Are we not all on the same team? Are we all not *sibkin*? Ghost Bears always speak of family and its importance, and none of you are acting like any family I want to be a part of! We all want to accomplish the same thing, so why do we not unite to work together?"

Lightning flashed and then thunder cracked.

Daniel laughed.

"You have fun with that, Alexis. I am going to lead us to victory." He turned, pulling on the straps of his pack. "Any of you who want to win, follow me. The rest of you losers can lick the freeborn's boots."

Alexis counted her *sibkin* off as they turned to follow Daniel. One, two, three, four, five of their sixteen. If any more turned to leave, they would lose the games as sure as anything. And unless they were assigned to one of the Clusters heading for the Star League Defense Force or to patrol the Draconis Combine border, there was little chance they would find any valor or victory in their careers beside this.

Perhaps that was why Daniel was taking it so seriously. He had to distinguish himself, even if he did absolutely the wrong thing and distinguished himself as a jackass instead of an exemplary Warrior.

"Sorry, Alexis," Jezebel said, turning to join Daniel.

"It is fine," Alexis said. She didn't want to make things worse by laying on the guilt, though on the street that might have been a perfectly sound strategy. "We will win regardless."

In fact, if Daniel was going to take a sortie straight up the center, she could use him. Could there be a better distraction than a loud group of Bearclaws getting caught?

Alexis looked around, counting the *sibkin* who remained. Including her, there were nine left. Of the sixteen, only six had left with Daniel. If she could pull it off, they would beat the Porbjorns and pull ahead a place or two.

"Is this everyone?" she said to those who had remained. Thomasin and Sophie remained right at her side. "Because if you want to go with Daniel, now is the time."

She scanned their faces one at a time, wondering if she could do something to make them all feel as one after Daniel had torn their spirits asunder. Some hid their faces under their rain hoods. Lewis wiped rain from his eyes. Anna dried her eyes with the crook of her elbow. Zoe didn't even bother trying to clear her face, it was caked in mud that ran in dirty rivulets down her cheek and neck.

Thomasin and Sophie both stood like Zoe, remaining silent in the rain, waiting for Alexis to give an order.

The togetherness she felt brought with it a fire that warmed her from the bitter cold of the rain.

She took a breath and it fogged up in front of her. "I am glad you all decided to stay. We really can win this. They will have patrols sweeping the entire delta, and they will have Daniel and his group to deal with. They will be loud and splash their way across and get caught, almost certainly."

"Aff," the rest said.

"And we have the ocean hemming us in on one side, and the forest on the other. Thomasin, is there any restriction from entering the forest?"

"Neg."

"Then we go there. We travel under cover or in the water where we can. We keep our trail invisible and move around the Porbjorns completely. Daniel's path is the most obvious, so that is where they will look. And, if Daniel is smart—"

"—you give him too much credit," Sophie muttered, folding her arms and narrowing her eyes.

"*Aff,*" Alexis said. "But he still wants to win. When he gets caught, they will ask him where we are, and I believe that no matter what he tells him, they will think we are close by, adding a layer of defense.

"Instead, we will go to the forest. That might help with some of the rain. But we stay in the water as much as possible to obscure our trail. They will almost certainly track Daniel back to this point. And we need to keep a watch out for the snakes. If you see one, call it out. We cannot afford to lose anyone to a snakebite."

They all nodded firmly.

They believed in her.

"Then let us go. We can still win this, but I need us all to work together to do it. Sunrise is in less than an hour, and we want to make it to the forest before the light appears. Are you with me?"

"*Aff!*"

"And you trust me?"

"*Aff!*"

Alexis held the straps of her bag and stepped into the stream. The water came up to her mid-shin, but to that point, her boots kept the water out and her socks dry. She did not expect that to last long.

"Follow me then, my fellow Bear Cubs. To victory!"

"To victory!"

KODIAK POINT
GHOST BEAR HEADQUARTERS
ANTIMONY
QUARELL
26 OCTOBER 3151, 1015 HOURS

"They still have not appeared?" Star Colonel Emilio Hall asked his second in command as he walked into the common room. The giant screen was tuned to the cross-training and games.

"*Neg.*" Star Captain Allison Rand stood at the back of the common room, which was filled with Ghost Bear Warriors watching the action. She pointed up at the proceedings. "It seems as though they have vanished completely."

"I imagine the Porbjorns are thrilled." Standing beside the Star Captain, Emilio took a moment to watch the footage and the Porbjorns it showed, standing sentinel in the rain across the perimeter they had to protect. "They look very tense."

"They caught the first group of Bearclaws an hour into the exercise, and have found no trace of the rest in all that time."

Emilio suppressed a laugh, grateful Rand was sufficiently distracted by the games to forget about her incessant talk of politics. It had grown obnoxious at best. "Should we send a search party?"

"You think they have gotten lost?"

Emilio shrugged. "Anything is possible in the rain, *quiaff*?"

"I suppose."

"But something tells me they are merely running out the clock. They have a solid forty minutes left before they are declared lost. Putting the Porbjorns on edge, thinking they have missed something, is a sensible strategy. And making them think they will win by default is a good way to get them to act in a sloppy fashion."

"I find watching the minds work of these young Ghost Bears fascinating," said Rand.

"You see? Hope in the next generation."

"*Aff,*" Rand said. "I am surprised to find myself learning from them as I watch the exercises. I have different ideas, depending on the situation, for how we can use the Fourteenth if we are called into action for the new Star League."

Emilio nodded. He had learned much, too, but did not want to dignify her gloating. "That is the strength of the constant renewal of our minds and Warriors. There is always a new way to look at a problem. We are by no means *solahma,* but our thinking can get fixed and rigid. The cadets always have something to offer."

"They truly are the future of the Ghost Bears," Rand said. "Losing them would be to lose ourselves."

"*Aff.*"

The audio from the screen grew louder as a commotion broke out on camera. The Porbjorns seemed to be caught by surprise, but the cameras could not seem to find what was going on.

"What is going on?" Rand said.

But Emilio did not know and said so.

They both edged closer to the screen. Behind the perimeter line stood a Ghost Bear. Not a Porbjorn, but a Bearclaw, in a much darker uniform and hefting her survival pack. The pack was covered in sticks and branches, obscuring it. Mud was caked across her face and Emilio got the distinct impression she must have crawled her entire way through the course in a makeshift ghillie suit.

And then another Bearclaw stood.

And another.

And another.

Eleven in all.

The Porbjorns were screaming, surrounding the incursion force, trying to figure out just what in the hell had happened.

The lead Bearclaw, a young woman Emilio recognized as the commander in the first match of the games, had the brightest smile on her face.

When the score was revealed, and the Bearclaws of Quarell were announced as the winners of the event, the common room erupted in cheers. There was something to be said for the home team advantage.

"*Seyla*, little bear," Emilio said with a smile. "You did it."

CHAPTER 19

COMITATUS-CLASS JUMPSHIP *ALIS FALCONIS*
RECHARGE STATION
LA GRAVE
JADE FALCON OCCUPATION ZONE
26 OCTOBER 3151

"Bears hide in dens," Khan Jiyi Chistu said, pointing up at the BattleROM footage on the screen as he paced back and forth in the briefing room. "It is the nature of bears, but especially Ghost Bears. The animal ghost bear is fond of ice caves. We will likely not have to worry about ice caves at our destination, but the theory is still the same."

Video played on the screen: first-person viewscreen footage of a battle. A Jade Falcon medium 'Mech approached the opening of a cave. The mouth gaped and looked pitch black on the screen. The MechWarrior switched their view to infrared and the inside of the cave brightened considerably. There were four Ghost Bear 'Mechs inside.

There was a flash of light, then all four enemy 'Mechs hit the unsuspecting Jade Falcon Warrior. The footage ended.

Jiyi looked out among the MechWarriors before him as they studied the footage. One of them flinched as the video came to its end and the MechWarrior died. "Tell me, is it to your advantage to let them hide?"

"Neg," answered the voice of a MechWarrior Jiyi recognized as Siamion.

"Then what would you propose to do to counter it?" he asked.

But Siamion did not have an answer. In fact, there didn't seem to be one immediately apparent to most.

Jiyi stood there, looking at their concerned faces, watching the gears turn inside each of their heads as they worked out potential solutions to the problem.

"Do not engage?" MechWarrior Natalya offered.

"That is a potential solution," Jiyi said, "but that risks you putting your back to them if they are in position to defend their objective or attack you. If you ignore them, they will come out eventually. Anyone else?"

"Would drawing them out work?" Star Commander Dawn asked.

It was exactly the answer Jiyi had hoped for, but he repressed a smile, hoping to draw out the rest of her promising logic. "How would you propose to draw them out?"

Dawn leaned forward in her chair. "In that situation, could the MechWarrior cause a rockslide at range, and force them to choose between staying put or being sealed in the mountain?"

"A definite possibility," Jiyi replied. He was pleased with Dawn's answer, but he still wanted something more. "That is certainly an approach I would recommend in dealing with situations like this. But what about situations that might not seem so straightforward?"

Jiyi advanced his presentation to another BattleROM. This time, a *Shrike*'s heads-up-display offered a view of a distant grove of trees large enough to hide an entire company of enemy 'Mechs. There were a number of trees splintered and pushed to the side where 'Mechs had already forced their way into the middle. The *Shrike* got closer to the trees and then strafed around it. As it circled the trees, missiles rocketed out from the inside, obscuring their point of origin almost completely. The *Shrike* strafed around further and launched missiles of its own into the thicket, but with nothing to target, they were largely ineffective.

Lasers lanced out from the trees and the damage readouts on the *Shrike* flashed yellow.

Jiyi paused the video. "What is a reasonable response to this situation?"

"Charge in and take as many as possible," said MechWarrior Maiden, a brutish *solahma* Falcon set in the old ways. "That *Shrike* likely outweighs and outclasses anything the Ghost Bears would have. And they could take all of that glory for themselves."

Jiyi nodded, but skepticism marked his face. "That is something they would expect a Jade Falcon to do. And in years past, it is something that would have occurred to all of us to do. But is it the most effective?"

Resuming the playback, the action happened just as Maiden had suggested it should. The *Shrike* entered the trees and found itself surrounded and mauled by the Ghost Bears hiding there until the playback went dead and the 'Mech shut off.

"I would argue no," Jiyi said. "The *Shrike* did take two of the 'Mechs with it, but upon careful analysis of this BattleROM, there were at least six Ghost Bears in their forest den and they were not engaged in *zellbrigen*. In this particular battle, they viewed the Jade Falcons as a hostile and dishonorable force after an attack using the Mongol Doctrine. I would wager there were actually ten 'Mechs—two full Stars. Too many to leave behind and far too many for one 'Mech to make a significant dent. So we have to fight smarter than they do. Now, I pose to you: how would you have dealt with this situation?"

MechWarrior Siamion sheepishly raised a hand. "It depends on the objective. If there was something to hold beyond the trees, they could have simply gone around."

"But that puts you in the same position we spoke of in the last scenario, with your back to the enemy. Never a good situation." Jiyi took a breath, realizing none of the situations they would find themselves in would likely be good, but he had to get them ready to recognize possible scenarios and adapt to them on the fly, not just resort to previous direct Jade Falcon tactics.

Their future depended on it.

Siamion continued his train of thought. "But if the objective was far enough from their position, we could create a defensive perimeter between the 'Mechs carrying out the objective and the enemy."

"So, working together, then?" Jiyi asked. "We work together to a point, but has it not been the way of the Clans to claim our own individual kills and coordinate by instinct?"

"Aff," the assembled MechWarriors muttered.

"I posit that this style of fighting will not serve us against the Ghost Bears. So how can we think less like the Jade Falcons of old, and more like the more intelligent and efficient Jade Falcons of the present?"

Deacon sneered. "These *dezgra* tactics are fine for spheroids and Ghost Bears, but what allure do they hold for us? The Jade Falcons cannot change overnight. You would have us abandon *zellbrigen* entirely, and fight free-for-alls and fight with dishonor."

Star Captain Quinn, who had been watching the briefing from the front row, stood up and turned, her hands balled into fists. "Are you questioning our Khan, Deacon?"

The man's eyes widened in surprise. "I, uh...no. I merely question the nature of these tactics."

Quinn took an aggressive step forward. "I see no difference."

Jiyi raised a hand. "Star Captain, it is fine. Let him speak his mind. We are doing things differently, and Deacon is the oldest of us here, so he has definitely seen some things that could enlighten us in his dotage."

The room chuckled at that, but Deacon fumed. "We have done things for hundreds of years because they *work*. We should not so easily dismiss them."

Jiyi furrowed his brow. "They 'work'? When you say they 'work', in what way do you mean? Did they work for the Jade Falcons on Terra? Because if you look around this room, these Warriors sitting here—this is the vast majority of the entire Jade Falcon *touman*. We are on the brink of extinction, Deacon. And the old ways are what brought us here. So please, tell me in what way they worked."

Deacon had nothing to say to that.

No one did.

The room stayed silent as they all thought about this. Maybe not for the first time, but with the gravity of their Khan's words behind it. Surely, they had to have considered how dire the situation was for *them* to be the saviors of the Clan. They must have all considered why they had not gone to Terra with the rest of the Falcon *touman*, why they had been left behind, why they had been elevated to the role of MechWarrior after their Clan had not seen fit to do so before.

"These are desperate times, my Falcons. I will not mince words about that. But we are on the precipice of rebuilding our Clan as a force to be reckoned with for now and all time. So, to preserve ourselves, we drill. We learn how to fight our enemies and we do it in unexpected ways. Let no one say the Jade Falcons do not have what it takes to win at all costs."

Deacon shrank in his chair. Suddenly he did not look so imposing a Warrior.

"You are right to question what we are doing now, Deacon. I do not mean to make light of your service to the Jade Falcons. I know you have fought for your Clan for your entire life. *Our* Clan. But I also know they left you behind and robbed you of your final glory on Terra, and left us all in a situation where we must build a Clan from scratch. You intend to do this with me, *quiaff*?"

"*Aff*," Deacon muttered.

"*Quiaff*?" Jiyi repeated, louder this time.

"*Aff!*" Deacon said, this time with much more conviction.

"Good." Jiyi turned to the rest of the assemblage, gathering his thoughts for a moment before continuing. "Before we continue our lesson, I want to offer one last thing for you to consider. Are you familiar with the Raging Bears? They are the Ghost Bears' Omega Galaxy. And they are tasked with fighting against Inner Sphere forces by using the Inner Sphere's own tactics against them. They do this because the Clans suffered far too many defeats at the hands of the Inner Sphere at Tukayyid and other places. Those defeats were possible because the Spheroids are not obligated to follow our Clan rules of honor in combat. The Ghost Bears can do this if we force a free-for-all in our Trials. Imagine that these Raging Bears are our opponent. Why can we not use their own tactics and ways of thinking against them? So, here we are. We study their tactics and we counter them. I have spent much time in the lands of the Ghost Bear during my post defending VaultShip *Gamma*. I have learned much from them. And when was it ever against the Clan way to learn about your enemy and exploit their weaknesses?"

And still, no answer came from those assembled.

Jiyi pointed back to the screen. "So, I ask again. What else could be done in a situation like this?"

MechWarrior Hosteen, a graying Warrior nearing the end of his run, looked back and forth to see if anyone else would offer an answer before raising a hand.

Jiyi pointed at him. "MechWarrior Hosteen."

"We can smoke them out?"

Jiyi furrowed his brow. He liked where Hosteen was heading, but had not puzzled out his method himself. "How do you propose to do that?"

"Use our lasers to start the forest ablaze?"

"It could work, but you could end up overheating your 'Mech. But the theory is sound. Rob them of the advantage of the cover, same as with the cave dens. This is how Ghost Bears think based on their traditions and culture. This is how they react. And the Fourteenth Battle Cluster stationed on Quarell is as traditional as it gets within the Ghost Bears."

Jiyi scanned the faces in the room. Their confusion and unease, for the most part, was being replaced with determination. He would take the unease on himself, still wondering if they would be able to pull it off. It did not matter how unsure he was, though, it was confidence he had to project. "We still have much training to do before we arrive at our destination. I want you all to be ready, so we continue to drill and study. *Quiaff*?"

"AFF," came their unified response.

ALIS FALCONIS
RECHARGE STATION
LA GRAVE
JADE FALCON OCCUPATION ZONE
02 NOVEMBER 3151

Star Commander Dawn wished she could sit on the command couch of a real 'Mech instead of a simulator, but when the day came for her to do that again, the fight would be real. In the meantime, she would have to content herself with practicing however she could, and the simulators were still a significant improvement over the training she had had to do in the infantry.

This time, she piloted a *Bane*, which gave her the distinct impression she would be piloting an assault 'Mech when they reached their objective, which suited her just fine. An assault 'Mech could do lots of damage and it would help her do her part. She had a lot of lost time to make up for.

"Star Commander Dawn," MechWarrior Hosteen said on the comm. This particular exercise had placed them in pairs to find ways to flush out Ghost Bear 'Mechs from their dens and enclaves. "The target area is up ahead."

"*Aff,*" Dawn said. But she was not seeing anywhere the Ghost Bears could hide. There were no hills or caves and no trees. The only thing that was ahead of them was a placid lake. "I do not have any 'Mechs on my scopes."

"Same. Where could they be hiding?"

Dawn's first thought was that they could be under the water, ready for an ambush, but that sounded further from Clan thinking than even a Ghost Bear would go. She scanned further beyond the target area. "There are outcroppings in the hills beyond the target area."

"But why would they give us this particular target area if they are not here?" Hosteen echoed Dawn's first instinct as well, but they sounded just as sheepish about verbalizing it. "Do you really think they could be under the water?"

"I mean, 'Mech cockpits *are* watertight."

"But their weapons would be useless from below."

"Only some of their weapons." Dawn switched to infrared mode, but the surface of the water appeared the same on her scope. A gently sloshing mirror, colored lighter than everything else because the water was much cooler than the rest of the area. It would make sense for them to hide there, given the parameters of the exercise and she said so. "I bet they are hiding beneath the water."

"Then how do we flush them out?" Hosteen asked.

It was a reasonable question. All of the *Bane*'s weapons were ammo-based. She boasted *ten* Ultra autocannons and four machine guns. She was deadly at long range, but at the mercy of how much ammunition she carried. She could not rely on lasers to lure out a target or paint it in the meantime. Every shot had to count. Shooting into the water with limited ammo did not make sense. But Hosteen was piloting a *Marauder IIC*, and was nothing *but* lasers.

Dawn switched back to her standard view on the HUD, trying to get more detail out of it. "Hosteen, fire into the lake. We will see if we can draw them out."

"*Aff.*"

The *Marauder IIC* fired its small lasers, bathing Dawn's entire console in ruby light. When the lasers subsided, steam rose from the boiling lake, but no 'Mechs appeared.

"Try it again," Dawn said.

Hosteen stepped closer, aiming down into the water before opening fire with his golden medium pulse lasers. Maybe he thought he would boil off more water with the shorter wavelengths and hotter beams.

Steam completely obscured the surface of the lake now, but it was enough to get the desired result. A gigantic *Mastodon* rose from the steaming water, rivulets dripping down its massive shoulder bay LRMs and dual PPC arms. As it moved backward, the assault 'Mech opened fire on Hosteen, unloading a fierce salvo of 40 long-range missiles that smoked across the lake, mixing with the steam and making the battlefield all that more chaotic. Half of them pummeled Hosteen's *Marauder*, exploding in a brilliant cascade of flame and fury.

Without waiting for further invitation, Dawn opened fire with her Ultra autocannons and machine guns, hoping to take the early advantage and blast as much armor off the *Mastodon* as fast as possible. Hosteen did not need to be told twice, either, firing a brilliant array of lasers and PPCs at their enemy. Half of their shots missed through the smoke and steam, but enough hit to see the *Mastodon*'s torso and arms crack with the impact.

"Let us hope," Hosteen said, "the lake holds no more surprises. In this case, one is more than enough."

"*Aff,*" Dawn said, backing up as she tried to keep outside the *Mastodon*'s firing arc, but keep it inside of hers. The *Mastodon* fired again at Hosteen, peppering his *Marauder IIC* with missiles.

Melted armor splashed into the lake, creating even more steam obscuring the view. The *Mastodon* stayed focused on Hosteen's *Marauder IIC,* ignoring Dawn entirely.

One assault 'Mech had enough armor to stand up to most attackers, but no assault 'Mech could stand up to two others and not suffer some consequences.

Although it took some time to break through the *Mastodon*'s 15 tons of armor, Dawn and Hosteen were eventually victorious. They limped away from the engagement and onto the next.

The pair ran through similar scenarios in different places. They caused a rockslide to trap a Star of Ghost Bears in a cave. They tried igniting a forest with Hosteen's lasers to smoke out a pack of Ghost Bears, but it did not work. That simulation ended poorly for them, and booted them when their 'Mechs were destroyed.

"I do not know how I feel about all of this," Hosteen told Dawn later in the mess hall.

"Which part?" There were a lot of potentially objectionable things happening; she could not be sure which one he meant.

"Well, any of it. The Jade Falcons are a shadow of their former selves."

Dawn smirked. "Is a shadow not enough? When a falcon swoops in, the shadow across the ground is often enough to freeze its prey in place."

"I wonder if the Ghost Bears will really believe we are the shadow with the falcon behind us, then. Do you think they even know about us and our survival? Or do you think they believe we *all* went to Terra and perished?"

Dawn shoveled more food into her mouth, tasteless rations meant to meet minimum nutritional standards rather than taste good. "I do not think the Khan would send us all the way into Ghost Bear space if anyone thought us truly talonless."

Hosteen ate more of his own nutrient-fortified paste. "I just worry. About a lot of things."

Dawn thought she knew what he meant. "*Dezgra* tactics?"

"*Aff.*"

"I am, too," Dawn said, swallowing another mouthful of mushy goo. "But are they still *dezgra* if the Khan is right? That this is how we have to fight to survive?"

"Would Kerensky say, 'Then we do not survive'?"

Dawn cocked an eyebrow. "I do not know what Kerensky would say. The more I discover about our history, the more I wonder if it has been taken to an extreme. The Wardens and the Crusaders all changed so much from the original teachings, so why do any of us pretend to know what Kerensky wanted or intended?"

"Because that is the way things are."

Dawn nodded. "But does that mean they always have to be that way?"

Hosteen shrugged. "All I know is I am told I should follow my Khan. And he seems trustworthy and intelligent. But will he make the right call for our honor as well as our Clan?"

Dawn found an answer inside her, but was surprised by it. Doubly so when she verbalized it. "What honor is there without a Clan in the first place?"

"A fair point."

"The Jade Falcons are going to survive, Hosteen, and we are MechWarriors in its new *touman*. We are no longer relegated to the dregs of the paramilitary police. And if the Khan is correct, we will be there at our destination to ensure our clan survives." Dawn's eyes drifted to a distant spot beyond her Starmate, many kilometers away. "Before this, we would have been nothing but footnotes in the history of the Jade Falcons, if we were ever even mentioned at all. But if we can truly succeed here, then we *will* be remembered. *Quiaff*?"

"It will definitely be better than the stories they tell of the police," Hosteen said, but did not get a chance to elaborate further.

An alarm sounded.

Time for another simulator drill.

Dawn sighed deeply and shoved a final spoonful food in her mouth as she stood.

Hosteen rose to his feet and picked up his food tray. "I just hope all of this drilling is worth it."

Dawn turned to him. "It will be as long as we have a Clan left at the end. And if we do not, then, at least we will have died fighting."

"We will know soon enough. Just one jump left."

Dawn left the mess and headed right back to the simulators. "One jump left," she repeated to herself.

CHAPTER 20

FELDSPAR
QUARELL
RASALHAGUE DOMINION
06 NOVEMBER 3151, 0920 HOURS

Alexis could not believe she was sitting in a BattleMech, ready to defend the vacant city of Feldspar and surrounding areas.

Their stunt in the last event had given them enough points to make it to second place and knock the Porbjorns down to third. That meant the Mektid Bears from Lothan were in first place, and would be laying siege to the city.

All Alexis had to do was defend the city. That was it. But she had no idea which direction they would be coming from—and she would have to coordinate the defense with Daniel.

Thanks to her performance in the stealth game, Alexis had been chosen to be one of two commanders; unfortunately, Daniel was the other. As one of the commanders, she got assigned a heavy 'Mech—an ancient 70-ton *Grizzly*. Daniel went out in a 60-ton *Mad Dog Mk III*.

That the Den Mother kept shoving Daniel into a leadership position after each subsequent mistake and loss was laughable. It did not matter how much the other *Ursari* argued that Daniel was not worthy of that position; the Den Mother insisted. His command of the other Star was a compromise between all the Bearclaw *Ursari* and the Den Mother to allow Alexis to even compete in the final competition, let alone command one of the Stars.

The *Grizzly* rumbled beneath her. The town of Feldspar was hers to defend, and there was nothing the Den Mother could do about it at that point.

"Bearclaw Cubs, report in," Alexis said.

"Cub One here," Thomasin said. Thomasin and Sophie both chose raptor-legged *Lobo*s. The *Lobo*s were good long-range fighters and boasted anti-missile systems. "Nothing on my scope yet, Cub Leader."

"Cub Two, same," Sophie said.

Lewis and Anna filled out the rest of the Star in a pair of *Solitaire*s. Essentially mobile laser cannons, the *Solitaire*s were capable medium-to-long range fighters, and then could take hits while dissipating their heat.

"Cub Three here, nothing to report," Lewis said.

"Cub Four checking in, it is quiet as a tomb out there," Anna said.

They had been patrolling for a solid thirty minutes since the official start of the exercise. Feldspar was small, wedged into a little valley and surrounded by hills. Two main roads led into and out of the small town, and there was no guarantee the Mektid Bears would use either of them. Alexis had studied their favored methods of attack, and found them very traditional in their thinking.

She had positioned all of the 'Mechs in her command on the hills, watching for any attacks from all directions. "Cub Three and Four," she said, knowing their *Solitaire*s were the fastest 'Mechs at her disposal, "I want you to keep scouting, head from hill to hill. The second you see something, hit it at long range and then fall back to the city."

"*Aff!*" they both said.

The colored dots that represented them on her HUD zoomed from one spot to the next, looking for anything that would even remotely resemble the Mektid Bear assault.

"Cubs One and Two," she said to Thomasin and Sophia, "I want you to keep closer to the city and patrol. Anything appears on your scopes, call it out."

"*Aff*, Cub Leader."

Alexis sighed, switching over to her command channel. Now she had to deal with Daniel. They had to coordinate their defense *somehow*, but she was not sure how that was going to happen. He had already refused to talk about tactics or an overall strategy, instead opting to stay close to the center of town. His 'Mechs did no patrols except for the immediate vicinity of the city center. Daniel's Star consisted of Jezebel, Zoe, Kaleo, and Yrsa. Jezebel and Zoe had each each chosen a *Rime Otter* as their medium 'Mechs. Kaleo and Yrsa took the extremely light and fast *Bear Cub*s to round out the second Star. As for Daniel, nothing he said could be trusted, and he could be counted on only to make the most foolish of moves. If they won the competition, it would be despite him instead of because of him.

"Bearclaw Alpha Leader, do you copy?"

"What do you want?" Daniel sneered into the comm.

"Report in. Any sign of the enemy?"

"If my Alphas saw anything, do you think I would just wait for you to ask me if we had seen something? Or do you think I would just tell you?"

"Honestly, Alpha Leader, I am not sure what you would do." Alexis tried to keep from laughing at him. "I have not expected you to do many of the things you have done in the games so far, but you persist in the most fascinating ways. One day, someone will write a book on the way you continually surprise your *sibkin*."

"Ha, ha, ha," he said. "Laugh while you can. When the glory of this battle is recorded, your name will be forgotten."

"I asked if you had seen anything, not for your fantasies. I have my *Solitaire*s patrolling on the nearby hilltops, and I have my *Lobos* between them in the city. What formation are you in?"

"As I have repeatedly stated, we have taken defensive positions in the city center, surrounding the capital to protect it. We will not be deviating from this strategy."

The city center complex was the enemy's target. The Mektid Bears merely had to reduce fifty percent of it to rubble to win full points on the exercise, and the glory of the entire cross-training exercises and war games.

"It might be wiser," Alexis started, despite her knowledge of Daniel's hard-headed stubbornness, "to keep up defensive perimeters that fan outward and collapse. If we just defend the target, they will be right there with everything they have."

"I understand," Daniel said.

That response sounded too gracious for Daniel, until she realized it dripped with sarcasm. He did not care what she said, one way or the other. He was going to camp at the objective and let them come to him. Which meant Alexis and her Star had to cover the entire circumference of Feldspar and the nearby hilltops to keep their defensive net as far from the objective as possible. It made sense to collapse the lines as they broke through and keep the enemy on the defensive as long as they could. It gave them more chances to win.

She could curse Daniel's name, but that would not do any good either.

All she could do was her best. Unfortunately, her best had to be enough to make up for Daniel's incompetence, and the blame would be on her if they failed. Though she suspected if they succeeded, the glory would all go to him, exactly as he had taunted her. Being a freebirth under a prejudiced Den Mother was not an easy position to be in.

"Cub Leader, this is Three. We have something," Lewis said. "Looks like they decided to make their move, coming in via the south road."

"Any other confirmations? Tell me what you see." Naturally, Alexis was up on the perimeter of the north road. As she waited for more teammates to call in, she turned her 'Mech around, figuring it would be faster to take the road all the way through town to reach the south road.

But could she really leave? The enemy's movement along the south road could be a feint. She did not expect them to arrive with their entire force, so the rest could be anywhere.

"Cub Three, stay there. Take a shot if you can get one. Cub Four, what do you see?"

"I am coming around to the next hill. I can get a look at them, and maybe we can get them in a kill box."

"Take your look," Alexis said, "and take a shot if you can, but unless their entire force is accounted for, I want you to scout another direction. Head to the east. Let me know if it is not all of them. At that point, I'll check north and Cubs One and Two can handle the west."

"Why is Alpha not taking any patrol duty?" Sophie asked, clearly annoyed.

"The usual," Alexis said. "When we have actionable intelligence, they will react. But as for patrol and the initial skirmishes, we need to assume we are on our own."

"There are twice as many 'Mechs out there than we are," Thomasin said. "How do they expect us to hold the line if they do not help?"

She would not dare say the obvious, though everyone would have figured it out, and Thomasin should have as well. Daniel wanted Alexis and her Cub Star to sacrifice themselves and soften up the targets so his Star could finish them off and take all of the glory.

But she did not want to say so on an open comm, especially since it could very well have been broadcast anywhere the games were aired, and right into Kodiak Point.

Alexis held her position for a moment, waiting.

"Cub Leader, this is Cub Three," said Lewis. "I only have visual on one Star. The other could be hiding or elsewhere."

"Cub Four, do you have a shot?"

"*Aff.*"

"Take it and get to the east. Fast. Cubs One and Two, report."

"Nothing here," Thomasin said.

"Nor here," Sophie said.

Alexis switched to the command channel. "Alpha Leader, we have one Mektid Bear Star coming in from the south road."

"South road," Daniel said. "Copy that."

But he made no move in his 'Mech. His entire Star remained around the city center.

"Are you coming to help?"

"Let me know when they breach the perimeter and when you find the other Star. Alpha Leader out."

He clicked off the command channel, and Alexis growled in anger. If they were going to survive, it was going to be by themselves. "Cub Three, report."

"A *Karhu* is out front—"

"That is their leader. Has it taken damage?"

"*Aff,* Four and I have both hit it. I am in position to hit it again, and Cub Four is headed east."

"That is correct, Cub Leader," Anna said.

Alexis tried doing the math in her head. At range, the *Solitaire*s could hit the *Karhu* with their heavy large lasers, which could do a considerable amount of damage. Two hits with a heavy laser could conceivably crack the ferro-fibrous armor on its center torso and expose its insides.

But only if they both hit it in the exact same place. It would likely take a few more hits than that.

If they were lucky.

The *Karhu* was not defenseless, either. Even though Lewis had the high ground and the element of surprise, it would not take long for the Mektid Bear Star Commander to get a lock on them. Its primary weapon was a plasma cannon, which could be devastating to the *Solitaire*s if it got a hit, as they were already prone to heat problems with their heavy laser suite.

"Cub Three," Alexis said, turning her *Grizzly* back around and heading up the north road, "take your last shot and pull back. I do not want to lose you."

"I do not want to lose me, either."

"Cubs One and Two, anything to the west?"

"*Neg,* Cub Leader."

Damn.

It felt like the enemy could arrive from anywhere, and Alexis' team was all sitting ducks.

The *Grizzly*'s top speed was less than half that of the *Solitaire*s', but Alexis had to make do as she pushed it to crest the hill of the north road, looking out at the rust-red hills and evergreen trees beyond.

And there they were in the distance. The Mektid Bears. Another *Mad Dog Mk III* led the way.

"I have eyes on the second Star," Alexis said. "They are coming up on the north road, trying to get us in a pincer maneuver. Any help your Star can provide would be helpful, Alpha Leader."

"Acknowledged," was Daniel's only reply.

Alexis did not bother to see if his Star rousted from their cowardly slumber. She sighted in on the *Bear Cub* running at the *Mad Dog Mk III*'s side, took careful aim, and fired with her Gauss rifle.

CRACK!

The slug missed the center mass, but sheared its left leg off in a shower of debris, sending the whole 'Mech falling forward with the force of its own momentum. In one hit, she had taken it off the battlefield.

"One of the light 'Mechs is down," Alexis said with smug glee. "Leaving nine, in case anyone else is keeping score."

With the other four 'Mechs of the second Mektid Bear Star facing her up the road, she felt confident in reorganizing the placement of her Star. "Cub Four, get in position to snipe at the north road. Cubs One and Two, guard the south road. Cub Three, fall back behind the line of support Cubs One and Two will create."

"Aff," they all replied, and sprang into action.

Alexis swore under her breath, figuring she would give Daniel one last chance. "Alpha Leader, we have all nine remaining 'Mechs accounted for. They are trying to put us in a pincer maneuver, approaching from the main road at the north and south end of town."

"Acknowledged," Daniel said again.

Alexis still could not tell if his response meant that he was going to help or not. *At least he heard me...?* "Any assistance you and your Star can provide will be helpful, and could mean the difference between us winning and losing."

Daniel did not respond.

Looking at the blips that represented his Star on her HUD's mini-map, it sure did not look like they were moving at all. She hoped he would at least move at the last second, come charging in as the heroic cavalry. In the meantime, she needed to do something about the incoming Mektid Bears.

The second *Bear Cub* in their pack saw what happened to their comrade, and the entire group tightened their formation behind the *Mad Dog Mk III*.

"Cub Four, set up from the side and take flanking shots on their approach. Pick softer targets. The more of them we can eliminate now, the easier it will be later. I will pick off what I can from the main road."

"*Aff!*" Anna said. The blip of her 'Mech on the map headed dutifully toward the hilltop that would give her the best shot at the lighter 'Mechs from the side of the road.

Alexis wagered she had one more shot at the heavy before she was a target herself, unless they decided to charge. Hitting the firing stud, the Gauss rifle roared and kicked again. In a blink, the impressive slug crashed into the *Mad Dog Mk III*'s torso, spraying chunks of armor onto the road. A solid hit, to be sure, but not enough to take the 'Mech down.

"Cub Leader, this is Cub Three."

"Report!"

"We have taken down the heavy."

"Excellent, take down the smaller targets first. The fewer Alpha Star has to deal with in the final defense, the better."

"They still are not helping?"

Alexis tried not to groan, backing up as fast as her *Grizzly* would allow her. She wanted to keep them in her sights, but gain as many seconds as she could without taking damage. "They have prioritized the defense of the objective."

The *Mad Dog Mk III* opened fire, but blocked the 'Mechs behind it from firing. It was a tradeoff, but Alexis assumed it knew what it was doing. The only weapons in range were its Ultra autocannons, which roared at her. Alexis was thankful they missed her entirely, though on her vidscreen she saw the wall of a building explode into dust and debris behind her.

Returning fire with her Gauss rifle, Alexis managed to nick the *Mad Dog*'s left arm. If she had hit it squarely, she might have knocked out two of its ER medium lasers, but no such luck.

"I am almost in position," Anna called out. Hopefully she could take them by surprise with devastating hits from her *Solitaire*, but Alexis refused to take anything for granted.

"Cub Leader, this is Cub One." Thomasin's voice was grim, and she braced herself for the bad news. "Cub Three is out. It is down to Cub Two and me."

"Is Cub Three alive?"

"Unknown, but I hope so."

"Hold out as long as you can."

The *Mad Dog Mk III* fired its autocannons again, and this time a high-explosive round smashed into her *Grizzly*'s torso.

A cascade of fire filled the front of Alexis' view screen as the round flared violently and cracked and melted her armor.

That is not good.

Alexis fired her Gauss rifle again, hoping to breach the *Mad Dog Mk III*'s front armor, but she hit it in the leg instead, shattering armor, but not slowing the heavy 'Mech's advance. She needed to readjust and be more careful.

From behind the *Mad Dog Mk III*, a *Bear Cub* and a *Lobo* broke formation and headed straight for the hill where Anna had taken aim. Alexis fired her full complement at the *Bear Cub*, and it withered below her. But the *Lobo* still charged for Anna.

"Another light 'Mech down!" she called out.

They would be doing better if Daniel were helping. With his help, there would be no need for a prolonged fight. But Alexis with her single Star had already improved their odds significantly.

"That's three down to one of ours," Alexis said proudly. "We are not doing too bad."

Except she spoke too soon.

"Cub Leader, we have taken their *Solitaire*, but Cub One is down."

Thomasin.

She hated that she could not protect him, and that he had likely done something foolish to protect Sophie. He would never admit to it, but that was how he operated. Just like he had claimed punching Daniel in the face was about Daniel, and not about Alexis at all. She saw right through him.

Or hoped she still would when this was all over.

"He better be all right," she said over the comm. What she did not say was that if he wasn't, Daniel was going to pay for it. "Now get out of there, Sophie, fall back to the objective and let them come to you. I do not want you to go down, too."

"*Neg*—" she began to argue, but Alexis cut her off.

"Sophie, I have enough problems with Ghost Bears not listening to my orders. I am the Commander of this Star, and I order you to the objective point at the city center."

After a long moment of silence, Sophie offered a begrudging, "*Aff,*" before slowly breaking away from the pack of Mektid Bears.

The *Grizzly* rocked with the force of another explosive impact and clouds of flame and smoke filled Alexis' view. The *Mad Dog* had hit her again.

The damage indicators on her torso flashed from green to yellow. She could not let the *Mad Dog* hit her center mass again with the Ultra autocannon. If it got any closer, it would turn the rest of her armor to slag.

Alexis shifted targets, drawing her Gauss rifle's reticule away from the *Mad Dog* and leading the *Lobo* still heading for Anna on the hill. It was a more difficult shot, but if she could make it, there was a chance she could take out the 'Mech and keep more of her Star intact and her compatriots alive.

There was no guarantee a MechWarrior would not die in one of these trials; two Cubs had already perished in the games, and several others had broken bones. They were firing live rounds and hot lasers and PPCs. Molten metal and slagged myomer was deadly no matter how friendly the combatants were. Cockpits got hit, even unintentionally. They were Clanners in competition. Even when they were family, people got hurt.

That thought did not comfort Alexis, but she did not have time to think about it anymore. With the simulators and more physical events, it was easy enough to set that aside. But then they handed a bunch of children—albeit well-trained children—incredible, deadly war machines and said nothing more than, "Do your worst."

Quite a loving family.

Shaking her head, Alexis refocused on her target and squeezed the firing stud. The Gauss round flew right past the *Lobo* and Alexis cursed herself for missing. Anna was going to die, and it would be her fault.

Alexis took another hit from one of the *Mad Dog*'s autocannons; thankfully, it ripped across her left arm instead of her torso. She had to ignore that and focus on falling back and lining up the next shot more capably.

Finally in position, Anna drilled the *Lobo* with the yellow fire of her heavy medium lasers, singing its torso armor and ablating the plating on its arm.

Knowing it was futile and she had to act on her own, Alexis still thought it was worth pleading with Daniel one more time. "If you are going to do something, do it now, Alpha Leader."

But Alexis knew he was not going to. She had to do something quickly. "Cub Star, fall back to the objective. We cannot do this ourselves."

"*Aff,*" Sophie said.

But no response came from Anna. "Cub Four, what are you doing? Fall back to the objective, do you copy?"

"I have a shot," Anna replied.

"Take it and fall back, now. That is an order."

"*Aff.*"

Alexis watched Anna take another shot with her medium lasers, but only one beam hit the *Lobo,* spilling molten metal across the hillside. Then Cub Four's *Solitaire* turned and ran back down the hill, heading for the perimeter of the city. Its top speed was almost twice that of the *Lobo,* so Anna would escape without a problem as long as the *Lobo* didn't get a targeting solution and blast it to bits. The *Solitaire* was well-armored for its weight class, but that did not mean it was Gauss-rifle proof.

Unable to decide if she should back up and keep taking the occasional potshot or head toward the city center and Daniel's Alpha Star, Alexis simply stood there and fired her Gauss rifle at the *Lobo* again. Maybe she could ensure Anna's escape and cover it, though that *Mad Dog* was getting awfully close to optimal range.

CRACK!

Her magnetic slug punctured the *Lobo*'s side, staggering it as its torso split apart, sending it crashing into the hillside.

"Mektid Bear *Lobo* is down," Alexis called out, just as the *Mad Dog* hit her with its Ultra autocannons again. Her left arm, where her Gauss rifle was, flashed yellow, then red, and then died on her display console, sending a jolt of feedback through her neurohelmet. She barely kept her 'Mech's balance as the rifle exploded.

"I have lost my Gauss rifle," she yelped when the pain in her head became more manageable. Shaking it off, she decided this was as good a time as any to make a run for the city center. If Daniel was not going to come help fight the battle, she would simply bring the battle to him. That was what he wanted, was it not?

She switched on her comm. "Cub Star, regroup at the objective. We have done all we can on our own."

"*Aff!*" they all called out.

And Alexis hoped, more than anything, that she had not made a mistake.

CHAPTER 21

KODIAK POINT
ANTIMONY
QUARELL
RASALHAGUE DOMINION
06 NOVEMBER 3151, 1047 HOURS

Star Colonel Emilio Hall should not have been surprised to see every vidscreen, noteputer, and monitor on Kodiak Point, from the commons area and conference rooms down to the 'Mech bay, tuned to the final hours of the final game in the *sibko* cross-training and war games event. To the credit of the *Ursari* across the Dominion worlds, it had been a rousing back-and-forth between the two *sibkos*. Naturally, the Star Colonel felt obligated to root for the Bearclaws since they were stationed on Quarell like the rest of the Fourteenth Battle Cluster, but he was equally proud of the Mektid Bears from Lothan for their strong showing as well. They had all done the Ghost Bears proud.

But then the competition heated up.

Drones and other cameras across Feldspar provided live feeds across the planet, giving the best view of the action one could get, short of the first-person feeds from a BattleROM. The Mektid Bears had made their move, attacking the city from both sides. According to the commentators, it looked like there was some disagreement between the commanders of two Bearclaw Stars, and they had been unable to decide if they were going to meet the Mektid Bears head-on or defend the city center, which was the ultimate objective of this scenario.

The score was about even, with both forces down a number of 'Mechs, although to Emilio's eye, the Bearclaws still had the advantage. They had taken down an entire Star's worth of 'Mechs and had still had the advantage of defending. The Bearclaws had taken out a lot more weight in 'Mechs than they had lost, too. Their Star leader, Alexis, had proven versatile in handling the superior force and calling out the threats to the defenders. There was a bit of disappointment in seeing the two Bearclaw leaders not working together better, but he could not argue with the results they were getting.

"This is going to be close," Star Captain Rand said. They were both watching from the command staff room, high up in the tower of Kodiak Point. The leaders of the various Stars from the Fourteenth stationed there had joined them. Refreshments were served, and they had turned the viewing of the final event into a party of sorts to celebrate the Ghost Bears who were coming of age.

"It will be. But every excellent match-up is."

"What would you do if you were attacking?" Rand asked him.

Emilio gnawed on that question for a moment. He did not know if Rand was trying to bait him into another argument. There was nothing he hated more, but as he chewed on the problem and thought back to his training in his *sibko* and learning of warfare and Jeet Kune Do, he knew exactly what he would do.

"First, I doubt I would have expected the Bearclaws to split their forces between a perimeter defense and objective defense, but I would want to remain flexible. It is said 'to attack, you must study the adversary's weaknesses and strengths, and take advantage of the former while avoiding the latter.' I might have aimed for the high ground around the city and avoided the road. I do like how the Mektid Bears split their forces geographically. It forced the Bearclaws to make some tough decisions, but they seem to be handling them well."

"And if you were defending?"

"I would have fanned my forces around the perimeter and collapsed back toward the objective as they moved closer. There is no reason for the Bearclaws to babysit the objective when there is so much ground to cover. It limits them where they do not need to be cornered. An unforced error."

"Agreed."

The room cheered, and Emilio turned his eyes back to the vidscreen. Alexis had pulled her Star back to the objective and laid waste to the *Mad Dog Mk III* harrying them, even without her Gauss rifle. With both of the Mektid Bear heavy 'Mechs down and both heavy 'Mechs of the Bearclaws still in play, it seemed there would be no problem for the Bearclaws to clean up the rest, though anything could happen. The odds favored the Bearclaws, but long odds were something Ghost Bears thrived on, cadets or otherwise.

The volume of the announcer casting the match got louder. *"This could be anyone's match. As the Mektid Bear Stars make their move on the objective, the Bearclaws must defend the city center. The terms of the match say the Mektid Bears must destroy the city center complex, not destroy the Bearclaws, so the Bearclaws are going to have to make much more offensive moves before that building collapses. Bearclaw Alexis, in charge of the Cub Star for that* sibko *team, did a valiant job taking out the other Mektid Bear 'Mechs, despite setbacks and infighting inside the Bearclaw* sibko.*"*

The images on the screens turned to the Mektid Bears. As each one got into range, they began firing beyond the Bearclaw 'Mechs in front of them and at the city center.

Emilio recognized the city center complex from his visit to Feldspar to parlay with the mayor months ago. It stood across the winding road from the mayor's modern home. The complex stretched across a city block, and was in a much older style than the mayor's house. Rocks made up most of the construction materials and foundation, and a high clock tower was the centerpiece of the complex, reaching up to the sky. The first shot from a Mektid Bear 'Mech in range did not do it well. So much of the history of the town of Feldspar came crashing down in a salvo of long-range missiles, bringing anguish to his heart.

Emilio hid it well—the last thing he needed was Rand commenting on more of his perceived weakness.

"Oh..." The commentator cringed as a cloud of dust and smoke billowed from the toppling tower. *"The Mektid Bears have taken the first shot against the objective. Although the damage looks brutal, that clock tower was not vital to the structural*

integrity of the complex. They need to destroy at least half of the complex in order to win, but something tells me the Bearclaws are not going to let that happen easily."

"The Mektid Bears are making a wise move," Rand said. "Stone is easier to destroy than myomer, and there is much more of it to blast."

"But they expose themselves to potshots from the Bearclaws."

Indeed, the video played out exactly as Emilio would have guessed. Once the Mektid Bears were in close enough, they ignored the Bearclaws completely, opting to destroy everything they could. The Bearclaws did their best to get in the way of the Mektid Bears and draw fire from the complex, disabling their enemies wherever possible.

The screen showed the official damage estimates at the bottom corner, and it climbed from ten percent to twenty, one missile and laser shot at a time. In the other corner was a counter in a different color, this one heading downward, and it was the number of Mektid Bears remaining. It fell from five to four as the number on the left, signifying the percentage of destruction, rose from twenty to twenty-five.

"It is going to be close," Rand said again.

And Emilio could not argue, they were already halfway there. Fifty percent destruction would be accomplished in no time.

Half of the Ghost Bears in the command room were on the literal edges of their seats, watching the battle play out. Sport like this was rare, and they all relished every moment of it.

"Ouch!" the commentator said. "It looks as though Star Commander Alexis, our pick for the most valuable Warrior for the Bearclaws, is out. But she is not taking fire from the Mektid Bears!"

The feed cut to a replay of Alexis' Grizzly doing its best to fire lasers into the fray of Mektid Bears, but taking shots from behind. Her other arm exploded into parts, leaving her 'Mech stripped and defenseless.

"Friendly fire!" the commentator shouted. "I cannot believe this! It appears as though Daniel, the commander of the Bearclaw Alpha Star, missed his target and taken the other arm from the commander of the Bearclaw Cub Star. I have never seen *anything like it! Is it a mistake? Or further evidence of their split and disagreement? In either case, it is very un-Ghost-Bear-like."*

Emilio *tsk*ed. That was a bad move and a completely unforced error, but cadets had to learn somewhere. He hoped this cub named Daniel would learn his lesson. According to the commentators, he had been nothing but a source of drama throughout the entire war games.

He would fit right in with Rand's Ghost Bears.

On the screen, the Mektid Bears kept up their barrage.

The remaining Bearclaws kept up their offensive fire.

The damage numbers climbed.

Alexis, in her armless *Grizzly*, rammed one of the Mektid Bear Light 'Mechs, toppling it to the ground and taking both out of the fight. Emilio nodded in awe. That was a bold move and the sacrifice of a true leader.

The number of operational Mektid Bears fell.

Star Captains and Star Commanders stood, unable to take the tension of the competition, waiting to see what the outcome would be.

At last, it came down to a final Mektid Bear. The Bearclaws had eliminated all the rest.

The percentage of destruction increased.

Forty-seven percent.

Forty-eight...

"It comes down to the last seconds. Forty-nine percent of the base has been destroyed and the Bearclaw Alpha Star leader—the one who damaged a member of his own force—comes charging in. Will he make it?"

The vidfeed zoomed in.

The Mektid Bears had one *Lobo* left, which faced off against a Bearclaw *Mad Dog Mk III*. All the Bearclaws had to do was destroy that last 'Mech, but all that *Lobo* had to do was fire one more shot at the crumbling city center. Finding a spot to shoot would be difficult for them, as they had to destroy a piece that had not already been shattered, but it would be easier than simply dying.

Fire exchanged back and forth.

The numbers hung frozen on the screen.

Forty-nine percent on the left.

One 'Mech left on the right.

The Bearclaws fired everything they had at the *Lobo*.

The last standing Mektid Bear fired everything *they* had at the complex.

The battlefield smoked ceaselessly from the missiles fired and dust kicked up in the building's destruction. Brilliant lights flashed in a mess of chaotic colors from all of the varied laser fire.

And then the numbers on the screen changed.

Fifty percent on the left.

At the same time, the number on the right clicked to zero.

The *Lobo* fell over, unable to support its own weight with all of its armor and inner structure slagged. After what seemed like victory for the Mektid Bears, Emilio could only hope the clever pilot still lived.

However, confusion took the room.

"What does that mean?" Star Captain Rand asked.

But Emilio only shrugged. He was not the arbiter of the rules. It was his job merely to offer a place to facilitate the games. The leadership of the *Ursari* decided the rules.

The commentator's voice filled the room. *"We are waiting on a final ruling from the* Ursari, *but it would appear that this battle was fought to a technical draw. The Mektid Bears and the Bearclaws both achieved their objectives—"*

The announcer's voice cut out abruptly.

Emilio's brow furrowed.

Someone else asked where the volume had gone, but Emilio realized there was nothing wrong with it when another voice came through the speakers.

"...I repeat, I am broadcasting on all open channels in hope that this message reaches Star Colonel Emilio Hall of the Fourteenth Battle Cluster... This is Jiyi Chistu of Clan Jade Falcon, and I am here on important business."

All eyes in the room looked to Emilio, though he was just as confused as everyone else. A thousand questions ran through his head, but the first had everything to do with what exactly a Jade Falcon would be doing in the Rasalhague Dominion.

He turned to Star Captain Allison Rand and nodded to her. "Get me a channel to them."

"*Aff,* Star Colonel."

The celebration of the games would have to wait, they had much bigger business to tend to.

CHAPTER 22

FELDSPAR
QUARELL
RASALHAGUE DOMINION
06 NOVEMBER 3151, 1105 HOURS

Alexis burned with fury.

It was bad enough they had lost, but she also had to suffer the indignity of friendly fire? And from *Daniel*, no less?

She sighed in her darkened cockpit, feeling—at the very least—lucky to be alive. Her comms still worked, independent of the rest of her 'Mech that had all but ceased to function after all the fire she took and the ramming maneuver that took her out. Her entire 'Mech was tilted at an odd angle; gravity tightened the straps against her chest, and *down* felt straight ahead.

So close, yet so far away. Curse it all.

"Did we win?" she asked, but no one seemed to hear her. If they did, they were ignoring her. Or her comm was receiving, but not transmitting. Or one of a hundred other things.

Instead, voices talked back and forth about how close it was.

And she was grateful to hear it sounded as though not a single one of the Mektid Bears or Bearclaws had lost their lives, though one of the Mektid Bears had suffered a broken arm, and Thomasin ended up with a concussion.

Then another voice came to her radio, filling every channel she could hear.

"I am broadcasting on all open channels in hope that this message reaches Star Colonel Emilio Hall of the Fourteenth

Battle Cluster...This is Jiyi Chistu of the Jade Falcons and I am here on important business. I repeat..."

The message repeated again before anything different happened. She could not tell if it was a recording, or if her mind was playing tricks on her to make her think his tone changed every time he repeated his message. She knew nothing about Jiyi Chistu, but had heard a lot about the Jade Falcons. They were murderous, for one. They would destroy cities and lay waste to entire planets if it fit their goals. But Jiyi Chistu's voice did not sound like it was murderous, nor did it seem to have any ill intent.

To Alexis' ear, he sounded downright...*happy*?

What could he have to be happy about? Based on all the news from Terra, even that which had filtered down to cadets in a *sibko*, the Wolves had mopped the floor with Malvina Hazen and her Jade Falcon zealots. They had lost their quest for Terra, and would never serve as the ilClan because they never would exist again.

At least she thought that was the case.

But here the Jade Falcons were.

At Quarell, of all places.

It did not make sense to her. But, after Daniel's friendly fire stunt, anything seemed possible. He would rather lose the exercise completely than allow her any modicum of victory. She wanted to strangle him. But he was still family. The thought of strangling him caused a pain in her chest.

Or perhaps that was just the harness cutting into her.

As she struggled to break free, she pondered that idea, letting the voice of Jiyi Chistu fill her ears, washing over her with its undertone of mischievous glee.

Eventually, after an eternity, a response to his message sounded in her ears.

"Jiyi Chistu of the Jade Falcons," said a voice Alexis recognized as Star Colonel Emilio Hall's. She knew him even before he introduced himself. "What business do you have on Quarell?"

It took a few moments for the reply to come through; there was a delay between Kodiak Point or wherever the Star Colonel was and the satellite feed and orbital relay that must have been transmitting the Jade Falcons.

But eventually, Jiyi Chistu's answer came.

"I am here to challenge you to an honorable Trial of Possession." Alexis could practically hear the oily smile in his words—perhaps her notions about the Falcons were correct. "And something tells me you will accept."

OVERLORD-C-CLASS DROPSHIP *FALCON'S SHADOW*
HIGH ORBIT OVER QUARELL
RASALHAGUE DOMINION
06 NOVEMBER 3151, 1114 HOURS

Star Commander Dawn listened to the complete exchange between the Khan and the Ghost Bears, since it was being piped through the entire DropShip. The Jade Falcons had made contact as soon as they were in range, and the Khan had flooded the frequencies with his message.

Dawn wondered how effective it would be to demand such a wide audience for his play if the Ghost Bears decided to not go for it. But the Khan sounded so confident as he called out their Star Colonel by name.

She supervised the 'Mech bay, overseeing the technicians and scrambling herself in zero-gravity, preparing all of the 'Mechs for deployment. She had never seen so many assault 'Mechs in one place, a veritable stable of *Bane*s, *Turkina*s, and *Marauder IIC*s. In one corner was the Khan's own *Gyrfalcon*, a medium 'Mech. There were lights and heavies scattered about as well, but Dawn's eyes were wide as saucers trying to fathom that many assault 'Mechs as she heard the Khan parlay with their intended enemy.

"I am here to challenge you to an honorable Trial of Possession," the Khan said, and the hairs on the back of Dawn's neck tingled. "And something tells me you will accept."

The man on the other end, the one the Khan had called out—Star Colonel Emilio Hall—had the temerity to laugh quietly. A reserved, smug laugh, full of unearned joy. If only he could see the might arrayed before her. Then he might not laugh so easily.

"What makes you so sure?" Hall said. "I thought the Jade Falcons were no more. That you had all flown to Terra."

"Some left, *aff*, and some died. But clipping the wings of a Falcon still leaves its talons and beak, *quiaff*?"

The banter back and forth between them was almost too much for Dawn to bear. It sounded like two people circling an argument, waiting for one to shove the other. A pissing match. She did not like such things. People talking plainly and straightforward should explain what they want, and if a fight must ensue to get it, then so be it.

It was the dancing around a subject she found so difficult to bear.

Fortunately, the Ghost Bear leader cut to the chase. "What do you want?"

"I propose a Trial of Possession. I come to claim the *sibkos* on Quarell participating in the cross-training and war games."

"You sound well-informed, Jiyi Chistu." Surprise tinged the Star Colonel's voice, and then resolve. "But I am afraid that is out of the question."

"I bid a single Trinary to fight for it."

"Very well, I bid the Fourteenth Battle Cluster."

Dawn knew very well that the Fourteenth contained no less than five Trinaries. If Khan Jiyi accepted that bid, the Jade Falcons would be wiped out completely. She looked around to the 'Mechs in the bay and wondered how they could possibly stand in front of the entirety of the Ghost Bear's Fourteenth Battle Cluster.

"You there!" she called to a tech who had floated away from an ammo container, "secure that!"

The tech turned around, tense as everyone listening to the exchange between the Khan and the Ghost Bears.

The delay between responses made listening to the conversation excruciating.

"That bid," said Khan Chistu, "does not seem fair or honorable, given our *rede*."

"Neither does showing up on a Ghost Bear world requesting a Trial for sixty or more young cadets."

"Hosteen!" Dawn called out to her floating comrade, standing over the 'Mech he hoped to be assigned to. "What are you doing floating there?"

"What does it look like?" He gripped the holds at the top of a *Turkina*'s cockpit, a tech behind him making final checks. "Preparing for war!"

"As are we all."

"Are you ready for this?"

"As I will ever be."

"Then," Khan Chistu said over the DropShip's speakers to the Ghost Bears, "let us start again on the right foot."

KODIAK POINT
ANTIMONY
RASALHAGUE DOMINION
06 NOVEMBER 3151, 1122 HOURS

Star Colonel Emilio Hall sat in his office, pursing his lips and smoothing his beard with this thumb and forefinger. He had just bid the entire Fourteenth Battle Cluster against the two offered Trinaries in this absurd Trial of Possession.

Who did this Jiyi Chistu think he was? And how could he be believed? As far as Emilio had heard, the Jade Falcons had been destroyed on Terra, and were a thing of the past. A nagging sensation twisted in his gut. How did he know he was not walking into a trap? Or if these people really were representative of the Falcons left behind.

The possibilities of what could be were endless, and Emilio could not be sure how to feel about it, but found himself vacillating between caution and skepticism.

As he considered his next response, Emilio looked across his desk to Star Captain Rand. "Do we have any intelligence about this Chistu person?"

Rand worked diligently at a noteputer. "We have had very few dealings with the Jade Falcons, but it appears Jiyi Chistu has appeared in some databases on Ghost Bear worlds. He was a Star Captain stationed with VaultShip *Gamma*."

"One of the merchant vessels?" Emilio's ears perked. He had long thought about starting such a program for the glory of the Ghost Bears as his Great Work in his retirement.

"*Aff.* The Ghost Bears have traded with the Jade Falcon Merchants extensively across the Dominion, and that is the only place where his name comes up."

"Interesting." Emilio thought for a moment, wondering why Chistu had not offered his rank. It was customary in the Clans to use full rank and Bloodname when introducing or addressing each other, especially in something so formal as a challenge for a Trial.

Something else was afoot here.

"How do I know," Emilio said to Jiyi Chistu, "that you are who you say you are? The Jade Falcons lost Terra, and your Khan was killed in that conflict—as well as all the Falcons sent to Terra."

As he waited for that message to reach the alleged Falcons, Emilio turned back to Rand. "Do we have any proof of his identity?"

"Other than his word and the transmission of Jade Falcon codes? No. And we will likely have no more confirmation until he lands."

"*If* he lands." Emilio wondered if all of this could have been a ruse, or part of some other bigger plan he could not yet see.

"*Aff.*"

"Reports of the Jade Falcons' demise have been greatly exaggerated." Chistu's voice crackled through the comm. The techs at Kodiak Point had eliminated the background noise from the war game broadcast and pulled it into the command channel so Emilio could respond. Unfortunately, according to the same techs, the Jade Falcons were also broadcasting the conversation back out on all frequencies, ensuring they would have an audience. "While it is regrettable what happened to our departed Khan Malvina Hazen, the Jade Falcons live quite imaginatively in our own occupation zone here in the Inner Sphere, neighboring on your borders."

"I see," Hall responded with great skepticism. "Your actions do not seem all that neighborly to me."

Minutes passed. Rand worked to obtain more information about Chistu, the Jade Falcons left in their occupation zone, and anything else that would be of use, but the details were thin.

"The Trial of Possession is a sacred rite between the Clans," Chistu continued unbidden, pleading his case with a joy Emilio could not help but like. Chistu did not sound like any Jade Falcon he had ever heard. "Our two Clans are no different. Whether it was Alaric Ward's taking of Ramiel Bekker for the Battle for Terra, or the infamous Trial that gave control of Reinar's Event Horizon to the Ghost Bears after a hundred-meter-dash against the Hell's Horses. It is something in our spirit."

Emilio could not argue with that. And the Trial of Reinar's Event Horizon was something the Ghost Bears talked of often with a chuckle. But what he could not do was put so many Ghost Bear cadets at risk. Especially those from other planets who were there on Quarell under his care and protection.

Star Captain Rand narrowed her eyes, suspicious, but Emilio was not sure how she hoped he would react. They had agreed to start the bid from scratch on more even footing. Hall needed to either overbid to the point of absurdity or refuse the challenge completely. With the information he had at the moment, there was nothing in this for him worth risking any loss of face. It would take something seismic to make him say yes.

Refusing completely tugged at his honor, but not in the same way accepting would. What message would it send to those wagered cadets about the nature of a Ghost Bear family that they could be so easily bartered away, especially after the performances they had turned in over the last month? They were nothing short of extraordinary. But refusing a challenge of Trial felt very un-Clan-like, even though outsiders might view the Ghost Bears as the most un-Clan-like of the Clans. Especially now, given their position inside the strictures of the Rasalhague Dominion.

"I agree, Jiyi Chistu of the Jade Falcons, but these cadets are the future of the Ghost Bears. As I said before, I will bid no less than the Fourteenth Battle Cluster for them, no matter how many times you wish to renegotiate the bidding."

Chistu might have been able to cobble together a single Trinary, possibly two, but five was out of the question. They were clearly in dire straits, and probably needed this more than Emilio would have guessed.

Emilio hoped his rebuke would be the end of it, until Chistu's response came back. "What if we make things a little more interesting?"

Chistu let the question hang there in the air. Dangling it lengthened the conversation—needlessly perhaps—and was designed to provoke a response. Emilio cursed inwardly because it worked. What *could* make it more interesting?

"I doubt that you can." Emilio did his best to sound blasé and dejected. "But what do you propose?"

"We will make it a double Trial. I will bid two Trinaries on the ground of your choosing for the right to take the cadets and make Jade Falcons of them. But it will also be a Trial of Possession for Clan Ghost Bear as well."

"And what would we be getting in if we are victorious?" Emilio wondered what a dying Clan could have that would make the lives of so many *sibkos* worth it? The answer hit him like a thunderbolt: *This is* all *that is left of the Jade Falcons.*

When Chistu finally responded, Emilio did not quite know how to reply. At first, he thought he misheard the Jade Falcon, but the stunned look on Star Captain Rand's face confirmed what he'd heard.

The incentive, according to Jiyi Chistu?

"VaultShip *Gamma.*"

FELDSPAR
QUARELL
RASALHAGUE DOMINION
06 NOVEMBER 3151, 1130 HOURS

Alexis sat in the back of the hover transport alongside the rest of the recovered cadets from the exercise, crammed between Thomasin and Sophie. She was still sore from the straps digging into her skin, though they had probably saved her life. They had to cut her out of the *Grizzly*, which was fine. She never wanted to pilot one again. Even if that 'Mech made sense for any battle she might fight in the future, she would never pick it. She never wanted to see the inside of a *Grizzly* again, or else she'd scream.

She kept her mouth shut, just like all of the other cadets. They had all listened intently to the conversation between the Jade Falcons who had arrived in orbit and Star Colonel Emilio Hall. Of *course* they were all listening. It was a very public parlay.

Anxiety gripped the transport, thick enough to cut. Everything Alexis had heard about the Falcons was unflattering at best. They were vicious monsters who slaughtered people like her in the streets. If she had picked the pocket of a Falcon, they would have been more likely to cut off her hand than toss her in a *sibko*. Alexis felt palpable terror from every corner of the transport's bay. Even Daniel, the picture of mediocrity that prevented him from ever feeling nervous, bit at his nails.

She didn't know if they were all thinking the same thing she was, but if they weren't, they should have been.

What if the Star Colonel *did* wager them away?

Worse than that, what happened if the Ghost Bears *lost*?

They were all Ghost Bears. They could not just become Jade Falcons, could they?

"What is a VaultShip *Gamma*?" one of the cadets up front— Lewis—asked the *Ursari*, Star Captain Diego. He had been given the task of the task of retrieving the fallen Bearclaws and Mektid Bears.

"VaultShip *Gamma* is a merchant ship, an invention of the Jade Falcons," Diego replied in the tone of a fascinated teacher. "Some of the Clans have VaultShips that carry all kinds of precious metals and important goods to trade across vast regions. Think of the DropShips you've studied, and then fill it with riches, and you will have some idea. That is what a VaultShip is. They are valuable prizes, run by the Merchant Caste, and worth the plunder of many planets."

"Not as valuable as us, though," Alexis said quietly, moving closer to Thomasin and Sophie.

"The Star Colonel will never do it," Thomasin whispered to her, sensing Alexis' worry. "You have nothing to fear."

"Thomasin is right," Sophie said. "There is no reason for him to wager us away. The Ghost Bears have all the wealth and precious metals we need. Why would he put us in harm's way?"

"He better not," Alexis said.

But that only made Thomasin laugh. "What would you do about it?"

"I don't know." Alexis fumed that Thomasin would never understand her frustration. He'd had his family forever, and she had not. She would *never* just wager them away like an object. How could one even consider such a thing? "I would march right up to him at Kodiak Point, slap the Star Colonel across the face, and challenge him to a Trial of Refusal. Or something."

"It is okay, Alexis." Sophie gripped Alexis' hand and squeezed it. "It will not even be an issue. Because if it is, you will not have a chance to slap him because I will do it first, I swear to Kerensky."

The voice of Star Colonel Emilio Hall interrupted through the radio system. "Jiyi Chistu of the Jade Falcons," he said, "It seems as though you are right. That would certainly make things a lot more interesting."

"This is the very reason I brought it with me. Scan the ships coming toward Quarellian orbit; we are transmitting our transponder codes now. You will find VaultShip *Gamma* is there. And I, on this open line, give the order for them to surrender to you if you engage in this unorthodox Trial of Possession and beat my Jade Falcons."

The chatter in the hover transport died completely.

Alexis held her breath, waiting—hoping—for Star Colonel Hall to swat this Jade Falcon Warrior's dreams out of the sky.

The Star Colonel's voice returned. "I will accept the bid of two Trinaries and match it with two Trinaries of the Ghost Bears' Fourteenth Battle Cluster."

Alexis could not have heard that right.

But she must have. The entire transport suddenly buzzed with anxiety and excitement.

Sophie's jaw dropped and she pulled away from Alexis. "He didn't..."

"He did, apparently," Thomasin said.

At the front of the transport, Star Captain Diego could not hide the shock or surprise on his face. This was not something any of them had seriously expected, and why should they have?

Now that it *was* happening, what did it all mean? Would they be put in some sort of holding pen while the challenge was being decided? Or would they be allowed to refuse? Why was she not getting a say in this? It was her life...

"For the battlefield," the Star Colonel continued, "I choose the area in and around the Pykon River Delta."

The comm went dead again as they waited through the delay for Jiyi Chistu to respond.

Star Captain Diego, ever the *Ursari*, found a teaching moment. "Can anyone tell me why the Star Colonel chose the Pykon River Delta?"

One of the Mektid Bear cadets raised their hand. Perhaps they felt sheepish answering the question of another *sibko's Ursari.*

"Yes, go ahead."

"Because he knows it well?"

"That is a good answer. Can one of the cadets from Quarell answer? Lewis, go ahead."

Lewis stood up. "Star Colonel Hall has no doubt studied Jade Falcon tactics. The Pykon River Delta, as we all found when we had to trudge through it, will make their swift, swooping tactics difficult. Between the thick wooded areas, the hills, the open rice paddies, and all of the swampy waterways leading out to the river and then the sea, it will negate some advantages of the Falcons' tactics."

"Very good," Star Captain Diego said.

Anna raised a hand before speaking anyway, "There are also no inhabited areas around for miles, merely minor fisheries and farms. The Mongol Doctrine will have little bearing on the fight if there are no nearby cities to raze or hold hostage."

"Excellent, Anna. You are all truly thinking like Ghost Bears."

Alexis stood, tears in her eyes, ready to scream. Anger twisted her stomach. "How are you all okay with this? They are betting with our lives!"

"Cadet Alexis?" Star Captain Diego asked allowed, confused by her outburst.

"Who just wagers away the next generation of their family?" She looked around at the crestfallen faces of all of her *sibkin* across the transport, and the Mektid Bears as well. Even Daniel looked affected, as though he'd taken a punch in the gut. "What kind of family is this?"

Star Captain Diego cleared his throat. "Cadet Alexis, I know the thought of Trials might be a little more difficult for you because of your upbringing, but if it something the Star Colonel agrees to with another Clan Warrior, whether they are in our clan or not, it is honorable and right. VaultShip *Gamma* would be quite a prize for the Ghost Bears."

"But what if he loses?" Daniel said, standing up in his seat.

Alexis could not contain the shock at his voice defending and supporting her.

Star Captain Diego furrowed his brow. "Then you would be Jade Falcons."

Daniel turned and looked back to Alexis, and for the first time, it felt like they were on the same team.

OVERLORD-C-CLASS DROPSHIP *FALCON'S SHADOW*
HIGH ORBIT OVER QUARELL
RASALHAGUE DOMINION
06 NOVEMBER 3151, 1138 HOURS

"Well bargained and done," Jiyi Chistu said. "Please send us the coordinates for the staging area at the Pykon River Delta. Jiyi Chistu and the Jade Falcons, over and out."

And all the Jade Falcon Khan could do was smile.

Star Captain Quinn's shoulders slumped, as though a great weight had just been lifted from her.

"You doubted the plan?" Jiyi asked.

"*Neg.* I doubted they would agree."

"They could not pass up the prize of VaultShip *Gamma.*"

"What made you know they would go for that bait? The Ghost Bears have all the riches they need, safe in their den of the Dominion."

"Human nature and the nature of the breeding of the clans. It is a prize and a challenge. It does not matter how civilized the Ghost Bears find themselves to be. Dangle bait in front of them and they will still come."

"I do not need to remind you, sir, that if we lose the VaultShip, then all hopes of rebuilding the Jade Falcons go with it."

"We will not lose the VaultShip. We cannot. And if we do lose it, then perhaps Clan Jade Falcon deserves to die."

"*Aff,* my Khan."

But Jiyi did not worry. The Ghost Bears had no idea what was coming. They had never faced a Jade Falcon like him before. They would be prepared to defend against a brutal Mongol horde, unthinking and unfeeling, mobile and ready to strike hard and fast. Instead, he would array a different sort of force against them, one they could not possibly withstand. They had no idea they had just walked into a steel bear trap. He just had to spring the jaws around their legs.

"Ready the 'Mechs," he said to his second. "Prepare the MechWarriors. Tomorrow, we go to battle."

CHAPTER 23

GHOST BEAR STAGING AREA
PYKON RIVER DELTA
QUARELL
RASALHAGUE DOMINION
07 NOVEMBER 3151

"No, Star Captain Rand," Emilio said, striding by the BattleMechs he had called to assembly for the Trial atop a hastily constructed boardwalk over the muggy marshland, "I do not believe these Jade Falcons pose a credible threat. If I thought they did, I would never have agreed to this Trial. If they came all the way here with VaultShip *Gamma*, it's my considered belief that this is everything the Jade Falcons have left."

"They did not come all the way here to simply gift us VaultShip *Gamma*," Rand said, following closely behind him on his swift walk toward the makeshift command center, swatting a mosquito in her path. The venom in her voice came with her annoyance. Nothing Emilio had done in the previous 24 hours had met with her approval.

"*Aff.* Of course not. They came to take our *sibkos*. Which means they are desperate. But what they do not know is that we have studied the Jade Falcons, and know how they think. We chose the fighting ground to undercut their most common tactics, swooping hit and run tactics. More than that, what MechWarriors do you think they are fielding?"

"What do you mean?" Suspicious, Rand narrowed her eyes.

"You have read the reports. You truly think Malvina Hazen just left an elite group of MechWarriors behind while she went to Terra? I doubt a single MechWarrior of worth is left, let alone two Trinaries' worth. This is a bluff if I have ever seen one. What is more, this is our chance to eliminate the rest of the Jade Falcons once and for all. Perhaps the Inner Sphere will finally have a chance at peace without their constant jockeying for power and the threat of their Mongol Doctrine."

"While I admit it would strain credulity that Malvina Hazen of all people left anything on the table in her march to Terra—especially when planets like Seginus reported them stealing food from civilians and destroying their industrial centers to take with them to Terra, it seems likely she left *someone* to protect their holdings in the occupation zone."

"I agree," Emilio said, doing his best to ignoring the stink of the swamp, "it is possible she left *someone* in charge. But based on what little you could dig up, Jiyi Chistu is not the sort of person she would place any trust in. He got sent on babysitting duty for a Merchant ship that continued operating in the Dominion in the Terran attack. Is it not more likely he is scrambling to use what scant resources he has to build *something* for those who are left? If we can destroy this last vestige of the Jade Falcons, who, as far as our intelligence reports claim, were all but destroyed on Terra, *and* take the VaultShip from them, it would please our new ilKhan greatly. Would it not?"

The makeshift command center was nothing more than a tent with communications and radar equipment inside. Emilio and the Star Captain stepped inside and found a bustle of activity. Technicians and laborers worked diligently to connect everything and create a fully functional command post as quickly as possible. No doubt the Jade Falcons were doing the same thing on the far end of the Delta, where they had been granted clearance to land their DropShips and begin their own preparations for the Trial.

"It is my belief," said Emilio, "that these are second-line MechWarriors. *Solahma* at best, and they think they can simply blunder through the Fourteenth. But we have more discipline and know-how. And we know how to fight them. No, Star Captain, I think you overestimate their chances."

"If you insist. I just do not believe the prize is worth the potential cost."

"We cannot afford to let this remnant of the Jade Falcons keep the VaultShip, and we would bring great glory to the Dominion if we destroyed them once and for all. Do not forget what brought our Clan so much shame in the face of the Wolves in our history. It is paramount that we not let this rabble escape to any corner of the galaxy. More than that, we will not lose the *sibkos*. They have no chance of winning. You have my most solemn oath on that."

Emilio turned his attention to Star Captain Mikaela, the Warrior in charge of the 23rd Battle Trinary, as she gave final orders to the MechWarriors in their Stars. "Star Captain, I trust your Trinary is ready for this challenge?"

"Ready and waiting," she said. "This will be fun."

"Do not be too eager, Star Captain," Emilio said. "We still have to win this battle."

"Spoken like someone who believes it might be a challenge," Rand said, still fuming beside him. "Even though he just claimed otherwise."

"There is a difference between confidence and overconfidence," Emilio reminded her. "And you, Star Captain Rand—I trust Trinary Command is sufficiently ready to fight this battle."

"They are always ready, Star Colonel."

Emilio knew they were ready; he commanded them. He just wanted something to divert Rand's objections. She would pollute the morale of the entire enterprise if she could. She did not believe in Emilio or the wager, which was fine, she did not have to. She just needed to follow orders.

Rand looked down to the noteputer she carried. "Your *Ursus II* is undergoing final ammunition loading. And, as requested, the OmniMechs have been outfitted to your specifications to best combat the Jade Falcons. Highly mobile and deadly up close for their swooping tactics."

"Excellent," he said, rubbing his hands together. "I assure you, VaultShip *Gamma* is a prize worth winning. But more than that, this is the last of Clan Jade Falcon. I thought you might be more pleased about eliminating them, since they are the sworn enemies of the ilKhan you are so eager to see us join."

Rand remained blank-faced. Mikaela nodded, agreeing with him.

Emilio looked on at the map they had come to, pondering where to best station his Stars. With 30 'Mechs at his disposal, there were going to be many battlefronts. But the Jade Falcons were nothing if not relentless. A frontal assault was as likely as a potential flanking maneuver. And since the battlefield encompassed the entire width of the region and split it between them so they would fight across it, rather than up or down, there were plenty of places the Falcons could strike from.

He merely had to divine their intent and actions, and decide where to strike before they could.

Even if he abhorred the politics that had plunged the Ghost Bears into endless bickering, Emilio relished the idea he could make their borders safer by eliminating the Mongol threat of the Jade Falcons. He focused on the map, feeling good about what they were about embark on.

"If we are to join the Star League after all, what better way to make up for our past and make an offering to the new ilKhan than to annihilate the rest of his enemies that lie on our own doorstep? Two green birds with one great stone."

"If that is how you can accept the vote, Star Colonel, then so be it," Rand said.

Glancing to the chronometer on the map of the Delta, Emilio nodded. "It is time. Let us do this."

"Aff!" the Star Captains said before they all headed to their 'Mechs.

Emilio smiled.

This final victory would make his retirement all the sweeter, and his Great Work would galvanize that VaultShip into something that would bring even more glory to the Ghost Bears.

JADE FALCON DROP ZONE
PYKON RIVER DELTA
QUARELL
RASALHAGUE DOMINION
07 NOVEMBER 3151

The *Falcon's Shadow* had deposited all the 'Mechs and Elementals of Khan Jiyi Chistu's attack Trinaries in the designated drop zone with aplomb, and he could not be more pleased. He had trained his Warriors for this very battle, and nothing would keep them from victory.

After all that time spent on a JumpShip's grav decks to drill and train, being in a 'Mech in the standard gravity of a planet could not be more refreshing. The command couch of *Emerald,* his *Gyrfalcon,* felt like home to him. He had not been in the cockpit for a long time, not for a real mission. Frankly, the deployment with VaultShip *Gamma* had not come with much chance for glory, and even less chance of needing to fight in a 'Mech. His purpose there had been purely pro forma, though it had ended up being to his benefit. He doubted anyone had ever ascended to the Khanship in the way he had. If Clan Jade Falcon lived and thrived, then no one would ever need to follow in his footsteps again.

Activating his comm, he opened a private channel to his second. "Star Captain Quinn, sitrep, please."

"All systems go." Her voice brimmed with confidence. "Based on your recommendations, we have divided the Warriors into Stars and assigned 'Mechs based on their performance in training over our voyage."

"*You* have done an excellent job, Star Captain."

"It is nothing, my Khan. It is what we will do as Warriors that counts."

"*Aff.* And they will sing songs of this day."

"Hopefully, they sing them about our victory, rather than that of the Ghost Bears."

"It will be the Jade Falcons. It will always be the Jade Falcons."

"*Aff,* my Khan."

"The time draws near for us to charge into battle. We are ready."

"*Aff,* my Khan."

He switched his comm to talk to the two Trinaries he had assembled for this dire mission. "Jade Falcons," he said in a booming voice. "Here we are. This is what we have trained diligently for. This is our purpose. You all heard the negotiation for the Trial. The future of the Jade Falcons rest in our hands, and will live by our deeds here today. Fight with no mercy."

"Aff!" they all sounded back.

Jiyi had other thoughts on his mind, though, and ideas for how to make the best of the situation and take as many Warriors home as he could. "But! Remember this is a formal trial of honor. The Ghost Bears deserve our respect and admiration for meeting us in this arena of combat, outgunned though they are, even if they do not know it yet. Adhere to the rules of *zellbrigen* for as long as the Bears do. Take as many Ghost Bear bondsmen as you can. We will make Jade Falcons of them all, and make our *touman* strong, and our Clan the best and brightest once again!"

"AFF!" they screamed again.

They were ready.

And Jiyi felt it, electricity arcing through their affirmations on the radio.

This was where they were supposed to be.

Of that he had no doubt.

He wondered about the cadets he would bring home with him. Where were they right now? Were they watching the battle unfold, wondering why their future would be decided in such a way? Or were they eager to meet their fate no matter what came? At least they would leave to a good home, where honor and glory would meet them.

It would be an adjustment, no doubt, but the Ghost Bears had nothing left to offer them.

They simply did not know it yet.

Glancing at the countdown on his HUD, Jiyi knew it was time. "Let us ride out to meet them!"

And ride they did.

CHAPTER 24

PYKON RIVER DELTA
QUARELL
RASALHAGUE DOMINION
07 NOVEMBER 3151

Star Commander Dawn suddenly understood why she had trained so much in an assault 'Mech during their voyage. For the Trial, she had been assigned a *Turkina*, named for the first jade falcon tamed by a human, the first Khan of the Jade Falcons, Elizabeth Hazen. A powerful 'Mech weighing a full 95 tons, the *Turkina* boasted squat raptor legs below a wide clamshell of a torso section. Its arms were nothing but autocannons and extended-range particle projector cannons. Its pauldrons housed twin racks of long-range missiles. In short, she was lethal at long range and would pick off as many Ghost Bear 'Mechs as she possibly could.

That was her job.

That was her *rede.*

Her Khan had commanded her to go forth and win, and that is what she would do. There was no way she would fail in her duties. She had fought too long and too hard for it.

Dangling above her in her cockpit was her necklace. St. Jude danced at the end of the chain with every step her *Turkina* took. As the patron saint of lost causes, he had already delivered her into the ranks of Jade Falcon MechWarriors. If her luck held, he would deliver all of those *sibkos* into the same ranks. They would fight alongside her and for her Clan. They would make the Jade Falcons something to be feared again.

Though she wondered if Jiyi Chistu was interested in ruling through fear. It seemed as though the Jade Falcons were finding a new trajectory, soaring through the sky, and that would be all right by her, too. She had no desire to be feared, per se, but she did want to be respected, something she had never been in the paramilitary police. And as far as she could tell, the new way of the Jade Falcons *would* command respect.

"Assault Stars Talon and Claw," came the voice of the Khan. "This is your Khan, Jiyi Chistu."

Dawn's ears perked up. She had been assigned command of Assault Star Talon.

"You will be the center anchor of our tight formation. You will lead and you will obliterate every enemy 'Mech you see. You did the exercises, you were put through the paces. When they arrive, your job is to pick them off as efficiently as possible and demoralize them. I want them to feel as though the battle is already lost. That is how devastating you will be. We will adhere to *zellbrigen*, but keep close together. If they miss and cannot keep to one target, feel free to focus your fire as you have practiced. It will speed the Trial and serve our purposes."

"Aff, *my Khan*," Dawn said in unison with the Commander of Claw Star.

But in that moment, with the voice of her Khan in her ear and his hopes for the success of the entire Clan pinned to her Star, Dawn wavered.

The situation for the Jade Falcons was desperate. It had to be for a washout like her to be playing so pivotal a role. Nothing hit the idea closer to home than that of her being important. She had spent the last few years coming to terms with the fact that she would not amount to anything in the annals of the Jade Falcons. And here, *the Khan himself* was commanding her into what he had described as the most important battle the new Jade Falcons might face in the midst of their rebirth.

How did she get here?

What if she was not cut out for this after all?

What if she failed?

"You will do my will and you will succeed, *quiaff*?"

"Aff!" they said again. Dawn had to force the reply out of her suddenly dry mouth, but she answered nonetheless.

"That is an order. Defeat is not possible."

"AFF!" they said a third time, and this time Dawn believed it—no matter what role she would play, she would do her best.

The Khan clicked off the line for the Assault Stars and continued his rotation, offering his wisdom and his orders to the next group in line.

The *Falcon's Shadow* had dropped them all off in the swamps of the Pykon River Delta on the east side. To their left was the swamps of the Delta itself and the water beyond. To the right were the hills and forested areas that fed the river and swamp. In both cases, there was ample cover, save for the wide-open swamp that had been illuminated on their HUDs as a rally point. Covering the entire battlefield was a low morning mist, creating a visual barrier that made the terrain more difficult to read and made the enemy seem further away, when they could even see them at all.

When the Assault Talon and Claw Stars were finally given the order to move out, the rally point was exactly where they headed, with Dawn leading the way.

Watching the dots of the Jade Falcon 'Mechs following her on her map left Dawn just a little bit dizzy. This should not have been happening to her.

Stop thinking of your unworthiness, she told herself. *You have earned this. Your initial opportunity was robbed from you, and this is your chance at glory and redemption.*

This is the way to salvation.

Not just yours.

For the Jade Falcons, too.

"We have incoming," the Khan said from his *Gyrfalcon* at the back of the formation.

And sure enough, across the swampy field and reflected on her radar were small dots of Ghost Bears on the horizon, marching through the swamp to meet them.

Her HUD began identifying targets and showing their effective ranges. The Khan's wager had been correct, and things were coming together exactly as he had predicted. Before her were a group of small and light 'Mechs that would fall before the long-range Assault Star behind her.

It was just like the exercise. She had figured out how to handle this intuitively, and here it was unfolding in front of her.

"Assault Star Talon, this is Talon Leader," she said. "We are coming up on our rally point. Dig in and open fire as soon as you find the closest target. We are not claiming targets for our own glory. Today, all kills are for the glory of Clan Jade Falcon!"

"AFF!" her Star replied.

"Position," she called out as she dug into the swamp and began looking for targets, "marked and locked in."

And that's when her targeting computer notified her that the Ghost Bear *Rime Otter* leading the charge had come into range.

"*Rime Otter* sighted," she said. "Target locked. It is mine."

Dawn opened fire on the *Rime Otter*, leading with her PPCs. Under the withering fire of her *Turkina*, the *Rime Otter* practically vanished. The *Marauder IIC*s with her fired at their targets. The *Banes* each fired across the distance with their Ultra autocannons. The PPCs melted everything they touched, and the Ultra autocannons pulverized armored torsos and limbs. Not all of their shots hit or killed, but it was enough to make at least one grease spot of the first of the oncoming Ghost Bears. The legs and arms of the *Rime Otter* she fired at again fell forward, attached to the bare outline of what used to be its torso.

It did not even have a chance.

Behind the *Rime Otter*, a long-armed *Grendel* suffered the same fate at the hands of another in her cadre.

The Trial had barely begun, and the Ghost Bears had already lost two 'Mechs with minimal effort.

Dawn smiled.

It was a good day to be a Jade Falcon.

BEARCLAW TRAINING FACILITY
COPPERTON
QUARELL
RASALHAGUE DOMINION
07 NOVEMBER 3151

Alexis watched as the Ghost Bear 'Mechs at the front of the formation were obliterated one by one.

"They need to get out of there. They need to scramble," she said, but her voice was lost in the din of Ghost Bear Cubs watching their future vanish before their eyes.

With the incursion and Trial issued from the Jade Falcons, no one seemed to care or remember that the final match was determined to be a draw on points. The *sibkos* across Quarell had been given the day off from duties and training to witness their fates play out at the Pykon River Delta.

The Bearclaws sat in the common area of the training facility where they normally reviewed BattleROMs and watched the Trial of Position unfold alongside the co-champions, the Mektid Bears. The competition that had intensified through the hallways of the training facility had vanished entirely.

The war games were over, and they were all Ghost Bears now, watching the unimaginable happen before them. They all sat at rapt attention, watching their future play out helplessly before their eyes. Even Daniel had turned pale, gripping his stomach as he watched as though he had eaten something rotten.

Nothing had made Alexis more enraged than being a bargaining chip in some game between two Clans, and she imagined the rest of the assembled Cubs felt exactly the same way. The room raged in a river of anxiety, and she felt its choppy waters as though they were all about to drop off a waterfall at the end.

Thomasin heard her comment and offered a belated reply. "The Star Colonel will not let them keep the upper hand like this. He will scramble sooner than later."

"How could he have made such a ridiculous mistake in the first place?" Alexis said. She wasn't sure if she meant the Trial of Position, or the opening march that had cost the Star Colonel four 'Mechs right off the bat while the Jade Falcons had not even suffered a scuffed paint job on a single 'Mech. It was probably both.

"In our studies of Falcon tactics, it was said they used up close hit-and-run tactics, relying on extremely agile 'Mechs coming in fast. This is not any sort of Falcon formation I have ever seen. They are not fighting like I would have expected Jade Falcons to fight," Sophie said. "The Star Colonel is walking right into a murderers' row as though he did not expect it either."

"He should have expected anything if he was going to gamble with our lives," Alexis said.

Thomasin's gaze went hollow as he stared at the screen, but to Alexis, it seemed as though he looked beyond it. "I will not be a Jade Falcon."

"I do not think we will have a choice," Sophie said.

Alexis thought on that. "Don't we? Do we have to abide by the whims of the Star Colonel?"

Neither Thomasin nor Sophie had a response to that. To them, she imagined it was unthinkable, and completely against their *rede* to turn against their Clan's customs. But to Alexis, she was accustomed to doing anything she had to in order to survive.

Alexis glanced across the room at the Ghost Bear cadets, one by one. Not a single one looked happy about what they saw playing out on the vidscreen. Daniel, normally a complete bootlicker, looked ready to start a riot and throw up all at the same time. It would not have surprised Alexis one bit if Daniel just started puking right there all over the floor.

And then she looked over to Thomasin. His strong jaw and Ghost Bear features, all reminiscent of the Bekker bloodline he bore, seemed too staid to become a Jade Falcon. When Alexis looked over to Sophie and her cute button nose, bright brown eyes, and slender neck, she did not know if the life of a Jade Falcon could be possible for her. Not that she was too delicate—though Alexis did think that of her before she knew Sophie to be a Warrior and Ghost Bear cadet. Sophie was quiet and unassuming, and it let people underestimate her.

She felt, deep in her core, that neither of them wanted to be Jade Falcons. They were Ghost Bears first and foremost.

And Alexis thought of herself as one, too.

The same held true for every single bear cub in that den.

The Ghost Bears had suffered through their own problems since the vote, but there had to be something she could do to keep them all together and prevent the Jade Falcons from tearing their world completely asunder.

Right?

"We have to do something," Alexis found herself saying.

"What?" Thomasin said.

"We can help. We can fix this. Can't we? We don't have to let the Jade Falcons just win, do we?"

Thomas furrowed his brow. "Like it or not, this is an honorable Trial."

"They can just wager us away?"

"Aff."

"And we cannot do anything about it?"

"What would you do?" Thomasin asked.

Well—there was one thing. It would be difficult. It would get them into a lot of trouble if they were caught.

But if she could save her *sibkin* from the indignity of becoming Jade Falcons, she would do it.

"I have an idea," Alexis said.

CHAPTER 25

PYKON RIVER DELTA
QUARELL
RASALHAGUE DOMINION
07 NOVEMBER 3151

From the safety of his *Ursus II* at the rear of the Ghost Bear formation, Star Colonel Emilio Hall watched as his brilliant opening strategy crumbled before him. He had advanced a knight in front of the safety pawns, and saw it sacrificed needlessly to an opponent's belligerent queen in ways he had not predicted. He had already lost most of a Star, which was bad, but not insurmountable. He could still fix this, but his intent to fight against predictable Jade Falcons tactics flew south for the winter. These were unlike any Jade Falcons he had ever seen, and he needed to adjust his tactics accordingly.

"This is not the battle we thought we were getting into," he said. "Those Assault Stars will chew us to pieces and we must deal with them."

"We are on it," Star Captain Rand said from her *Kuma*. The growl of anger in her voice grated against his ears. But, true to her duty, she led the heavier 'Mechs from the forward-facing Stars in a break for the center of the Jade Falcon formation. "Watch that fire and get in range as fast as you can."

"The swamp is slowing us," MechWarrior Justin said.

"We will overcome," came the voice of MechWarrior Reinhart.

Emilio was grateful they were fighting on his side this time, and aiming their efforts at the Jade Falcons. He had not enjoyed being under their fire in Feldspar, and knew they were capable. Now they had the anger of their Star Captain, too, which made them twice as deadly.

These Falcons would learn to never poke a sleeping Ghost Bear.

Emilio saw a handful of Jade Falcon blips circling the perimeter, trying to cut the Ghost Bears off from the Delta in a flanking maneuver. "We cannot let them hem us in either. We want all of our options, and they cannot take any from us. Star Captain Mikaela, I will leave that to you to handle."

"*Aff*," Mikaela said, and a group of Ghost Bear blips peeled off to head in that direction.

"I am tagging these 'Mechs as heavies. A group of *Thunderbolt IIC*s and *Hel*s," said a MechWarrior Emilio's computer tagged as Hixson.

"Approach with caution, destroy with prejudice," Star Captain Mikaela said.

"*Aff*," came the response.

Chaos.

Chaos was before him.

It was not the decisive start Emilio wanted, but he would make it work as best he could. Scanning the battlefield, he wondered what he could turn to his advantage. The swamp land had done nothing for him and his Ghost Bears, as the Jade Falcons—except the ones trying to flank—had opted to stand still. Now it was working against his Warriors.

If it was not working for them, they needed to change the conditions of the battle and win by other means. *The best laid plans of Bears and men...*

Closer inland, away from the Delta, were hills and valleys and many trees they could hide in. They would need to pull back and make hit-and-run attacks and snipe from cover positions. "Ghost Bears, those not engaged with the Assault Stars of their center formation and those defending our flank, head for the trees and hills to the west and take up firing positions."

Dutifully, the Ghost Bears followed his commands. They would have to work together if they were going to overcome such an immediate deficit, but they could do it.

They had to.

They had no choice.

Emilio shifted his *Ursus II* to the left, changing trajectory and leading the rest of the 'Mechs into the cover of the terrain and swampy forests. The Jade Falcons might have divined their opening strategy better, but Star Colonel Emilio Hall still had many tricks up his sleeve. He had not been given command of the Fourteenth Battle Cluster for no reason

Khan Jiyi Chistu could not help but feel thrilled, watching the battle unfold from the command couch of his *Gyrfalcon* at the back of the Jade Falcon formation.

The Ghost Bears were in complete disarray, scrambling in three different directions while his Jade Falcons held their positions and herded the Bears exactly where he wanted them. So far, the losses were manageable. To his count, only two green dots on Jiyi's HUD had winked out, signifying the loss of only two 'Mechs. They were in an excellent position, and the Ghost Bear Star Colonel had played right into his hands.

"Assault Stars," Jiyi said, "eliminate every Ghost Bear 'Mech in firing range as long as they send 'Mechs at you. As soon as they reassess their strategy, we will determine the next course of action. And do your best to disable rather than kill. Again, we want to bring these Warriors home with us. They are honorable, and doing their part for the Ghost Bears. I am sure they will do their part for the Jade Falcons as well."

"*Aff*, my Khan," Star Captain Quinn said from her 70-ton *Flamberge*. He had left her in command of the second Trinary in their assault, though at the moment there was no need for the split command. He had everything under control until the Ghost Bears had exhausted their resources, throwing their 'Mechs like water against the rocks of the Jade Falcon shore.

When the fighting got more intense, Jiyi would definitely need to delegate more. But for the moment, as he listened to the battles being fought individually, he was confident. He had prepared for this since the moment he had left Sudeten, and drilled his MechWarriors with every contingency plan he could think of. If the Ghost Bears pulled a victory from the mess they were in, it would not have been due to lack of planning on Jiyi's part.

And he did not expect them to act dishonorably. The Ghost Bears were a lot of things—family-oriented, obstinate, slow to react—but dishonorable was not among them.

Jiyi oriented his *Gyrfalcon* behind the Assault Stars that anchored his position as he let the rest of the 'Mechs begin their flanking maneuver, wanting to keep an eye on the battle himself. He stuck close by in case something untoward happened, but with the assault Star screening him, he had no targets. He could have taken a larger 'Mech into battle, but *Emerald* was a place of power and comfort for him. There was nothing that could change that. *Emerald* simply felt like home. He could not have imagined his predecessor, Malvina Hazen, fielding any 'Mech other than her *Shrike* onto the battlefield. *Black Rose,* as she called it, had become a symbol of her ferocity. Granted, the *Shrike* was an assault 'Mech, and Jiyi's *Gyrfalcon* was a medium, weighing a mere 55 tons. But he had no problem surviving every battle he had ever fought in. And he would not die in this battle today. Of that he was sure. He had too much work left undone.

No, his survival was all but assured in his mind.

"They have engaged our Heavy Star in the south," Star Captain Quinn said.

"As they should," Jiyi replied. "Let us see how much damage they can do there without the range advantage."

"*Aff,* my Khan."

Jiyi split his attention between the immediate view on his screen of the Assault Star ahead of him, still without any losses, and the radar display on his HUD, giving him a shorthand view of the battle and the engagement zone. The *Thunderbolt IIC*s and *Hel*s flashed back and forth against the heavies the Ghost Bears sent against them. Lights winked off here or there.

The Assault Stars did their best against the oncoming forces, taking 'Mechs out as fast as they could arrange it. It would only be a matter of time until the assaults began taking losses, but for now, things were going well. It took so much effort for the Ghost Bears to even get in range, he could not imagine why they were still coming, unless it was pride—another thing that filled the Ghost Bears to overflowing.

"Carry on, Falcons," he said to those in his command. "Victory is at hand..."

Star Commander Dawn tracked the clumsy spray of laser fire from the enemy *Kodiak* and watched it hit three of her Star's 'Mechs and she understood the Khan's plan in keeping them so close together. She blasted it and called out to the rest of her Star, "Target the *Kodiak*! It just broke *zellbrigen*!"

"AFF!" they replied.

She fired her PPCs, but missed. Something was wrong with her targeting system. She had taken very few hits, but one of them had managed to damage her aiming system, and no matter how much she adjusted her aim, it was off from her visual sight. Wondering if her missiles would do better, she fired a battery of them across the battlefield and watched them explode in a checkered pattern across the charging Ghost Bear. *At least something works.*

The rest of the Star opened fire against the *Kodiak*. PPC blasts and laser blasts cooked armor off its arms and legs, just as the Khan had directed, but not enough to stop it. The *Kodiak* had enough time to aim a shot right at her with its large laser and Ultra autocannon. The laser ablated much of the armor from her left arm and the autocannon round smashed a hole right in the center of her torso. The flashing indicator lights on her armor flashed yellow over the arm and torso to reflect the damage. "Damn," she muttered.

Despite the dread in her belly and unsure feelings about her survival, her cognitive dissonance was enough that she had almost hoped to get through the engagement without a single bit of damage.

At least, that was how the Khan had made her feel about their odds. That they would arrive on the planet, blast the Ghost Bears, take the *sibkos*, and be gone in a matter of hours. Rarely did battles ever go like that, but Dawn had never been in one of this scale before.

"I am taking significant damage," Siamion called out. The 'Mech behind the *Kodiak* had challenged him as their next target.

The Ghost Bears had not adapted to their fighting style yet, though Dawn expected them to at any point. She was grateful for the respite, though. If the *Kodiak and* its compatriots had opened fire on her en masse, there would be little left of her 'Mech to lead the rest of the battle.

Siamion's indicators on Dawn's HUD shifted from green to yellow. And his left leg flashed red, noting the spot where he had taken the most damage. "Watch it, Siamion."

"I am doing my best, Star Commander."

Should she order them to pull back into the formation? Did her nominal command of the Star even give her the right to make such commands, changing the fundamental makeup of the formation the Khan had shaped them into? But then she realized it was decidedly her job to do so. There was no reason she would have been assigned a command, no matter how nominal, and not be able to use it. It was her judgement focused on this particular Star that would see them through the battle. There were six Stars fighting, three to each Trinary, and there was no way the Khan could keep track of all of them.

"Pull back," she finally said. "Withdraw and take a position to the rear of the formation."

Watching Siamion's 'Mech react to her commands and back up exactly as ordered, pulling back behind the main line, filled Dawn with awe. She had grown accustomed to controlling her own 'Mech, but seeing her ability extend to the 'Mechs of others filled her with a thrill she had not expected.

Command was real power.

And she had never really had it before.

It felt good.

"Natalya," Dawn said as she adjusted her own aim and took another shot at the *Kodiak* bearing down on them. "Watch your aim. We do not want this *Kodiak* to get any closer."

"*Aff,*" Natalya said.

Dawn's shots still missed the *Kodiak*, but Natalya's Ultra autocannon struck true. The shell hit the 'Mech's hand, exploding it into tiny bits of shrapnel and destroying the four medium lasers it housed.

"Good work, Natalya." A shot that did that much damage and eliminated that many weapons from an assault 'Mech was always a good thing.

"Thank you, Star Commander."

"Do we stand, Star Commander?" asked Maiden. "Or do we pursue?"

Looking at the dwindling number of Ghost Bears and the relatively small losses of the Falcons, it was an easy choice for Dawn, even if it took her a moment to express it. "As long as they come for us, we stand and fight, MechWarrior Maiden. If they turn to run, we reassess."

The 'Mechs coming toward her Star were screening the withdrawal of the other Ghost Bears heading west. Even then, only a few 'Mechs approached, leading with that challenge-broken *Kodiak*.

"My Khan," she said, feeling odd about being able to talk directly to the Khan for clarifications, "With most of their forces fleeing into the woods, what are your further orders for my Assault Star? Do we charge and gain ground, or stand sentinel?" Her voice almost wavered, but she held steady.

"I see the Bears fleeing to their dens, Star Commander Dawn. Let them go. We have a different plan for them. Focus your Star on eliminating those who come for your Star and take whoever you can as bondsmen. You are performing well, keep it going."

"*Aff*, my Khan."

Planted firmly in the swamp with her *Turkina*, Dawn felt like a steel fortress defense, attacking anything in range. But she had to take down the *Kodiak* first. For an assault 'Mech, the *Kodiak* was lightning-fast, maxing out at well over 60 kilometers per hour, at least a dozen more than her *Turkina*. But her *Turkina* had an advantage in that, just like its namesake, she could fly if she had to. And if Dawn needed to get through the swamp and change directions, that was exactly how she planned to do it. It would help minimize the effect of the sludge she stood in and keep her maneuverability up.

The *Kodiak*, as fast as it was, still struggled against the mud and muck of the Delta. Dawn understood why the Ghost

Bears had chosen this area, but it had turned into a detriment for them very quickly.

"I am still taking fire," Natalya said.

Maybe the Ghost Bears were targeting the Falcons more judiciously. The 'Mech behind the *Kodiak* had decided they were going to take down Natalya, come hell or high water.

Dawn did not have a moment to think or react as the *Kodiak* hit her again. Its Ultra autocannon round offered a thunderous *CRACK!* against her torso and the flashing lights on her display blinked from yellow to red. "Maiden, cover Natalya and let her get behind you. The rest of you, keep your fire on the *Kodiak*. More hits like that and my inner structure will be exposed, and I will be as good as dead."

"Aff," called Maiden and the rest of them.

If they could get through this without losses, it would be a feather in her brand-new Star Commander cap.

"I am going down!" Natalya yelled.

So much for no losses...

Natalya had crossed behind Maiden, but that opened up a different hole, and the Ghost Bears pounced on it, a salvo of missiles sailed toward the damaged *Bane.*

Dawn sighted it in her 360-degree viewscreen and watched the *Bane,* a devastating assault 'Mech with raptor legs and autocannon arms, lose integrity and stagger backward until it crashed into the marshy terrain in a huge splash.

"Damn it," Dawn growled.

She brought her eyes back to the *Kodiak* and fired her aim-addled PPCs again. A bright flash of azure light filled her screen; she had led far enough to the right to make up for the errant targeting. The PPC blasts cremated the *Kodiak* at the knees and dropped it, falling forward as it succumbed to all the damage it had taken.

Dawn exhaled, feeling the relief wash over her like a cool breeze in the heat of her *Turkina.* That *Kodiak* had been the only 'Mech that had taken shots at her. But she knew that feeling would be short-lived. The Ghost Bears still had five 'Mechs charging toward the Assault Stars, and had taken down three Jade Falcon 'Mechs total—two from Claw Star and Natalya from her own Talon Star.

But with the *Kodiak*'s cockpit intact, once the smoke had cleared and the mist of the battle had burned off some, Dawn would claim that Ghost Bear as a bondsman and bring them into the Jade Falcon fold.

But first, there was work to do.

"I claim the *Kuma* for my next target!"

"Aff, Star Commander!"

CHAPTER 26

PYKON RIVER DELTA
QUARELL
RASALHAGUE DOMINION
07 NOVEMBER 3151

Emilio called for those in his command to watch their fire. The cluster of Jade Falcon Assault 'Mechs anchoring their forward position were packed together like Ghost Bears huddling for warmth—not at all like Jade Falcons. The targeting carets of that cluster all bled into each other, and he wondered if a targeting computer would be able to tell them all apart. "Do not miss your shots!"

He knew what would come of such sloppiness, and he could not afford it. Especially not with the loadout of 'Mechs Jiyi Chistu had fielded for the Jade Falcons.

But it happened anyway.

MechWarrior Hamnet's lasers hit two different Jade Falcon 'Mechs with one blast. Then MechWarrior Andor did the same thing to a different pair of Falcons.

"Damn it," Emilio said as his open frequency chimed on.

Then the voice of Jiyi Chistu filled the cockpit of his *Ursus II*, full of swagger and certainty. "Star Colonel Hall, this is Jiyi Chistu."

"This is Star Colonel Hall," he said, cursing himself further under his breath. He knew what this would be about, and there would be nothing for him to protest. "We are a little busy here, so please make this quick."

"The rules of *zellbrigen* have been broken, Star Colonel, repeatedly. The Jade Falcons have met you with honor and called single challenges—"

"—and you have also clustered your 'Mechs together so tightly they can barely be seen as more than a single target." Emilio did not believe the argument held much water, but he had to try to dispute the Jade Falcon's claim. An all-out melee would not suit the fight for the Ghost Bears at all. Especially not if they caused it.

If Emilio were being honest with himself, he had hoped the Jade Falcons would have been the ones who had forced the melee, because then he could pounce on them and take the VaultShip and minimize the risk to the *sibkos*.

"I do not recall anywhere in the rules of honorable combat that dictate the proximity of my 'Mechs from one another, nor their need to move."

Emilio wanted to snarl back, but kept his composure. "We have met you in honorable combat, Chistu."

"And yet your 'Mechs have sloppy aim and cannot keep to their declared targets. I am now declaring this a melee, and the rules of *zellbrigen* are null. We will take bondsmen as we defeat them. I expect you to do the same."

"If that is your wish, but know that freed from the constraints of *zellbrigen*, I have many more tactical options at my disposal," Emilio bluffed.

"If it were to your advantage, Star Colonel, would you still be dickering here with me as such?"

Emilio had no response, nor did he need one. Jiyi disappeared from the open broadcast channel, back to his own devices and to command his own troops. And that left Emilio feeling off balance. The tension began in his temple and at the back of his neck and he had to suppress the anger he felt. Anger was not becoming of him, he knew he had to swallow it down and bury it in the snow of his heart.

His tactics had not worked, and the loadout he had chosen was woefully inadequate to meet the task against the Jade Falcons. The nullification of *zellbrigen* could be a gift, loss of honor be damned. He could reassess and redeploy.

Perhaps he had not been bluffing Jiyi Chistu after all. He just needed to determine what his next move was before it was too late.

He would not miss an opportunity again.

The future of these cadets depended on it.

BEARCLAW TRAINING FACILITY
COPPERTON
QUARELL
RASALHAGUE DOMINION
07 NOVEMBER 3151

Watching the shifting winds of the Trial of Possession, Alexis had never felt more like throwing up in her life, and she had been through high-G centrifuge training. The helplessness she felt was tempered by the fact she was putting her idea in motion, and it would begin with a whisper.

Alexis leaned forward and whispered in Anna's ear that a plan was being hatched, but she needed help to fix this.

"Mine?"

"Yes, Can I count on you?"

"Of course."

"There's more than that, but I need someone specific as well."

"Whose?" Anna asked quietly.

"Daniel."

Anna froze when she heard the name. Of course she would.

Alexis knew he did not want to be a Jade Falcon any more than she did. And if she could not count on him to stand up now, she knew he would never be counted on by anyone.

Thomasin and Sophie had both tried to talk her out of it when she had told them the plan, but when she gave them her reasoning, they did not argue.

"Do you trust me?" Alexis leaned even closer than she had before.

Anna nodded.

"And will you follow me?"

Anna nodded again.

"Then pass the word."

Anna nodded a third time. And, as Alexis leaned back, Anna leaned forward and passed the message along.

As the message spread, wildfire through her *sibkin*, she watched everything else *but* the Trial. The *Ursari* at the corners of the room watched the holoscreens and feed of the Trial with the same horror on their faces as the cadets. Even the Den Mother. Alexis figured it was good to know Star Captain Sasha Ivankova could feel *something* other than disdain. For the last month, Alexis had been convinced the Den Mother had only one mode, vindictiveness, aimed solely at her. The Star Captain kept her arms folded, standing by the doors at the far end of the commons area.

Another Den Mother, the one from Mektid Bears, stood at the other end at the doors there. The *Ursari* weren't specifically guarding the doors, but it certainly seemed like that could have been the case. There was also nothing that said that they could not move around or talk.

There was nothing formal about this assembly.

Alexis wondered if the *Ursari* were being lax because they thought there was no reason to discipline anyone for less than model behavior because there were drastically increasing chances that none of the cadets would be Ghost Bears for much longer. Why invest any further in the future of likely Jade Falcons? With the turns the battle had taken and the departure from honorable combat, it became more and more likely.

Someone close to the front row coughed loudly.

Yrsa. One of Daniel's Star from the final game. Alexis wagered she heard the message. And she was the last step on the way to Daniel, but she looked conflicted and turned to ask what Alexis assumed was a follow up question to clarify a point.

"Are you sure this is going to work?" Sophie leaned in and whispered to Alexis.

"It might not. But we have to try, *quiaff?*"

"*Aff,*" Sophie admitted.

"We obviously cannot leave it to the leadership." Alexis pointed up at the holoscreen where, as if to accentuate her point, another Ghost Bear 'Mech collapsed, toppling under the focused fire of the unleashed Jade Falcons. "They would give us all up without a second thought."

"They are already," Thomasin added to the conversation.

"They do not want to lose us, how could they? They would be set back a generation without us," Sophie said.

Alexis watched as Yrsa finally leaned over to Daniel, her lips so close to his ear Alexis could imagine the breath on her own ear as Yrsa spoke.

"He is not going for it," Thomasin said. But they only had the view of the back of Daniel's head and his posture. His arms were crossed, guarded. Every time he had turned around to see the countenance of those assembled, his face looked drawn with emotion.

"He will, Thomasin," Sophie said, and squeezed Alexis' hand. "He is a fool, but he is not stupid. This is our best chance."

"We cannot trust him," Thomasin continued.

"Perhaps not," Sophie told him. "But I trust Alexis. And you should, too. We will get through this and it will work. I would follow you anywhere, Alexis."

"I know," Alexis said, trying to tune out her *sibkin* and focus in harder on Daniel now that the message had been delivered.

He lowered his head, then pulled it back into a haughty laugh Alexis could hear from across the room. Daniel caught himself and covered his mouth to stifle the noise. Alexis held her breath as Daniel shook his head. Then her eyes widened when he stood up, pretending to stretch.

She had him.

Daniel turned and made as though he were doing a lap around the commons area, just to stretch his legs, but he caught Alexis' eye and cocked his head in the direction of the back of the room. Taking the hint, Alexis stood and headed to the perimeter to make a lap in the opposite direction.

Eventually, they both walked to the rear wall of the common area, meters away from any *Ursari* and with their backs to the wall.

"What do you want?" he asked finally, never taking his eyes from the holoscreen.

Alexis turned her head away from him and kept her voice low, doing her best to prevent it from looking like they were having an actual conversation. "We have to stop this."

"For once, I agree with you. But I do not see how we can."

"If you can create a distraction and let Thomasin, Sophie, and I make it out of here unnoticed, I will make it happen."

"Ha," Daniel said too loudly. He continued his derision. "You think I will just create a commotion here and let the three of you escape? They will hunt you down like dogs, Falcons or Bears, and you would be easy prey."

Alexis stopped herself from rolling her eyes and looked over to Star Captain Ivankova. She stood there severely by the far door, at rapt attention on the holoscreen. Then glancing up to the screen herself, she watched a Jade Falcon *Bane* take a blow to its leg, snapping it off and toppling it.

The room erupted into a cheer, and covered by the din, she continued her conversation, "Listen, I am not going to run. You do not like me, but I am a good Ghost Bear, and I care about my family. I do not want to be a Jade Falcon, and I know you do not either. I do not want *any* of us to be Jade Falcons. And the adults are unwilling to do anything about it, so we have to. So will you help or not?"

"What is your plan?"

"It would be better for both of us if you do not know." The plan was brazen, but Alexis had come to learn that the more brazen the plan, the higher the potential payoff. Maybe it came from her time in the streets. Maybe it came from her time as a Ghost Bear. Wherever it came from, that idea was her guiding light.

"Think I am going to betray you?"

"I know it is a possibility if your past actions are to be believed. But I am going to put my trust in you now. But if I tell you, it would only complicate things. Now, will you help, or would you doom us all to a Falcon's nest?"

Daniel thought about it as the cheers subsided, and the talking in the room fell back down to a dull roar.

He sighed heavily. "What do you need me to do?"

Alexis grinned.

Alexis sat back down between Thomasin and Sophie.

"Well?" Sophie whispered.

Alexis watched Daniel take his place back at the front of the room and sit down. "I gave him the one job that played to his ego and would allow us to leave."

"And what was that, exactly?" Sophie asked, her brow furrowed.

It was then that Daniel stood up in front and turned to the assembled *sibkos.* He bellowed in a loud and arrogant voice, "Fellow Bear Cubs, this injustice cannot stand!"

Sophie adopted a skeptical look and tone. "He is giving a *speech*?"

"*Aff.*"

"Star Colonel Emilio Hall has failed us!" Daniel raised his arms, orchestrating the crowd like a conductor. "And what can we do about it?"

The anger in the room rose.

"Cadet Daniel," the Den Mother said, "Sit down."

"*Neg*, Star Captain. We have to come up with a plan to resist this, and I am here to lead!"

As the *sibkos* grew restless in front of Daniel's goading, Star Captain Ivankova moved from the door and closer to the ringleader, leaving the door behind her unguarded.

"Now?" Sophie said, eager to help. They all were.

"Not yet," Alexis told her.

Daniel raised a fist. "We cannot let this stand! We will not let this stand! Who will join me?"

Their *sibkin* in the Bearclaws rose to their feet. They knew something was up, even if they did not know the exact details.

Alexis got to her feet and pulled Sophie and Thomasin with her. Sophie tried to move to the door, but Alexis stopped her. "Not yet." She looked over to the Mektid Bears, and saw they had not yet fallen into any sort of unrest.

The Den Mother reached Daniel. "Cadet Daniel," she said, "I understand your frustration, but you are on the path to being a proud Ghost Bear, a true *ristar*. Now act like it."

"What of you, Mektid Bears?" Daniel said, ignoring the Den Mother. "Will you put aside our difference and stand with the Bearclaws?"

And when the Mektid Bears stood, Alexis nodded. "Now."

The three of them crouched behind the crowd and made for the door the Den Mother had left to deal with Daniel. As they moved, Daniel glanced over at them and nodded briefly. The Den Mother's attention almost shifted to the door, but he interjected in time to draw her gaze back to him. "But Den Mother, are Warriors not to have some say in their fate?"

"You are not yet a Warrior, Bear Cub."

"But I will be, and I wish to be a Ghost Bear!"

The restless class of students shouted, "SEYLA!"

That's when Alexis made her move across the gap to the door. In a crouch, Alexis, Thomasin, and Sophie made it into the hallways.

"This way," Alexis said. "Straight for the communications center."

She waved them ahead and Thomasin sprang into the next corridor, running to the end of it. Sophie followed, with Alexis bringing up the rear.

The three of them were so in sync they kept time with their sprinting steps. They had trained for years together, and in their time coupling and getting to become better friends and members of each other's Ghost Bear family, they had practically grown to be one person.

In fact, Alexis thought of the three of them as spiritually linked in the same way the founders of the Ghost Bears, Hans Jorgensson and Sandra Tseng, had connected with the Ghost Bear that saved their lives. They had decided it would be better to die together than be separated by the system of the Clans, and they had come out stronger.

If anything, Alexis thought the rebellion she was leading to keep her friends in the Ghost Bears was the most Ghost Bear thing they could do: Die trying to keep their family together, if that's what it took.

CHAPTER 27

PYKON RIVER DELTA
QUARELL
RASALHAGUE DOMINION
07 NOVEMBER 3151

The smoke cleared and the rising sun burned off the rest of the fog, making the battlefield look completely different to Star Commander Dawn. Before her lay the wreckage of a half-dozen Ghost Bear 'Mechs. The rest had retreated to their dens and warrens, just as the Khan had predicted they would, taking cover in the trees and mountainous areas beyond.

The Khan had commanded his forces to stay put rather than pursue, let the Bears lick their wounds as the Falcons sought new members to bring into the fold of their reemergent Clan.

"None here," MechWarrior Bria said, standing over a downed *Ursus.* "Shot straight through the cockpit."

"Damn that Jade Falcon efficiency," Dawn said wryly.

"It is lethal." Bria maneuvered their *Bane* to the next 'Mech. "We do a thorough job."

"Aff," Dawn said, approaching the *Kodiak* in her *Turkina.*

The Ghost Bear assault 'Mech was face down in the swamp, water edging up around its back. Dawn hoped its crew compartment was still watertight, else the Bear inside would have drowned. Not the death she would wish on a Warrior of any stripe.

Using one giant, clawed foot of her *Turkina,* Dawn did her best to get the *Kodiak*'s cockpit out of the water. It was a complicated maneuver even for the most experienced MechWarrior, but Dawn managed it without tipping her own 'Mech over.

Swamp water splashed as she levered the *Kodiak* onto higher ground, draining all of the collected liquid down each line of damage in its chassis. The damage to its legs and arms was extensive, melted in misshapen ways. But Dawn was delighted to see the cockpit remained whole and unspoiled.

Keying her PA system, she called out to the powerless Ghost Bear pilot below her. "Ghost Bear MechWarrior. This is Star Commander Dawn of the Jade Falcons. You have fought honorably and well. Surrender now, and no further harm will befall you, for I will claim you as a bondsman for Clan Jade Falcon."

No sound or unusual sight issued from the *Kodiak*, but the pilot *must* have heard her. That is, unless they were knocked unconscious, which was not unheard of after a 'Mech the size of a *Kodiak* went down. Dawn thought MechWarriors never talked enough about concussions, but they were commonplace.

"Ghost Bear MechWarrior," she called out again, and this time it worked. The hatch at the top of the *Kodiak* separated from the rest of the 'Mech and opened. A Ghost Bear came out, hands raised. She was a tall, thick woman with long, red hair pulled into a bedraggled bun, looking very much like the Scandinavians that had colonized Rasalhague in the first place.

"What is your name?"

"Khodaverdi," she called up, her face dirty and sweat pouring from her body, sadness writ large on her face, "of the Ghost Bear Fourteenth Battle Cluster, Twenty-Third Battle Trinary."

"No longer," Dawn said. "As I told you, you are now my bondsman, and I claim you for the Jade Falcons."

"Aff." Khodaverdi looked around at the swamp before her, as far as the eye could see. "What? Am I just supposed to walk?"

"Aff. Head due north. This *Bane,* piloted by MechWarrior Bria, will accompany you."

"Aff, Star Commander," Bria said. "It will be done."

Just as the *Bane* lined up behind Khodaverdi, who had started taking long, wading steps through the marshy territory, Dawn heard a loud whistle outside her 'Mech, then a lock tone from sensor console. Looking up, she saw it: a salvo of missiles arrowing right for her, a spiraling trail of smoke leading from the wooded area. Dawn braced herself for the explosive impact just in time. About half the missiles hit her across her arm and torso, but the damage indicators did not move from their yellow warning state.

"Get out of here!" she told Bria.

"You are going to have to ride with me," Bria called out to Khodaverdi, offering a leg for her to climb onto. Once Khodaverdi secured herself to the handholds that normally carried Elementals, the Bane let loose and jogged back for the Jade Falcon Drop Zone.

Dawn covered their escape, firing into the woods, but she had no idea where the Ghost Bears were. This was exactly the problem the Khan had predicted in his training, but they had not been able to figure out a reasonable response to the woods. The water and the caves were easy enough to mitigate, but the fens that turned to trees eluded them.

"Incoming! They are breaking through!" Siamion said, the sound of explosions echoed through their transmission.

Dawn glanced over to see their 'Mech, an enormous *Marauder IIC*, buckle under the withering force of enemy fire. The fusillade perforated one of its arms, searing it off. Siamion's torso melted in a wave, boiling as it hit the water of the marsh. The *Marauder*'s nose took a face-full of missile fire and then a bright blue particle projector blast. The whole 'Mech keeled over.

"Siamion!" Dawn yelled into her comm.

But he was gone.

Dead.

Another in her command lost.

The reality of it felt delayed for a moment. Like she could not comprehend the loss, but then, after what felt like eternity trapped in a split-second, it kicked her in the chest like a mule.

Siamion was dead.

Dawn thought of those who had fallen so far, and wondered how the others were faring, Hosteen in particular. The life of a real MechWarrior was a constant ceremony of loss, and she hoped not to lose him, too.

Cycling through different enhancements on her viewscreen, Dawn sought one that would give her some advantage or indication of where the fire was coming from before she became the next casualty.

When a laser cut through the trees, she backtracked it and pinpointed a general area of where the enemy might be, so she pulled her trigger and pushed her firing stud all at once. Missiles snaked from her shoulder pauldrons and the blue flash of her particle projector cannons filled her screen. The missiles exploded against the trees in rapid succession and the PPC shot cut through others, but Dawn doubted she had hit anything of importance or consequence.

She wanted to rush in, to destroy those who had felled Siamion, but by herself that would be folly.

The more sensible move would be to pull back and regroup. She started walking backward, trying to get further out of her attacker's range. Firing her missiles and PPC in the same direction again, Dawn hoped she kept them worried and unsure of her position. Off balance and on the move, the same way she was.

More than anything, she hoped they ceased firing long enough to let her get away, back to the rallying point without losing any more of her Assault Star. There were only three of them left, including her. It would not do to allow her numbers to dwindle further.

"Let us go. We regroup with the others and head where the Khan commands!"

"*Aff!*"

And so they went.

BEARCLAW TRAINING FACILITY
COPPERTON
QUARELL
RASALHAGUE DOMINION
07 NOVEMBER 3151

The doors to the communication center were larger than the others down the central corridor. A great big set of double doors, fastened with an old-fashioned cross bar as though it were an old hunting lodge. Except the cross bar was metal, and it had an electronic locking mechanism keeping it in place. The only bigger doors in the facility led to the 'Mech bay.

"Okay." Thomasin looked the lock up and down. "What now?"

"I've got it," Alexis told them, reaching in for the locking mechanism. "Just keep a look out and keep the coast clear."

"Aff," Sophie said.

The pair of them pulled back to the cross hallway, keeping watch for anyone who might stop them. Though Alexis wondered why anyone would want to stop them, unless they *wanted* the Jade Falcons to steal them all.

Opening the panel for the lock, the wiring was not actually all that complicated. It worked with a simple keycard system. The lock should have been more than adequate to keep out the average cadet, but Alexis had been a thief.

A gifted one.

As gifted as she hoped to be as a Ghost Bear.

"I've almost got it."

"Hurry," Sophie said.

"I doubt they even know we are gone yet," Thomasin said.

"There are cameras everywhere," Sophie reminded him.

Alexis shushed them both. "They are watching the Trial, too. Now let's go."

Something *clicked* behind the panel, and she pressed the button that lifted the cross bar across the door. With a quiet *whir*, the door opened, revealing the communications room on the other side.

Alexis' eyes widened.

For some foolish reason, she had expected the communications center to be empty, but on the other side of the massive door were a pair of technicians in Ghost Bear blues, sitting at their stations, watching the Trial on a massive holoscreen against the far wall. Their backs were to Alexis and her cadre, and they had not noticed the door had opened. There was still a chance to make this happen, but they would have to be careful.

Alexis turned to Sophie and Thomasin and raised a finger to her lips. Then she pointed to each of them and then to either side of the room. They would cover the techs while Alexis found a way to enact the rest of her plan.

Thomasin nodded, his jaw tightened in resolve, and he tiptoed into the back of the room. Sophie followed close behind. As they passed the threshold of the door, Alexis knew they had reached the point of no return. What happened next would be forever in their record and would define them for the rest of their lives, however long that might have been.

As her compatriots moved into position behind the techs, ready to pounce, Alexis spotted the console she sought and crept toward it.

When they were all in position, she nodded.

And they sprang forward...

PYKON RIVER DELTA
QUARELL
RASALHAGUE DOMINION
07 NOVEMBER 3151

Jiyi watched from the safety of his *Gyrfalcon* and the relative comfort of his cooling suit as his Jade Falcons returned with new recruits from the Ghost Bears. The heat in his 'Mech had not required much supervision; while he ached to get into battle himself, he knew he needed to be careful. They would replenish their *touman* with veterans and cadets alike, and it would be to their benefit, but only if their strategy came off flawlessly and they were victorious in the Trial.

The Khan guarded the rally point and watched his 'Mechs gather around, ready for him to direct them to the next offensive as the battle shifted. The early losses of the Ghost Bears boded well, but Jiyi would not count them out yet. The Ghost Bears would put up a fierce fight, especially now that they had been bloodied, and would not relent until they had been vanquished.

"They are on the move!" one of his Star Commanders called over the comm. "Do we pursue?"

"Aff," he said. "Give them no quarter, and do not hesitate to focus fire. Take them down as fast as you can."

"*Aff,*" replied the Star Commander.

But then the radio squelched, and a new voice spoke, "Jiyi Chistu of the Jade Falcons, do you hear me?"

Checking the dials and readouts on the console below him, it was a frequency-wide broadcast, just as he had sent out to make his own challenge. The voice sounded as though it belonged to a young woman, and the hurried desperation told him everything he needed to know about her state of mind.

He adopted a curious tone for his reply. "This is Jiyi Chistu of the Jade Falcons, to whom do I have the pleasure of speaking?"

"I am Cadet Alexis of the Bearclaws *sibko,* broadcasting from our Den in Copperton."

Jiyi's face scrunched in confusion. "Star Colonel Emilio Hall, I imagine you are behind this. What is going on here?"

But Hall had no response, maybe he could not hear it?

"I am not acting with the permission of the Star Colonel, but as a member of the Rasalhague Dominion and a Clan cadet, I have the right to call for a Trial of Refusal on behalf of all of the *sibkos* in your wager."

Jiyi grinned. He had to hand it to this kid—she was bold. "The political rights of Dominion citizens do not apply to Jade Falcons and so I must refuse your trial, Little Bear."

Star Colonel Emilio Hall barged in on the line. "Cadet, what is the meaning of this?"

"We do not wish to be the subject of this Trial, and wish to determine the outcome for ourselves."

"Little Bear," Jiyi said, "I understand your feelings and even admire them, but leave this to the real Warriors."

"I will do no such—" the line from the open broadcast went dead.

"Jiyi Chistu," Star Colonel Emilio Hall picked up over the static. "Let us continue unimpeded. My apologies for this interruption."

Jiyi laughed. "Let us continue. May the best Clan win."

BEARCLAW TRAINING FACILITY
COPPERTON
QUARELL
RASALHAGUE DOMINION
07 NOVEMBER 3151

"It is no surprise to me to find you here like this. But you are caught red-handed," Star Captain Ivankova said to Alexis. "I think you will end up going with the Jade Falcons even when we win the Trial of Possession. You will be much better suited there. Turn around. Now."

Alexis turned around. Her microphone had gone dead. Cut off from another part of the facility.

In the next row of consoles, the techs were tied up with their mouths bound and held down by Thomasin and Sophie.

All three of them rose slowly and raised their hands in surrender.

Ivankova stood in the only doorway, blocking any escape Alexis could choose. Behind her were a score of Ghost Bears and She was well and truly caught.

"They should never have put you in a *sibko*." Ivankova stepped closer to Alexis, getting right in her face. "You are not Ghost Bear material. We all know it—and you know it, too."

But Alexis had had enough. If she was going to get flunked out of her *sibko*, she would tell Ivankova what she really thought. There was nothing left to lose.

"I'm more Ghost Bear than you, Star Captain," she said. "And you know it."

Ivankova smirked. "Enlighten me, thief. You cannot even speak properly. What makes you think you could live in our society and actually become a Warrior?"

"You think a lack of contractions are the mark of good Ghost Bear? Speaking without them is a show. A mask. The heart of a Ghost Bear is in family, and that's something you haven't understood for years. You treat the kids under your charge like garbage. You don't respect me or any other freeborn, as though that matters. It has not mattered to our Khan for as long as I've been alive, and by all accounts, she is as set in the old Bear ways as you. You despise me because I'm better in so many ways than so many of your precious Trueborns, and it pisses you off."

Ivankova snarled. "The Ghost Bears pulled you off the streets, gave you a home, and this is the respect you give us?"

Alexis locked eyes with Ivankova. "*Us?* There is no 'them' or 'us,' Den Mother. And that's what you do not understand. I *am* a Ghost Bear. I have been since the day I joined the Bearclaws. And you were too stubborn to see it."

"There is more to being a Ghost Bear than being in a *sibko* or learning to be a MechWarrior."

"And there is more to being a Warrior than your rank. You are just a bully. All the Ghost Bears are, if you think you're a fine example."

"You insolent whelp. You will pay for this." Ivankova's eyes cast over Thomasin and Sophie. "And you two, what do you have to say for yourselves? You ought to have known better."

Sophie straightened in defiance. "You are a bully. You deny the talent in front of you, and you do not care about us. You never have."

The look on the Den Mother's face told Alexis she had underestimated Sophie, too. Just because she was small and quiet, no one ever assumed she was going to be the one to cause a problem. But a fierce fire burned within her.

The Den Mother slowly shook her head. "How dare you. Everything I do has been for the benefit of you all. I am your Den Mother, that is my oath and my *rede*."

Thomasin picked up where Sophie left off. "Then why have you done nothing to stop this Trial?"

Ivankova's straight and severe posture deflated almost imperceptibly. By millimeters. Weary. "You have no idea how the real world works. You are cadets, and you still have so much to learn. Do you really believe there is anything I *could* do to stop this?"

Alexis had no answer to that. And even if she had, the Den Mother continued with a sneer. "None of us can interfere with an honorable Trial of Possession. It is not the Clan way. It is against our *rede,* and your thoughts and deeds toward deleterious effects prove I have failed in training you somehow, and you have not learned. My discipline with you three has clearly been far too lax. I will contemplate your punishment as you wait in the brig."

Ivankova stepped aside, and the *Ursari* behind her flooded into the room, grabbed Alexis and her companions in tight grips, and took them away.

CHAPTER 28

PYKON RIVER DELTA
QUARELL
RASALHAGUE DOMINION
07 NOVEMBER 3151

Star Colonel Emilio Hall found the losses of the last hour incomprehensible.

The loss of *zellbrigen* in the Trial was a blow, to be certain, but perhaps it was a gift, too. He needed to find a new strategy, and fast. They would not last long hiding in the forests and caves. They needed to start evening the odds, and if they did not have to deal with individual challenges anymore, that opened a larger array of options for him.

The Jade Falcons had not fought like any Emilio had ever heard of or encountered. As he began parsing the data he had collected over the course of the battle, he realized they fought like he would fight if *he* were in *their* position. He was not facing the average, Mongol Doctrine Jade Falcon and devotee of Malvina Hazen. He faced Jade Falcons that fought against Ghost Bears with the knowledge of how Ghost Bears fought, and had adapted to their tactics. They were not the brutal Mongols everyone was led to believe Jade Falcons were, and assuming so was a mistake that would weigh heavy on his head. If he lost, Rand would immediately challenge him to a Circle of Equals. These Falcons were something else entirely. And when one spent their time studying an enemy to counter their attacks, it would always do well to study the *correct* enemy.

"*Stravag,*" he said.

Callisto rumbled beneath him as he weaved a path through the forested area beyond the marshlands of the Pykon River Delta. He needed a more complete picture of what was happening before he could launch an effective counterattack. The Jade Falcons could catch him by surprise once, but they would not do it again.

"Mikaela, sitrep."

"We are falling back as ordered, but we lost more than a Star against their flanking force of heavy 'Mechs. *Thunderbolt IICs* and *Hels*. They came loaded for Bear."

The Star Colonel suppressed a groan, thinking about what commands to give them. He needed to take the early advantage from the Jade Falcons and create a scenario more suitable to the 'Mechs he had insisted the Ghost Bears field. But he had already lost more than half a Trinary. There would be no more opportunities for him to be caught unawares. "*Aff*, they did, but that does not mean we cannot be ready for them. Take to the trees and the hills beyond. We will make them come to us this time, in places where their range and firepower will mean less, and it will be a completely different situation."

"As you command, Star Colonel."

Emilio switched channels on his radio and dialed it in to his second. "Star Captain Rand. This is Star Colonel Hall, come in."

"I copy, Star Colonel." Her voice was formal and curt, her anger palpable.

She did not say it, but he knew she blamed him for what happened.

Of course she did.

Emilio blamed himself as well. But that sort of anger was not going to help any of them, and it was not going to help win a battle.

"Sitrep."

"There is a Star in the woods screening our—" Rand struggled to find the right word or phrase through her barely contained rage. "—our change of position. We are setting up where we can along the way, but we have no final destination."

Emilio expanded the map of the area on his viewscreen and chose the place where they would make their stand and change the course of the battle: a large bowl just over the next rise beyond the trees. If he could position his 'Mechs there, he would have rocks to his back, and he could keep his guns aimed at the ridge so the Jade Falcons would no longer have any advantage with range. They could snipe Jade Falcons one at a time as they showed their heads. They would have to focus their fire, but with Chistu declaring an end to *zellbrigen,* it made sense as the best strategy available.

"I have dropped a pin on your map; this is your waypoint. Bring your Warriors there. If there are suitable caves and outcroppings, split off 'Mechs to hide in them. We can launch an attack from their rear if the concealed Warriors can go unnoticed."

"*Aff.*"

"And be sure to keep the suppressing fire up from the forest. We do not want to let them have an easy advance."

"*Aff.*"

Her answers were curt, with an edge that could have cut Emilio if she had been standing in front of him. She harbored anger toward him, and he understood, but he could not think of any way to mitigate that at the moment. As long as she followed his orders, that would have to be good enough. They could have this out afterward—assuming they both survived the Trial.

Emilio always preferred Warriors that followed him because they wanted to, because they believed in him, because they believed in the Ghost Bears. He hated this strain of obstinance, strife, and divisiveness that had grown from a tiny crack to a chasm inside the Fourteenth lately. It had started long before the vote. It had been a streak inside the Ghost Bears as long as he could remember. Even before the Freeminders had risen and been absorbed. No, it was really the founding of the Clan. Being a family meant disagreeing with each other in ways that could hurt sometimes.

Perhaps it was just the Ghost Bear way.

It happened when no one was looking, and no one had quite realized it until it was too late.

But Emilio felt it.

They were coming undone somehow.

Frayed at the edges.

Or maybe that was just how the battle made him feel. He could not lose those *sibkos.*

Switching back to the wide—but encrypted—Ghost Bear frequency, Emilio kept his fingers on the pulse of the chatter.

"Falcon down," one MechWarrior said. Emilio's computer tagged them as Timothy, Star Commander of the 'Mechs defending the forest, laying down the suppressing fire that covered the Ghost Bear change in venue.

It was working. The Falcons were converging on the path he wanted them to take, he was leading them right where he wanted them to be, and they were moving more slowly than he would have wanted to if he were in their position.

They would whittle away at these Falcons and still leave with victory, the riches of VaultShip *Gamma*, and the final destruction of the last remnants of the Jade Falcons.

For as happy as he was at those prospects, that grim thought of the fraying Ghost Bears kept Emilio from smiling.

He would have to consider what to do about that at a later time—for now, he had a battle to win.

"Falcon down!" a voice said over Jiyi Chistu's command channel—the last sound he wanted to hear.

He could not afford to lose *any* of his Warriors. Adding more to the loss would only make his gambit a higher price than he wanted to pay. Yes, Jade Falcon Warriors should want to die in battle, but those battles should be in conquest, for glory, not merely cobbling the Clan back together.

He vowed not to waste the sacrifices of the Jade Falcons who had come with him and spilled their blood on Quarell. "Star Captain Quinn, sitrep."

"We have pulled a number of bondsmen from the wreckage of the initial assault, and are bringing them back to the rally point. The Assault Stars have pulled back to cover those returning with new Jade Falcon Warriors. The Ghost Bears continue to snipe from the trees."

"Advance slowly," Jiyi said, weighing his options. Then, he remembered the training exercises. One MechWarrior stood out in his memory. Jiyi switched frequencies on his radio, to one of the more mobile, mixed Stars in his *touman*. "MechWarrior Hosteen."

"*Aff*, my Khan."

"The Bears have created a den of the forest. Take the Point of Salamanders from your Star into the trees."

"*Aff*, my Khan." His voice sounded nervous, unsure of where this was leading.

"It is not a suicide mission. Your job is simple. Burn it down."

A trill of delight entered the MechWarrior's voice. "*Aff*, my Khan."

Hosteen had been at the rallying point in his *Nova*, a fast 'Mech for its 50 tons, hardly more than a frame with a dozen medium lasers strapped to it, ready to melt down even the strongest 'Mechs and thickest armor. The Salamanders were the chosen battle armor of a Point of Elemental infantry Jiyi had brought , wagering their weapons would be useful and, indeed, they had been. They were old and scorned; the Elementals who piloted the Salamanders did so begrudgingly, but they had their uses. His predecessor had used the battle armor and their flamers to torch cities, burning everyone alive and reducing places to ash while the residents fled the flames in terror. Jiyi found the destruction of a single forest on the path to victory a much more honorable use of the Salamanders.

Now Hosteen raced his *Nova* by Jiyi, the entire Point of Salamanders perched atop the 'Mech. Jiyi was pleased at how quickly they had sprung into action. As they charged up the initial incline and reached the top, the Ghost Bears began firing at them from the trees.

On one hand, Jiyi was delighted to see the Bears changing tactics to match his strategy, but it was also going to make his life more difficult. Hosteen was taking fire from at least four different angles, and Jiyi could just imagine what the BattleROM footage would look like. They were concentrating on him alone, and carving up his armor. He would have to do something drastic to even make it to the tree line.

Before Jiyi could say a word, Hosteen hit his jump jets, and the pummeled *Nova* soared into the air. Lasers shot from the trees missed, burrowing into the hillside or flying high into the air. The *Nova* didn't quite soar like a Falcon—it didn't have the wings like a *Gyrfalcon* or a *Shrike*—but the idea was similar and just as effective.

Jiyi watched in awe as, when the *Nova* reached the apex of its jump, the Salamanders hit *their* jump jets, flying even higher over the fray and far out over the cover chosen by the Ghost Bears.

"Brilliant." Understanding their plan in a heartbeat, Jiyi felt confident both that it would work, and that it was safe enough to follow. "Jade Falcons, to the ridge. All of us. We move in force to sweep in behind them."

Looking out his cockpit, he saw Hosteen's battered *Nova* land hard at the edge of the trees, one of the Salamanders still gripped tight to his leg.

A laser fired from the safety of the woods scored the *Nova*'s front, leaving a molten gash on the tip of its nose right beneath the cockpit. That didn't stop Hosteen from opening fire into the woods.

Another laser cleaved the still-attached Salamander in two, dropping most of the armored Elemental from the *Nova*, though its magnetic claws still kept its legs stuck to the 'Mech.

A gruesome, bloody sight, but Jiyi could not look away.

As if to avenge their fallen comrade, the rest of the Salamanders began dropping into the trees. The 'Mech and Elementals began laying waste to everything around them, medium lasers and flamers blazing.

The Ghost Bears fired back, taking another Salamander out. Others fired at the advancing Falcon forces, but their aim was obscured by the conflagration and most of the shots missed. Missiles poured out from the smoke. The Salamanders edged further in, igniting more trees, while the *Nova* stood at the edge and fired in, felling trees with his lasers to rob the Ghost Bears of even more cover. The Ghost Bears focused in on the *Nova*, cutting its arms to ribbons, but the fire became less concentrated as the Bears switched targets to the Salamanders wreaking havoc on the black and white trees, setting the whole place ablaze.

Flames licked the trees and a column of white smoke wafted up into the air in an ominous column.

It was working.

Another laser flash-melted the armor over the *Nova*'s left knee actuator, spilling slag on the ground. Hosteen could not take many more hits.

In the shadow of the flickering flames, Jiyi knew he had to do more and push forward faster. According to the dots on the HUD's mini-map, there were only three Salamanders left, but they were getting deeper and deeper into the thicket, burning everything. There were no blips for the obscured Ghost Bears, so they must have either fled or died in the fire.

Jiyi would be happy with either result, as it meant his forces could continue their march to victory.

"Jade Falcons, this is our time. Through the fire we will be reforged, reborn like an emerald phoenix. We march to the doom of the Ghost Bears and the future of our Clan. Will you follow me?"

"AFF!" his Jade Falcons bellowed.

Jiyi led the charge in his *Gyrfalcon* through the flames. He dodged some of the Ghost Bear wreckage and wondered where the rest were hiding. They had found safety by pulling back, and it was incumbent on the Jade Falcons to rob them of that safety.

More missiles turned and twisted through the smoke, so fast Jiyi could not track where they had come from. They sailed past him and crackled against the 'Mech beside him—a hefty *Turkina* his computer marked as Star Commander Dawn. The missiles did little damage to her armor. The *Turkina* was a stout 'Mech, and it would take more than that to drop her. The flayed *Nova* of MechWarrior Hosteen limped proudly but impotently on his other side for one more step before it collapsed in the trees.

Danger lay ahead. For him and his MechWarriors.

And he had superior numbers and tactics. But for as happy as he was at that prospect, the grim thought of the Jade Falcons becoming annihilated kept Jiyi from smiling.

He would have to consider what he could do about that later—right now he too had a battle to win.

CHAPTER 29

Star Colonel Emilio Hall pushed forward, working to create a gauntlet for the Jade Falcons to pass through. The Ghost Bears would chip away at the opposing force and leave them with nothing. And when they reached the final ridge, it would be over. He had learned in his study that practically all offensive action is indirect, and every agile maneuver and feint were put in place to draw an opponent into a scientific plan.

Glancing down to all the blips on his map—each place they left a Ghost Bear in wait—he felt more and more satisfied about his plan. It was a murderer's row of 'Mechs, all tucked away in spots that would allow them to strike the passing Falcons as they pursued the bulk of the force down the ravine, over the ridge, and into the bowl beyond. As the Jade Falcons passed through his crucible, the Ghost Bears would focus on the biggest, longest range 'Mechs first, robbing them of their advantage by the time they reached the ridge.

The Falcons still had so much of the range advantage, since they had brought such large 'Mechs. After retreating through the forest, Emilio worried they would still be able to snipe the Ghost Bears as they built the trap. Time was short, but he was confident his Ghost Bears would see it through and ensure that the *sibkos* stayed on Quarell.

"They are coming through the thicket!" MechWarrior Reinhart called out. "Or what is left of it."

Reinhart had the first hiding position in the chasm, ready to strike once the Jade Falcons passed. He would halt the advance, at least for a moment, and then the next 'Mech would step out. Gurdel.

This was it.

The plan was sound.

It held close to everything he believed about tactics and strategy. The tenets of his training as a Ghost Bear. His study of Jeet Kune Do and the other ancient martial arts. Everything.

It was time to execute it—and the Jade Falcons with it.

"Each of you hold the line!" Emilio called out. It would serve to keep the Falcons off balance, jumping at shadows and unsure of where the next attack would come from. "We will beat them. Just wait to strike until the time is right!"

Emilio watched as the lead Jade Falcon 'Mech, a *Gyrfalcon*, stepped out of the flames, flanked by larger 'Mechs—a *Bane* and a *Turkina*—on either side. The Star Colonel was not facing the right way to fire upon them, but all he had to do was lead them through the ravine and get them to follow. They still had an advantage with their numbers, but it was dwindling. He would beat them back to a standstill.

The *Gyrfalcon* jumped forward, and the two assault 'Mechs to either side of it stomped ahead. Then, through the smoke and flames, more 'Mechs stepped through.

"This way!" Emilio said. "We will take them!"

He led the majority of his 'Mechs to the top of the ridge. They would retreat into the bowl, then turn and make their stand, giving them the cover they needed until the Falcons broke through the gauntlet and crested the ridge themselves. Then the Ghost Bears would blast them with everything they had from all sides.

Taking one last look at the Jade Falcons marching through the flames, Emilio knew heading over the edge and down into the shallow valley was the right move, but it still felt a little bit like retreating.

"Over the top!" he called to his Ghost Bears, and they followed.

The formation came down the bowl's slope and Emilio lost visual on the battle. But he heard the fighting start.

"We have one 'Mech down! A *Bane*," Reinhart said.

"They are stopping to fight," Gurdel said.

Emilio pulled his line down to the center of the bowl and turned them around, ready to blast the first Jade Falcon to show its face.

"Another down!"

"Gurdel is out!"

Emilio glanced down at his control panel and saw Gurdel's dot wink out.

The rest of the battle sounded like a chorus of shouts as they spoke to and over each other about what was going on so Emilio could be ready, along with the rest of the Ghost Bears assembling their line and aiming at the lip of the rise.

"They are marching forward again."

"Let loose with the next phase."

"A *Thunderbolt IIC* has fallen."

"So has a *Hel*!"

"Three Elementals are down!"

"The rest are running!"

Would the Elementals try to flank the Ghost Bears? Or were they simply leaving the battle since they had outlived their usefulness in this particular conflict?

"Why are you firing on Elementals?" he asked. "Attack the long-range targets, those were your orders."

"Aff," they all replied after the reminder.

He knew how difficult it was to see the larger picture sometimes, and Emilio hoped he had not lost sight of that bigger picture, too. It would have been easy to do, waiting at the bottom and not seeing anything with his own eyes. But he kept tabs as best he could.

His command channel chimed, and he switched over, keeping an eye on the transponders on his console. It was Star Captain Rand, who stood at his side in her *Kuma*, guns aimed up and ready for the attack. "This had better work, Star Colonel."

"It will," he assured her. "Is there anything else?"

"I wanted to let you know if we lose these *sibkos*, I am holding you personally responsible."

"That is something else we have in common, Star Captain." Emilio winced when he saw another Ghost Bear blip on his dash disappear. But the data showed the gauntlet of Bears in their dens, each leaping out to chew through the Falcons, were sufficiently evening the odds and wearing their opponents down.

"I will stand by you now, Star Colonel," Rand said. "But I *am* warning you."

"We will not fail, Star Captain."

"With all due respect, Star Colonel, we had better not."

Star Commander Dawn pivoted to her right just as another Ghost Bear 'Mech came out of the rocks and foliage to attack just ahead of her. A *Kodiak*.

They had held their assault 'Mechs for the end.

"Another assault, marked and locked," Dawn called out, dragging her aiming reticle across the *Kodiak*'s torso. A lock tone sounded, and she pulled the trigger and hit the firing stud. Her autocannons barked and spat shells across the distance, and her particle projector cannons exploded in brilliant blue light, all of them hitting the *Kodiak* square.

"Keep on them," Khan Jiyi Chistu said over the comm. "All forces on the *Kodiak*. They think to whittle us down, but we work together, *quiaff?*"

"*Aff!*" Dawn repositioned and aimed again as the *Kodiak* chose her as its target. Its claws rose up and its golden lasers fired in her direction.

Dawn was relieved to find most of the lasers had missed, and quietly thanked St. Jude for the help with her lost cause. A few of the lasers had cut into her 'Mech's left arm, but the damage was too slight to add to her worries. She would live to fight another day, or at least to fire another shot.

She launched a salvo of missiles at the *Kodiak*, then fired her autocannons again, worried she was going to run out of ammo sooner than later. It was the constant problem of a target-rich environment and a 'Mech dependent on ammunition-based weapons. Before this engagement, Dawn could not have imagined a scenario where she *could* have run out of ammunition.

The *Kodiak* convulsed with the shots, spraying chunks of armor across the rock face behind it. More missiles came in to hit it, and a battery of lasers cut into it, tracing a line down its arm and torso, melting armor and exposing its under-layer. But it was not out for the count yet, and riposted with its Ultra autocannon.

In a blink, the shell whizzed right by Dawn, and she could not believe her luck—until she realized the *Hel* behind her had taken the hit and dropped. The *Kodiak* had not been aiming for her, and Dawn had been so wrapped up in the situation she had forgotten she was not the only target in the milieu. Firing her PPCs at the *Kodiak,* she hoped she could take it down once and for all, but she was not that lucky. One of the shots missed, impacting against the rock of the chasm behind the assault 'Mech. The other one hit the *Kodiak*'s shoulders, where it kept its short-range missiles.

Dawn did not know if her shot had made the *Kodiak*'s SRMs go haywire or if the 'Mech pilot thought it was the perfect time to fire them, but missiles launched from the 'Mech in three different, twisting directions. Some of the missiles crackled against Dawn's *Turkina*; another about-faced backward into the rock wall and exploded against it. A third sailed off into the pack of Jade Falcons somewhere, and she lost track of it.

The number of yellow lights on her damage readout increased, and several were threatening to turn red.

Dawn could not take much more damage, but she so badly wanted to stay in the engagement. More lasers and missiles crashed against the *Kodiak*.

Dawn pulled her trigger again and fired her autocannon at it. Direct hit.

The shell blasted through the *Kodiak*'s center mass and it staggered back, lost its balance, and fell back against the rocky wall it had stepped away from.

Dawn sighed in relief.

One more test passed.

And one more minute of surviving this battle, the most important of her life. She wondered if that would be *every* battle from now on. Each would be the most important, the most dire, the one that could cost her life, the one that could make or break the glory of her Clan.

Dawn pushed her *Turkina* forward, closer and closer to the drop-off into the bowl. Then she got an idea, and a 'Mech with a machine gun would be perfect. She looked down to see if anyone from her Star had survived, someone she could give the order to.

But they had all succumbed. Only she remained.

Another Ghost Bear 'Mech stepped out from the side of their phalanx, slowing them in their ambush. But it did so right behind Dawn's firing arc.

A second 'Mech, a *Mad Dog Mk III*, stepped out of a cave further ahead and Dawn had a choice to make. The closer 'Mech could do much more damage to her, and it had stepped out on her already damaged left side. But it would almost certainly get a hit on her as she turned around, which would also open her up to the *Ursus II* up ahead. Did she fire at the *Ursus II*? Or turn around?

Without another thought, Dawn went for the *Ursus II*. The Jade Falcons behind her would take care of the *Mad Dog*. They would have to. She only hoped they did before she was destroyed.

"I am on the *Ursus II*," she called out. "The *Mad Dog*, get the *Mad Dog*!"

She stepped forward, hoping to make herself a more difficult target for the *Mad Dog*, and waited for a missile lock tone. As soon as its comforting beep sounded, she launched her last battery of missiles at the *Ursus II*, pummeling the 'Mech in a series of explosions.

She smiled and wished she could wipe the sweat from her brow through her neurohelmet.

The *Ursus II* was hurt, but was not going down that easy.

It fired its pulse lasers at her, and she could not tell if it missed, or if it was aiming at a 'Mech behind her.

Her eyes darted up to the St. Jude medallion and she thanked it again. Lost causes seemed to be her specialty now, and they were partners in the task of her staying alive through this chaotic conflagration.

Another salvo of missiles sailed from behind, right over Dawn's head, and detonated across the *Ursus II*, staggering it.

From the sky, a *Gyrfalcon* landed right next to the *Ursus II* and opened fire with both extended-range lasers, cutting right through the Bear's damaged torso from both sides.

Dawn unleashed another pair of particle projector cannon blasts, which sealed the deal.

The *Ursus II* collapsed into pieces.

"Now for the *Mad Dog*," Khan Jiyi Chistu said from his *Gyrfalcon*. His 'Mech, *Emerald*, pivoted around to aim at the *Mad Dog Mk III* beside her with its lasers.

Dawn stepped back and turned, hoping she could catch the 'Mech in her arc at some point. The Khan's cyan lasers cut into the *Mad Dog*'s side.

The *Mad Dog* continued to aim up at Dawn with its Ultra autocannon. A shot in the wrong place with that beast, and Dawn would be out of this fight. But all she could do was hope the rest of the Jade Falcon 'Mechs could take it down before it could take a shot.

Not even St. Jude could help her with that one.

The report of the *Mad Dog*'s cannon brightened her viewscreen. When her 'Mech rocked hard with the impact, Dawn knew it was a brutal hit.

The *Mad Dog*'s aim had been hurried, though. The shot, brutal as it was, had taken her left arm clean off at the actuator, robbing her of her autocannons.

"*Stravag!*" Dawn pulled back and turned with another step just in time to watch the *Mad Dog Mk III* take more damage from the other side; lasers boiled off swaths of its armor and missiles crashed into it, sending debris flying.

Dawn fired at it with her remaining PPCs, hoping she could hit shooting from the hip.

The PPCs shots missed.

She glanced up to St. Jude again.

If there was a time she ever needed his help, it was at this moment. This was the most lost she had been since ascending to the rank of MechWarrior—

Turquoise light illuminated the area, and the rest of the *Mad Dog*'s armor cooked right off its torso from its right side.

St. Jude had saved her one more time, working through Khan Jiyi Chistu.

Relief blew over Dawn like a cool wave on the shore.

One more test passed.

One more battle to fight.

"Onward," the Khan commanded.

And for Dawn, there was nothing left to do but obey.

After the ordeal of the crucible, Khan Jiyi Chistu looked down over the ridge into the bowl and saw the Ghost Bears only had sixteen 'Mechs left.

Only sixteen 'Mechs.

Just one more than a Trinary.

And they kept up their withering fire, more bees than bears, angry and swarming together.

That was all that stood in his way. And he would not let them take his victory from him, no matter how outnumbered he was.

He had a mere fourteen 'Mechs left.

Just one less than a Trinary.

The Ghost Bears were good. Forcing the Jade Falcons to run the gauntlet was a wise strategy. It had ground his force down and caused devastating losses, and bought the Ghost Bears time, but getting stuck in the low ground was foolish, and they would pay dearly for it.

That did not mean they were defenseless. As soon as the Jade Falcon forces crested the ridge, the firing began. Some lasers hit, some missed. Missiles twisted across the bowl, but that soon ended as they ran out of ammunition after the prolonged engagement.

"Orders, my Khan?" Star Captain Quinn asked, eager to end the fight.

"Fan out. Cover the ridge. Send the fastest 'Mechs to the edges and keep the Bears contained in the circle. Keep the firing up."

"*Aff*, my Khan."

His Jade Falcons followed his orders to the letter. Each of them, no matter how damaged, kept up their suppressing fire and spread out around the semi-circle of the ridge. All of their fire poured into the bowl like thunder and lightning. Lasers in various blues, greens, and golds shot back and forth in a stunning light show bright enough that the Khan's viewscreen automatically dimmed from the brilliance.

But the Ghost Bears did not remain simply standing in a line as they fired; they adjusted to the Falcons and their pattern across the ridge's lip.

Jiyi sliced across Bear 'Mechs with his lasers and remained unscathed, but he lost two more 'Mechs from his *touman.* But then so did the Ghost Bears, and Jiyi could not see how this would not end in anything but the complete destruction of these Ghost Bears. It did not matter that they still had one more 'Mech at their disposal than he.

Jiyi sidestepped *Emerald* when a laser singed it across its arms. According to his readout, the damage was nothing more than superficial. He had been there for every stage of the battle and had even led the charge for much of it, but had avoided being significantly damaged so far.

He took it as a sign that he had been right, and his actions were justified.

Both sides out of ammunition and missiles, the Ghost Bears and the Jade Falcons now exchanged laser and PPC fire consistently. The battle would take forever at this rate. The Ghost Bears lost another 'Mech—a *Rime Otter* at the center of the formation, which crumpled under a scathing blast of gleaming yellow laser fire.

Jiyi's eyes narrowed. He knew what had to happen. He could not afford to play this long game of attrition. He either had to charge them and end it or come up with something else.

He switched his radio to an open, public frequency and donned a bright grin to match the tone of his voice. "Star Colonel Emilio Hall, do you copy?"

"This is Star Colonel Emilio Hall." He sounded out of breath and weary. As anyone would.

"This is Jiyi Chistu. You have put up a brilliant fight worthy of your codexes. The Warriors have shown the care you put into training your *sibkos,* truly. It was a more difficult fight than I expected and that is to your credit."

"Your kind words are appreciated, Jiyi Chistu. But not as much as your defeat will be. What was it you want? As you can see, I am still fighting a battle."

Jiyi chuckled. "I offer you and your remaining Ghost Bears *hegira.* You would be free to accept this defeat with no further losses, and march proudly back home under your own recognizance."

"I know what *hegira* means. And it is bold of you to offer it in the middle of a battle you have not yet won."

"You began this particular engagement with one more 'Mech than I did, and now you have one less. We have the high ground and the advantage. There is no sense in sending more of your admirable Warriors to their death."

"I would like to offer your Jade Falcons *hegira,* and I would suggest you take it before my Bears catch their breath."

It had been worth a shot.

Hall was a shrewd commander, and Jiyi had meant everything he said in praise of his opponents. The *sibkos* these Bears had trained would be valuable to the Jade Falcons for generations. "What if I admit, reluctantly, that we are at a stalemate? Surely neither of us wish to throw any more Warriors at this problem."

"Then you would still be overly optimistic about your chances, but closer to reality than your initial offer of *hegira* would imply," Star Colonel Hall said with a joyous bravado despite his exhaustion that Jiyi could not help but like.

"You are piloting an *Ursus II, quiaff*?"

It took Hall a moment to answer. Perhaps he could not decide if there was something to be lost in giving that information. "*Aff,*" he said finally. "*Callisto* is its name."

"And I pilot a *Gyrfalcon. Emerald,* I call it."

"Wonderful," Hall said, his voice dripping with sarcasm.

"What if we stop this conflict and wager the rest of our mutual Trials on a personal duel?" Jiyi asked. "Our 'Mechs are evenly matched. You and I can end this for the rest of our Warriors and do it more quickly. Afterward, we can both go home and let them tell stories of this day."

A de facto cease fire began as Jiyi waited for an answer. All of the firing ceased as they waited for the response to come in.

Smoke rose from the battlefield and began to lift as everything calmed, even for just a moment.

Seconds ticked on, but no response came. That Hall had not rejected him outright meant he was considering it.

Jiyi hoped it could be that easy. "What say you to my offer, Star Colonel? It would certainly be to both our advantage. And if you lose, I will still offer you and the rest of your people *hegira*, and my assurance that you yourself will remain a Ghost Bear."

The Jade Falcon Khan wondered if taunting his opponent would work. He could offer the idea that maybe the Ghost Bear was afraid he would lose, but Jiyi thought better of his opponent. Nothing so base as goading would work with as worthy an enemy as Hall.

"Very well," Hall said, finally. "I accept."

And Jiyi's face stretched into a wide smile.

It worked.

CHAPTER 30

BEARCLAW TRAINING FACILITY
COPPERTON
QUARELL
RASALHAGUE DOMINION
07 NOVEMBER 3151

Alexis had her wrists bound in cuffs. Star Commander Diego had been the one to clasp her hands together, apologizing the whole time. He apologized to her and let her know he wished she would have talked to him before putting their plan in motion, but he simply did not understand. None of the *Ursari* did. The future was not theirs, and they would never understand what the cubs were going through.

The three of them—Alexis, Thomasin, and Sophie—sat together in the spare cell of the brig.

"What do you think she is going to do?" Alexis asked them. She assumed they had more experience with the Ghost Bears in this sort of situation than she did. The sort of cells she had been thrown into when she was younger before she joined them were a lot scarier and dirtier. And there was always an inevitableness to her release.

Now, she was not so sure.

Sophie, her hands also bound in cuffs, leaned back against the metal wall. "I think she means to teach us a lesson."

"But what about that crack about tossing us to the Jade Falcons even if the Star Colonel is victorious?" Alexis eyed them both. "Can she do that?"

Thomasin shook his head. "*Neg*. The only way would be in a Trial like this. You did the best you could, Alexis. We all did. Even Daniel. The Bearclaws are behind you. They will not forget what you tried."

The door to their cell slid open, and Star Captain Diego stood in the doorway. The somber look on his face brought news and not the good sort.

"Star Commander," Alexis said. "I imagine the Den Mother is still upset."

Diego grimaced. "I think that would be putting it mildly."

"I had to do something," Alexis said, her heart getting in the way of her head. "I could not sit idle while this hung over our heads. Do they not teach us to act decisively?"

"You would have made a fine Warrior."

Alexis did not like the tone he took. And the words. *Would have*. Past tense. "They mean to wash me out?"

Diego's eyes glassed over, and his voice grew grim. "Cadet Alexis, I believe the Den Mother means to kill you. It came up more than once in our discussions."

A shiver ran up Alexis' back.

Thomasin's mouth slacked open. "You cannot be serious."

"She is not allowed to do that," Sophie said, bucking up from her seat.

Diego shrugged. "And she may not, but she is seeking a way. She compared you three to rabid dogs."

Alexis could not fathom so severe a punishment, but she did not regret her decision one whit. "I would still do it all over again, Star Captain."

"I do not doubt you, little cub," Diego said, casting his eyes to the ground. "But you should have known that you cannot interfere with a Trial of Possession. If you had taken your plan further, you may well have caused the Star Colonel to lose by default, and you would have caused the very outcome you hoped to avoid. And disrespecting the Den Mother...that would always end badly for you. She is an excellent Warrior, but a severe *Ursari*. And stubborn."

"More Ghost Mongol than Bear," Alexis said.

Diego gave her a stern look, as though she should have known better to make a statement like that.

A breath caught in Alexis' throat, and she found her urgency and concern again. "Has the Trial been decided?"

"*Neg*," the *Ursari* said. "But they are changing the terms of the Trial. Star Colonel Emilio Hall and the Falcon Chistu have agreed to a personal duel. *Ursus II* against *Gyrfalcon.*"

"Will he win?"

"*Aff,*" Diego said.

Alexis felt no conviction from him, though. Anything was possible. "And if he does not?"

"I imagine if the Den Mother finds no way to end your life, then at the very least your life as a Ghost Bear will end. Instead, if the Star Colonel loses, she will be all too happy to put you in Jade Falcon green."

Alexis looked into the Star Commander's eyes, searching for some compassion. "Is there *anything* we can do?"

"*Neg.*"

She found compassion in his eyes, but also sadness.

He stepped back into the corridor, behind the edge of the door. "I just thought you all should know. Good luck, little cub. You are going to need it."

She tried to meet his eyes, but he refused to. The door slid shut. Alexis looked around their tiny cell and found some small comfort. At least she had Thomasin and Sophie.

Alexis was surprised to see Thomasin holding tears back. Yes, he was a Ghost Bear and a Warrior, but also human. There was no shame in crying, and Alexis told him so.

He looked to her without a word.

A single tear fell down his cheek.

Sophie's eyes gazed at the single window to the outside, her stare a thousand kilometers away. "She means to kill us, truly."

Alexis shrugged. "That is what the Star Commander said. But who knows? Could it be a story they just tell us to make us think about what we've done? I certainly have no idea."

Thomasin wiped the tear from his face with both of his cuffed hands. Then he gripped the seat below him between his knees, letting his knuckles go white. "I would rather die than be a Jade Falcon."

Alexis furrowed her brow. "Why?"

"They are monsters. You have heard the stories."

"I wonder if those are just stories," Alexis said, thinking back to the Den Mother, "and maybe the Ghost Bears are the real monsters."

Thomasin kept his jaw tight. "And I would still rather die a Ghost Bear."

"Knock that off, Thomasin," Sophie said. "We vowed to follow Alexis, and she did her best for us. If we die, at least we die with honor."

"You are not the least bit upset? Or worried?"

"*Neg.* It will all turn out. I will have the both of you with me until my end. Bear or Falcon, it makes no difference."

Sophie looked between the two of them. Thomasin shook his head and spun to look at something—anything—else. Alexis leaned her head on Sophie's shoulder. Sophie reached up with both bound hands to comfort Alexis, caressing her face softly.

"Shh," Sophie said, playing the strong one. "It will be okay, Alex."

"We are going to die," Alexis said. And the tears finally came. First leaking quietly, then she sobbed. "Your end is bound in ours and imminent. We are going to die because we wanted to save our family."

"Shh, shh." Sophie ran her fingers through Alexis' hair and brushed the tears away from her cheek.

Alexis tried to center herself, to calm her tears. Her chest felt untethered, as though all the feelings inside her were going to float away into space and never return.

She had faced the inky, black mirror of her death before, and never thought she would have to do it again until she was a full-fledged Ghost Bear. It was a possibility every day on the street as a child. If she did not act to steal or grift, she would not eat, and simply waste away into nothing. But she could *do* something about that. There were actions she could take, stratagems she could employ, schemes she could engage.

Here, she was helpless.

Nothing she could do would save her life.

Handcuffed and stuffed in a cell to die or worse with no possible way out except the green of the Jade Falcons.

Alexis imagined Ivankova's face, her lean cheeks ruddy with anger. They should have killed her. If they were going to die for their attempt to keep their family together, at least they could have ended her reign of tyranny.

Nothing had prepared Alexis for the unsettling feeling of vulnerability that grew in her heart. There had *always* been something she could do to save herself, but now there was nothing. Her hands were literally tied, and every trick in her book had been exhausted. She was left with nothing.

She thought of allies she might have. When she became a Ghost Bear, there had always been someone she could rely on.

Perhaps there could still be help, but she had no idea what the situation was with those that had helped them. Daniel in particular.

"If we do face death or Falcons," Alexis said to Thomasin and Sophie through her hyperventilating, "I am glad it will be with the two of you."

CHAPTER 31

PYKON RIVER DELTA
QUARELL
RASALHAGUE DOMINION
07 NOVEMBER 3151

Star Colonel Emilio Hall smirked. Clouds had rolled in, and the rains had begun. It rained on the Delta every day, but usually first thing in the morning. Evening rains were not unheard of, but it felt poetic.

His *Ursus II* and Jiyi Chistu's *Gyrfalcon* stood on opposite sides of the very edge of the Delta, back in the swampy marsh and running creeks. A circle of BattleMechs surrounded them, the remaining Ghost Bear and Jade Falcon forces.

Star Captain Rand stood to his left at the twelve of the circle's clock face, right at the top of the Delta, in her *Kuma*. She had survived the battle, despite the loss of her 'Mech's left arm and large laser. She had also scolded him for agreeing to the personal duel to finish the Trial.

But Emilio had a better chance to win on his own, one on one.

Across the way, Chistu, in his winged *Gyrfalcon*, waited for the signal to begin, just as Hall did in his *Ursus II*.

As they continued their tense wait for the start of the duel—to be signaled by their seconds' coordinated firing of lasers across the field—Emilio took a deep, cleansing breath, closed his eyes, and thought back to his teachings. Jeet Kune Do had taught him that to understand combat, he had to approach it in a simple and direct manner. He had to shed his mind of preconceived notions and take things as they came. That had been his problem when he began this Trial, but it would not be a problem as he finished it.

The only thing he needed to know about Jiyi Chistu was that he was unknowable.

Any strategy or tactic—matter how Inner Sphere or Clan in nature—was possible. Not that Chistu had resorted to *dezgra* tactics, per se. Emilio felt confident in his assumption that the Jade Falcon Warrior had clustered his forces together at the start to force a melee on purpose. Chistu fought like a man possessed of a need to survive.

Hall admired it.

And wished they could have been faced with similar goals instead of conflicting aims.

Waiting for the start, Emilio double-checked his systems. The damage he had taken was superficial, singes across his arms and legs. Several missiles had exploded on his torso, but his damage readouts were all still in the green. He had exhausted all his missiles, unfortunately. Emilio guessed Chistu's beaked bird of a 'Mech had expended its ammo, too, leaving this to be purely an energy weapon fight. Or worse, a melee—something Jade Falcons excelled at.

"I wish you luck, Star Colonel Hall," Chistu said.

"To you as well, Jiyi Chistu," Emilio replied. "May the best Warrior win."

Any second.

Emilio thought about the Bear Cubs on the line.

And what they must be feeling.

And the one who had made that call during the Trial. Such a bold and foolish move, but he had to admire it.

Emilio vowed he would do everything he could to save them.

Lightning flashed white across the battlefield, and for a split second, Emilio thought it was the start of the duel.

But the light was colorless, not like a laser flash at all. Then thunder followed with a bellowing *CRACK*.

Then the lasers came, shimmering across the battlefield, and the fight was on.

Like a good student of tactics, Emilio waited for his enemy to act first to determine the best course of action. He would flow like water in his 'Mech and meet Chistu as he went, not as he thought he might go. He had already lost too much assuming Chistu would fight like a Jade Falcon. He would not make that mistake again.

The *Gyrfalcon* took flight on its jump jets, leaping into the air like a great bird of prey. Emilio got the sense, looking at his readouts, that Chistu was coming toward him on his arc, so he would not be where Chistu expected when he landed.

Emilio charged forward, positioning his *Ursus II* below the apex of the *Gyrfalcon's* arc, then began to turn, hoping to line up a shot.

It was a risky maneuver, but it put them at an equal disadvantage. They would both need to turn to get a firing solution.

From the side of his viewscreen, Emilio saw Chistu come down hard, stressing the knees on his raptor-style legs to take the impact of the landing. Emilio kept his turn up and saw Chistu turn as well, but before Chistu had been in his spot for the span of a second, he jumped again.

Emilio could not to turn fast enough to get a shot in, but neither could Chistu, so they were still at an impasse.

There was no discerning Chistu's plan of attack. There seemed to be no rhyme or reason to it. He landed, pivoted his firing arc, and jumped again. He would overheat before he even fired a shot, unless the wings were as good at heat dissipation as the stories said. But there must have been some reasoning to it, since he had not taken a shot either.

Was it a stalling tactic?

Or meant to confuse him? If that was the case, it was working.

Emilio worked to get Chistu in his firing arc, pivoting and redirecting with every jump the Falcon made. After what seemed like a hundred jumps across the muddy terrain, Emilio finally matched his aim with Chistu's landing, splashing down into one of the water's tributaries.

"You are mine, Chistu." Emilio thumbed the firing stud and unleashed everything he had left.

The brilliant array of different lasers sent a veritable rainbow of color reflecting off the ponds and water. The blue-green large laser cut across the *Gyrfalcon*'s wings and the rest of them slashed savagely across the right arm.

First blood had been drawn.

But the *Gyrfalcon* returned fire. Chistu focused his lasers on the broad center mass of Emilio's *Ursus II*, disintegrating tons of armor as the numbers on *Callisto*'s armor integrity fell, and his damage schematic lights flashed from green to yellow.

This duel was going to be more difficult—and more evenly matched—than the Star Colonel had thought.

But it would take more than that to bring down a Ghost Bear.

BEARCLAW TRAINING FACILITY
COPPERTON
QUARELL
RASALHAGUE DOMINION
07 NOVEMBER 3151

Handcuffed in front of the entire Bearclaw *sibko*, Alexis stood defiant, her head held high. The Den Mother, pacing in front of her, Thomasin, and Sophie with her hands tensed behind her back, would not break her. Alexis had already won, even if there existed a possibility that she might lose her life today.

"Bearclaws," Star Captain Sasha Ivankova said loudly over the lowered sounds of the battle playing out on the holoscreen behind Alexis, speaking to the assembly of cadets in the common hall. Alexis spied Daniel right there in the front of the crowd, smirking, keeping up appearances. "I want you to look at the three cubs before you. There is a single word I want you to think of when you look at them."

Ivankova turned to Alexis and her compatriots. Fire burned in her eyes with the intensity of an exploding star.

Alexis returned the bright glare. The Den Mother would not intimidate her or make her feel small. Never again.

"*Dezgra*," Ivankova said. "*Dezgra* is the word I want you to think of. It is a word that will mean many things over the course of your career as a Ghost Bear. And it will be something you must constantly work to avoid. I want you to look at these three, and see their faces every time you think the word *dezgra.*"

Alexis tightened the muscles in her jaw and bit at the sides of her cheeks to keep from screaming. *Dezgra?* Ivankova did not know the true meaning of the word, and never would.

"The *dezgra* shown here is some of the worst." The Den Mother looked back to the crowd and continued pacing back and forth to pontificate. "And it is made even worse by the fact that they did so under the banner of the Ghost Bears. You all know the story of our founding. Of how, rather than be separated from each other in different Clans, our founders decided to die together. In the frozen climes of Strana Mechty, huddled together for warmth, ready to perish for their beliefs, a ghost bear came upon them."

If there was something else Alexis hated about the Ghost Bears, it was how often lessons came back to the founding of the Clan. This was not the time for it and Alexis knew it. She saw the eyes of the cadets in front of her, of Anna and Lewis, of Yrsa and Jezebel, all of the rest, dividing their attention between the proceedings, her story, and the holoscreen and the battle over their fates on the holoscreen behind them.

Ivankova did not care and did not stop. "This would have been their end. Ghost bears are vicious predators. But this ghost bear found them kindred spirits. Instead of eating them for their meat, the ghost bear huddled up to them for warmth. For three days it warmed and fed them. And when their strength had returned, so too did they return home. Ultimately, they convinced Nicholas Kerensky to let them create a new Clan, one based on family, and the compassion the ghost bear had shown them. It is something our Clan does, and is found in none other."

Ivankova paused, then turned back around, walking the line again. "What do you think would have happened to Sandra Tseng if she had attacked the ghost bear, even though it was sharing its warmth and food?"

The Den Mother let the question hang there, Alexis and the rest of her *sibkin* wondering if it was rhetorical or meant to be answered.

Finally, Daniel answered nervously, "It would have killed them."

Ivankova stopped and looked to him. A smile widened across her face, more cat than bear, ready to eat a canary. "Very good, Cadet Daniel. It would have killed them."

She looked out over the rest of the *sibko*, eyes wide, like she had just revealed the meaning of life. "And is that not what these three have done to me? Their Den Mother. It is my job to keep all of you safe. It is my job to keep you warm and fed, nurtured in mind and body, to ensure that you become the best of what the Ghost Bears have to offer. And if you disobey me in such a fashion, is that the Ghost Bear way? Is that what one does to family?"

Either the assembly took this question as rhetorical as well, or perhaps the battle raging beyond them gripped them too powerfully.

Ivankova continued after a long pause. "I would have hoped the rot had not infected the rest of you, but unfortunately it has. Their plan did not get as far as it did without help. And I would like to know more about it."

The Den Mother's penetrating gaze scanned the crowd, and then she said, "Daniel, to me."

Confused, he approached her at attention and offered a salute. He was involved, and Alexis would never understand why the Den Mother preferred him over everyone else. She would never suspect him.

"Yes, Den Mother?" he said after she saluted him back.

"What do you know about this insurrection plot?"

To his credit, Daniel gave nothing away. He kept his jaw clenched tight, and Alexis was actually impressed. "Nothing, Den Mother."

Ivankova turned back to the rest of the cadets and the *Ursari* standing around them in a wide circle. "Does anyone else know anything about these *dezgra* and their plan?"

Alexis realized there were no answers because the Bearclaws and Mektid Bears were all behind them. No one wanted to sell them out. Even Daniel. The belonging she had hoped for rose in her chest, and for the first time ever, she felt like a full member of her *sibko*.

"No one will come forward?"

Daniel remained silent, as well as the rest of their *sibkin.*

The Den Mother stepped closer to Daniel. Uncomfortably close. "And you, Daniel? You are sure you have nothing to say?"

"*Aff*, Star Captain."

"You disappoint me."

"Star Captain?"

"If these three, Alexis, Thomasin, and Sophie, are the troublemakers of the *sibko,* then you are its traitor. You were the star cub, and now you are its biggest disgrace."

Daniel looked as though he'd been struck across the face. His mouth slackened and his eyes widened. "What?"

"You think me a fool? Your display was the distraction they needed to escape. Take your place with Alexis, Thomasin, and Sophia."

"Den Mother?" he asked, his voice cracking.

Alexis could not believe it when Ivankova pointed to a spot next to her and Daniel dutifully marched there and turned to face the rest of the *sibko.*

"Now. Star Commander Diego, I leave it to you to remove the patches from their uniforms. They are no longer fit to wear the insignia of the Ghost Bear. *Seyla.*"

Shocked but still following orders, Star Commander Diego approached the front. He stepped up to Alexis's face, apologies writ large in his sad eyes.

Alexis refrained from saying a word as Diego gripped the Ghost Bear patch on the shoulder of her uniform and ripped. Or tried to, anyway. She had sewn it on herself, and had done a good job. It did not tear away easily, and she almost smiled at the effort it took him to finally rip it from her sleeve.

With the removal of the patch, there was also a freedom that came with it. Watching Daniel suffer alongside her, it clicked in her head that the rot was in the Ghost Bears. It was in the leadership and the culture. Losing her patch almost came as a relief.

Diego moved to Sophie, gripping her patch as the Den Mother continued her speech.

"You will see the extent of my mercy," Ivankova said. "After today, these four will no longer be Ghost Bears, and will serve as an example for all of you."

Diego tore the patch from Sophie's arm, the ripping sound echoing through the hall. To Alexis' eyes, Sophie looked just as relieved as Alexis felt. Then, setting his jaw, he moved to Thomasin, who was barely able to contain his composure. His chin quivered and his lip trembled. Thomasin's grief acted as a counterweight to the relief Alexis thought she felt, and her heart broke as Diego ripped Thomasin's patch off.

The sound of the rip masked the sound of his strangled sob. Thomasin did not deserve this treatment, because ultimately it was because of her that he was receiving it.

With Alexis, Sophie, and Thomasin completed, that left Daniel for the Star Commander.

Diego looked back to the Den Mother, almost to ask if she was sure he should be doing this, and she nodded to him.

Ugly tears streamed down Daniel's face, but he kept his posture straight. He was going to take it.

A day ago, Alexis would not have been moved by this display and might have even rooted for it. Now it came with sadness. Daniel had come through when it mattered most, when it was life or death, and now he was losing everything he had.

The Den Mother glared at Daniel, marked with shame for her favorite student. "We will wait to see the final outcome of the Trial of Possession. If the Ghost Bears prevail, we will find a way to mete out further punishment to these unworthy cubs."

The finality of her words deepened the pit in Alexis' stomach. She did not want to punished any more than she had been since she met Star Captain Sasha Ivankova, and maybe the alternative was not so bad.

"If the Ghost Bears somehow manage to *not* prevail...well, then..." The Den Mother smirked. "Then they will be the newest Jade Falcons, and I will deliver them to this Jiyi Chistu myself. And I leave their punishment to you all in your new lives."

Ivankova turned to Alexis.

She resisted the urge to spit in the Den Mother's face.

"Do you have any last words before we await the outcome of the Trial, Alexis?"

Alexis' muscles tightened. And she fought every instinct in her body to fight. All she did was say a single, defiant word that would show that she would meet this fate with dignity. "*Neg.*"

PYKON RIVER DELTA
QUARELL
RASALHAGUE DOMINION
07 NOVEMBER 3151

Khan Jiyi Chistu leaped again in his *Gyrfalcon*. He loved the idea of toying with the Ghost Bear Star Colonel, but really he just wanted to make sure his opponent did not have a chance to gain his bearings and get off another good shot.

Hall was an excellent 'Mech pilot, but he was too predictable in his attacks. Or counterattacks, rather. Part of that predictability came in the notion that he seemed to prefer parries and ripostes rather than an out-and-out offensive. He waited to see what the attack was before responding. Jiyi had only wished he could have noticed that pattern sooner.

Crashing down into the swamp once more, water splashed up high enough to reach the middle of his viewscreen, but the cameras and sensors were covered in rainwater anyway, so none of it mattered.

Lightning flashed, illuminating the *Ursus II* with its back exposed, and thunder *cracked* to mark the pull of Jiyi's trigger.

The *Gyrfalcon*'s lasers flashed blue-green, ablating the armor across the *Ursus II*'s back. A solid hit, but not enough to take his opponent down. But Jiyi had planned this moment well.

Finally able to maneuver himself behind the *Ursus II*, he had time to take a second shot before the Ghost Bear managed to drag his aim across Jiyi's 'Mech.

Damage indicators lit up across his console. *Emerald* had definitely seen better days, but never in a more difficult and righteous fight for its life.

Catching the *Ursus II* on its side, the lasers whittled a chunk from an arm and ablated a chunk off its torso. Rain sizzled against the meaty Bear 'Mech where it had been hit. Steam rose from the wound.

The Ghost Bear side-stepped again, pivoting his firing arc.

Normally, at this point, Jiyi would have launched up again into the sky, hoping to put the Ghost Bear off balance. But that was not going to happen this time. The jumping had been a feint for this moment.

Jiyi charged.

The *Ursus II* had expected him to jump, and so it took a moment for Hall to react.

Jiyi aimed the colossal arm cannons of his *Gyrfalcon* right at the heart of the Ghost Bear and fired. The twin lasers flensed off armor across the arm and side of the *Ursus II*, sending melted gobbets to the ground below in waves that brought steam rising from the shallow swamp water below.

The *Ursus II* stepped around further, still trying to get Jiyi into his firing arc.

Juking to the left, hoping to keep from getting shot, Jiyi fired again, carving more armor from the *Ursus II*. The Ghost Bear 'Mechs looked like giant bears to begin with, bulky and large, and this bear began to look like it had come out of its winter hibernation, all dangling skin and sinew, rather than the fat one would expect.

Hall fired back as fast as he could manage, his medium pulse lasers flashing at Jiyi's 'Mech, vaporizing slabs of armor across *Emerald,* solid hits that brought the damage indicators across his torso into the yellow, verging on red.

Jiyi had one more shot at ending it, else he'd be ended himself.

But one shot was all he needed.

The *Gyrfalcon's* cyan lasers sliced right through the center of the *Ursus II*, turning the inner structure and its gyro into slag.

The *Ursus II* crumpled over, the internal structure no longer able to hold the weight of the top portion.

"Yes!" Elation and relief washed over Jiyi Chistu. He could not keep from smiling. He would not have to give up the VaultShip to the Ghost Bears, and that meant something. That relief came laced with joy like frosting on a cake.

He had just ensured another generation of Jade Falcons would live to fight another day, and he could now build something special in the Occupation Zone.

"We did it," he said to the Falcons assembled in the circle around him. "You have all fought well and we have won this Trial of Possession. You have taken Ghost Bears as bondsmen, and we will grow our *touman.* Our visit to Quarell has been nothing short of an unmitigated success. Each of you who made it through has won a place of honor in our Clan."

There were shouts across the radio, his surviving Warriors excited at their victory. Jiyi looked at the wreckage of the *Ursus II* and hoped Star Colonel Hall had survived. If he had perished in the fight, Jiyi worried he would not find so magnanimous a Ghost Bear to deal with in his absence. "Now, we just need to ensure the Ghost Bears do not renege on the deal."

"*Aff,* my Khan," Star Captain Quinn said, unable to hide the relief in her voice. It must have been a strain on all of them. "Excellent work."

"Thank you, Star Captain. Order the DropShip in and ready our departure as soon as we have taken possession of our prize."

"*Aff,* my Khan."

CHAPTER 32

BEARCLAW TRAINING FACILITY
COPPERTON
QUARELL
RASALHAGUE DOMINION
08 NOVEMBER 3151

Alexis still could not quite fathom the idea of being a Jade Falcon.

And since her illusions about the Ghost Bears were slowly fading, she had no idea if she should believe the stories she had been told about them.

Even though the Falcons had "won" her, would they resign her to a similar fate, as Star Captain Sasha Ivankova wanted? Would they simply kill her for not being a Trueborn?

The Den Mother kept Alexis, Daniel, Thomasin, and Sophie in handcuffs as they marched them to the transports alongside the rest of the Bearclaws and the Mektid Bears. The mood among the two *sibkos* was somber overall. There was anger there, but Alexis could not determine if the anger was for the Ghost Bears for losing them, for her and the others for not saving them, or for the fact that they were going to be Jade Falcons.

It would take two transports to get them all loaded and sent off, one for the Bearclaws and one for the Mektid Bears. The Den Mother for the Mektid Bears led that *sibko*, his walk a sad, slow trudge.

And then, they would all be taking the trip to Antimony together.

"There has to be a way out of this," Thomasin whispered.

But before Alexis, Sophie, or any of their *sibkin* could respond, the Den Mother hissed, "Shut your mouth."

Thomasin clenched his jaw and obeyed.

But Alexis whispered back to him, "You do not have to listen to her anymore."

The Den Mother's gaze snapped back to Alexis, glowering. Alexis thought the look would have killed a lesser being, but not a true Ghost Bear. But Alexis didn't think she was much of a true Ghost Bear, because apparently part of being a Ghost Bear was surrendering children to the enemy.

"All right," the Den Mother said when they arrived at the hover transports. "You four, in."

She ushered Alexis, Daniel, Thomasin and Sophie into the transport, but instead of loading in the others, she closed them inside by themselves.

"What is she doing?" Sophie asked.

"Who cares?" Daniel said through a sniffle. "We are lost."

"We will fight this," Thomasin told Daniel, "Whatever it is."

But Alexis knew. Ivankova was still trying to keep them separate, even as she lost control of them. She was going to drive one last wedge between them. She never thought she would succeed in uniting Thomasin and Daniel.

The sound of Ivankova's voice carried—albeit muffled— through the transport's door. "You Ghost Bears Cubs, this is the last time I address you as Ghost Bears. According to the *rede* of our Clan, you have been lost in a Trial of Possession. You will be Jade Falcons. Though this might seem a dishonor, know that it is your honorable duty to accept it."

The Den Mother could be callous and cold, but it seemed beyond reasoning that she would be happy to just hand the kids she had spent years training over to the Jade Falcons and tell them nothing more than to just get over it. She had done nothing to prevent their loss, either. The Den Mother was supposed to be an example of Ghost Bear ideals, and hadn't *she* been the one to tell the story of the Clan's founding? Shouldn't she have been offering them food and warmth, comfort and safety?

Alexis wanted to scream that she was a hypocrite, but it did not matter.

After their ride, she would likely never see the Den Mother again.

Another relief.

"I need you to remember," the Den Mother continued, "that those four *stravag* washouts in the transport already have dishonored themselves. You do not have to suffer their dishonor any further. Mete out what justice you would upon them, in this life or the next. They were *dezgra* Ghost Bears; I imagine they will be *dezgra* Jade Falcons as well. *Quiaff*?"

"*Aff!*" their *sibkin* called back, the harsh edge of their bark passed undiminished through the transport walls.

Alexis' heart sank deep in her chest when Ivankova opened the transport back up and her *sibkin*—former *sibkin?*—filed in. They came up the center aisle between the benches and began taking their seats.

Alexis narrowed her eyes, staring them down, wondering if their anger was for her or for the Den Mother. Yes, she was handcuffed, but that did not matter if she had to defend herself if they decided to attack them. She had been in tougher scrapes than this.

Daniel cowered next to her. Thomasin and Sophie sat straighter, willing to meet whatever came.

Looking back to the doors of the transport, Alexis watched as the Den Mother began to close them. "Farewell, Ghost Bears," she said. "And good luck."

The doors locked shut, darkening the compartment, leaving them all alone.

As the transport started forward on their way to Antimony, Alexis looked to Daniel and took in a deep breath. Then she looked to the rest of the *sibko*, and held that breath close, waiting for what came next.

KODIAK POINT
ANTIMONY
QUARELL
RASALHAGUE DOMINION
08 NOVEMBER 3151

Though his left arm was in a sling, and he still felt the pain from the bruises across his face and ribs, Star Colonel Emilio Hall was not much worse for wear after the Trial of Possession. He wished he would have won, but there was nothing to be done about it now. The tenets of Clan life and honor dictated that he hand the cadets over, but they said nothing of magnanimity. He would bring that on his own.

They were to meet for the handoff in front of the Kodiak Point complex. Each of the *sibkos* on Quarell had gathered there; the Berserkers, Bjornsons, and Bearclaws were situated at attention on the right side of the building. The Dragonbears, Mektid Bears, Porbjorns, and Werebears stood similarly on the left.

Just over fifty of the Ghost Bears' best and brightest, sent off to roost in Falcon's land.

"A shame," he said to himself, looking down at his shoes, polished to mirrors. He did not relish his next meeting with Star Captain Rand. The last thing he wanted was to have to face her I-told-you-sos and angry disappointment—not to mention having to meet her in a Circle of Equals.

There was nothing more severe than the feeling of letting down people you cared about. They were his family, even if he did not know each of them personally.

But honor demanded honor.

Emilio thought Jiyi Chistu might arrive by palanquin. Something about his demeanor insisted that would be a possibility. Instead, he came in a line of hover vehicles and transports he had probably hired in Antimony. It made sense that he would have had access to enough Bear-Krona to do it, with VaultShip *Gamma* still in his possession and them plying their trade across the Dominion.

Chistu arrived in the first car and stepped out onto the circular ferrocrete drive that fronted the complex. He was dressed in a drab olive Jade Falcon work uniform. His brown curly hair was unkempt, and he had a scar over his right eye—unsurprising to Emilio, he could not think of a Jade Falcon he had ever met without such a scar.

Chistu's broad smile turned somber and business-like when he came to greet Emilio. "Star Colonel Emilio Hall," he said, extending a hand to shake. "I am truly happy that you lived through the Trial. It would have been a shame for any Clan to lose a warrior as you."

Emilio met Chistu's handshake and found it firm, but not excessively so. "Jiyi Chistu. It is a pleasure to meet you, though I wish the battle would have gone the other way."

"I am sure you would have. VaultShip *Gamma* would have been an immense prize."

"I hope to show the *sibkos* that the Clans do not always have to be in constant conflict. Our *rede* is such that we can honor our principles even when we lose."

"Admirable, Star Colonel. I appreciate your sense of chivalry. If all Clan Warriors thought as we did, imagine what we could accomplish?"

"Aff," Emilio said, his voice hollow. This Trial would be a stain on his codex for the rest of his life. He felt the terror emanating from the neat rows of cadets that would be handed over like a chest of pirate booty. He had not been lying. He did want to show them an example of being gracious in defeat, but it still hurt like hell. "I hope you will allow them to keep some of their identity as Ghost Bears, even as they grow wings to fly as Jade Falcons."

Chistu's blue eyes glinted in the afternoon light, and he could barely contain the smile that seemed so readily apparent. Perhaps he was simply trying not to gloat, struggling, and not being very good at it. "You have shown them the strength of the Ghost Bears. I hope they never lose the equal measures of ferocity and wisdom that you have shown both on the battlefield and here today."

Chistu turned to his second, a woman who looked to Emilio like a much younger Malvina Hazen, but with kinder eyes, blonder hair, and no scar. "Star Colonel, this is Star Captain Quinn, my second in command."

Emilio nodded to her, and she nodded back.

"Star Captain," Chistu said to her. "Please, get them loaded up."

"*Aff*, my Khan."

Emilio suppressed his reaction to her words, hoping his eyes did not widen too much. This man was the *Khan* of the Jade Falcons. This really *was* everything they had left. And he had failed to eliminate them. The realization was yet another blow to his pride.

Chistu turned back to Emilio as Star Captain Quinn began the transportation of the *sibko*s, looking sheepish at the slip of his title.

"I see," Emilio said, "why you obfuscated your title in our negotiations."

"I felt it would only complicate the situation for us both."

"*Aff.*"

"But we are no worse for wear. We have both made it here with our lives, and live to fight another day, *quiaff*?"

"*Aff.*"

"And that is all we can ask for in these troubled times."

Hall furrowed his brow, processing all the information he was being given. The more he thought, the more he believed that this was likely the *entire* Jade Falcon *touman*. They had nothing else. They were those left behind.

"That is fair enough," he said politely.

"I thank you again for your honorable conduct, Star Colonel." Chistu extended his hand to shake once again, and Emilio accepted it. "It is in short supply in these dark days."

"I hope to meet on the battlefield again one day," Emilio said, and it was no lie.

"One day," Chistu said. "But let us hope it will not be too soon."

The Jade Falcon Khan turned his back to Emilio, effectively dismissing him, as his Star Captain began loading the *sibkos* onto vans and transports. Emilio took the time to turn and salute as the former cubs went by, hoping to offer some honor to the sacrifice they were forced to make through no fault of their own.

For the most part, they were fresh-faced youngsters, ready to lay down their lives for the Ghost Bears, had they been asked. This was just a different type of sacrifice.

A few saluted on their way by. Others would not even look at him. Some had bruised faces and arms, and he wondered if the cross-training exercise had really been that hard on them.

One passed him by, patches torn from the shoulder of her uniform. She locked eyes with him and paused just a bit in her step.

Her accusing glare held blazing fury in it.

Not fear. Emilio would have recognized that much easier.

No, in her face he saw resolve—and disgust.

And it withered him to his core. In its place blossomed the shame of failure and anger at himself for his defeat. He had been tasked with protecting them. All of them. And he had lost all of them in a duel. He could do nothing about it.

She shook her head disapprovingly as she passed, judging him personally responsible. Tears threatened to form in his eyes as his emotion overtook him.

Emilio had failed.

He had failed all of them. But he had failed that cadet in particular, in a way she would never forget for the rest of her life as a newly minted Jade Falcon.

And neither would he for the rest of his life as a tired, old Ghost Bear.

Khan Jiyi Chistu watched the first of the cadets load up into the last transport van. He clapped his hands and rubbed them together.

This was work well done.

They had done it, even though it had cost them.

The Ghost Bear Star Colonel had stood at attention, watching each new Jade Falcon go by. His neatly pressed uniform and perfect posture never wavered in the wind. It was a worthy sign of respect as the *sibkos* were led to their transports and loaded up just a few at a time.

"I only wish I could have bid him into the *touman,* too," he told Star Captain Quinn. And he meant it. The offer of *hegira* meant to sweeten the pot might have been too high a cost.

"Who?"

"The Star Colonel." He would have made a fine Galaxy Commander, when the Jade Falcons had a Galaxy in their command once again. Perhaps Jiyi would come back for him and take the Trial. Though he wondered if the Ghost Bears would continue standing for other Clans coming and taking their best Warriors in Trials every so often, as had happened with Ramiel Bekker, and these many, many cadets.

"I see," Quinn said, pressing no further. She had no qualms leaving it at that. And she had likely also become accustomed to the riddles Jiyi would sometimes answer with. Questions answered with more questions.

It was not because he was difficult, but because sometimes he just needed the time to think of the right thing, and more data always brought it to him.

Quinn loaded the last of the *sibko* cadets into the transport. The head of the caravan had already left, heading out to the spaceport on the edge of Quarell's capitol, where they would find the *Falcon's Shadow* waiting to take them to their new home.

"How many total?" Jiyi asked Quinn.

"Almost sixty, plus the half-dozen bondsmen added to the *touman*."

"And how many did we lose?"

"Almost half. A full Trinary."

"Hmm." Jiyi lost himself in thought again, spinning possibilities in his mind for what the next moves might be.

The last door of the last hover transport closed, and it snapped Jiyi back into the present. "Let us go quickly," he said.

"Of course, my Khan."

"I would hate to see our hosts here on Quarell change their mind about our prize."

She nodded. "*Aff*, my Khan."

CHAPTER 33

KODIAK POINT
ANTIMONY
QUARELL
RASALHAGUE DOMINION
08 NOVEMBER 3151

Emilio Hall watched the last Jade Falcon transport pull away. Jade Falcon *Khan* Jiyi Chistu was in that last hover car, heading off to rebuild his *touman* in the most devious and underhanded way Emilio could think of.

Desperate times, though.

He understood it, though he could not agree with it. But Emilio's part had been played. He had been outmaneuvered by a clever foe. Shaken his hand as the Bear Cubs he had lost watched, powerless.

Emilio decided the word he felt was *conflicted.*

He could suppress the rage and disappointment, temper that with the cunning and likability of the Warrior he had just lost to, and end with little more than internal conflict. Once he had made his reports and informed the Khans of what had happened, he would either be removed from command, or things would stay in place. At least, until Rand came for him.

But they would want to know what he had learned about the Jade Falcons. They were not dead. They were not missing or vanished. They were here. Real. In the flesh and in their 'Mechs.

Emilio walked through the empty halls of Kodiak Point, finding them hollow. The last month, thanks to the life brought by the visiting *sibkos* and their cross-training and war games exercises, the halls had bustled every day to overflowing. Their youth and inventiveness had brought a spark to Kodiak Point, and invigorated of his Warriors across all stripes.

And now...nothing.

The halls were empty. The Bjornson, Berserker, and Werebear *sibkos* had all been staying at Kodiak Point. The place was going to feel vacant after their departure regardless, but Emilio had not expected this level of despair to permeate every echoing step.

Heading to the command center his office opened on to, he wanted to make his report about Chistu to the Khans immediately. It was intelligence they were going to need, if they had not already heard from the Watch.

But Star Captain Allison Rand stood there in his way.

Her back was turned to him, but she stood there trembling.

"Star Captain?" Emilio asked.

He stepped cautiously into the room and stepped around her, trying to get a better look at the front of her. Rage radiated from her like a heater.

"You must go after the *sibko*s and rescue them," she said through gritted teeth.

Emilio furrowed his brow. "*Neg*. Honor demands I do nothing."

Rand turned, revealing a noteputer she held, its screen full of dense text. "I insist."

"Yet, I refuse. What is this about, Star Captain Rand?"

He felt it there, hanging in the air. Something left unsaid. Her face tightened with anger.

She handed him the noteputer to let him read what had made her so upset.

It was a decrypted communique from the Ghost Bears Khans. He read it and then read it again, because he could not believe it. His stomach dropped out from beneath him.

All of the ways he felt conflicted before magnified. Confusion took over. "What does this mean, he rejected the vote?"

"IlKhan Ward rejected our vote out of hand."

"That is what it says. But he cannot just tell us to hold the vote again until it is unanimous."

"He said we are not dedicated enough to the new Star League." Rand paused for a moment, taking a breath to contain her rage. "For the Ghost Bears, it was all or nothing, and he does not understand the *rede* of our Clan. If we cannot agree unanimously, there will be war with the Star League."

"It does not say here that it will be war. He rejected the vote. This is not a bad thing, per se. The vote was close, many will rejoice." If that was how she read it, despite the fact it did not say that in so many words, it would be a problem for more than just her. "This is not a calamity. At least not yet."

Many thousands—billions, even—would think just like her, and react just like her. The unrest would increase, and there was a very real chance the Rasalhague Dominion would tear itself apart. Slowly. World by world.

And it all started with a simple message from Terra.

Rand's eyes narrowed and her tone rose with her passion. "I say again. You must go recover those *sibkos.* We will need every Ghost Bear we have for what comes next. This refusal from the ilKhan bodes poorly for our Clan, and the entire Dominion."

Emilio could not believe what he was hearing. "To renege on the Trial of Possession would be *dezgra,* no matter what situation the Ghost Bears are in. Do you not see that?"

"I demand a Trial of Grievance."

He frowned. "For not committing dishonor?"

"For not doing what is best for the Ghost Bears. With your vote to keep us from joining, you have put the entire Dominion at risk. You are a traitor. And now you continue your treachery. I will supplant you and do what is right."

"What is right is to not dishonor ourselves and accept the results."

"How dare you? You say this only because the result was what you want—"

"How dare *you,* Star Captain," Emilio said, cutting her off, noticing that her hand got closer and closer to her sidearm. His brow furrowed. *Would this really end in threats of violence?* "You forget your place. I admit, I did not want the Rasalhague Dominion to join the Star League. But when my views were outvoted, I accepted it. Now that they have been overruled, frankly, I think I might be relieved, but the light of morning might prove that thought otherwise. But to say I am a traitor for exercising my vote and best judgement is beyond disgraceful."

"We must maintain the stability of the Ghost Bears. This is a test that will break us."

"Continue reaching for your pistol, and see how broken we have become."

She paused. Her hand hovered over the grip.

Emilio tried to examine everything he knew and everything he thought he knew about his second in command, trying to figure some way out of the situation. She seemed too far gone. Though he could read her moves and see her intent, he was battered and broken, which gave her the advantage. She would be faster on the draw than he. And, as he thought about it, no matter how honorably he had fought, he could not think of the last time he had won in any combat save for his sparring matches with her.

Perhaps he had become *solahma,* and had not even realized it.

Talking her down was his only way through the fray, and he hoped it was possible in the frenzied state she was in. It radiated from her like a fiery warmth. "Are politics a reason to kill a superior?" he asked finally.

"Sedition is."

"What sedition? I voted. I accepted a Trial. I lost. It is regrettable, but it happens."

"Fix your mistake. *Now.* Give the orders, or I will."

Emilio looked her in the eyes, wondering if she had the heart to do it. She was a Ghost Bear, through and through. She cared about family and the Dominion. "I understand your disappointment about the *sibkos.* I share it. And I understand your disappointment about the vote. I empathize with you. So much of my life these last months has been coming to terms with what I considered the lost vote. I understand you are bitter because even though you won, the ilKhan has taken that victory from you. But that is no reason to do this."

"You know nothing of what I feel." Her fingers still hovered over her sidearm.

"I know you feel betrayed. But sometimes, that is what being in the Clan is like."

"Not the Ghost Bears. You have lost your way."

"Star Captain, the Ghost Bears have always evolved. They have changed so much during my lifetime, and they will change again. They will weather this storm. You are too young to remember how the Clan changed before we absorbed the Freeminder movement. And neither of us were even alive when we came to Rasalhague. We hold our values together thematically and spiritually, but in practice, they change with the times, like all things." Hall smiled, thinking back. "We do not wear the bear pelts of our barbarous ancestors."

"Blasphemy."

Emilio sighed.

There would be no convincing Rand. So he would simply ignore her. She had not drawn her sidearm yet. He could pretend that there was no threat at all, and then not have to report or challenge her about this. She was raw from the vote. He could understand that and sympathize. There was no need for him to make it worse.

"I understand you disagree with me," he said carefully. "But I have to file a report with the utmost urgency, so if you will excuse me."

He turned back from her and walked toward his office. He would file the report to let the Khans know of the Jade Falcons and their transformation or reemergence or whatever it was they had experienced. They would want to know immediately.

And showing his back to the Star Captain was the ultimate example of trust he could offer her. It was all he had. All he could do.

Leather creaked quiet and he heard the *swoosh* of swift movement. He spun to see, but the sidearm went off with explosive force, and suddenly he could not feel anything.

The ground came to his head, faster than he would have thought possible.

"You left me no choice," the Star Captain said, but she sounded far away and underwater.

A ringing in his ears accompanied his fading vision.

And then Emilio realized he had been undone.

He was no more.

Star Captain Allison Rand could hardly focus beyond the faint smoke rising from the barrel of her gun. But beyond it lay Star Colonel Emilio Hall.

Dead.

There was nothing to be done about it.

He had left her no choice.

She tried to reason with him. She tried challenging him by the *rede* of their Clan. But he would not listen to reason, nor duty, nor honor. She had *had* to kill him.

Allison had already begun to think of him as a traitor when he had voted against the Star League. But it became obvious when he had accepted the Trial of Possession, risking Ghost Bears for something as inane as a VaultShip. How could she not? He had turned his back on the way of the Ghost Bear. He had lost his mind before the vote, otherwise he could not have voted to refuse. But he got his way anyhow. He must have been involved in this plot to plunge the Ghost Bears into chaos and have the new Star League Defense Force led by the Khan of Khans turn their back on them completely.

No.

It *had* to be done.

It took her a moment, staring blankly at him, to realize she had to spring back into action.

If she hurried, she could still save the *sibkos* and undo these *dezgra* actions. They had already lost so much with the ilKhan's refusal of their legitimate vote. She would not allow the Ghost Bears to lose any more than that.

With her hand shaking only slightly, she lowered the pistol and put it back in the holster at her hip. Strangely, she could not take her eyes off the Star Colonel—or what was left of him.

He had fallen in mid-turn, so his body twisted there on the command center carpet. Blood pooled beneath him, and his eyes remained wide open in a death stare.

Allison had seen death up close before, and this body should not have sent her heart thumping as it had. She had been left no choice, and he had died in combat, at least. Though his codex would mark him as a traitor for the rest of Ghost Bear history. How could it not?

She took in a deep breath and tried slowing her heart rate, but realized she had lost control of it completely. It did not matter. She did not need to remain calm to issue her orders.

Turning back to the console on the desk, she keyed the comm to alert the Warriors waiting to defend their Clan inside Kodiak Point. They were always at the ready, and she needed them now more than ever.

"Ninety-sixth Battle Trinary. Star Captain Paugh. This is Star Captain Allison Rand, do you read me?"

"*Aff*, Star Captain, what may I do for you?"

"Scramble the Trinary."

"What are the orders, Star Captain?"

"We are betrayed. The ilKhan has rejected our vote to join the Star League, the Star Colonel has been killed, and the Jade Falcons are stealing our Bear Cubs. Go to and bring them back. They are loading up at the spaceport, and if you hurry, you might catch them. Launch the fighters if you have to."

Paugh hesitated, unable to mask her shock and surprise, but responded satisfactorily for the Star Captain. *"Aff."*

Allison clicked off the comm and straightened her uniform. Then she took another deep breath, doing her best to feel pleased with herself for doing her duty, reminding herself she had done only did what she had to do, and the Khans would be forced to side with her. The Star Colonel's death was a necessary price to pay, and she knew they would see it her way.

CHAPTER 34

From the back seat of his hover car, Khan Jiyi Chistu watched the transports drive across the spaceport's landing pads until they found themselves in the lee of the *Falcon's Shadow*. He could not have been more delighted with the outcome of this mission.

Well, he thought, *I have not quite done it yet.* He would not truly pat himself on the back until he had safely lifted off Quarell, never to see it again. The Ghost Bears would never again think to do another cross-training and war game trial with their *sibkos* so close to the Jade Falcon Occupation Zone. Had their games been held closer into the Rasalhague Dominion, they would have likely been safe from his machinations.

Likely.

But maybe not.

Jiyi smiled confidently, but a swirl of anxiety lay hidden in his belly like a zephyr of wind out of a clear blue sky. There was something more on the way, something he was missing. It had been too easy, and there was the nagging thought in his head that if he had just lost so many cadets, he would find some way to retaliate. Perhaps there was a Ghost Bear among them who felt the same way, and would risk their honor to strike out at them.

Knowing himself to know his opponents, Jiyi just did not trust his victory yet.

"Star Captain Quinn," he said.

"*Aff,* my Khan?"

Staring out at the transports and vans used to bring the *sibkos* to the landing platform, he thought preparedness would be the best strategy. "Be wary."

"Of the Ghost Bears? That Star Colonel was no Bear, but a vole, eager to throw himself into Jade Falcon talons."

"It is not him I am worried about, though I would not underestimate him either. He is a fine Warrior and an honorable one. No, there is something off about this whole situation. Surely not everyone agreed with his handling of it. The reports we have taken from Quarell since we landed paint a picture of political unrest distracted by the *sibko* war games. I do not believe the Star Colonel would cause a problem, but the frayed edges of that painting tell a tale of Ghost Bears who might take matters into their own hands."

"Shall I mobilize 'Mechs on the landing platform?"

"*Neg.* Not yet, anyway. Just keep an eye out and put your ear to the ground."

"*Aff,* my Khan."

His hover car stopped at the end of the line, and Jiyi was quick to get out. He wanted to greet some of these *sibko* cadets personally before their long voyage. They had to be made to feel like they were at home. And, if his knowledge of the Ghost Bears maintained accuracy, he would want to make them feel like *family.* After the success of his raid, though, he felt confident he knew the mind of the Ghost Bears.

The cadets filed out of the backs and sides of the mismatched, too-small transports they had convoyed to and from the spaceport, and Jiyi approached a group of them.

"You there, cadet," he called out.

The cadet, a tall, young woman, turned to greet him, standing at attention. He decided that with her determined attitude, dark skin, and even darker hair, she would be much more suited to wearing Falcon green than Ghost Bear blue.

"My Khan," was all she said.

Jiyi grinned. They had already come to know their place, wearing Falcon colors in their hearts already.

"What is your name and where were you from?"

"Cadet Hamilton, my Khan, and I was trained on Thun as part of the Dragonbears *sibko*."

"And how did the Dragonbears do in your competition?"

"We did not win, my Khan."

He smiled. He heard they had ended up coming up in last place. A diplomatic answer. "And do you feel your *sibko* deserved to lose?"

"Neg."

"What would you have done differently?"

"I would have studied our opponents more thoroughly before and during the war games. And I would have thought differently about how to approach the stealth ops."

"But you learned from these war games and ops, *quiaff*?"

"Aff."

"Then you did not lose. You are still in your *sibko*, and the goal of every exercise is to teach you. You win—even when you lose—because it shows you how to be better for the next engagement, *quiaff*?"

"Aff," she said again, and other members of her *sibko* nodded. They were scared, but he wanted to reassure them and show them things would be fine. He would show them the Jade Falcons were not the monsters they had probably been told about in their nursery schools and cadet trainings.

"Good." He gave her a satisfied nod. "Very good. Now carry on. We have no time to waste."

He remembered another group of cadets that had come through down and defeated, and he wanted to see about them. Their demeanor told them they had not been damaged in the games, but had suffered in some other way. He wanted no bad or broken apples in his *sibko* bunch.

He found one of them a few conveyances ahead, spotting them easily by their torn patches.

"You, cadet," he said to the boy who stood closest to him. Behind him cowered a second boy who might have been taller if his shoulders weren't slumping so badly. His eyes were red-rimmed and puffy. Had their transfer really caused tears? "What is your name and from where do you hail?"

The first cadet turned, but his demeanor was not as crisp as Hamilton's. He was hardly at attention, unimpressed, and Jiyi picked up anger from the kid like a seismic reading off the charts. The kid only tightened the muscles in his jaw, not wanting to answer at all.

"Your Khan has asked you a question, cadet."

"Thomasin," came his pained reply.

"Thomasin. And where do you hail from?"

"Quarell. Here."

"And what happened here?" Jiyi pointed at spots where patches had been ripped from his shoulder.

"Being a Warrior in training has its hazards."

Jiyi knew a bit about that. He had almost died in his *sibko,* and was only one of three that graduated. The others had washed out or were killed. The Jade Falcons had been a lot harder on cadets in his day than Ghost Bears ever were. "I know the feeling. But here you are, *quiaff?*"

"Aff," Thomasin said with no energy. But his eyes shifted to something beyond Jiyi, and his face brightened.

"They have come to rescue us!" The cadet behind Thomasin yelled with a genuine glee that could be problematic for Jiyi in the future.

He turned to look, wondering what had caught the boy's attention. The Khan's eyes scanned the horizon and sure enough, there were 'Mechs there, coming from the direction of Kodiak Point. "Of course," he muttered.

"You are never going to win, Falcon scum," Thomasin said.

"We are Ghost Bears!" the boy behind him said.

Jiyi turned to the boy and smiled grimly. "I am sorry you feel that way. I am sure your heart will change in time."

"Never!" he said, and then spit at Jiyi's feet.

Fire burned in Jiyi's eyes. He looked to the left and saw a group of cadets from a different *sibko* watching, wide-eyed. He snapped his fingers and cocked his head, beckoning them to him.

"Cadet Thomasin and his friend have asked for help to their bunk. I would appreciate if you gave it to them."

"*Aff,* my Khan."

Thomasin raised a finger at the Ghost Bear 'Mechs coming. "They are coming for you, Jade Falcon Khan!"

His compatriot struggled against the grips of their *sibkin*. "If you manage to get us out of here, we will escape and find our way home long before we become Jade Falcons."

Jiyi ignored the boys and nodded to the other cadets as they gripped Thomasin's arms. They dragged both boys toward the *Falcon's Shadow*. He understood they were afraid and angry. And, frankly, they were acting like Warriors. But Jiyi did not have time to have a personal discussion with each cadet about their fears. There were incoming Ghost Bear 'Mechs and a timetable to keep.

He turned back toward the end of the convoy and shouted, "Star Captain Quinn!"

"I see it," she said from closer by than he expected. "Orders?"

"Let us get to the DropShip and see what we can mobilize quickly."

"*Aff.*"

Together, Jiyi and the Star Captain ran for the boarding ramp of the *Falcon's Shadow,* passing by Thomasin and the other cadet being dragged there, kicking and screaming. "We will escape!"

"We will never wear Falcon green!"

"Charming kids," Jiyi told the Star Captain.

"They are certainly fierce."

"We need to get everyone aboard quickly. The longer we tarry, the more damage they can do and the more we risk them undoing all the work we have accomplished here."

"*Aff,* my Khan."

They made it to the entry ramp and into the central 'Mech bay of the *Overlord-C*-Class DropShip, the only one that had any fully operational 'Mechs inside. Half were significantly damaged.

Technicians bustled back and forth, already set to work repairing 'Mechs. MechWarriors young and old stood by the door, welcoming the new Jade Falcons as they boarded with smiles and open arms.

"What do we have ready?" the Khan asked Quinn.

"A few assault 'Mechs. We have a whole Star ready to go, but who would pilot them? And how would we get them back on board in time? There is at least a Trinary out there. Defending with our 'Mechs, riding out to meet them, would be suicide."

Jiyi nodded. "Then we hope the DropShip can save us if they do not scramble fighters."

"Excuse me, my Khan," said a voice from behind Jiyi.

Jiyi turned. "MechWarrior Hosteen?"

"My Khan, I would like to volunteer."

Jiyi offered a grim smile. Hosteen had performed admirably in the Trial. He was older, bordering on the age when he would be deemed *solahma* and sent for other duties. But that time had not yet come, and Jiyi still needed every Warrior he could get. "You realize that you would ride out, the doors would close, and we would leave."

"*Aff.* It would be an honorable end to cover your escape."

"I would volunteer, too," came the voice of another rank-less MechWarrior behind him. She, too, looked to be nearing *solahma* age.

In moments, he had five volunteers, an entire Star. They could keep the 'Mechs far enough away from the loading zone and spaceport that they would have a chance to get away, and the DropShip could deal with any fighters they scrambled on its own.

Jiyi did not like the prospect of leaving these Warriors behind. His Jade Falcons desperately needed officers.

But they could tell he was hedging.

"My Khan," said Hosteen, "it would be our honor to do this for the Jade Falcons. Take the cadets and rebuild. Promise us that you will rebuild the Clan to its former glory, and let us live on through future generations."

Jiyi clenched his teeth and his eyes almost watered. "That is my solemn oath."

"Then we will go," Hosteen said. "There is no time to waste."

"We are Jade Falcon!" the second volunteer said.

"*We are Jade Falcon!*" the rest repeated, and then they scrambled to their 'Mechs, ready to die for the survival of the Jade Falcons. Jiyi watched as MechWarrior Hosteen passed by Star Commander Dawn. She offered him and the passing *solahma* a perfect salute as they went by.

Jiyi snapped to attention himself, matching her salute.

"*Seyla*, my Falcons," he said quietly. "*Seyla.*"

Star Captain Allison Rand drove her *Kuma* out to battle. She saw the sprawling spaceport and its lone control tower reaching to the sky. The Jade Falcon DropShip stood below it in the distance almost half as tall, resting in one of the deep blast pits that marked the ferrocrete field. Magnifying her view, she saw the Ghost Bear cadets lined up, entering the DropShip one or two at a time. Processed into the Falcons like objects rather than people.

Anger rose within her.

"Faster!" she told the Ninety-Sixth, spittle spraying onto the viewscreen in front of her. "We cannot lose them!"

The cadets at the open bay of the Jade Falcon DropShip suddenly scrambled in different directions, making Rand's brow furrow. She wondered what was happening, but that wonder only lasted a moment.

The Falcons were mounting a counterattack. 'Mechs began streaming out of the bay.

Looking down at her map and the metrics of distance between her and her prize, the Jade Falcons would be able to keep her and the Ninety-Sixth occupied for only so long. And his JumpShip was scrambling fighters to protect the DropShip. So she, too, would scramble fighters and take out the DropShip as a last resort. She did not want to hurt any of the cadets, though destroying them and keeping them from the Jade Falcons was worth the cost. That was the *rede* of the Ghost Bears: to eliminate the fugitive enemies of the Clans.

The Jade Falcon 'Mechs shifted direction, maneuvering around their own convoy of transports and the mess of cadets trying to get out of the way, and began running toward her position at top speed.

The blips on her radar showed only five 'Mechs.

Confusion washed over the Star Captain, and she wondered what sort of trick this was. She had brought fifteen 'Mechs of the Ninety-Sixth, plus a Star from the Command Trinary. The Jade Falcons were outnumbered with everything she had at the ready. They would crumble beneath the firepower of twenty. It was a grim calculus, but that's how the math worked out. These five 'Mechs were doomed to die. Perhaps not quickly—they were assault 'Mechs, every one—but they would fall to the superior firepower of the Ghost Bears, and she would then set her sights on the DropShip. Once it was secure, they would return the Ghost Bears to their proper family.

Allison cursed the Star Colonel Hall for putting her in this position, then opened her comm. "Star Captain Timothy. Have Charlie and Bravo Battle Stars split off to engage with the interlopers."

"Consider it done, Star Captain."

"Alpha Command and Battle Stars, follow me to the DropShip. We *will* stop them."

"*Aff!*"

But the incoming Jade Falcon 'Mechs—her computer tagged them as a *Turkina*, two *Thunderbolt IIC*s, and two *Marauder IIC*s, all long-range assault 'Mechs—were moving to intercept her and her sortie, rather than the Stars coming straight for them.

It was a screening maneuver.

Magnifying her view once again, focusing on the DropShip, Allison saw the last of the Ghost Bear cadets stagger into the doors, which closed behind them.

"It is a suicide attack!" she said to those under her command. "These *dezgra* fools mean to escape!"

Looking down to her maps and the distance between them, Allison feared she would not be able to catch them before they took off completely.

Her mind racing with possibilities, Star Captain Rand decided she had one course of action left to her.

"Eradicate these 'Mechs." Then she switched her comm to radio back to Kodiak Point and the fighter wing. "Launch the fighters against the DropShip. Do it now. And send word to our space forces to launch an attack to capture or destroy VaultShip *Gamma*."

Allison had her computer mark the lead 'Mech. A *Turkina*. She aimed straight for it. These five Falcons would pay for their Clan's treachery with their lives if it was the last thing she did.

CHAPTER 35

OVERLORD-C-CLASS DROPSHIP *FALCON'S SHADOW*
JORGENSSON-TSENG SPACEPORT
ANTIMONY
QUARELL
RASALHAGUE DOMINION
08 NOVEMBER 3151

From the command center of the *Falcon's Shadow,* Jiyi watched two battles play out. The most immediate was that of the Jade Falcon pilots running through checklists and ignition sequences to take off as quickly as possible, while gunners got to battle stations in case the incoming Ghost Bear 'Mechs and fighters got within range. The second battle was on the monitor in front of the chair he had strapped himself into.

"Faster on the entry ramp retraction!" someone said.

"We are locking in our launch sequence now!" came another voice.

"Hurry!"

"Aff!"

"No!"

"That one over there!"

"Ghost Bear fighters incoming!"

The cacophony of the bridge was enough to break many concentrations, but not Jiyi's. He opened a radio communication to the Ghost Bears, hoping someone would be listening. Especially the Star Colonel, who did not seem as though his character would allow such *dezgra* actions. "Star Colonel Emilio

Hall, this is Jiyi Chistu of the Jade Falcons. We are under attack by rogue Ghost Bear forces after your promise of honor in loss of the Trial and safe passage."

No response came.

"I repeat, Star Colonel Emilio Hall, please come in."

The radio sputtered, and a sharp voice came through. "This is Star Captain Allison Rand."

"Where is the Star Colonel?"

"Dead. For betraying the Ghost Bears. I am in command now. And we are correcting his mistakes."

That news greeted Jiyi like a slap across the face. Anger rose in him; Hall was a fine Warrior and did not deserve such an end. "You know this dishonors both you and the Ghost Bears?"

"The Star Colonel dishonored us first. We now work to gain it back. There will be no parlay and no negotiation. I will not fall to your oily words, Falcon. And I will not be talked down. Rand, out."

The radio cut out abruptly.

Jiyi sat back, wide-eyed. "Well, so much for that working. But it was worth a shot."

As the DropShip made its final checks to depart, he focused on the monitor and the work of MechWarrior Hosteen. It was a glorious thing Hosteen was doing—that all of them were doing. They went out against a vastly superior force, apparently led by this Star Captain Allison Rand. It was a name Jiyi vowed not to forget, surely their actions would be worth a line in the Remembrance.

By that time, the firing had begun. Being in the assault 'Mechs he had brought to bedevil the Ghost Bears, the defending Falcons had a range advantage from the start. The Ghost Bear 'Mechs took the early hits with aplomb, but they started to lose 'Mechs before the Jade Falcon Assault Star had lost a single one.

He tuned in to their radio channels, listening to Hosteen command the battle.

"Luca!" Hosteen shouted, "watch your flank!"

"*Aff*, Hosteen."

"Erika, they are coming in hot. You have four circling and a fifth coming for you."

"There is another coming up over the landing pad!"

"Luca, get out of there!"

But Luca screamed before his radio squelched and his smoking, shattered 'Mech fell over on the monitor.

One down.

Jiyi needed to say a word to those laying down their lives as the DropShip readied for departure. Lifting the transmitter and pressing down on the button to activate it, he took a moment to summon the right words.

"Jade Falcons, this is your Khan. I want you to know that you are engaged in the great work of ensuring our survival. It has been my honor to fight alongside you. It has been my honor to serve as your Khan. I will make sure your names are added to our histories. You will be added to our Remembrance. Your genetic material will be used to ensure that more Jade Falcons are given the traits you possessed that brought us to this victory."

Jiyi hoped they could hear his words.

He hoped they *felt* them.

"It has been our honor, my Khan," Hosteen said, the sounds of laser and missile fire coming through behind his words. "And we will hold out as long as we can to screen your escape."

"I know you will. Thank you for giving your Clan the chance to survive."

"It is what we were born to do, my Khan," Hosteen answered.

There was a flash on the bridge and Jiyi looked up, his focus momentarily broken. The Ghost Bear aerospace fighters had scrambled and made their circle around to the *Falcon's Shadow.*

The DropShip's crew was loud enough Jiyi could hear them as well.

"—We have incoming!—"

"—Are the laser batteries operational?—"

"—Crews are returning fire!—"

"—We cannot let them through the screen!—"

"—Continue with the forward batteries, then, do not let anything get through!—"

"—Taking damage.—"

Glancing around, Jiyi realized he would not want to be in battle with any other group of pilots and Warriors. They were all the best who had ever fought, from Hosteen and the *solahma* charge to meet the Ghost Bears all the way to the bridge of the *Falcon's Shadow.*

They were all willing to lay their lives on the line for him and his schemes to save their Clan, and in that moment, he understood the truly awe-inspiring nature of that power. The grave nature of the situation made hairs on the back of his neck stand on end. "We need to get this DropShip in the air, or their sacrifice will be in vain."

"*Aff,* my Khan," the ship's captain, Cliff, said, turning to nod in deference. "We are doing our best."

"I know. And I know you would offer nothing short of your best. Your Khan appreciates it." Jiyi looked back down to the monitor of the ground battle.

The Jade Falcons had lost another 'Mech. One of the *Thunderbolt IIC*s. It was inevitable. Half of the Ghost Bears had circled around them and headed straight for the DropShip, opening fire as soon as they were in range.

"Cliff," Jiyi said, "How soon until we take flight?"

"We are at least five to eight minutes away from liftoff. Sooner if we can manage it."

"All possible speed," Jiyi said. Or else all of their work would be for naught.

Star Commander Dawn led the next batch of new Jade Falcon cadets to their quarters, gesturing them inside two or four at a time through the expansive DropShip. They were lucky to have as much room as they did for bringing the *sibkos* home.

Dawn could not imagine what these kids were going through, but caught herself. First, were they really kids? They were only a few years younger than her. And second, they were soon-to-be Warriors, and they were trained to deal with any adversity.

Then she put herself at that age in their position, and knew she would have been an angry mess, too. She would not have wanted to switch from the Jade Falcons to another Clan. And she would not want to feel as though her chance to be a Warrior could be robbed from her.

The last two cadets seemed different than the others. Their patches were torn off their sleeves and the edges of their uniforms were frayed. They looked resolute, sure, but beneath that veneer was obvious fright.

"I am Star Commander Dawn," she offered to them as she led them to their bunk. "What are your names?"

"I am Alexis," the one in front said with a tinge of exasperation and even more exhaustion.

The other did not seem to want to speak.

"This is Sophie," Alexis said.

"Is everything all correct with both of you?"

"It has been a long day."

"*Aff.* But I can assure you that it is over—"

The lights overhead sputtered, and the DropShip rocked, as if impacted with missiles near their quarters. All three of them looked up, expecting the whole thing to cave in.

"Do not worry," Dawn said, reassuring herself as much as the cadets. "These *Overlord-C*s are sturdier than you can imagine. It will take quite a bit of time for them to punch through."

Alexis nodded.

"Here you are." Dawn hit the button that slid open the door. The room was cramped. Barely enough room to maneuver, and two well-made bunks on the other side.

The one named Sophie went in first and climbed immediately to the top. Alexis lingered there in the doorway.

"It will not be so bad, little one," Dawn said, trying to be reassuring. "The Khan is not what you have heard of the Jade Falcons. And you will have a good home now. You are Jade Falcon."

Alexis looked down to her shoes and her eyes glassed over. She did an excellent job of hiding her tears. "I just wanted a family. This wasn't supposed to..."

Dawn tilted her head like a curious robin looking for a worm, considering the empty space where Alexis' patch should have been. "Did something else happen today?"

"*Aff,*" Alexis said, and her tears came closer to the front.

"They think Warriors are machines with no emotions, and they try to train us that way, but that is not how humans work, no matter how much they have tampered with our genes."

"I am freeborn," the girl said, almost in tears at her sputtering confession.

"All the same," Dawn said softly. "You will do fine. And if you need anything, come see me. You have friends here. Stick close to them. It does not have to be lonely."

The girl, Alexis, considered her words and her features softened. Dawn's word had given her heart. "Where is Thomasin?"

"I do not know who that is."

"He was a cadet that came here with me. He spit at the Khan, and they dragged him away with another, Daniel."

"Do not worry. I do not believe the Khan is the sort to resort to capital punishment. Especially not of children, and doubly so knowing the stress and shock you are all under."

"Will you find out? And look out for them?"

"You have my word."

"Truly?"

"My word is my bond, little one."

Without another word, the girl threw herself forward, embracing Dawn. Dawn had not expected that, nor was she quite equipped to know what to do when the girl buried her face in Dawn's shoulder.

Awkwardly, but with as much warmth as she could muster, Dawn put her arms around the girl and patted her on the back. "It will be okay. I promise."

"Thank you."

"It is nothing. Just be sure to be at the briefing. After we break orbit, the Khan wishes to address you all. You will be there, *quiaff*?"

"*Aff*," Alexis said, sniffling into Dawn's shoulder. "We will be there."

They separated, and Dawn backed up a step and put her hand on the button to close the door, but before she did, she looked at both girls once more in turn, smiling warmly to each of them. "I know this is scary, but I promise you are safe and in a good place."

"Thank you," Alexis said, as though she had never received such a kindness.

"You are Jade Falcons. And I will see you at the briefing." Dawn engaged the door, which slid shut quickly.

JORGENSSON-TSENG SPACEPORT
ANTIMONY
QUARELL
RASALHAGUE DOMINION
08 NOVEMBER 3151

From the command couch of her *Kuma,* Star Captain Allison Rand used her heavy large laser to melt right through the cockpit of the last Jade Falcon 'Mech, a *Turkina* that had given far too good of a fight. The green-and-gunmetal *Turkina* crumpled into a mess of melting armor and myomer at odd angles.

Looking up to the Jade Falcon DropShip, Allison knew her Trinary and extra Star could not bring an *Overlord-C* class ship down on their own, but with her fighters attacking and the VaultShip being pursued, anything they could bring to bear was going to help.

The *Overlord-C* could hold *three* Trinaries, so the DropShip would likely repel that many in an attack. And it had the armor to allow it to turtle for hours if it needed to. But if the Ghost Bears could get a DropShip of their own in the air to keep the Falcon DropShip docked...

"Press the attack!" she said into her radio.

Looking down at her display and on her wraparound viewscreen, she saw the Ninety-Sixth coalesce into a tight formation and approach the DropShip to find positions to continue the offensive. In the air, she saw the DropShip lasers flash in the distance, and then a Ghost Bear aerospace fighter erupted into fireball and fell to the ground in a blazing heap.

Another got shot out of the sky and nearly hit the DropShip itself.

"We cannot let them get away!" she shouted, anger shooting the words out of her throat.

As she traversed across the spaceport's landing surface, Allison thought of every cadet aboard that DropShip and what they must have been facing. It could not have been an easy prospect to believe that their superiors had simply given them away.

She hoped the attack would give them hope that perhaps they would keep their lives. She hoped that they could rescue them if possible, and wanted them to know that the Ghost Bears were coming, and they might not have to die as Jade Falcons after all.

But that was when the DropShip's engines ignited and it lifted up from its blast pit, heading toward the sky.

"Hurry!" she called out. "We can still hit it from the ground!"

She planted her *Kuma*'s feet into the ground and fired her heavy large laser again, flashing cyan, bright but almost invisible against the Quarellian sky. From her sides, the smoke trails of a dozen salvos of long-range missiles twisted up the horizon, all aiming for the DropShip. Their explosions peppered one by one across its thick carapace, barely denting it at all.

It would take so much more than they had to stop it.

She switched her radio channel to engage their command center. "Kodiak Point, this is Star Captain Allison Rand. Send everything we have at that DropShip. We cannot lose it."

"Star Captain Rand," the control center from Kodiak Point responded, "they have chewed the OmniFighters to pieces."

They only had ten fighters in the Star, and by her rough visual count, there were only a few left. "Scramble more from the Delta Fighter Trinary."

"Star Captain, they are in the next hemisphere, and the DropShip will be beyond orbit by the time they can make it here."

"Send them anyway!"

"*Aff*, Star Captain."

As the DropShip got further and further away, out of range of her Trinary's weapons, all she could think of were the cadets aboard the ship and what horrors would await them.

"*Stravag!*" she shouted, smashing her fist against her command console.

CHAPTER 36

OVERLORD-C-CLASS DROPSHIP *FALCON'S SHADOW*
QUARELL SYSTEM
RASALHAGUE DOMINION
08 NOVEMBER 3151

Alexis tried to find a place in the back of the briefing room where they had been directed once the battle was over and they were out of range of any potential Ghost Bear rescue. She held Sophie's hand the entire time.

Worry burned inside her, and as they waited for the Khan to address them, she looked around for Thomasin and Daniel. She wanted to know they were safe. That feeling for Thomasin felt natural, but feeling that for Daniel shocked her. She was truly saddened to see neither of them in the room. Even in trouble, she thought they might have been required to be at the briefing.

The din of her *sibkin* and the captured Jade Falcon bondsmen grew louder. They all grew impatient waiting for their new Khan, but Alexis did not see Thomasin anywhere.

Nor did she see Daniel.

She could not be sure, but she did not see a few she might have recognized from other *sibko*s that they had spent the last month competing against. This was definitely not everyone. Others must have been in trouble with the new Khan, too.

"I do not see Thomasin," Sophie said, whispering softly in Alexis' ear.

"Me, neither."

"Do you think he's okay?"

"I hope so. Star Commander Dawn said she would make sure he was. And I got a good feeling from her."

"I am glad one of us did. She is a Falcon, Alexis."

"So are you now, Sophie."

Sophie *harrumphed* and settled deeper into her seat.

Everyone went silent when the Khan finally entered the room. He marched in with purpose, wearing a Jade Falcon officer's uniform, but instead of a tie, his collar remained open. He seemed more casual than she would have guessed, but his countenance was grim, and he strode to the podium with purpose. Behind him, the large screen showed nothing but an illuminated Jade Falcon logo on a green field.

Gripping both sides of the lectern, the Khan looked out over the *sibkos* and right into Alexis with his sea-storm eyes. She found a softness there she did not expect. His exterior was exactly what she would have imagined from a Jade Falcon: unkempt, barely shaved, trademark eye scar. But there was something soulful about him that Alexis found inspiring. Charming, even.

She *wanted* to listen to him.

At least she could hear what he had to say, and then decide whether or not he was worth spitting on. Thomasin had not given him that chance.

"Cadets," he said finally. His voice sounded more likable in person rather than over the radio, threatening to steal them all. "I know all of you did not expect to wake up this morning Ghost Bears and go to sleep as Jade Falcons. It would not have been my first choice if I were you, either. I know some among your *sibkin* have decided they would rather die trying to escape than wear the green of Clan Jade Falcon. You will notice they are not here with you now."

She never thought Daniel and Thomasin would have agreed on anything, but she supposed that this was the one topic they were bound to find common ground and build a new *sibkin*ship.

"I do not blame them. In fact, I admire them for their spirit. They will be joining you soon, as long as they are able to behave and embrace their new future. For them, and even for the rest of you, I understand your resentment. You had no intention of being here."

The Khan cast his gaze across the *sibkos.* As his eyes passed over Alexis, a shiver crept up her back.

He continued. "Which of you called the Trial of Refusal on behalf of each of you?"

Alexis shrank, her shoulders hunched, and she looked down at her feet.

To their credit, none of her *sibkin* pointed her out. She could not be sure how the Khan would react to such insubordination.

"It is okay," the Khan said. "No harm will come to you for admitting the truth. Which one of you is Alexis?"

Sheepishly, Alexis raised a hand. "I am, my Khan."

Those last words were so difficult to say, especially as she braced for his anger.

Instead, he beamed. "Alexis?"

"Aff."

"Cadet Alexis, your spirit is admirable and the very spirit we need injected into our renewed Jade Falcons. You have my respect and admiration."

This level of praise and acceptance from the Khan of her new Clan made Alexis' head swim. But it also rippled through her chest like a balm.

"I promise you," the Khan continued, "*all of you*—that you will have a better future as a Jade Falcon than you would have had as a Ghost Bear. None of you are Warriors yet. You would have had a chance to wash out or fail your Trial of Position and end up in a lower caste. That will not happen with you in the Jade Falcons. You will be Warriors, even if you fail your Trial. Granted, you might end up in the infantry at that point, but you *will* fight and have a chance at glory."

The Khan looked across the room and managed to find Alexis' eyes again. She did not know how to accept his words or praise.

He seemed to lock eyes with *everyone* in the room and she wondered if the others felt the same. Were they simply guarding against his promises? Or believing them?

"The Ghost Bears are a fine Clan," he said matter-of-factly, "but there are many, many Ghost Bears and few battles they fought. How many Ghost Bears shine bright enough to earn a place in the histories? How many stand out as Warriors? How many battles do Ghost Bears even fight these days? They sit fattened for winter in decades of hibernation. The odds of you being remembered as a Ghost Bear are infinitesimal. But as a Jade Falcon? We have so many fights ahead that you will unquestionably be bathed in glory."

Someone down in the front row actually gasped at this pronouncement. Alexis could not tell if it was in excitement or disbelief. Possibly both.

Sophie squeezed Alexis's hand tighter, and could practically feel her competing doses of excitement and anxious energy.

"I will be honest with you all," said the Khan. "You might have heard many stories of the Jade Falcons. Many of them may even have been true once. But the Jade Falcons are changing. Some might say drastically. We adapt to survive, and in this, we are family now. We will not be caught quarreling among ourselves, as you saw the Ghost Bears do. Some of these changes will benefit you all, my new cadets. The future leaders of Clan Jade Falcon are very likely sitting in this room right now. The best among you will win that honor."

Alexis' *sibkin* practically *ooh*ed and *aah*ed at that prospect.

"How many of you are freeborn?" he asked finally.

A half-dozen hands in the room raised. Alexis was surprised to find herself confident enough to raise her own hand as well. Sophie had nudged it up on its way for her, but it was raised nonetheless.

"You. Cadet Alexis. You have the spark that makes this a certainty." The Khan pointed right at Alexis. "What was your last name before joining the Ghost Bears?"

Alexis barely found her voice. "Zarnofsky."

"How would you like to see Zarnofsky elevated to a Bloodname for the Jade Falcons? Prove yourself worthy, and a new branch of our family tree shall begin. You will become a legend, because you will be the first of your line." The Khan looked around the room to the rest of the freeborns with their hands raised. "That would make you all legends."

They lowered their hands—Alexis a bit slower than the rest.

"Welcome to the Jade Falcons, Alexis Zarnofsky. And all of you. This is your new family, and I promise we will take care of each other."

Alexis soaked his words up like a sponge.

It was everything she had ever wanted to hear a leader say.

Squeezing Sophie's hand, Alexis took in a deep breath and smiled. Perhaps she would like being a Jade Falcon after all.

For the first time in a long time, Alexis felt like she was home.

EPILOGUE

ANTIMONY
QUARELL
RASALHAGUE DOMINION
21 NOVEMBER 3151

From the command couch of her *Kuma,* Star Captain Allison Rand listened to the local news stations. Unrest and riots in the streets of Antimony. Of Tholos. Of Silver Summit and Paralia. From the Pig Iron Plains to the hills of Emporio. Even in the smaller towns of West Enterprise and New Santorini.

She pushed her 'Mech forward, marching step by step to the Prime Minister's residence.

Prime Minister Erika Gulbrand, a prominent refuser, had locked herself in the governor's mansion. From there, she had broadcast a message to the people of Quarell, telling them there would be no revote, nor would there be a recount. The vote was final and, apparently, so was the ilKhan's decision if they did not find a way to formalize a unanimous vote or a unilateral decision from the Prime Minister and the Ghost Bear Khans.

As the ranking Ghost Bear in the military on Quarell, and an ardent joiner, Allison Rand had decided to lead the coup to remove Gulbrand and fix the vote so the Ghost Bears and the new Star League could once again be whole.

Turning the corner, she saw Star Captain Ahmed in his *Kodiak,* guarding the official residence. Many of the Ninety-Sixth had been traitors and refusers. When it became apparent what was happening, they had left with their 'Mechs and created a resistance against the joiners.

"Ahmed," Rand said on an open radio signal. "I am still disappointed by your decision to abandon your post in betrayal."

"I am defending the sanctity of the Ghost Bears and the sanctity of the democratic process of the Rasalhague Dominion, Star Captain. As well as the wishes of the ilKhan. You must stand down."

"Clan Ghost Bear does not recognize you as anything but a traitor. Stand down, or we will attack."

"I do not wish to fight, Star Captain," Ahmed said. Lying, most likely.

"Do not test me, Ahmed."

"I do not aim to test. We are protecting the duly elected civilian government of this planet. We will not attack first, merely retaliate for any hostile actions."

Allison had a choice to make, as did so many Dominion citizens across every world in Rasalhague.

She took a deep breath...

Steeled herself...

And pushed her *Kuma* forward into the fight.

HAMMARR SPACEPORT
HAMMARR
SUDETEN
JADE FALCON OCCUPATION ZONE
09 DECEMBER 3151

Grateful to be home with a new batch of Warriors no matter how costly the Ghost Bear Star Colonel had made their wager, Jiyi loved the feeling of walking on solid ground once more. He could not help but smile as he took in the fresh air. The Warriors he had brought and the would-be Warriors he had won filtered out of the DropShip behind him, all stretching their legs and squinting in the bright sun of Sudeten.

Their new home. At least, until the Jade Falcons found a better one to call their headquarters.

The Khan saw Merchant Factor Jodine come out from the spaceport to great them, and his smile broadened further. "Merchant Factor Jodine!"

Stone-faced, she stepped up and struck him right across the face. "If you ever even *think* of risking my VaultShip again, I will kill you."

The assembly of Warriors behind the Khan pouring from the DropShip stopped and all stared, wide-eyed. No one ever talked to a Warrior, much less a Khan, like that if they expected to live.

It took Jiyi a moment to shake off the blow, but when he gained his wits again, he laughed, long and loud. "This is *exactly* the spirit of the new Jade Falcons."

She turned away from him, still fuming.

But Jiyi put on a show for the Warriors and cadets surrounding them, all waiting to understand how to react to such a sight. Normally, a Merchant would *never* strike a Warrior and live, let alone live long enough to threaten them afterward.

Instead, Jiyi spread his arms like a carnival barker. "You all see this? Honor and respect are not exclusive to Warriors! I have offended the Merchant Factor, a vital part of our society. There is no question about it. I wagered VaultShip *Gamma*—*her* ship, the ship of the leader of our Merchant caste—without warning her, all in my bid to win the new blood our Clan needed. It worked. But she did not deserve this."

They all looked on, curious. None of this made any sense to them. No Clan Warrior had ever offered such respect to a member of the Merchant caste.

And he understood their confusion.

"If the Jade Falcons are to survive, closer bonds of fellowship with the other castes are required. Warriors will lead, but that is because we are the tip of the spear. But we are all part of the same weapon, and one cannot strike without the rest, *quiaff*?"

The Warriors and cadets looked skeptical, but he would have time to work with them all and change their attitudes. It would be a change for the Falcons, too, but as he said, it was necessary for their survival.

The Jade Falcons were being reborn.

Right before their eyes.

Of course, it would be difficult for some. But they would learn, or they would perish.

And Jiyi would do anything to ensure the Jade Falcons would not perish, and so he would endeavor to teach them how to learn and adapt.

Alexis debarked from the DropShip with Sophie at her side.

"I still do not like this," Thomasin said from behind them.

"Neither do I," Daniel said.

"Of course you do not," Alexis told them.

It had only been a couple of weeks since they had been let out. Their new green uniforms actually suited both of them. In Thomasin's case, Alexis thought it brightened his eyes and brought out hints of green in them, too. For Daniel, it was fine. They had botched the tailoring on his, so the uniform was not as flattering as it could have been.

"These are the worst."

"Why would we like these?" Thomasin asked.

"Because you like Sophie and I too much," Alexis said with a silly smirk.

Sophie stopped and pulled Alexis to a halt with her, allowing Thomasin to catch up. Daniel straggled behind.

Thomasin wrapped an arm around Sophie and Alexis. "I suppose if there is any reason, it is that. Ghost Bears or Falcons, we are still family."

"And we always will be," Alexis said.

"Give me a break." Daniel passed by them, annoyed.

They had befriended him, but he had not changed *that* much.

The four of them kept pace at the back of the crowd, filing out with the rest of the cadets.

Alexis looked out to the horizon of Sudeten, and thought this would make as good a home as any. She studied the crowd of Warriors and cadets, and caught sight of Star Commander Dawn, who came over to see them. "Alexis, Sophie, it is good to see you doing better."

"Thank you, Star Commander Dawn," Alexis said.

"And thank you for your help with him," Sophie said, tousling Thomasin's hair.

"Hey," Thomasin protested, letting go of Alexis and Sophie. "But seriously, Star Commander Dawn, I am truly grateful for your help."

With the sun in her face, Star Commander Dawn squinted. "I knew you would see the light."

"I hope we will see you around," Alexis said. She had very few friends, and it would be good to have a tried-and-true Warrior among them.

"You will," Dawn said, putting her hand on Alexis' shoulder. "You will all take your Trials soon, and your entry into this new family will be complete. And we will be Warriors together, and do exactly as our Khan commands."

"I did not know the Jade Falcons believed in family so much," Sophie said.

Dawn furrowed her brow. "Nor I, but I think, as the Khan says, there will be a new way of things for the Jade Falcons. And with so many former Ghost Bears now among our ranks, family is something us old school Falcons will have to get used to."

"That sounds like exactly what we need," Alexis said, and meant it. "Family."

I am Jade Falcon, she thought, looking up at the brilliant blue sky. The Jade Falcons would be all the family she ever needed.

And with them, she would soar.

ACKNOWLEDGMENTS

This book would not have been possible without the support of my family and my kids. They are so gracious in their tolerance of me working as hard as I do on my writing.

I would be nowhere without my writing group, the Salt City Genre Writers and the rest of the League of Utah Writers. I feel like we are all impostors, and they do their best to remind me that I'm where I'm supposed to be.

I want to thank the entire crew at Catalyst Game Labs and the entire fact check team who did their best to keep this manuscript on the straight and narrow. I'm still relatively new to *BattleTech*, and their guidance and patience has been nothing of amazing. They are nothing less than a fine bunch of people. John Helfers, Katherine Monasterio, Philip A. Lee, and Michael A. Stackpole were specifically invaluable resources who helped make this a better book. And I also want to call Ray Arrastia out specifically for pointing me at this story, bringing me in, and believing I was the right person for the job. I hope I did it justice.

MORE BATTLETECH FICTION
BY BRYAN YOUNG

A TEST OF LOYALTY...

Clan Jade Falcon's war efforts draw closer to Terra, but to conquer this ultimate prize, the Falcons' vicious Khan, Malvina Hazen, must be able to trust all of her warriors to carry out her commands without hesitation—no matter how much death or collateral damage they will cause. For Malvina, victory is the only thing that matters, and those who stand in her way suffer swift and brutal elimination.

Star Captain Archer Pryde is an unconventional Falcon MechWarrior who chafes at carrying out his Khan's terror tactics, but he delivers results in combat, so Malvina has turned a blind eye to his beliefs so far. But when civilians on a conquered world revolt against their Clan masters, innocents are caught in the Falcons' crosshairs. Archer and his fellow MechWarriors must prove their mettle to Star Colonel Nikita Malthus, the Khan's vindictive advisor, by carrying out their scorched-earth orders to the letter. But are these orders a betrayal of what it means to be a true and honorable Jade Falcon? With both his loyalty and honor in question, Archer must run the gauntlet between duty and principles, or risk his own destruction...

BEAR CUB
Light—25 tons

EXECUTIONER (GLADIATOR)
Assault—95 tons

GRIZZLY
HEAVY—**70** TONS

GRENDEL
MEDIUM—**45** TONS

GYRFALCON
MEDIUM—55 TONS

HEL (LOKI MK II)
MEDIUM—55 TONS

KARHU
HEAVY—65 TONS

KODIAK
ASSAULT—100 TONS

KUMA
HEAVY—60 TONS

LOBO
MEDIUM—40 TONS

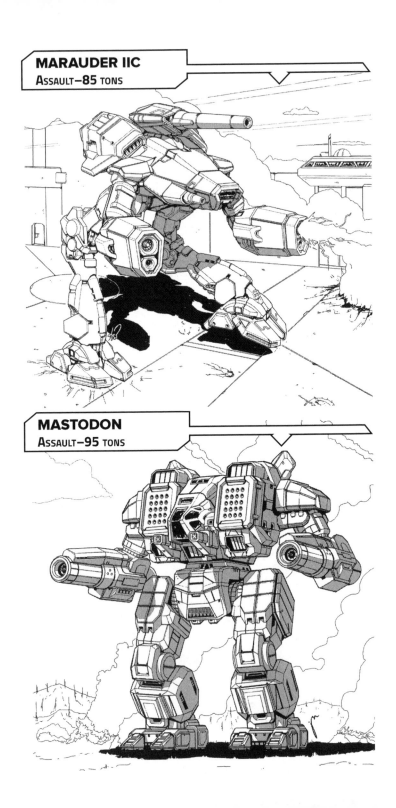

MARAUDER IIC
Assault—85 tons

MASTODON
Assault—95 tons

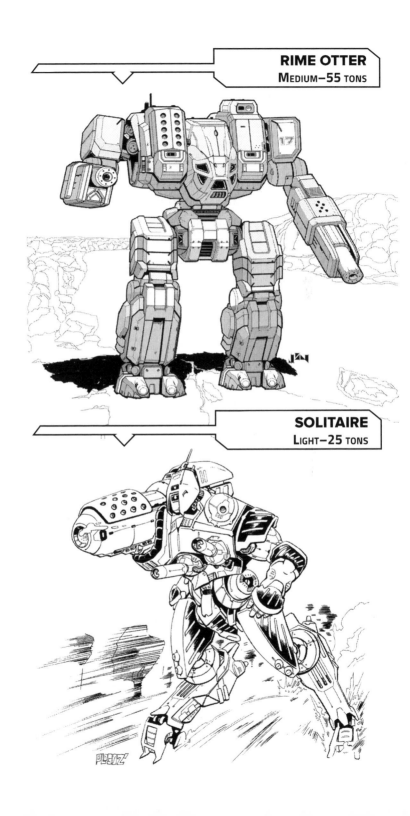

RIME OTTER
MEDIUM—55 TONS

SOLITAIRE
LIGHT—25 TONS

THUNDERBOLT IIC
HEAVY—70 TONS

TURKINA
ASSAULT—95 TONS

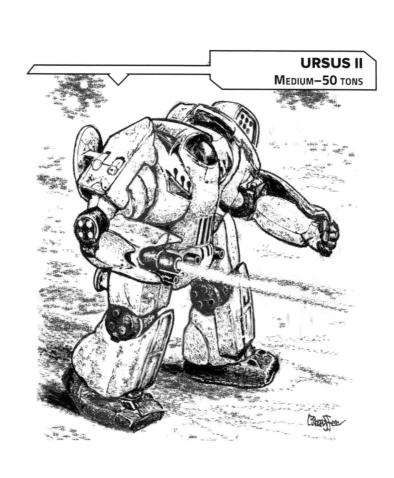

URSUS II
MEDIUM—50 TONS

BATTLETECH GLOSSARY

Clan military unit designations are used throughout this book:

Point: 1 'Mech or 5 infantry
Star: 5 'Mechs or 25 infantry
Binary: 2 Stars
Trinary: 3 Stars
Cluster: 4-5 Binaries/Trinaries
Galaxy: 3-5 Clusters
Nova: 1 'Mech Star and 1 infantry Star
Supernova: 1 'Mech Binary and 2 infantry Stars

ABTAKHA

A captured opponent who is adopted into his new Clan as a warrior.

AUTOCANNON

A rapid-fire, auto-loading weapon. Light autocannons range from 30 to 90 millimeter (mm), and heavy autocannons may be from 80 to 120mm or more. They fire high-speed streams of high-explosive, armor-piercing shells.

BATCHALL

The ritual by which Clan warriors issue combat challenges. Though the type of challenge varies, most begin with the challenger identifying themselves, stating the prize of the contest, and requesting that the defender identify the forces at their disposal. The defender also has the right to name the location of the trial. The two sides then bid for what forces will participate in the contest. The subcommander who bids to fight with the number of forces wins the right and responsibility to make the attack. The defender may increase the stakes by demanding a prize of equal or lesser value if they wish.

BATTLEMECH

BattleMechs are the most powerful war machines ever built. First developed by Terran scientists and engineers, these huge vehicles are faster, more mobile, better-armored and more heavily armed than any twentieth-century tank. Ten to twelve meters tall and equipped with particle projection cannons, lasers, rapid-fire autocannon and missiles, they pack enough firepower to flatten anything but another BattleMech. A small fusion reactor provides virtually unlimited power, and BattleMechs can be adapted to fight in environments ranging from sun-baked deserts to subzero arctic ice fields.

BLOODNAME

A Bloodname is the surname associated with a Bloodright, descended from one of the 800 warriors who stood with Nicholas Kerensky to form the Clans. A warrior must win the use of a Bloodname in a Trial of Bloodright. Only Bloodnamed warriors may sit on Clan Councils or hold the post of Loremaster, Khan, or ilKhan, and only the genetic material from the Bloodnamed is used in the warrior caste eugenics program.

BONDCORD

A woven bracelet worn by bondsmen who has been captured and claimed by a Clan member. Warrior-caste bondsmen wear a three-strand bondcord on their right wrists, with the color and patterning of the cords signifying the Clan and unit responsible for the warrior's capture. The cords represent integrity, fidelity, and prowess. The bondholder may cut each strand as he or she feels the bondsman demonstrates the associated quality. According to tradition, when the final cord is severed, the bondsman is considered a free member of his or her new Clan and adopted into the Warrior caste. Each Clan follows this tradition to varying degrees. For example, Clan Wolf accepts nearly all worthy individuals regardless of their past, while Clan Smoke Jaguar generally chose to adopt only Trueborn warriors.

BONDSMAN

A bondsman is a prisoner held in a form of indentured servitude until released or accepted into the Clan. Most often, bondsmen are captured warriors who fulfill roles in the laborer or technician castes. Their status is represented by a woven bondcord, and they are obliged by honor and tradition to work for their captors to the best of their abilities.

CASTE

The Clans are divided into five castes: warrior, scientist, merchant, technician, and laborer, in descending order of influence. Each has many subcastes based on specialized skills. The warrior caste is largely the product of the artificial breeding program; those candidates who fail their Trial of Position are assigned to the scientist or technician caste, giving those castes a significant concentration of Trueborn members. Most of the civilian castes are made up of the results of scientist-decreed arranged marriages within the castes.

The children of all castes undergo intensive scrutiny during their schooling to determine the caste for which they are best suited, though most end up in the same caste as their parents. This process allows children born to members of civilian castes to enter training to become warriors, though they belong to the less-prestigious ranks of the freeborn.

CHALCAS

Clan term referring to a person or belief that challenges the Clans' rigid caste system.

CIRCLE OF EQUALS

The area in which a trial takes place is known as the Circle of Equals. It ranges in size from a few dozen feet for personal combat to tens of miles for large-scale trials. Though traditionally a circle, the area can be any shape.

CODEX

Each Clan warrior's personal record, contained on a bracelet as a digital file. It includes the names of the original Bloodnamed warriors from which a warrior is descended. It also records background information such as a warrior's generation number, Blood House, and Codex ID, an alphanumeric code noting the unique aspects of that person's DNA. The Codex also contains a record of the warrior's military career.

CRUSADER

A Crusader is a Clansman who espouses the invasion of the Inner Sphere and the re-establishment of the Star League by military force. Most Crusaders are contemptuous of the people of the Inner Sphere, whom they view as barbarians, and of freeborns within their own Clans.

DEZGRA

Any disgraced individual or unit is known as *dezgra*. Disgrace may come through refusing orders, failing in an assigned task, acting dishonorably, or demonstrating cowardice.

DROPSHIPS

Because interstellar JumpShips must avoid entering the heart of a solar system, they must "dock" in space at a considerable distance from a system's inhabited worlds. DropShips were developed for interplanetary travel. As the name implies, a DropShip is attached to hardpoints on the JumpShip's drive core, later to be dropped from the parent vessel after in-system entry. Though incapable of FTL travel, DropShips are highly maneuverable, well-armed and sufficiently aerodynamic to take off from and land on a planetary surface. The journey from the jump point to the inhabited worlds of a system usually requires a normal-space journey of several days or weeks, depending on the type of star.

FLAMER

Flamethrowers are a small but time-honored anti-infantry weapon in vehicular arsenals. Whether fusion-based or fuel-based, flamers spew fire in a tight beam that "splashes" against a target, igniting almost anything it touches.

FREEBIRTH

Freebirth is a Clan epithet used by Trueborn members of the warrior caste to express disgust or frustration. For one Trueborn to use this curse to refer to another Trueborn is considered a mortal insult.

FREEBORN

An individual conceived and born by natural means is referred to as freeborn. Its emphasis on the artificial breeding program allows Clan society to view such individuals as second-class citizens.

GAUSS RIFLE

This weapon uses magnetic coils to accelerate a solid nickel-ferrous slug about the size of a football at an enemy target, inflicting massive damage through sheer kinetic impact at long range and with little heat. However, the accelerator coils and the slug's supersonic speed mean that while the Gauss rifle is smokeless and lacks the flash of an autocannon, it has a much more potent report that can shatter glass.

HEGIRA

Hegira is the rite by which a defeated foe may withdraw from the field of battle without further combat and with no further loss of honor.

ISORLA

The term for spoils of battle, including bondsmen, claimed by victorious Clan warriors.

JUMPSHIPS

Interstellar travel is accomplished via JumpShips, first developed in the twenty-second century. These somewhat ungainly vessels consist of a long, thin drive core and a sail resembling an enormous parasol, which can extend up to a kilometer in width. The ship is named for its ability to "jump" instantaneously across vast distances of space. After making its jump, the ship cannot travel until it has recharged by gathering up more solar energy.

The JumpShip's enormous sail is constructed from a special metal that absorbs vast quantities of electromagnetic energy from the nearest star. When it has soaked up enough energy, the sail transfers it to the drive core, which converts it into a space-twisting field. An instant later, the ship arrives at the next jump point, a distance of up to thirty light-years. This field is known as hyperspace, and its discovery opened to mankind the gateway to the stars.

JumpShips never land on planets. Interplanetary travel is carried out by DropShips, vessels that are attached to the JumpShip until arrival at the jump point.

KHAN (kaKhan, saKhan)

Each Clan Council elects two of its number as Khans, who serve as rulers of the Clan and its representatives on the Grand Council. Traditionally, these individuals are the best warriors in the Clan, but in practice many Clans instead elect their most skilled politicians. The senior Khan, sometimes referred to as the kaKhan, acts as the head of the Clan, overseeing relationships between castes and Clans. The junior Khan, known as the saKhan, acts as the Clan's warlord. The senior Khan decides the exact distribution of tasks, and may assign the saKhan additional or different duties.

The term "kaKhan" is considered archaic, and is rarely used.

LASER

An acronym for "Light Amplification through Stimulated Emission of Radiation." When used as a weapon, the laser damages the target by concentrating extreme heat onto a small area. BattleMech lasers are designated as small, medium or large. Lasers are also available as shoulder-fired weapons operating from a portable backpack power unit. Certain range-finders and targeting equipment also employ low-level lasers.

LONG-RANGE MISSILE (LRM)

An indirect-fire missile with a high-explosive warhead.

MACHINE GUN

A small autocannon intended for anti-personnel assaults. Typically non-armor-penetrating, machine guns are often best used against infantry, as they can spray a large area with relatively inexpensive fire.

PARTICLE PROJECTION CANNON (PPC)

One of the most powerful and long-range energy weapons on the battlefield, a PPC fires a stream of charged particles that outwardly functions as a bright blue laser, but also throws off enough static discharge to resemble a bolt of manmade lightning. The kinetic and heat impact of a PPC is enough to cause the vaporization of armor and structure alike, and most PPCs have the power to kill a pilot in his machine through an armor-penetrating headshot.

POSSESSION, TRIAL OF

A Trial of Possession resolves disputes between two parties over ownership or control. This can include equipment, territory, a person, or even genetic material. The traditional *batchall* forms the core of the trial in order to encourage the participants to resolve the dispute with minimal use of force.

REDE

A promise or oath that reflects on the swearer's honor is considered a *rede*. Breaking a *rede* is considered extremely serious, and is sometimes punishable by death.

REMEMBRANCE, THE

The Remembrance is an ongoing heroic saga that describes Clan history from the time of the Exodus to the present day. Each Clan maintains its own version, reflecting its opinions and perceptions of events. Inclusion in The Remembrance is one of the highest honors possible for a member of the Clans. All Clan warriors can recite passages from The Remembrance from memory, and written copies of the book are among the few nontechnical books allowed in Clan society. These books are usually lavishly illustrated in a fashion similar to the illuminated manuscripts and Bibles of the medieval period. Warriors frequently paint passages of The Remembrance on the sides of their OmniMechs, fighters, and battle armor.

SEYLA

Seyla is a ritual response in Clan ceremonies. The origin of this phrase is unknown, though it may come from the Biblical notation "selah," thought to be a musical notation or a reference to contemplation.

SHORT-RANGE MISSILE (SRM)

A direct-trajectory missile with high-explosive or armor-piercing explosive warheads. They have a range of less than one kilometer and are only reliably accurate at ranges of less than 300 meters. They are more powerful, however, than LRMs.

SIBKO

A Clan word for "sibling company," the primary means by which Clan warriors are raised and trained. Sibkos are generally collections of Trueborn children produced by the same geneparents, and number upwards of one hundred children. Freeborns who have proven themselves fit for warrior training are also placed into sibkos and undergo a training regime designed to make them the best warriors possible. Here they begin training in skills necessary for their individual role, whether as MechWarriors, aerospace pilots, or Elementals, until around their 20th birthday when they either pass their Trial of Position and become a full warrior, or fail. Those who fail their trial are relegated to the civilian castes, though some progressive Clans do allow a secondary Trial of Position to allow potential warriors the chance to rank in a second-line unit.

SUCCESSOR LORDS

After the fall of the first Star League, the remaining members of the High Council each asserted his or her right to become First Lord. Their star empires became known as the Successor States and the rulers as Successor Lords. The Clan Invasion temporarily interrupted centuries of warfare known as the Succession Wars, which first began in 2786.

SURAT

A Clan epithet, alluding to the rodent of the same name, which disparages an individual's genetic heritage. As such, it is one of the most vulgar and offensive epithets among the Clans.

TOUMAN

The fighting arm of a Clan is known as the *touman*.

TROTHKIN

Used formally, *trothkin* refers to members of an extended *sibko*. It is more commonly used to denote members of a gathering, and warriors also frequently use it when addressing someone they consider a peer.

TRUEBIRTH/TRUEBORN

A warrior born of the Clan's artificial breeding program is known as a Trueborn. In less formal situations, the Clans use the term Truebirth.

WARDEN

A Warden is a Clansman who believes that the Clans were established to guard the Inner Sphere from outside threats rather than to conquer it and re-establish the Star League by force. Most Wardens were opposed to the recent invasion of the Inner Sphere.

ZELLBRIGEN

Zellbrigen is the body of Clan rules governing duels. These rules dictate that such actions are one-on-one engagements, and that any warriors not immediately challenged should stay out of the battle until an opponent is free.

Once a Clan warrior engages a foe, no other warriors on his or her side may target that foe, even if it means allowing the death of the Clan warrior. Interfering in a duel by attacking a foe that is already engaged constitutes a major breach of honor, and usually results in loss of rank. Such action also opens the battle to a melee.

BATTLETECH ERAS

The *BattleTech* universe is a living, vibrant entity that grows each year as more sourcebooks and fiction are published. A dynamic universe, its setting and characters evolve over time within a highly detailed continuity framework, bringing everything to life in a way a static game universe cannot match.

To help quickly and easily convey the timeline of the universe—and to allow a player to easily "plug in" a given novel or sourcebook—we've divided *BattleTech* into eight major eras.

STAR LEAGUE
(Present–2780)

Ian Cameron, ruler of the Terran Hegemony, concludes decades of tireless effort with the creation of the Star League, a political and military alliance between all Great Houses and the Hegemony. Star League armed forces immediately launch the Reunification War, forcing the Periphery realms to join. For the next two centuries, humanity experiences a golden age across the thousand light-years of human-occupied space known as the Inner Sphere. It also sees the creation of the most powerful military in human history.

(This era also covers the centuries before the founding of the Star League in 2571, most notably the Age of War.)

SUCCESSION WARS
(2781–3049)

Every last member of First Lord Richard Cameron's family is killed during a coup launched by Stefan Amaris. Following the thirteen-year war to unseat him, the rulers of each of the five Great Houses disband the Star League. General Aleksandr Kerensky departs with eighty percent of the Star League Defense Force beyond known space and the Inner Sphere collapses into centuries of warfare known as the Succession Wars that will eventually result in a massive loss of technology across most worlds.

CLAN INVASION
(3050–3061)

A mysterious invading force strikes the coreward region of the Inner Sphere. The invaders, called the Clans, are descendants of Kerensky's SLDF troops, forged into a society dedicated to becoming the greatest fighting force in history. With vastly superior technology and warriors, the Clans conquer world after world. Eventually this outside threat will forge a new Star League, something hundreds of years of warfare failed to accomplish. In addition, the Clans will act as a catalyst for a technological renaissance.

CIVIL WAR
(3062–3067)

The Clan threat is eventually lessened with the complete destruction of a Clan. With that massive external threat apparently neutralized, internal conflicts explode around the Inner Sphere. House Liao conquers its former Commonality, the St. Ives Compact; a rebellion of military units belonging to House Kurita sparks a war with their powerful border enemy, Clan Ghost Bear; the fabulously powerful Federated Commonwealth of House Steiner and House Davion collapses into five long years of bitter civil war.

JIHAD
(3067–3080)

Following the Federated Commonwealth Civil War, the leaders of the Great Houses meet and disband the new Star League, declaring it a sham. The pseudo-religious Word of Blake—a splinter group of ComStar, the protectors and controllers of interstellar communication—launch the Jihad: an interstellar war that pits every faction against each other and even against themselves, as weapons of mass destruction are used for the first time in centuries while new and frightening technologies are also unleashed.

DARK AGE
(3081-3150)

Under the guidance of Devlin Stone, the Republic of the Sphere is born at the heart of the Inner Sphere following the Jihad. One of the more extensive periods of peace begins to break out as the 32nd century dawns. The factions, to one degree or another, embrace disarmament, and the massive armies of the Succession Wars begin to fade. However, in 3132 eighty percent of interstellar communications collapses, throwing the universe into chaos. Wars erupt almost immediately, and the factions begin rebuilding their armies.

ILCLAN
(3151-present)

The once-invulnerable Republic of the Sphere lies in ruins, torn apart by the Great Houses and the Clans as they wage war against each other on a scale not seen in nearly a century. Mercenaries flourish once more, selling their might to the highest bidder. As Fortress Republic collapses, the Clans race toward Terra to claim their long-denied birthright and create a supreme authority that will fulfill the dream of Aleksandr Kerensky and rule the Inner Sphere by any means necessary: The ilClan.

CLAN HOMEWORLDS
(2786-present)

In 2784, General Aleksandr Kerensky launched Operation Exodus, and led most of the Star League Defense Force out of the Inner Sphere in a search for a new world, far away from the strife of the Great Houses. After more than two years and thousands of light years, they arrived at the Pentagon Worlds. Over the next two-and-a-half centuries, internal dissent and civil war led to the creation of a brutal new society—the Clans. And in 3049, they returned to the Inner Sphere with one goal—the complete conquest of the Great Houses.

LOOKING FOR MORE HARD HITTING BATTLETECH FICTION?

WE'LL GET YOU RIGHT BACK INTO THE BATTLE!

Catalyst Game Labs brings you the very best in *BattleTech* fiction, available at most ebook retailers, including Amazon, Apple Books, Kobo, Barnes & Noble, and more!

NOVELS

1. *Decision at Thunder Rift* by William H. Keith Jr.
2. *Mercenary's Star* by William H. Keith Jr.
3. *The Price of Glory* by William H. Keith, Jr.
4. *Warrior: En Garde* by Michael A. Stackpole
5. *Warrior: Riposte* by Michael A. Stackpole
6. *Warrior: Coupé* by Michael A. Stackpole
7. Wolves on the Border by Robert N. Charrette
8. *Heir to the Dragon* by Robert N. Charrette
9. *Lethal Heritage* (The Blood of Kerensky, Volume 1) by Michael A. Stackpole
10. *Blood Legacy* (The Blood of Kerensky, Volume 2) by Michael A. Stackpole
11. *Lost Destiny* (The Blood of Kerensky, Volume 3) by Michael A. Stackpole
12. *Way of the Clans* (Legend of the Jade Phoenix, Volume 1) by Robert Thurston
13. *Bloodname* (Legend of the Jade Phoenix, Volume 2) by Robert Thurston
14. *Falcon Guard* (Legend of the Jade Phoenix, Volume 3) by Robert Thurston
15. *Wolf Pack* by Robert N. Charrette
16. *Main Event* by James D. Long
17. *Natural Selection* by Michael A. Stackpole
18. *Assumption of Risk* by Michael A. Stackpole
19. *Blood of Heroes* by Andrew Keith
20. *Close Quarters* by Victor Milán
21. *Far Country* by Peter L. Rice
22. *D.R.T.* by James D. Long
23. *Tactics of Duty* by William H. Keith
24. *Bred for War* by Michael A. Stackpole
25. *I Am Jade Falcon* by Robert Thurston
26. *Highlander Gambit* by Blaine Lee Pardoe
27. *Hearts of Chaos* by Victor Milán
28. *Operation Excalibur* by William H. Keith
29. *Malicious Intent* by Michael A. Stackpole
30. *Black Dragon* by Victor Milán
31. *Impetus of War* by Blaine Lee Pardoe
32. *Double-Blind* by Loren L. Coleman
33. *Binding Force* by Loren L. Coleman
34. *Exodus Road* (Twilight of the Clans, Volume 1) by Blaine Lee Pardoe
35. *Grave Covenant* ((Twilight of the Clans, Volume 2) by Michael A. Stackpole

76. *Daughter of the Dragon* by Ilsa J. Bick
77. *Heretic's Faith* by Randall N. Bills
78. *Fortress Republic* by Loren L. Coleman
79. *Blood Avatar* by Ilsa J. Bick
80. *Trial by Chaos* by J. Steven York
81. *Principles of Desolation* by Jason M. Hardy and Randall N. Bills
82. *Wolf Hunters* by Kevin Killiany
83. *Surrender Your Dreams* by Blaine Lee Pardoe
84. *Dragon Rising* by Ilsa J. Bick
85. *Masters of War* by Michael A. Stackpole
86. *A Rending of Falcons* by Victor Milán
87. *A Bonfire of Worlds* by Steven Mohan, Jr.
88. *Isle of the Blessed* by Steven Mohan, Jr.
89. *Embers of War* by Jason Schmetzer
90. *Betrayal of Ideals* by Blaine Lee Pardoe
91. *Forever Faithful* by Blaine Lee Pardoe
92. *Kell Hounds Ascendant* by Michael A. Stackpole
93. *Redemption Rift* by Jason Schmetzer
94. *Grey Watch Protocol* (*The Highlander Covenant, Book One*)
     by Michael J. Ciaravella
95. *Honor's Gauntlet* by Bryan Young
96. *Icons of War* by Craig A. Reed, Jr.
97. *Children of Kerensky* by Blaine Lee Pardoe
98. *Hour of the Wolf* by Blaine Lee Pardoe
99. *Fall From Glory* (*Founding of the Clans, Book One*) by Randall N. Bills
100. *Paid in Blood* (*The Highlander Covenant, Book Two*) by Michael J. Ciaravella
101. *Blood Will Tell* by Jason Schmetzer
102. *Hunting Season* by Philip A. Lee
103. *A Rock and a Hard Place* by William H. Keith, Jr.
104. *Visions of Rebirth* (Founding of the Clans, Book Two) by Randall N. Bills
105. *No Substitute for Victory* by Blaine Lee Pardoe
106. *Redemption Rites* by Jason Schmetzer
107. *Land of Dreams* (Founding of the Clans, Book Three) by Randall N. Bills

YOUNG ADULT NOVELS

1. *The Nellus Academy Incident* by Jennifer Brozek
2. *Iron Dawn* (*Rogue Academy, Book 1*) by Jennifer Brozek
3. *Ghost Hour* (*Rogue Academy, Book 2*) by Jennifer Brozek
4. *Crimson Night* (*Rogue Academy, Book 3*) by Jennifer Brozek

OMNIBUSES

1. *The Gray Death Legion Trilogy* by William H. Keith, Jr.
2. *The Blood of Kerensky Trilogy* by Michael A. Stackpole

NOVELLAS/SHORT STORIES

1. *Lion's Roar* by Steven Mohan, Jr.
2. *Sniper* by Jason Schmetzer
3. *Eclipse* by Jason Schmetzer
4. *Hector* by Jason Schmetzer
5. *The Frost Advances (Operation Ice Storm, Part 1)* by Jason Schmetzer
6. *The Winds of Spring (Operation Ice Storm, Part 2)* by Jason Schmetzer
7. *Instrument of Destruction (Ghost Bear's Lament, Part 1)* by Steven Mohan, Jr.
8. *The Fading Call of Glory (Ghost Bear's Lament, Part 2)* by Steven Mohan, Jr.
9. *Vengeance* by Jason Schmetzer
10. *A Splinter of Hope* by Philip A. Lee
11. *The Anvil* by Blaine Lee Pardoe
12. *A Splinter of Hope/The Anvil* (omnibus)
13. *Not the Way the Smart Money Bets (Kell Hounds Ascendant #1)* by Michael A. Stackpole
14. *A Tiny Spot of Rebellion (Kell Hounds Ascendant #2)* by Michael A. Stackpole
15. *A Clever Bit of Fiction (Kell Hounds Ascendant #3)* by Michael A. Stackpole
16. *Break-Away (Proliferation Cycle #1)* by Ilsa J. Bick
17. *Prometheus Unbound (Proliferation Cycle #2)* by Herbert A. Beas II
18. *Nothing Ventured (Proliferation Cycle #3)* by Christoffer Trossen
19. *Fall Down Seven Times, Get Up Eight (Proliferation Cycle #4)* by Randall N. Bills
20. *A Dish Served Cold (Proliferation Cycle #5)* by Chris Hartford and Jason M. Hardy
21. *The Spider Dances (Proliferation Cycle #6)* by Jason Schmetzer
22. *Shell Games* by Jason Schmetzer
23. *Divided We Fall* by Blaine Lee Pardoe
24. *The Hunt for Jardine (Forgotten Worlds, Part One)* by Herbert A. Beas II
25. *Rock of the Republic* by Blaine Lee Pardoe
26. *Finding Jardine (Forgotten Worlds, Part Two)* by Herbert A. Beas II
27. *The Trickster (Proliferation Cycle #7)* by Blaine Lee Pardoe
28. *The Price of Duty* by Jason Schmetzer
29. *Elements of Treason: Duty* by Craig A. Reed, Jr.
30. *Mercenary's Honor* by Jason Schmetzer

ANTHOLOGIES

1. *The Corps (BattleCorps Anthology, Volume 1)* edited by Loren. L. Coleman
2. *First Strike (BattleCorps Anthology, Volume 2)* edited by Loren L. Coleman
3. *Weapons Free (BattleCorps Anthology, Volume 3)* edited by Jason Schmetzer
4. *Onslaught: Tales from the Clan Invasion* edited by Jason Schmetzer
5. *Edge of the Storm* by Jason Schmetzer
6. *Fire for Effect (BattleCorps Anthology, Volume 4)* edited by Jason Schmetzer

MAGAZINES

The march of technology across BattleTech's eras is relentless...

Some BattleMech designs never die. Each installment of *Recognition Guide: IlClan*, currently a PDF-only series, not only includes a brand new BattleMech or OmniMech, but also details Classic 'Mech designs from both the Inner Sphere and the Clans, now fully rebuilt with Dark Age technology (3085 and beyond).

STORE.CATALYSTGAMELABS.COM

Made in the USA
Columbia, SC
25 July 2022

63911412R00189